PRAISE FOR GAIL R DELANEY

"This book is a MUST READ... This may be my favorite book of all time... one of those rare books for which a five heart rating seems sadly inadequate."

— THE ROMANCE STUDIO

"Delaney's characters are what makes this science fiction story shine! ...*Revolution* is a story packed with adventure, excitement, and love..."

— SALLY PINK REVIEWS

"I love Sci Fi Rom, but I'm a hard sell... Finally, I found a book that gives me exactly what I want! *Revolution* is a living, breathing, vivid, and all too possible glimpse into our future with characters I felt I knew personally.

And Michael... he's a mystery I want to see unfold."

— GOODREADS REVIEW, 5 STARS

The Phoenix Rebellion
Book One

Revolution

Part One of the Future Possible Saga

REVOLUTION

THE PHOENIX REBELLION BOOK ONE

GAIL R DELANEY

Irish Eyes
Books

To: Jamie and Shalon for poking, prodding, harassing and generally being a pain until I said I'd give a futuristic a try. Thanks, you two!

To: Jenifer, the other half of my brain.

To: Rick and Amanda. You'll probably never have any idea the inspiration you gave me, but the least I can do is say 'Thank you'.

THE FUTURE POSSIBLE SAGA

THE PHOENIX REBELLION QUARTET

BOOK ONE: REVOLUTION

BOOK TWO: OUTCASTS

BOOK THREE: GAINING GROUND

BOOK FOUR: END GAME

PHOENIX RISING QUARTET

BOOK ONE: JANUS

BOOK TWO: TRIAD

BOOK THREE: STASIS

BOOK FOUR: LIBER

THE FUTURE POSSIBLE SAGA
STORYTELLING STYLE

The Future Possible Saga is a continuous timeline, in which any give book extends the story of the book prior to it and sets up for the next book while also telling its own story. The books must be read in order to have full understanding of the saga.

This means each book has its own story arc, but also extends the greater saga story arcs.

There will be cliffhangers, but as the author I will always provide you with a payoff within the book you're reading. Each book has its own plot, it's own storyline, and its own resolutions. Each book (with the exclusion of the final book in the saga) will have setup for the next book. These may or may not be considered cliffhangers by some. But, be aware, they exist.

The good news is the saga as told through The Phoenix Rebellion quartet and Phoenix Rising quartet is complete. You don't have to wait for a cliffhanger resolution. Just continue to the next book.

I hope you enjoy, and complete the journey with us.

OUT OF ASHES HUMANITY WILL RISE AGAIN

THE ARETH: LONG LOST BRETHREN OR WOLF IN SHEEP'S CLOTHING?

By: Paul M. Anderson

February 4, 2008

(A/P — WASHINGTON, DC) Except for the most isolated and primitive parts of this planet, nearly everyone in the world knows of our visitors from the stars. Aliens, who look like us, miraculously speak every major language on the planet, and claim to be the very generators of our existence. Some of us O.G. earth-dwellers have accepted their promises of a better world without hesitance, arguing that to believe we were alone in the universe would be sanctimonious and egotistical. Others beg for prudence, their words often falling on deaf ears, as it would seem if the rulers of the world's major countries are any indicator.

But who are the Areth? What else do we really know about them? And if their claims are true, what does it mean for the human race and everything we have ever known to be true?

Whatever your religious affiliation may or may not be, it has always been a generally accepted truism that the people of Earth came from, well, Earth. Whether you believe Divine Intervention placed us here, or you believe we crawled from the primordial goo and sprouted legs, it all happened on this Big Blue Marble. Makes sense, right?

Not according to the newest inhabitants of our ever-shrinking planet.

Let me give you the long and the short of it, just in case you *have* been living in a cave for the last few months.

Last week, at a press conference held at the White House following a lengthy closed-door meeting with President Bush, Warrick made the following statement. Again, for those of you in the dark, Warrick is apparently the Areth's version of the Prez—the Big Cheese—High Honcho—The Boss.

> *"Ten thousand years ago, an exploration ship was lost in this part of the galaxy and its inhabitants assumed dead. We now know those scientists found their way to this planet, and survived despite the primitive elements. Ten centuries apart have changed us, made us separate— Human and Areth—but we are at the core the same. We are brethren."*

Long story short, they are our ancestors. Not Adam and Eve. Not hunchbacked cavemen with buckteeth and uni-brows. A bunch of highly advanced 'aliens' from the other side of the galaxy spawned us.

Freaky, huh?

So, what *about* Adam and Eve, and every other belief we have held on to for more generations than any of us can count? Do we just say, "Okay, sure. Sounds good. You must be right; you *are* the superior race and all"?

I don't know about the rest of you, but I've watched way too many science fiction movies to swallow this cock and bull story. The second you fall for it is when their eyes glow, a ten-foot tongue comes flying out of their mouth, or you find out you have some reptilian embryo clawing its way out of your gut.

Rev. Jedediah Quinn said yesterday during a highly publicized sermon from his megachurch in Tallahassee, Florida, *"To throw aside our faith in God and the very teachings of the Word would be an abomination. These Areth are not our forefathers. The same God created both Man and Areth, but God put us here, not them. Our history is our own, our past our own, and our future should be our own."*

Science has proven that, at least on a genetic level, we are indeed made up of the same DNA soup as the Areth. Our hearts are in the same place, they beat at pretty much the same rhythm. Their blood isn't green. They don't have large, bulbous heads and clawed hands. So, what sets us apart? How have we evolved differently over the last ten thousand years or so? Apparently, the Areth don't like to 'get it on.'

That's right. No hanky panky.

If that's the future, you can have it. I don't want it. I like things *just* the way they are.

Apparently, the Areth recreate themselves through cloning. And remember how your college buddies told you if you didn't use it, you'd lose it? They were right...

So, they show up and say they're our long lost brethren. They want to move in and mingle amongst us lesser-developed Areth wannabees. Why? What do we have to offer them? And why should we let them stay? Other than the fact that they have some big honkin' space guns, they claim they want to 'share' their knowledge. They want to teach us how to improve our world, make ourselves better, stronger live longer.

Did I mention they live to be close to five hundred years old?

And look damn good doing it, too!

I'm not claiming I know what we should do. I'm not even sure I have a solid opinion yet. The scales tip back and forth... No sex? No way... Live longer? I could deal with that... as long as I can keep the sex.

Paul Anderson signing off... Live Long and Prosper... May the Force be With You... Stay Shiny... Nanu Nanu... So Say We All.

PROLOGUE

3 July 2050, Sunday
London, former United Kingdom
Continent of Europe

The humid, heavy air slapped her face when CJ Montgomery stepped out of the air tram terminal into the afternoon sunshine. The sky was overcast, but each burst of sunlight through the clouds warmed the summer air, making her hair cling to the back of her neck and her dress stick between her shoulders.

She stepped clear of the crowd and pulled a pair of dark glasses from her shoulder bag, careful not to open the satchel any further than necessary. Her vision caught on a single item, and her insides tensed. Immediately reining in her expression, she slipped on the glasses and walked away from the station.

CJ clutched the bag to her side as she strode down the sidewalk, her high-heeled sandals beating a cadence against the stone; her heart beat twice as fast against her ribs. She drew a shaky breath, hoping she managed to look calm to the citizens that passed her going the other direction.

Three blocks from the air tram station she reached the designated open-air café, and with a nod to the nearby waiter, sat at a vacant table.

1

The yellow and white striped umbrella overhead shielded her from the direct sunlight as the clouds shifted. CJ debated about holding her bag in her lap, but remembered what she had been told. *Act normal . . . draw no attention to yourself.* A woman holding her bag as if her life depended on it might draw suspicion. Steeling her nerves, she leaned sideways and set the bag on the ground beside her chair.

"What may I get you, ma'am?"

CJ looked up, slipping her dark glasses off her face. "Water with lemon, please. And a fruit plate."

The waiter nodded and weaved his way back through the maze of tables and patrons.

Her insides jumped, flipping and twisting of their own free will, and CJ analyzed the wisdom of what she was about to do. All her life, she had taken the Areth, and everything they told her, as truth—believed every step forward in science and medicine was for the *good* of mankind, for the good of them all. Was she right to throw all that away now? After everything she had given up for her conviction, could she accept what had been right in front of her?

Images of what she had seen, the video files and data records of past experiments, flashed through her mind and her stomach rolled.

Yes.

This was right.

There was no other choice.

A shadow fell across the table, and CJ leaned back in expectation of her lunch.

"It's a beautiful day, though unseasonably warm," said a deep, enticingly smooth voice over her, lightened by an accent she didn't immediately recognize. "Almost as beautiful as you, darling."

CJ looked up. A man towered over her, his broad shoulders blocking the sun and his dark skin gleamed in the heat. She carefully schooled her features and smiled. "Thank you, sweetheart."

He pulled out the chair beside her and released the button of his jacket before sitting down. The metal legs of the chair scraped across the tile as he shifted closer. He removed his dark glasses to reveal equally dark eyes. As he leaned one arm on the table, CJ shifted forward, closing the distance between them, and he took her hand.

Every nerve and muscle in her body wanted to jerk into spasms of panic, and a small voice in her mind screamed to run. *This was too much! Too insane! She was a doctor! A geneticist! Not a damn spy!*

"You did very well, Doctor Montgomery. No one followed you today, or for the last several days. I would assume that your actions have gone unnoticed."

CJ blinked. "You've been watching me?" *Who else is watching?*

He smiled, revealing startling white teeth, and somehow the ease of his smile let her relax a small degree. "Doctor Montgomery, what we are doing—you and I—brings risk to both of us and the people I represent. We needed to be cautious."

CJ released a breath. "I'm just not used to this."

"No one would expect you to be."

The waiter returned with her lunch, and CJ sat back so he could set it on the table. The man with her ordered a glass of pineapple juice with a soy tofu sandwich, and CJ did her best not to wince. She took a sip of the water, relishing in the cooling effect as it spread out from her chest. Her hand trembled as she set the glass down, and her companion reached out to gently squeeze her fingers. To anyone watching, they were merely a close couple having lunch.

Nothing could be further from the truth.

"What happens now?" she asked.

"You give me what you have. I take it back to my people. If all goes well, we will contact you again."

"How long?"

"I can't say for sure. When we're sure it's safe."

She nodded, and poked at her cantaloupe with the tines of her fork. Her appetite was non-existent, had been for the last month. CJ swallowed hard and took another drink of her water.

"I can see in your eyes you've seen the truth."

She strangled a laugh and shook her head. "I have a feeling I've only seen a small portion of the truth. And that is what sickens me the most."

"It will be an immense benefit to have you with us, Doctor."

She tried to smile, but knew her façade was slipping. "Please, call me CJ."

He did smile, and it was genuine enough to make her feel better. "Of course. And I am Damian Ali."

CJ nodded. "Thank you, Damian."

"For?"

"For making me feel not quite so cloak and dagger about all this."

The waiter arrived with his sandwich, and CJ curled her lip when she looked at it. Excluding his taste in cuisine, Damian Ali seemed like a man she could trust. Something she desperately needed right now. Something concrete and solid . . . something she could believe in. She hadn't felt that in years. Not since . . .

CJ swallowed again. Her heart was yet another victim of the Areth and their cold-blooded ways.

They ate their food, and Damian shared conversation with her; asking her questions about herself and some about her work almost like a friend would over lunch. He told her he had been born in Trinidad, which helped give context to his soothing tone. She almost felt real. Like this wasn't some game, a roll she was playing. As they finished, Damian waved to the waiter and handed the young man his payment card.

"When should I—"

"Not yet," he answered, cutting her off.

When the waiter returned with the card, the two of them stood and moved back onto the sidewalk. After walking several steps, he nodded slightly and CJ reached into her bag for her glasses, curling her fingers around the small microslide she had guarded with her life for the last week. With it held against her palm by only two fingers, she dropped her hand to her side.

Damian took her hand as they walked, his fingers lacing through hers, the microslide pressed between their palms.

"You are very good at this."

CJ laughed. "I'm too frightened to be anything else."

"You'll get better at it. Less frightened. More determined. We all have our reasons for doing what we do, but none of us are anything less than determined."

He walked with her to the air tram terminal. Damian turned to her, pulling her into an embrace. As his hand slipped free, the microslide went with it, and CJ's breath hitched in a momentary wave of panic. Damian pressed his lips to her cheek, speaking softly in her ear.

"I am sure I will see you again soon, CJ."

She could only nod. Then he released her and headed down the street. Several feet away, he turned back and waved and she lifted her hand, but couldn't bring any sound from her throat. With a shaking hand, CJ pushed some hair back off her forehead.

Well, Caitlin June . . . if you're dead in twenty-four hours, you'll know why.

CHAPTER ONE

5 October 2051, Thursday
Alliance Center for Genetic Advancement
Santa Fe, New Mexico
Former United States of America

"*S*ecurity Enforcement, please report to D-Wing immediately. Code 423. Code 423. Repeat. Security Enforcement staff, report to D-Wing immediately to subdue unruly subject."*

Victor raised his head, looking away from the streaming data on his computer screen. He hadn't really seen any of it for the last three hours. The computer-synthesized voice echoed through the facility speaker system, and he heard rapid footfalls in the hall outside his office as the security staff nearest his lab headed for D-Wing.

He looked to the clock on the wall. Nearly 2130. If he left now for his apartment, he could rest for a few hours before returning in the morning. The thought of leaving one sterile, silent place for another held no appeal for him. Victor glanced at the couch in the corner of his office. Perhaps a few hours' sleep here would be sufficient. Sleep was sleep. It didn't matter where to him.

Even sleep didn't appeal.

He rubbed his hands over his face, pushing his fingers into his short black hair, and tried to focus again on the twisting computer generated double helix, each genome illustrated in a different shade. His eyes saw it, but nothing registered in his mind anymore. After three decades of looking, he felt no closer to finding the key than when he had begun. Victor knew the key was right there, twisting and swirling in shades of blue and red, but he'd be damned if he could see it—the patch that would solve his race's most pressing problem.

At times like this, he swore he *knew* the answer but something blocked it from surfacing, from letting him see. One of the many holes in his memory he couldn't fill, perhaps.

With a sigh, he stood and left his office, heading toward the small kitchen at the end of the hall. Most of his kinsmen thought he was peculiar for enjoying the strong coffee the Earth scientists brewed, but he had immediately found a taste for it, and it helped his senses stay alert on these late nights.

He poured a cup and dumped three packets of sugar in it, stirring until the grit was gone from the bottom of the cup. The aromatic liquid was slightly bitter, but it still tasted good and the warmth spread through his chest as he sipped it. After another couple swallows, he topped off the cup and poured another, adding the same amount of sugar to it. He stared at the second cup, wondering if the intended recipient would want it the same as he, then added some milk from a carton in the refrigerator.

The halls were nearly silent as he headed for the elevator, carrying both paper cups of coffee. The section his office was housed in held mostly laboratories and other offices, and at this time of night they were empty. The soft glow of security lighting chased away some of the shadows, but the echo of his footfalls sounded much louder than they would during the day. He rode the elevator down several levels and continued his walk, hoping the coffee wouldn't be too cold by the time he reached his destination.

This wing of the facility wasn't as quiet as the labs. Many of the subjects were still awake, moving around in their rooms. Victor heard shouting at the far end of the hall, and knew it had to be Alexander. The sedatives were no longer working, and the painkillers had lost their effectiveness. He was in pain all the time now, and growing harder to handle. Victor had heard his superiors speak of alternatives, and knew euthanasia had been discussed. Alexander was a failure, and his body no longer served the purpose intended by the scientists who created him. It angered Victor, but he held his tongue. One too many times he had raised his concerns, and one too many times his judgment had been called into question. If he wasn't careful, he would find himself back on the *Abaddon* orbiting overhead.

Or worse . . . downloaded into stasis for a hundred years as punishment for questioning his superiors.

He reached cell 914 and leaned against the steel door, putting his mouth near the metal mesh screen that allowed the guards to hear what might be happening inside. "Michael? Are you awake?"

"Yes," came the simple answer.

Victor shifted the coffees into the crook of one arm so he could press his thumb to the bio-reader beside the door lock. The pad lit up, scanning him for genetic markers to confirm his identity, and the lock disengaged. Footfalls echoed from down the hall, and Victor knew a guard came on his rounds. He pulled open the door and stepped into the cell, closing it behind him.

The small space was dark except for a single reading lamp over Michael's head that shed a circle of light around the bed. Michael sat at the head of the bed, his back against the wall and his knees drawn up, his arms resting on his raised legs. His light brown hair was in need of a cut, but he probably didn't care, and neither did the orderlies or guards responsible for him. The heavy lines on his cheeks and between his brows made him look much older than his twenty-five years.

"You don't often come this late."

Victor crossed the room and held out the extra coffee to him. "Milk and sugar?"

"I'll take it any way I can get it."

As Michael took his first drink of the coffee, Victor retrieved the only chair in the room and carried it to the side of the bed, not wanting to drag it across the floor and draw too much attention. He sat down and set his foot on the side railing of the bed. Folded open on the blankets near Michael's bare feet was a paperback book, its cover bent and worn.

"What are you reading?"

"*The Martian Chronicles.*"

"Is it interesting?"

Michael shifting his position to sit cross-legged and picked up the book, staring at the open pages. "Bradbury was wrong on his assumptions. You're not golden. Or telepathic."

Victor chuckled. "And I'm not from Mars."

Michael's eyes squinted, staring at Victor. "You aren't, are you?"

"From Mars?"

"No. Telepathic."

He laughed again. "If I were telepathic, I wouldn't have to ask how you like your coffee."

Michael nodded slowly, accepting the answer, and shifted again, bringing one leg up to rest his arm on it. He was restless, as usual. Victor often found him pacing, and wondered what went on in his mind to have him so agitated. He had watched Michael grow up here, had even seen him the day his associates brought him here as a three-year-old child. It hadn't been until the last few years that Victor had come to know him. There was more behind Michael's eyes than anyone here understood, or even considered.

Most of the lifetime subjects had resigned themselves to their lives, but Michael would never concede to a life here. Not since he mistakenly learned the one fact about his existence that angered Kathleen to the point of murderous rage. That fact—that name—gave Michael strength. Victor knew that, and anyone who thought otherwise was a fool.

Michael took another drink of the coffee, looking at Victor over the rim. He was a man of few words, but Victor had known Michael too long.

"I thought you might like a coffee."

"There's more on your mind."

Victor took one last sip of his coffee, which was now too cold. He held the cup between his laced fingers, staring down at the swirling design on the surface of the dark liquid. "You know me well, my friend."

"Friend? Is that allowed?"

Victor raised his eyes and looked at Michael, who stared back unwavering. Then Victor shifted his gaze to the book now resting on Michael's leg. "Tell me about this book."

15 October 2051, Sunday
Parson's Point, Maine
Former United States of America

J stood at the corner of Nick's porch and inhaled deep. The air was heavy with the scent of leaves, pine, and earth, and the sky was a brilliant blue softened with long wisps of cirrus clouds. It had been a long time since she had been outside a city, or anywhere *green* like this.

A long time since she had been *here*.

She closed her eyes and reached out her hand to lay it on the rough birch log, enjoying the tactile sensation beneath her fingertips. CJ leaned into the wall, inhaling slowly to let the scent of the wood fill her head. With the smell came more memories than she could ever count or categorize, and she smiled.

She opened her eyes, dropped her hand away from the side of the cabin, and stepped down onto the ground. Stone and dirt crunched beneath her shoes as she walked along the side of the house toward the lake. Nick wasn't inside, but he might be down at the dock. The sound of a low voice carried on the breeze, accompanied by the scraping of wood against wood. Her heart skipped, and she paused at the corner of the cabin.

Nick was on the dock, crouched down on the edge as he tied a small boat to the mooring, his long, sure fingers knotting the rope. A soft breeze blew in off the water, swirling fallen leaves from the ground and stirring his hair. Last she saw him, his hair still had been mostly brown with just the slightest touches of gray at the temples. Now, he was almost completely silver with brown showing through to indicate what it once had been. Dear god, he was still the most beautiful man she had ever seen.

She knew he'd hate her choice of words.

A small dog, not much more than a mass of white and brown fur, sat on the dock beside Nick, its tail swishing back and forth. Nick said something, and the dog's tail went faster. He stood, and CJ swallowed the hitch in her breath.

Eight years ago, Nick Tanner had made her heart skip a beat with a glance and turned her body to molten heat with a touch. Seventeen years her senior, she never once saw him as anything but absolutely virile and masculine. Now, so many years later, the effect was the same. He wasn't perfection, wasn't the ideal in the eyes of most, but CJ thought any woman whose heart didn't skip when they looked at him just had to be dead. A square jaw and chiseled features gave him the look of strength, and his dark eyes were shadowed reflections of his soul. His lips were finely sculpted, thin, and straight, and the lines on his cheeks only brought out his features.

He ruffled the shaggy fur that hid the dog's face, and stood to his full height. The first time she saw him, he had been wearing his Earth Force dress blues and the uniform had accentuated his six-foot three-inch frame. Not nearly as much as faded denims and the blue plaid shirt he

9

wore now. The breeze caught the open shirt, pulling away from his chest, letting her see the gray tee shirt beneath, and she knew he was as strong and lean as he had ever been. The silver hair added time to his forty-seven years, but everything else defied it.

CJ closed her eyes for a moment, steeling her resolve. She wasn't here to relive past love affairs. Nothing about this visit was for her. It didn't matter how seeing him made her feel. She was here *for* him, and to convince him of the truth.

Her heart knew there was no chance of anything else. She had hurt him far too badly for that.

"Come on, Dog. Let's go get some lunch."

CJ's eyes snapped open at the clear sound of his voice, and she stared transfixed while he moved off the dock toward her. She knew she should speak, but the ability was lost to her as he smiled at the antics of the mutt hopping along beside him. Then the dog stopped mid-stride and turned in her direction, sniffing the air. CJ held her breath, and thought momentarily about disappearing around the corner of the cabin and running.

No. She couldn't. This was too important.

The dog yapped and bolted toward her, and CJ held out her hand, wondering whether she would lose a finger or just end up with a slobbered palm.

"What's your problem . . ." Nick called after the animal, but the question trailed off as he looked up and their gazes connected.

CJ reached out her hand to find strength in the wall of the cabin. The smile on his lips dropped away in an instant, and his eyes darkened. Nick squared his shoulders a degree and shifted his stance, setting one foot uphill with his knee bent. He stared at her, showing no sign of surprise, but absolutely no sign of pleasure. If anything, the cold steel in his eyes almost frightened her.

"Hello, Nick," she finally managed to say, petting the dog who had chosen to sniff and lick over any kind of attack.

"Leave. Now." His voice was flat, emotionless, despite the demand.

"I have to tell you something—"

"No."

He strode toward her with purpose, and CJ held her breath as he brushed past her. She turned and reached for his arm to draw him back, but the fury in his eyes when he spun around to glare at her made her drop her hand away. CJ retreated, bumping the wall of the cabin.

"Do you hate me so much you can't even listen to what I have to say?"

"Hate," he forced through clenched teeth, and the cold levelness of his voice made CJ swallow her breath. He took the one step needed to close the space between them, stepping so near she had to hitch her chin up to hold his stare. "Now, *there's* a word."

Then he was gone, storming off to the front of the cabin, leaving CJ swaying in the space he left behind. She drew a breath, blinking rapidly, and leaned back against the wall. Perhaps General Castleton had been right. She wasn't the person to do this. They should have waited until the mission was done, the task accomplished, and then Nick Tanner could have been told the truth. If they failed, he never would have known.

She couldn't let things go. Couldn't let him go another day without knowing the reality. She owed him that much.

CJ steeled her nerves and pushed clear of the wall, walking back to the porch. The dog had already forgotten her, and was sprawled out in a spot of sunshine, not bothering to lift his head when she approached. The front door was closed, but she hedged her bet that Nick never fixed the lock. The knob turned and she stepped inside. The cabin was dark, and slightly warmer than outside from the glowing embers still in the fieldstone hearth. Very little had changed in eight years. The flat monitor on the wall had been upgraded, and the rug in front of the fireplace might be different, but everything else was just the same as she remembered, from the soft leather couch with the red and blue woven blanket on the back to the handcrafted wood cabinets in the kitchen. The air smelled of burning hickory and bacon, with an underlying aroma of the soap she knew he used.

Her eyes burned and she blinked hard to keep back the tears. She refused to let this turn into *anything* to do with her. Nothing she felt, nothing she wanted, would come into play. Tonight, she would condemn herself for being stupid and naïve, but not now.

She closed the door and stepped inside, her shoes muffled by the braided rug covering the wide plank floor. CJ walked past the end of the couch and looked to her right to the archway leading to the joining bedroom. There was no door, nothing blocking her view to the large wrought iron bed that sat against the far wall, or to keep her from seeing Nick where he sat on its edge, his elbows resting on his knees with his head down.

CJ swallowed the lump in her throat and forced herself to enter the room, unprepared for the onslaught of memories that bombarded her when she curled her fingers around the cool metal framework of the footboard. Nights of lovemaking, mornings of waking in his arms . . . they all came back in a vicious wave.

"What part of *leave* was confusing?"

CJ closed her eyes against the hate and anger in his voice. "I will leave—"

"Yes, you will."

"You have to hear this first, Nicky."

His head snapped up and he glared at her. "There is *nothing* you can tell me that I want to hear."

CJ released the footboard and slipped a trembling hand into the hip pocket of her dress, her fingers curling around the microslide she had tucked away there. She extended her hand, palm up, and unfurled her fingers. Nick sat up, staring at the slide, his dark brown eyes darting up to meet hers momentarily. She nodded, jutting her chin toward it.

"Go ahead. See for yourself. Then, if you want me to leave, I will."

Nick stood, the old bed creaking at the loss of his weight. His fingertips brushed her palm as he took the microslide and strode past her into the main living space. CJ took a moment to breathe deeply, closing her eyes. Her skin tingled where his fingers had touched. Clearing her throat, she turned and followed him. As she stepped into the main room, Nick opened the data receptacle on the monitor and placed the disk inside. He didn't spare her a glance as she moved beside him, punching in the command codes to open the file and run the program.

The screen flickered and a video began to play. CJ was far too familiar with the contents, having watched it again and again. The image spanned a large common room filled with men and women of all ages, dressed in loose, light clothing. Some sat together in small groups, some curled into themselves near the wall, rocking to the rhythm of an unheard beat. Orderlies and nurses stood on the outskirts, distributing medications to some, removing one or two for experiments that CJ hadn't yet been able to define or determine.

"What am I looking at?"

She pointed to the far right corner near the bank of bar-covered windows. A single man stood, facing out into the sun, with his feet set apart and his hands linked behind his back in a stance all too familiar to CJ. He was tall and lanky in build, even that was obvious through the baggy clothing he wore. His hair was brown, the same color she imagined Nick's had been a lifetime ago. Even now, looking at the younger man, CJ's heart skipped. The reality excited her, yet broke her heart in the same instant.

"Here," she said. "Magnify and enhance."

Nick touched the screen and the image paused. He tapped with his pinky and a menu appeared. With deft fingers, he relayed the commands and the video shifted, magnifying the image two hundred percent so the single man filled the screen. His back was still to the camera.

"Resume."

Nick tapped again and the video restarted. CJ's pulse quickened. She knew the moment she wanted approached. She stepped closer to Nick, her shoulder brushing his arm. He didn't move away, his focus on the screen, and she wondered if he felt the same niggling sense of familiarity she had the first time she saw it. She glanced quickly up at him. His gaze was intent on the monitor, a deep crease digging in above his nose as he focused.

Another man entered the view dressed in a white lab coat with his hands pushed into the large front pockets—Victor. That was all she knew about him. His singular name he'd either adopted or had assigned to him when he and his race arrived on Earth. He had dark hair and defined features, and the two men stood nearly at the same height, the doctor only being slightly shorter. If she didn't know what he really was, she would suspect his family to be from Belize, or that general part of the world. He looked to be about CJ's age, around thirty, but as an Areth his apparent age meant nothing. Her own supervisor at the lab didn't look much older than Nick, and she knew he was nearly four centuries old.

"Get ready to pause again," she said softly.

He held his hand over the monitor, not touching it.

The doctor stopped and spoke, and the focus of their attention shifted. For one brief moment, he looked straight at the camera.

"Now."

Nick tapped the screen.

"What the hell . . ."

His words mirrored CJ's own reaction the first time she saw the young man's face. It was like seeing Nick Tanner twenty years before. The same eyes, the same angled features, the same lips.

"Who is this?" he demanded, only briefly looking at her before focusing again on the screen.

CJ cleared her throat to try and push through the thick emotions threatening to choke her. "His name is Michael Tanner. Your son."

CHAPTER TWO

*N*ick leaned back in his chair, scrubbing his face with his palms. His foot bumped the leg of the kitchen table and the personal access tablet set upright in front of him shook with the force. With a frustrated groan, he lowered his hands and crossed his arms over his stomach keeping his slouched position.

The small monitor glowed with the video Caitlin had brought him. Nick had programmed it to magnify and loop over the same thirty-second strip, focusing again and again on Michael's face as he first spoke to the doctor then turned and looked into the camera.

Again and again.

Michael.

It was unsettling and almost bizarre. Looking at Michael was like looking at himself, the resemblance was so close. There was no denying they were kin. His son . . . the thought choked him and made his eyes ache. Nick rested his head on the high back of the chair, the heels of his hands pressed against his eye sockets until spots of light flashed in the darkness.

He heard the door open, and her soft footsteps approaching across the living room accompanied by the clicking of Dog's toenails as they approached doorway of the kitchen. She stood there for several moments, watching him. However, Nick didn't move.

"I don't have all the answers, but I'll tell you what I can," she finally said, her voice soft and rough.

"How do you know he's my son?"

"The people that gave me this information were able to access a limited amount of his medical and personal records. He was born 14 March 2026 in Richmond, Virginia."

Nick's throat closed in, and he swallowed painfully, lowering his hands to look at her. She stood with her shoulder leaned against the doorjamb, her arms crossed and her elbows grasped in her hands. The breeze outside had mused her short, blond hair leaving it in soft curls around her cheeks and chin. He saw the glimpse of cobalt blue earrings through the curls, setting off the color of her eyes.

"The records list his paternal contributor to be Captain Nicholas Michael Tanner. Michael's entire DNA profile was kept in his medical files and has been compared to your own in your military records. Your DNA matches with ninety-eight percent surety. You are his father. And his maternal contributor is an Areth scientist named Kathleen." Her voice cracked as she spoke, and her words split through his head like a spike.

Nick shot out of the chair with such force it fell backwards, bouncing off the edge of the sink before it hit the floor. "Kathleen wasn't . . . she *died* giving birth to our son," he shouted. His stomach twisted, and he curled his fists, forcing himself to tamp down the rage. "My wife was not Areth," he forced out through clenched teeth.

Caitlin's eyes glistened bright with unshed tears, but she didn't look away from him. He watched as she swallowed, pressing her lips together, before she spoke. "I'm sorry, Nick. She was. And as far as we know, she isn't dead."

His heart pounded in his ears and he couldn't think. Nick pressed his wrists against his temples, trying to push back the chaos. He needed air, and headed for the door. Outside, he drew oxygen in through his nose and gripped one of the porch posts to keep himself upright. She followed, but kept a safe distance back to stand in the doorway.

"Where is he?"

"An Alliance facility outside of Santa Fe, New Mexico."

"What kind of facility?"

"Genetics research is the official designation."

Pain shot down the side of his neck as he ground his teeth together. "How long has he been there?"

Caitlin stepped onto the porch beside him, her hand resting on the post below his own, but not touching him. She leaned into it, her cheek close to the wood. When she looked into his eyes, his gut clenched in a vicious amalgamation of hate and pleasure that just added to the burning fury.

"Twenty-two years."

Nick's knees could no longer hold up his weight, an unseen fist punching his gut. He dropped into a crouch, letting his back brace against the porch railing. With his elbows on his bent knees, he pressed his thumbs to his forehead and closed his eyes. His chest hurt, and Nick wondered if this was what a heart attack felt like as spots of light danced in his vision and his temples throbbed.

He squeezed his eyes closed until they ached, and felt the hot tears escape he wished he could deny, running down his cheeks. Nick swallowed, struggling to push back the images that wouldn't leave his mind. Kathleen . . . her body still and ashen . . . lying on the stainless steel table, her face turned away from him, and the tiny body—blue and cold —that the doctors had kept hidden from him. He remembered falling to his knees and screaming at anyone who could hear to save them, bring them back.

"I don't—" He tried to pull air into his chest, but it hurt so much he could barely gasp. "I don't understand. Why would they take my son? "

Caitlin knelt beside him, tears running down her cheeks, and he couldn't look into her face. Couldn't take seeing the gentleness and compassion. Not now. Because he wanted it.

"My son . . ." he choked again.

"I don't know," she whispered, her voice cracking. "I don't know, Nicky."

She reached up and touched his hair, smoothing her hand back from his temple, and something tore apart inside him. It ripped through him with a vengeance, stealing the last weak grip he had on control. Nick grabbed hold of Caitlin and hauled her to him in a rough embrace—she wrapped her arms around his head and shoulders and cradled him against her breast.

*C*J stood in Nick's kitchen, watching out the small window over the sink to where he stood on the dock. He hadn't moved in at least twenty minutes, his hands pushed into the back pocket of his jeans and his face turned toward the sun as it set behind the tree line on the other side of the lake.

He had left hours ago, and she had no idea when he had returned. Half an hour ago, she had glanced outside and saw him standing at the end of the dock. That was where he had been ever since.

She took a deep, steeling breath and turned away from the sink. The day was over, and it was time for her to go. CJ turned and walked to the door, pausing to rest her hand on the cool leather of the couch. She looked around the space and her chest restricted. If she wanted to let herself, she could relive a thousand wonderful memories that took place here. It seemed like a lifetime ago. It almost was.

CJ was a different person now—she knew that. She had been so young when she fell in love with Colonel Nicholas Tanner. Young and willing to believe everything the Areth told her. Nick had warned her time and again—sometimes teasing and sometimes with such cold seriousness it had made her skin rise in gooseflesh—that she shouldn't take them for their word. In the end, she had taken their word over his.

A decision she immediately regretted, and now . . . now, she knew just how naïve and stupid she had been.

CJ swallowed hard against the raw emotion. She couldn't let him see how much being here hurt. Not because she couldn't admit she had been wrong—in the right time and place, she would gladly tell him. Now was not the time, and this was not the place. CJ didn't want Nick to think she came here for any other reason than the truth.

Michael.

With one final glance around the living room, CJ went to the door and stepped outside. The night air had cooled, and a soft breeze rustled the leaves. Peepers sang to each other, and somewhere in the distance, a loon called out. CJ almost hated to move or speak, not wanting to disturb the peace and calm here on Nick's lake. There were so few untouched places left on Earth.

She stepped down off the porch and followed the same path she had taken when she found him that morning. The only indication from Nick that he knew she was there was a slight turn and tilt of his head as he glanced at her over his shoulder. The hem of his flannel shirt blew in the breeze, otherwise he didn't move.

CJ crossed her arms and drew in a long, slow breath. The scent of evergreen and earth filled her senses.

"I have more questions," Nick said, breaking the silence. His voice was rough and heavy, weighing down the air and pressing against her.

"I'll answer what I can."

He turned his head more, and in the moonlight, she saw the glisten of his eyes as he looked at her. "How long have you been with Phoenix?"

The question surprised her, but she did her best to hide it by clearing her throat. "Just over a year."

"You didn't think I knew about them." It was a statement, not a question.

"Not many people outside the group do."

He turned away, offering no further explanation. CJ took a step closer, standing on the edge of the dock. "Why did you think of Phoenix?"

Nick shrugged. "No one else would give a damn about something like this." He turned to face her, his hands still pushed into his back pockets, pulling his tee shirt tight across his chest. "What do they plan to do?"

"Michael isn't the only human at the facility. A plan is being engineered to go in and extract as many as possible, Michael being one of them. Along with as much information as can be gathered."

"Isn't that going to alert the Areth to the existence of the entire Phoenix organization?"

"They already know there are people of Earth who oppose them, and this wouldn't be the first time one of their facilities has been broken into. We'll just be another dissention group. We won't have a name. Not yet."

Nick shook his head. "This is insane. Do you know anything about their security? Their systems?"

CJ hitched her chin and squared her shoulders, meeting his stare. "We know everything we need to know. There are more people involved than you could ever imagine."

He shook his head again, looking past her to the cabin, seeming to think about what she had told him. "When does this all happen?"

"Within the month."

Nick nodded slowly. "Fine. I'll be ready to leave in five minutes."

He started to move past her, but CJ stopped him with her hand against his chest. "No."

"No?"

She shook her head. "No. You aren't coming with me."

"The hell I'm not!"

CJ shifted her hand, unable and unwilling to fight the urge to move her palm over his heart. The steady beat pounded against her palm, the heat of his body coming through the fabric of his tee shirt. She focused on her hand, and the contrast of her skin against the dark color of his shirt.

If she looked up, she wasn't sure she would be able to speak. Not with him standing this close. Not with her senses so aware of him.

"Nicky, I didn't come here to recruit you or to get your help—"

"Then why did you come? Why *you*, Caitlin. Why were *you* the one who came?"

She did look up then, meeting his stare. His dark eyes were black in the moonlight, his hair silver, his features shadowed.

"I came because I know what losing your son did to you. No matter what happens, I wanted you to know he's alive. If this mission fails, I want you to know so maybe there can be another chance."

"You were the only one who could do that?"

She shook her head. "Probably not, but=t I was the only one who understood. Because, no matter what happened, I know you, Nicky. Better than anyone else on Earth."

He stared down at her, the muscle along his right jaw jumping sporadically. Slowly, CJ let her hand slide down his body, only taking her fingertips away when they reached his waist. She thought she felt a slight tensing of his stomach muscles beneath her touch but knew that whatever reaction there was, it was probably more one of distaste and anger than anything else. It felt good to touch him. If even for a few moments.

"I'm coming with you," he said slowly, his voice solid and cold as steel.

CJ shook her head. "No, Nicky. Please."

"Do you expect me to just sit here on my ass and wait for you to come back with Michael? If that's the case, you shouldn't have come at all. If you know me as well as you say—"

"I knew you would want to know either way."

He spun away from her, raking a hand over his hair as he marched to the end of the dock, his other hand against his hip. "Damn it, Caitlin!"

Silence settled over the lake, and CJ barely dared breathe as Nick hung his head and stood with his back to her. She could only imagine the things he was trying to process. She had hit him with so much. A cold, evening breeze came through the trees, chilling her arms, and she hugged herself. The day was gone.

"I have to go."

"Caitlin . . ." he said slowly.

"I'll be back in a month with your son. I swear to you, I'll bring him to you. Or I'll die trying."

He turned back to her again. "*You* are going in after him?"

CJ nodded.

"Damn it, Caitlin. This is dark ops extraction, not some genetics lab experiment!"

CJ gave him a small smile. "Some things have changed in the last eight years, Nicky."

"No."

She smiled wider. CJ knew that one word was Nick's answer to everything. *No* she wasn't going in after Michael. *No* she hadn't changed. *No* she wasn't leaving him in Parson's Point. *No* to whatever point of the conversation he didn't like. That was Nick Tanner.

She still loved him for it.

"I have to go."

She turned and headed back toward the cabin and her vehicle she had brought in that morning. Nick reached her before she took three steps, grabbing her elbow to spin her around to face him. The action brought her almost flush against his chest and she had to raise her chin to look up at him.

"We'll get Michael out," she said softly, reaching up to lay her palm against his cheek. Nick didn't move either into or away from her touch. Caitlin tried to smile and dropped her hand, pulling free of his hold. He didn't call out after her again as she walked the path and climbed into her vehicle.

She glanced back as she engaged the hovermode and the compact vehicle lifted up from the ground to move away from the cabin. Nick stood where she left him, his tall form a shadow against the moonlight, still and straight.

CHAPTER THREE

27 October 2051 — Friday
Alliance Center for Genetic Advancement
Santa Fe, New Mexico
Former United States of America

*M*ichael sat on the ground in the corner of the small exercise yard, his knees raised, and his back against the concrete wall behind him. He had spent the last hour running the perimeter of the yard, and now his lungs burned and the muscles of his legs twitched with the exertion. Dust clung to the perspiration on his back and chest. He draped his tan linen tunic over his knees and enjoyed the cool feel of painted cinder block against his back.

The sun overhead was hot, but the walls around the exercise yard were tall enough that shade was abundant except at the highest point of the day. It was still early enough the sun wouldn't break past the eastern watchtower for another twenty minutes. Michael let his head fall back to rest on the wall, closing his eyes as his tired muscles recovered from the workout.

He heard the approach of Alexander's dragging shuffle, and shielded his eyes before he opened them. The large, severely deformed man—if he still qualified as a man in the eyes of some—stopped beside him and dropped to the ground to sit. His facial features were lopsided, not aligned symmetrically, and his small eyes were set wide apart. A tongue too large for his mouth poked from between cleft lips. He held out one dirty shoe in his large hands, deformed with the two center fingers of each melded together to form one large, almost useless digit. A broken lace was pinched between meaty fingers and he held it out along with the shoe.

Michael knew very little about Alexander, only that Alexander had been at the facility much longer than he. No one knew for sure how old he was, only that his mind was trapped somewhere in the past, never growing or maturing. Probably for the best, because if he had, he might actually understand what his captors had done to him. What they were responsible for.

It was bad enough Michael knew and could do nothing about it.

"What do you need, Alexander?" Michael asked, already knowing, but wanting to encourage Alexander to try and verbalize.

Alexander held out the shoe and lace with a soft grunt, scooting closer to Michael on his rear end. Dust swirled up from the dry earth.

Michael shook his head. "I don't understand, Alexander. You need to tell me."

"Pfif, pleefff," Alexander said, his tongue and lips fighting to form the words his mind knew. Spittle ran down his chin, and he wiped it away with the back of his hand. "Miffl."

Michael smiled and took the shoe.

Alexander smiled so the expression made his nose and eyes seem even more unbalanced, and laughed softly. The sound reminded Michael of when he was younger, and had been in the exercise yard when a storm came in unexpectedly. Thunder had rolled over the compound, vibrating in the air, and dark clouds had blackened out the sun. He shifted to cross his legs and rested the large shoe in his lap to tend to the broken lace.

The capacity for cruelty from the Areth, even in its most subtle form, always amazed him in the worst possible manner. Alexander was incapable of doing much on his own beyond struggling through feeding himself. Dressing himself was impossible. The deformities in his hands didn't allow it. Each day, the Areth orderlies in charge of his care struggled with him to dress him in shirts with buttons, pants with zippers and shoes with laces.

While Michael, on the other hand, was given shapeless pull on tunics of colorless linen and thong sandals.

Of course, he knew why. They were afraid. Afraid of what he would do with anything else. Just two days ago they had taken away his reading light and everything else that ran on electricity in his cell. Once the sun went down, he was in the dark.

Apparently, Mother was angry.

Probably because he called her Mother again.

Michael smiled as he knotted the two ends of the broken lace together and loosened the shoe. "There. Good as new. Let me have your foot."

Alexander obeyed, rocking on his hips to plop his massive, dirty foot in Michael's lap. Michael wiggled the shoe over Alexander's stubby toes. He tied the lace and patted Alexander's leg.

"All set."

"Fanfff, Miffl," Alexander sputtered with a wide grin.

"Good. Why don't you go find a ball? If you do, I'll roll it here with you."

Alexander smiled widely, his distorted features twisting into a face only Picasso could appreciate, and struggled to his feet, kicking up a cloud of dirt in his battle. Michael waved his hand in front of his face, clearing the air, as Alexander shuffled off in search of a ball. Unfortunately, the exercise period would most likely be over before he returned. Michael knew that just the offer to play meant a great deal to Alexander.

Twin shadows fell across him, and he looked up to see Jaeger and Rocco standing over him, dressed in the customary white uniforms of the laboratory assistants. With a sigh, Michael used one hand as support and moved to his feet. He dusted off his pants and slipped the tunic over his head. Rocco gripped Michael's elbow and Jaeger grabbed the other.

Jaeger and Rocco led him past the other prisoners, even though the Areth preferred the term patients or subjects. Some turned away, not wanting to meet his gaze because they knew what was in store for him. Others looked him in the eye, offering silent encouragement. None of them had anyone, left here to rot and die at the will of their captors. The only connections they could make were with each other, no matter how fleeting and inconsequential.

They stopped at the entrance back into the facility, and Jaeger took a security badge from his pocket, swiping it in the electronic lock. He pressed his thumb to the bio-scan pad and the door clicked open. The air inside the facility was cooler, but the bright florescent lights burned at Michael's eyes as the two big Areth pulled him along. Thoughts of what might be in store for him crossed his mind, but he knew it did little good to try and figure out the motives of the Areth. What he had done at birth to glean their hatred and scorn, he may never know. He would most likely die here, in this place, as much in the dark as the day he arrived.

They stopped at the elevator, and Jaeger again accessed the security panel. Michael counted the dings as the car approached. *Three . . . Four . . . Five.* The doors opened, and a woman stood inside, her head down as she scanned a tablet held in her hands. As she stepped forward, she nearly ran straight into Rocco and stopped short.

"Oh, I'm sorry," she gasped, her head coming up.

She was beautiful. Michael didn't have the memory of many women with which to compare her to, but surely she had to be beautiful compared to most. Her pale blond hair fell just past her chin, and a natural wave had it curling around her cheeks. The white lab coat she wore hid her figure, but she was tall in comparison to most women he had seen. Human women, anyway. Bright blue eyes connected with his, and she gasped, her mouth falling open as she blinked.

"Excuse us, Doctor Montgomery," Rocco said.

"Oh, yes. Of course." She stepped aside, folding her paperwork against her chest.

Michael watched her as Rocco and Jaeger forced him into the elevator, turning so they again faced out. Doctor Montgomery stood in the hallway, her intense eyes staring. Michael arched one eyebrow, and was amazed when he actually thought he saw her lips tip up in the smallest of smiles.

The door closed and she was gone.

They rode in silence down to the laboratories where Mother did her best work. Quiet and secluded, she was far less likely to be disturbed. After several more security checks, they reached her lab. Neither Jaeger nor Rocco said a word as they unceremoniously lifted him into a stainless steel chair and secured him. The nylon straps dug into his wrists and ankles, and the leather thong at his throat made it hard to swallow. When they were done, both men turned in unison and headed for the door.

He sat there for several minutes, and knew the solitude was merely for effect, before the door opened again and Mother entered. Her brunette hair was curled into an intricate twist along her skull, and only the faintest signs of age marred the corners of her eyes and lips.

"Hello, Michael," she said, her voice as cold as the stainless steel chair he was strapped to.

To her assistants and peers, in the nature of the Areth to be known by only one name, she was called Kathleen. Michael knew this woman as much more. Torturer. Nightmare giver. Bloodhound. Worst of all . . .

"Mother."

*C*J forced herself to remain calm as she walked across the lab adjacent to her office. She nodded to a couple of the other scientists, and stopped to speak briefly with one of the lab technicians who had a question. The whole time, her heart pounded furiously in her chest and the top of her head felt like it was going to float away.

"Make sure the samples stay in the centrifuge for at least an hour to obtain the maximum separation," she instructed as she moved away from the last station.

She made it to her office and stepped inside. CJ's hand trembled as she gripped the doorknob. She released a shaky breath as the latch clicked. For about five seconds she contemplated closing the blinds, but knew that it would only attract more attention rather than allow her the privacy she needed.

This was not good. So not good!

As an Earth scientist working in a Coalition facility, on the surface she was considered an equal with her peers. In the six weeks she had been here, she had not been told of the human patients kept in the west wing. The only reason she knew of their existence was because of Michael, and because she came here looking. They were the Areth's dirty little secret.

She had inadvertently come face to face with one of them.

Michael.

Good God, he was his father's son.

CJ walked to her desk on shaky legs and sank into her chair, resting her head against her palm. This could ruin everything. What would her superiors do now? Would they confront her about seeing him? Would they question her? Would they demand her silence, or would they act as if it were nothing to be concerned about? Worst yet, this could put her under their scrutiny. They would be watching her now, looking for signs of some reaction. She was, after all, human. What would a human scientist feel about her Areth counterparts holding humans as lab rats?

The fact she had inadvertently stumbled onto him wasn't what worried her the most.

Where were they taking him?

And why?

CJ turned to her computer, and rested her fingers on the keyboard, her touch bringing the machine to life. She stared at the main screen, and wondered where to even begin. It was highly doubtful she would be able to just punch a few keys here and there and find out what they were doing with him, and why. Wasn't that what she had been doing for the last month and a half?

She groaned and covered her eyes with her hands, the precarious line she walked finally sinking in. If she dived into the computer base and started digging around, they would know in an instant what she wanted and why. Just the fact that she saw him was bad enough; to draw more attention could make things monumentally worse.

CJ's stomach clenched and a nervous sweat broke out over her whole body.

Dear God, please don't let this ruin everything. I promised him. I promised Nick.

*O*ictor drained the last lukewarm swallow of coffee and tossed the paper cup in the trash receptacle beside his workbench. He had a fleeting thought whether he was developing an addiction to the caffeinated brew, recalling medical journals he had read from decades before. He smiled.

In human history, there were worse things to find pleasure in than coffee.

Without warning, a sharp pain shot from the base of his skull and spread like acid in his veins. Victor pressed his eyes closed against the wave of nausea that gripped him. He slipped from the stool he had sat on, and barely stayed on his feet as he held onto the edge of the table. Dark spots shifted in his vision and his head felt as if it was going to split. Then, just as quickly, the pain ebbed back and the knot in his gut released. Victor sucked in sharp gulps of air and wiped a shaky hand across his damp upper lip.

The attacks were growing more frequent, as often as once a week now. Striking him with no warning, no known cause, ending as quickly as they started. He had run every test he could think of, and had determined nothing.

Yet, he was still reluctant to bring the matter to the attention of his superiors. Something in the back of his mind told him not to. They couldn't know.

He straightened, feeling his strength return. The headache was only a dull throb now, pulsing at his temples in rhythm with his heartbeat. Another half hour and it would be gone. It was a familiar routine now.

The lab door opened, and Barnabas looked in. "Victor, I am glad to find you here. We need to speak."

Victor ran a hand over his black hair and made his way back to his stool, sitting down. His knees still felt shaky, and he didn't want to run the risk of collapsing in front of the facilities lead scientist. "What is it?"

"There was an incident today with one of the subjects."

"Who?"

"Michael."

Victor's stomach clenched again and a cold sweat broke out over his body, but he focused on maintaining a steady and unemotional expression. "What sort of incident."

"I should clarify. Our new human geneticist, Doctor Caitlin Montgomery, inadvertently saw Michael today."

Victor leaned back and crossed his arms over his body. "I see. How did this happen?"

"He was being taken to Kathleen's lab. Rocco and Jaeger used the east entrance elevators, and Doctor Montgomery saw them."

"Has she said anything? Did she recognize him?"

"No. However, Terence and Kathleen have concerns. Justifiable ones."

"How can I help?"

Barnabas tapped his knuckles on the granite tabletop, his other hand scratching at the salt-and-pepper beard that lined his jaw. "I had concerns bringing her to this facility, considering her history. Keep an eye on her. See if she says anything. Asks any questions."

"And give the appropriate answers if she does."

"Exactly. You know, as well as I, the importance of this facility."

Victor bit down, curling his fingers into fists beneath his arms. "I will see to it."

Barnabas nodded and turned to leave. Victor called out to him as he reached the door, and he stopped. "Why did Kathleen have Michael? I thought her experiments were complete for the time being?" he asked.

Barnabas smiled a smile so cold it almost made Victor shake. "You know Kathleen. She needs her amusements."

Victor bit down harder. "Of course."

*M*ichael prayed for death.

It was the only salvation from the pain that had taken over his body with no mercy. His nerves crackled, his skin sizzled like burning meat. The world was a black pit, with no up or down, no point of reference. Whether he was lying down, or still strapped to Kathleen's chair of torture, he didn't know.

His own blood pounded in his ears like someone beating on the steel door of his cell with a hammer. Every breath he took felt like raw wool scraping against the inside of his ribcage.

Silently, he begged for it to end.

Cold liquid touched his lips, and the touch of a hand supporting the back of his head. Michael swallowed greedily, relishing in the refreshing sensation as the water washed down his parched throat. The cold spread through his fevered chest, making him shiver. He tried to open his eyes, but couldn't tell if he had or not. Everything was black.

A cold cloth wiped across his face and throat, and Michael closed his eyes again, although nothing changed in his line of sight. He tried to focus, and realized he was lying on his back. By the familiar lumps and bumps, it had to be his own bed in his own cell—which explained the darkness.

The cool touch returned, extinguishing the fire that burned beneath the surface of his skin as it ran along his throat and shoulders. He couldn't move, lacking the strength to even lift his arm.

"Who is there?" he asked, his voice rough and shallow in the darkness.

"You must be silent," said a low voice near his ear. "Or it will be trouble for both of us, my friend."

Michael swallowed again, his throat dry already. "Victor?"

"Quiet. You need to rest."

Michael couldn't argue, the heavy weights of sleep pulling at his limbs. He wished only to close his eyes and slip into oblivion, to escape the pain.

"Drink some more," Victor whispered near his ear again. "I have dissolved some electrolytes, analgesics, and antibiotics in the water. I am sorry, but I can do little else."

The hand once again supported his head and Michael drank the water. Some ran from the corners of his mouth to drop to his chest, but he continued to gulp it down. When the flow stopped, Victor eased him back onto the bed and Michael released a heavy breath.

"I'm so tired, Victor." He could barely force his own voice from his throat.

A warm hand curled over his shoulder. Moments later, the cloth returned to clean his face and cool his skin. Time passed, and whatever Victor had given him slowly began to take the edge off the pain. The pounding in his ears lessened, breathing was easier. The sheet beneath him no longer felt like sandpaper on his bare skin.

He felt Victor beside him, leaning in to speak close to his ear. "I can't stay, Michael. I've done all I can. If I do more, someone will question it."

"You shouldn't have come," Michael said, his voice hoarse.

There was no answer. The blanket whispered in the dark as Victor pulled it over him. Michael blinked slowly, still seeing no change in the darkness. He wondered for a moment if he was blind. Once again, he felt Victor's hand on his shoulder, and then the touch was gone. Moments later, the sound of his cell door clicking closed echoed through the pounding in his ears.

He was alone.

CHAPTER FOUR

28 OCTOBER 2051, SATURDAY
PHOENIX COMPOUND
OUTSIDE COLORADO SPRINGS, COLORADO
FORMER UNITED STATES OF AMERICA

"*H*ey, Nia. Uh, oh . . . looks like someone took a digger."

Jace Quinn smiled as he stepped into the base's makeshift infirmary, wagging his fingers at the little girl who sat on the edge of one of the beds, her hair a mass of blond curls around her head. She smiled, showing a gap between her front teeth, and her cheeks flushed pink.

Nia looked over her shoulder at him as she wrapped a bandage around the girl's knee. "Nothing too serious. Sabrina tripped on her untied shoelaces. We're going to make sure they're tied from now on, right?"

Sabrina nodded, glancing at Jace. "Yes."

Nia lifted Sabrina down off the bed, and Jace ruffled her hair as she ran by and into the hallway. "She still didn't tie her shoelace," he said, listening as the soft footfalls died away.

"Nope. She'll be here again."

The compact personal access tablet attached to Jace's belt beeped, and he snapped it off to read the flashing message. *Lt. Quinn—Meeting in Control at 1330 for all key personnel. Gen. Castleton.* He glanced at his watch, and noted he had almost an hour and a half. Plenty of time. Jace clicked the PAC in place at his waist.

"How's your other patient?"

Nia groaned and rolled her eyes. "Whoever said 'physician, heal thyself' obviously didn't have her in mind."

Jace chuckled. "I'll go check on her." He headed for the back of the infirmary wing as Nia cleaned up the bandage remnants left on the bed. Jace stopped at the doorway, turning. "Oh, and it was Jesus Christ."

She looked up. "What was?"

"Luke chapter four, verse twenty-three. *And he said unto them, Ye will surely say unto me with this proverb, Physician, heal thyself: whatsoever we have heard done in Capernaum, do also here in this country.*"

Nia tilted her head, arching one eyebrow. "Wow, I'm impressed."

"Don't be. Dad and Grandpa were preachers." He tapped the jamb as he left, walking through the dark storage room to another closed door that led to the attached living quarters.

Jace opened the door and listened as he entered the main room. The entire space consisted only of three rooms; the main room that served as kitchen and dining area with a long couch for relaxing, the bedroom, and the bathroom. The main room was dark and empty except for a kettle of water heating on the small stove, steam curling from its spout. Jace took a clean cup from the sink and filled the tea diffuser kept by the stove. As the kettle whistled, he lifted it from the heat and poured boiling water over the diffuser into the cup. The scent of mint filled the air, rising up from the fragrant tea. Cup in hand, he headed for the attached bedroom.

Lilly was buried deep in the bed, the blankets pulled up to her chin, with just a tuft of damp blond hair, still wet from the shower she'd practically fallen asleep in, splayed across the pillows. Jace set the mug on the bedside table and sat down on the mattress, resting his hand on one of the lumps.

"I brought you some tea."

A muffled groan was his answer. Jace chuckled softly and tugged at the blankets until they slid down her body, revealing his wife's pale and tired face. She turned into the pillows, hiding from him with another groan.

"Come on. You'll feel better if you drink the tea. It's mint."

"Who's the doctor here? You, or me?" she grumbled.

Jace didn't answer, but tugged gently on her hand until she conceded to sit up, running a hand over her hair. Golden locks curled around her cheeks, unruly and untamed from lying in bed, and her ice blue eyes were red-rimmed. Even sick and rumpled, she was beautiful to him. As she sipped from the cup, he moved around to sit against the headboard and Lilly reclined back against him, resting her head on his shoulder so he could circle his arm around her body.

"Thank you for the tea," she said, her voice cracking.

"I wish I could do more."

Lilly chuckled wryly. "It amazes me. We've cured two-dozen diseases in the last two decades. Even created a vaccine for HIV. Yet, we can't cure the common cold. After hundreds of years of suffering, there's not a damn thing we can do but ride it out."

Jace kissed her hair and smoothed it beneath his fingers. She scooted closer and he wrapped his arms around her, holding her close. Her body was hot, either from a fever or from hiding beneath the blankets. He felt the heat emanating from her through his utility pants and tee shirt.

"Are you feeling *any* better?"

Lilly nodded. "Some, yes. I'll be fine in another day or two." She snorted a small laugh and coughed, covering her mouth with the side of her fist. "Just in time to leave again. I can't believe this. I'm only here for two weeks, and I spend a week of it sick in bed."

Jace pressed a kiss to the exposed skin where her neck met her shoulder. "I'm not one to ever complain about having you in bed for a week." Lilly laughed softly and he smiled against her throat. He moved his lips to the sweet spot beneath her ear, tracing his tongue along her skin. "I miss you."

The familiar heat Lilly never failed to illicit in his blood quickly grew from a slow simmer to a rolling boil, but Jace tamped it down and wrapped her in his arms to hold her in a firm hug. She just smelled and felt so good. These short times together—two weeks here, a weekend there—only made him hungry for her all the more.

"When is your next trip home?" he asked, resting his cheek against her hair.

"I will be here for the New Mexico extraction. We have no idea what kind of physical condition those prisoners are going to be in. I want to be here when you come back." She ran her hand along his arm, her innocent touch making his nerves spark. "And I want to be here when you go."

"To see me off?" he said with a lilt to his voice.

"Have you ever gone on a mission that I wasn't here to see you off?"

"Not since the day I convinced you marrying an AWOL Earth Force lieutenant was somehow a good idea."

Lilly chuckled and sniffled, sliding her left hand beneath his until their fingers interlocked. The simple gold band she only wore on base clicked against the matching one that never left his hand. "Who says you were the one doing the convincing?"

Jace laughed out loud, pulling her closer to press another kiss to her temple. "Fair enough. I should go and let you get some more sleep." He bent his neck and allowed himself the brief, tempting pleasure of kissing the curve of her neck.

Lilly drew in a long, slow breath through clenched teeth as her hand came up to cup the back of his head, holding him in place. Her fingers laced into his hair, and every nerve in his body shot to life when she softly whispered his name.

"Lilly . . ." he groaned in answer.

"Don't go, Jace. Not yet."

He drew in a slow breath, filling his senses with the scent that clung to her skin. A heady mix of musky floral, spicy citrus and the underlying warmth that he knew simply as *Lilly*. Today it was tinged with the scent of mint and menthol, but erotic all the same. Jace closed his eyes and curled his fingers into the soft cotton of her tank top. He swallowed hard, his throat dry.

"Do you want me to stay until you go to sleep?"

"I want you to stay," she said, her voice raspy. "But I don't want to sleep."

"Are you sure?"

She moaned as he sucked her earlobe between his lips. Her voice was a husky whisper as she spoke, sliding her hand over his to guide it to her breast. "You know, it has been medically proven that lovemaking has many beneficial side effects. Other than the obvious . . ."

Jace found the hem of her top and slipped his hand inside, finding the soft skin of her stomach. She moaned softly as he skimmed his fingers around her bellybutton. "Yeah? Like what?" He flattened his palm against her skin and slid it beneath the waistband of the loose shorts she wore.

She arched against him, drawing in a sharp breath, releasing it on a long hum. "Um, during sexual arousal the body releases histamine that can relieve congestion and the natural increase in blood flow can lessen headaches."

Jace smiled against her hair. "I love it when you talk biology. What else?"

Lilly pulled her lower lip through her teeth, her eyes closing, as he imprinted in his mind how every inch of her body felt. "Slow, prolonged lovemaking helps cleanse toxins from the system," she finally said with hitched breath. "And the natural elation of mood and release of tension from orgasm helps the body rejuvenate itself."

Jace shifted them together until they lay horizontally across the bed, the headboard behind his back, so he could look down at his wife. He pushed up her top until her breasts were exposed, running his thumb along their undersides as he kissed the soft line of her jaw. "I can do slow. I can do fast. Baby, I'll do whatever you want."

"I can't say I was all that surprised to hear from you, Nick."

Nick looked across the small elevator car to General Bob Castleton, his former Earth Force commanding officer, and now the C.O. of the Colorado Phoenix base. The years had been fairly kind to Bob, and approaching seventy he still looked healthy and fit to lead an army. Nick shifted the strap of his duffle on his shoulder.

"Wasn't that the point when you sent Caitlin?"

The general shifted to an at-ease stance, his hands behind his back and his feet set apart as he faced Nick. "There's no real point in making things into something they're not, Nick. Therefore, I'll be straight. I didn't want CJ to go see you because I knew you'd see it this way. It wasn't a ploy. But I knew once she went, and once you knew, that you'd come."

"Did you want me to know at all?"

General Castleton winced, the deep lines at the corners of his eyes becoming more pronounced. "I didn't know what the right call was. But once CJ knew that was your boy, there was no talking her out of it."

Nick nodded, believing the man. In the ten years he served under Castleton's command, he had never known the man to sugarcoat anything, or to be anything but straight cut honest. The elevator shifted and bounced to a stop, and the doors opened. Dog came to his feet, keeping close to Nick's leg, and Nick reached down to scratch his ear. He understood the animal's trepidation. Being twenty floors below the surface wasn't his idea of a good time, either.

"My key people will be meeting with us at 1330. We have some time if you want to look around."

Nick glanced left and right. Gray painted hallways stretched in both directions with similarly painted pipes running along the ceilings. Hydrogen cell lights cast a soft glow every few feet, and colored stripes on the floor provided directions for those who knew the coding. It reminded him of half a dozen other military bases he had been on throughout his career.

"Nah, I'll figure it out on my own."

Castleton nodded and motioned to his left. "We'll just head to Command and wait for the others."

Nick shifted the duffle to hang down his back, the strap hooked on two fingers at his shoulder, and walked beside the general. Dog padded along behind him, eliciting smiles from the few men and women they passed in the hall. He figured they didn't keep too many dogs down here, but leaving Dog behind to fend for himself wasn't an option.

"Does she know?" Nick asked after walking a few minutes in silence.

"That you're here? No."

Nick cleared his throat, disguising the chuckle threatening to escape. General Castleton looked at him sideways before continuing down the hall.

"You didn't mention to her we know each other?" the general asked.

"No. But I'm guessing you didn't either."

Castleton didn't have to answer. They reached the end of the hall, which opened up to a large command center banked on two walls with computers and monitors behind smoky glass panels. Nick dropped his duffle just inside the door to retrieve later. An octagon-shaped holovid table sat in the center of the room, at which stood a broad shouldered black man and a woman with golden-red hair that cascaded down her back in soft waves. The man wore military issue utility pants and a black shirt that nearly blended into the deep color of his skin. His head was shaved bald, and it gleamed beneath the hydrogen lighting.

The woman wore a filmy lavender dress that flowed around her in multiple layers, accentuating her curves beneath. Her skin was nearly translucent and as she looked up, Nick was startled by the rich jade color of her eyes against the pale glow of her skin. Her eyes angled slightly, giving them an exotic, almond shape accentuated by the high angle of her cheekbones and hinted at some sort of distant Eastern heritage. He had seen beautiful women, but she was something else altogether.

Breathtaking.

What the hell was she doing in a place like this?

"Good afternoon, General," the man said, standing straight. Nick noted the lack of salute. This was, after all, nowhere near an official military station.

"Captain, I'd like you to meet Colonel Nicholas Tanner. Nick, this is Captain Damian Ali."

They shook hands, and Nick made a mental note never to challenge Damian to an arm wrestling match. The redheaded woman watched each of them with keen interest, her gaze shifting between each of them as they spoke, and her eyes focusing on their lips. Something about the way she moved, silent and graceful, and the intensity of her concentration, both unnerved and captivated him.

"Nick, this is Beverly Surimoto. Her parents were among the founding members of Phoenix over thirty years ago, and she is still with us."

Nick extended his hand, and she slipped hers inside his grasp. Her long, elegant fingers brushed the inside of his wrist as her thumb tangled with his. A strange tingling shot up his arm, like bubbles in his veins, and a light sensation flowed up the back of his skull. The hairs on the back of his neck stood on end, and warmth wrapped around him. Nick blinked, staring at her, and thought for a moment he saw a flash of surprise in her eyes. She smiled, and a soft voice emanated from a small brooch pinned near her collarbone.

"It is a pleasure to meet you, Colonel. We are honored to have you here. Please rest assured that we are all working with everything in our power to bring your son home again."

The warmth wrapped around his shoulders, almost as real as an embrace, and Nick pulled back. As soon as the contact broke, the sensation fell away. Nick rested his hand on the back of his neck, rubbing slowly across the short hair there.

"Thank you."

"Beverly is deaf," General Castleton explained. "She can read your lips and understand as easily as someone who can hear. She speaks through a neurological link connected to the speech center of her brain."

Nick just nodded, staring at the small brooch.

Beverly smiled, and Nick tried not to look completely freaked that she was talking to him without her lips moving. "Don't worry, Colonel. It will take some time to get used to. I understand."

Dog whimpered beside him, and Nick glanced down, realizing he had completely forgotten the animal was with him. Dog had remained quiet, absorbing everything much like Nick himself. When he looked down, he caught Beverly following his actions. Her mouth fell open and her eyes brightened as she crouched down, reaching for the rag mop that sometimes passed for a dog.

"He's precious," her 'brooch' said as she scratched Dog's ears and ruffled his fur. Dog licked her knuckles and ate up the attention.

The room slowly filled with more people. Individuals ranging in age from their early twenties to much older than the general, men and women alike. General Castleton introduced him around, but Nick gave up much hope of remembering after the third or fourth introduction. As everyone settled around the table, each pulling up a chair, a man came running down the hall on the other side of the room. He stopped short as he stepped into the room, pausing to finish tucking the hem of his tee shirt into his pants and smooth his hand over his dark hair. He was in his early to mid-thirties, and had the looks of a man who had spent most of his adult life in the military.

"Sorry," he said on a huff. "Did I miss anything?"

General Castleton cleared his throat. "No, Jace. Take a seat. Nick, this is Lieutenant Jason Quinn. Jace, Colonel Tanner has just joined us—"

"No way!" Lieutenant Quinn exclaimed as he gripped Nick's hand, pumping it hard. "*The* Colonel Nick Tanner?"

Nick slid a glance at the general before looking back at the lieutenant. "I guess."

Quinn grinned, setting his hands at his hips. "Damn. I spent five years on the Force trying to break your wormhole flight records. Almost did once. Came within three seconds, but I lost my O_2 boosters."

Nick leaned back in his chair, linking his hands over his stomach. "So, *you're* the hotshot Gomer who tried."

He smiled wide, bouncing on the balls of his feet. "Yup. I would have, too. Except for those damn boosters. How did you compensate for the manual trajectory manipulations necessary while still adjusting for the—"

"Lieutenant, could we please focus on the matter at hand?" General Castleton interjected.

Quinn cleared his throat, nodding at the general before he found an empty chair beside Damian. He ran his hands over his hair again, smoothing a tuft that didn't seem to want to lay flat.

"So . . . Lilly feeling better?" Nick heard Damian ask, a chuckle in his voice.

Quinn smiled wider, nodding his head as he focused on the details loading on the individual screens in front of them. "Hell, yeah."

"Damian, I want you and Jace to work together with the colonel after our meeting today. Bring him up to speed on all the details. He's going in with us, understood?" General Castleton stated.

Both men nodded in agreement, not missing a beat.

"What is there new to cover?" the general asked.

"General," came a familiar female voice from the hallway behind them. "I have some new information that may change our plans."

Nick sat back in his chair and slowly turned. Caitlin looked down, her gaze connecting with him and her mouth fell open. He couldn't help his smile, and to be totally honest, didn't really want to. She stared at him, her lips moving with unspoken words as he pressed his hands against his knees and stood. Her eyes followed him.

"Hello, Caitlin."

CHAPTER FIVE

*D*amian offered her his chair, and CJ sank into it before her legs gave out completely. She forced herself to look away from Nick, to give herself time to think. Half a dozen questions collided in her head in the same moment, throbbing in her temples, demanding answers. The loudest of all being *how did he get here*?

She scooted closer to the table, smiling quickly at Jace and Beverly. CJ tried to hide how flustered she was at Nick's presence by folding her hands in her lap and focusing on the data on her monitor until she could look up with some measure of confidence. It wasn't that she couldn't maintain a professional demeanor with Nick Tanner in the room, it was just . . . he wasn't supposed to *be* in the room!

CJ took a data disk from her pocket and slid it into the port nearest her station, loading the command to send the information on it to all the monitors at the table. "I was able to gather more detailed information on the security systems that should help us bypass them when the time comes, along with a detailed floor plan of the facility. I have determined the prisoners are being kept in what the Areth call D-Wing, which is here." She tapped her own screen, and a corresponding red dot flashed on the screens of everyone present.

Damian leaned over her shoulder to view the information. "What floors are they kept on?"

"The cells are on the third floor. I hope to have medical information on as many of them as I can obtain. So we can adequately treat anything we might face for whomever we're able to bring out."

"I'll let Lilly know," Jace said, adding, "She's sick."

CJ nodded, and looked back to the monitor, still avoiding the dark eyes of the man just four chairs to her left. "They're putting up a solid front for this facility. Everything on the surface appears completely ethical. They have me working on a genetic filtering process to immobilize and eliminate Guillain-Barre Syndrome. For all intents and purposes, they haven't questioned me or limited me." She took a deep breath. "Yet."

"You said you have information that might change our plans," General Castleton said, leaning back with his arm extended across the tabletop. "What is it?"

"We may need to move faster than we planned. I don't know yet."

"Did something happen?"

CJ forced herself to look at Nick when he asked the question, meeting his gaze. His expression was intense and dark, with his eyes hooded as he rested his elbow on the arm of the chair and curled his fingers over his lips. She nodded, slowly, before answering.

"I inadvertently caught them transporting . . ." She paused, contemplating for a brief moment the ramifications of the whole truth versus trying to somehow cushion the blow. "Michael yesterday afternoon. I stepped out of an elevator as two Areth guards were preparing to bring him in."

The only change was a straightening of his lips behind his fingers, and a muscle jumped along his jaw. CJ didn't look away, even when the general spoke.

"Do you know what they were doing?"

"No." Her voice cracked, and she cleared her throat, speaking again. "No, but wherever they were taking him, he wasn't a willing participant. He wasn't physically fighting them, but they were strong arming him."

Nick's eyes slid closed.

"Are you concerned for his wellbeing?" the general asked.

CJ finally pulled her focus back to the general. "For the immediate future, yes, I have concerns. To be honest, General, we have no idea what they are doing to any of the prisoners there. My concern also lies in the fact the Areth now know I am aware of his existence. They may make it more difficult for me to continue my intelligence gathering. They may implement more stringent security measures. I don't know yet what their response will be. I don't believe my being away this weekend will cause questions because I mentioned that I was going away prior to the incident. But any future contact or travel might be closely monitored."

"Perhaps moving up the extraction isn't the answer, General," Damian said from behind her chair. "Perhaps we wait until sufficient time has passed that we can be confident Doctor Montgomery's loyalties are no longer in question."

CJ looked to Nick, who sat silent but watched the general—waiting for his judgment call. She held her breath.

"I don't think we should change anything," Beverly said, raising her hand to draw everyone's attention to her. She swept her hand around the table, indicating each of them as her synthesized voice spoke. "We have all put a great deal of time, effort, and detail into carefully planning this mission. Attempting to change too much now could lead to mistakes. Something we cannot afford." She tapped the monitor with her palm. "We know what we have to do and why we have to do it. And we know when."

All eyes turned to General Castleton, who sat silent for several moments, tapping his fingers on the table. He drew in a sharp breath and sat forward, linking his hands together. "We stay status quo for now, until something happens to change the plan. I want to talk again tomorrow before you return to New Mexico, CJ. In the meantime, make sure the Intel you brought back is downloaded into the main computer. Damian and Jace, the two of you are to go over the security information over the next week to make sure we don't meet up with any surprises."

Everyone nodded their agreement and the group disbursed. CJ stole a quick glance at Nick, who hadn't moved since she'd spoken Michael's name. His fingers still curled across his cheek to partially cover his lips, and his brown eyes stared past everyone to some indistinct point on the far wall.

CJ touched Jace's arm as he stood, standing with him. "How sick is she?"

Jace smiled, patting her hand. "Just a cold. She says she'll be fine in a day or two. And she's the doc, after all."

"Tell her I'll come see her this evening."

Jace promised he would, and took the microslide from her, stating he would download the information for her. CJ smiled as he walked away, noting the swagger that always seemed to take over his stride whenever his wife was on base, and wondered if he knew about the strawberry-shaped mark Lilly had left behind just peeking from the collar of his tee shirt.

"CJ, would you mind showing Nick to his quarters? The empty one across the hall from you," General Castleton stated from the hallway door as he left, allowing her no time to answer.

She looked to Nick again, but he still hadn't moved except to rest his other hand on Dog's head. His pet had been so quiet and well behaved through the meeting that she hadn't even realized he was there. CJ remembered reading once that pets could be finely tuned to their owner's feelings and emotions, and she wondered just what Dog sensed in Nick right now. Perhaps it explained his silence.

Command had returned to normal function, with only a staff of two others monitoring systems on the other side of the room. CJ drew in a fortifying breath and walked to the chair that General Castleton had left empty, turning it to face sideways so she could look at Nick, and sat down. She crossed her legs and folded her hands in her lap, waiting, but he didn't move.

Finally, she cleared her throat. "Nick."

He slowly lowered his hand and turned to look at her. The storm stirring his eyes was enough to catch her breath, but she didn't turn away. "You should have just brought me with you. Saved yourself the shock."

Just like that the storm subsided and the darkness was tamped down. He buried it, and forced himself to appear unfazed by what was going on. She pulled her lower lip through her teeth and tilted her head. "Let me guess. You served with General Castleton on Earth Force?" His eyebrows arched, waiting for her to continue. "And he'd already asked you once to join Phoenix but you said no."

Nick smirked and shrugged one shoulder. "Don't panic. He made it clear you didn't know and that you weren't sent as recruitment bait."

CJ looked down at her hands, rubbing her thumb over her knuckles. He still knew her well enough to know that those had been the first thoughts to come to mind. Nick was not a man who liked being manipulated, and if he suspected for a minute that bringing him to Phoenix had been her true intention, he'd never trust another word she said.

Not that she entertained the thought that he trusted her now . . .

"If I had known—"

"You would have come anyway."

The deep timbre of his voice made CJ look up and for one moment she saw a flash of something kind and warm in Nick's eyes. Then he blinked and looked away, and it was gone. CJ cleared her throat and braced her hands on the arm of the chair, pushing up.

"I'll show you to your quarters."

*N*ick stood behind Caitlin as she punched a code into the numeric key lock outside his new quarters, and heard the lock disengage. She pushed down the handle and opened the door.

"I'm sorry for the archaic number pad lock, but this facility was decommissioned within the first few years after the Areth came. We focused on keeping the base security and computer systems up to date, but never felt personal security was a concern."

"No problem."

"I can show you how to update the code to whatever you want before I go."

He just nodded and walked into the space that was his new home.

For now.

It was about as far from Parson's Point as he could get.

There were no windows and the only light came from the hydrogen gel lamps recessed into the ceiling and along the walls to create a more natural light. The walls were utility gray, and the space was small but functional. A small kitchen area was to his left with just enough room to turn around. Two tall stools sat on the outside of the counter to serve as seating. To his right was a desk with a PAC already set up and ready for use. Straight ahead was an open doorway through which he saw a bed.

Nick walked through to the bedroom, Dog on his heels, and dropped his duffle in the middle of the full sized bed. Dog jumped up and flopped to his side, stretching out on the blankets. Normally, Nick would have told him to get down, but he figured he'd let it go. The dog deserved a little slack. He had behaved himself thus far.

Standing at the foot of the bed, he saw another door that led to the bathroom. He'd lived in smaller places. It actually reminded him of the military quarters first given to him and Kathleen after they married.

For just one beat of his heart, his chest squeezed and he had to swallow against the wave of smothering rage that hit him.

"You can eat here if you like, but there is also an open cafeteria on level twelve. The PX is there. No credits necessary. Just take what you need. We don't have a lot of surplus, but we've managed to have enough."

Nick kept his back to her as she spoke, but he knew she had moved to the doorway of the bedroom, stopping short of stepping inside. They stood like that for several minutes, in silence, before he heard her restrained intake of air.

"I'll leave you to unpack or do whatever you'd like."

He counted her footfalls as she walked away. *Five . . . Six . . . Seven*

"Caitlin . . ."

"Yes?"

He turned slowly. She stood near the door, her arms crossed. Nick walked toward her and she slowly hitched up her chin as he approached, holding his gaze with her blue eyes. When he was within a few inches of her, he stopped, pushing his hands into his pockets.

"Michael – what did he – how did he–" He didn't even know what questions he wanted to ask. How did he look? The question sounded asinine, even to his own ears.

"When I saw him, he looked good. He looked just like you." Her voice was so soft it almost didn't reach him. "I only saw him for a minute, and I saw you in him, Nick." She paused, her head tilting as her gaze narrowed slightly, studying him. "Your eyes. Your height." Her gaze shifted down, to settle on his lips. "Your mouth. He even has your smile."

"My smile?"

She nodded, looking back up at him. The tension that had seized him when her gaze focused on his lips eased, but the heat that immediately sparked in his blood didn't get the same message. How could everything south of his shoulders still respond so hard and strong to her when his brain remembered so clearly what she had done?

"He does the same thing with his eyebrow that you do."

Without thinking, Nick arched an eyebrow, and Caitlin smiled brightly, a soft chuckle making the base of her throat bounce as she tipped her head back.

"Yes, that. Then he smiled, and I saw you."

Nick swallowed hard against the heaviness that settled in his chest, squeezing his lungs and tightening his throat. He stepped away from her, moving to one of the stools along the counter, and curled his fingers around the back. His knuckles whitened with the grip, and he leaned into the hunched stance. Caitlin didn't move from where she stood, only turning to watch him.

"Do you think they've hurt him?"

"Now? Or in the last twenty-five years?"

"Ever."

He heard her draw a breath, and the tremble moved through her as she released it. "Nicky—"

"Don't answer that. I don't think I want to hear."

Two shrill beeps sounded from a hidden speaker over their heads before General Castleton's voice echoed in the room. *"Colonel."*

Nick straightened and glanced toward the source of the unseen voice. "I'm here, sir."

"When you're settled, please return to Command. We'll begin preparing you for the mission. Time is growing short and we have a lot to cover."

Caitlin shifted her gaze to meet his, and her lips pressed together as she stared at him. Nick stared back, recognizing the unspoken argument already forming in her head. "I'll be right there."

Two more beeps indicated the communication link closed. Caitlin wrapped her arms tighter around her body, gripping her elbows, and curled her lips between her teeth as she slid her stare away.

"Go ahead." He hitched his chin toward her. "Say it."

She turned sharp on the balls of her feet and headed again for the door, talking over her shoulder. "Anything I have to say is irrelevant at this point."

"You still don't think I should be here. Or going on the mission."

Caitlin stopped at the door, her fingers curled around the handle, and looked back at him. "I have no problem with you being *here*, Nick. Being with Phoenix. But you should not be going to New Mexico."

"Why?"

"Because it's too close! Too personal for you," she said, her voice rising as she waved her free hand back at him.

Anger pushed out against his chest, making him overheated and his hands fisted. "He's my son, Caitlin. I couldn't—"

Her frustrated groan cut him off as she bumped her forehead against the door. "I should have listened to the general. I should have just waited until Michael was safe then brought him to you."

Nick walked across the small space to her, standing close but not close enough to touch her. "You think I'll do something stupid."

She raised her head from its resting position and met his gaze, her blue eyes shifting as she looking at him. "Stupid, no, but I think you'll do anything to get Michael out. Even if it means . . ."

Her voice cracked, and she pressed her lips together, not finishing the thought.

"You're right. I would."

Caitlin shook her head. "You can't."

Nick raised his arm to rest it on the wall beside the doorframe, leaning into it. The stance shortened his height enough that they were almost eye level. "Which one of us is too close now, Caitlin?"

She drew a sharp breath, her body shaking, but she didn't look away. Every instinct in his body screamed to lean in and kiss the worried tension from her lips, and to take the rest of the day to relearn her body all over again. He wondered if she still liked it on top, or if she still had that 'trigger spot' on the back of her neck that always had her humming in seconds when he kissed it.

Nick clenched his fist and bit down hard. The air around them was heavy and static, sparking on his skin. He knew she felt it. He saw it when she shifted her gaze to his lips for a split second before staring into his eyes again. He swallowed, and forced himself to remember.

Never again.

"I'm going in after my son, and one way or another, he's coming out," he said, his voice rough and low between them. His breath stirred the wispy hair that framed her face. "If I don't come out with him, I guess that's just one more thing on your conscience."

She sucked in a sharp breath, her spine straightening, and Nick saw the immediate shine of moisture fill her eyes. Something had changed in Caitlin June Montgomery in the last eight years, because she didn't allow a single tear to fall. She pushed down the handle with a decided click and yanked the door open, the disturbance of air brushed across his face. He didn't move until the door closed again on its own, echoing in the silence of the small room.

Nick rested his head on his arm and closed his eyes. His chest ached with the breath he had held from the moment the words left his lips. Some part of him had wanted her to deny, or argue, to fight back, to maybe apologize for what she had said and done eight years ago. Just as much as he wanted it, he also knew he wouldn't have accepted it. Not now, not yet.

He drew a long breath and set his hand on the door handle, still warm from her palm. Nick ran his thumb over the smooth metal.

"Damn it," he cursed to the empty room and shoved the handle with far more force than necessary. "Come on, Dog."

The soft click of paws followed him out into the empty hall.

CHAPTER SIX

"It is with great pride and the utmost faith and confidence in our future that I announce the election of the New World Congress. For the first time since our brethren Areth have returned home, we will govern the people of Earth jointly. No longer the government of Humans and the society of the Areth, we are now one and the same.

"There will be no more boundaries. No more limitations. No more obstacles. We are all one. Ruling and moving together toward a world where we all can grow and thrive. The Areth have brought to us advancements in science, medicine, and technology that even our greatest scientific minds could only dream of four decades ago. They have helped us unite every nation together, wiping out war and obliterating famine. We are no longer a divided world of separated people, but one cohesive race. And now, we have extended the hand of faith once more to our brethren the Areth and reach to the stars."

*N*ick stood in the back of Command, watching President Hargrave speak on the large vid screen encompassing most of one wall. Hargrave was the seventh World President to be elected since the dissolution of individual nations and the creation of a One World government in 2017, this being his second term in office. By the sounds of his speech, the Areth had just as tight a grip on his short hairs this term as they had his last.

With a disgusted huff, Nick crossed his arms over his chest and leaned back into the wall behind him. He remembered the day the first World President was put into power. He was thirteen, and the Areth had been on Earth almost all his life. He barely had any recollection of an Earth before them. When he was born, his father was half way around the world, a United States Marine fighting a war Nick would only ever understand in textbooks. He remembered clearly his father's opinion of the New World Order. Mark Tanner was very vocal in his mistrust.

Nick was almost glad his father hadn't lived long enough to see how far things had fallen.

Warrick, an Areth face that every human on the planet could identify by now, replaced President Hargrave on the view screen and launched into an equally flowery and eloquent diatribe about the union of Areth and Humans after ten-thousand years of separation. He rambled on about how worthwhile the last four decades had been to bring us to this point.

It sounded like the gears slipping on Nick's old outboard motor.

"I never thought I'd see the day when we'd just roll over and die like this."

Nick looked sideways to where the general now stood, seeing in the man's deflated expression that they shared the same thoughts. He glanced back at the screen. A political reporter, no doubt fed her opinions and commentary directly from the Office of the President or Warrick himself, gave her report on the speech. She eloquently reiterated the importance of the New World Congress, and hit again on each point both Hargrave and Warrick had made.

"How is it ninety percent of the World's population falls for this crap?" Nick asked, not really expecting an answer. Like General Castleton, he didn't get it.

Castleton shook his head and gave a heavy sigh. Nick didn't say anything further, knowing there was no justifiable explanation. None that he could accept. The Areth had come promising longer lives, better health, better living. To most, whatever trade-offs they asked for seemed worth it.

The commentator went on for several more minutes, but as interest died down the gathering in the command room slowly disbursed. He scanned the dwindling group, his eyes drawn to the familiar form standing near the other door. She leaned with her shoulder into the wall, her arms across her body in a stance he had seen her adopt frequently. One leg was bent, her foot resting on the point of her toes, her head tilted as she spoke to Beverly Surimoto. Beverly must have said something to make her smile, because her lips tipped up and he saw just a flash of teeth. Even from here, he knew the expression was restrained.

Beverly touched her arm, and after one more smile between them, she left Caitlin alone. As she moved away, Caitlin's gaze shifted and connected with his across the space of the room. The small bow of her lips relaxed, and the dimples in her cheeks disappeared as she stared, unwavering. Familiar heat shifted through Nick's limbs to collide in his gut, and he clenched his teeth against the unwanted and uninvited— *undeniable*—reaction to her simple glance.

Her shoulders dropped as she released a breath, and she looked away. The connection broke and some of the building tension ebbed, but not nearly all of it. His focus shifted to unabashedly watch the slow sway of her backside as she walked down the hall.

"How long you going to keep your head up your ass when it comes to her?"

Nick jerked his head around to stare at the general. Castleton stared right back, daring Nick to deny or argue the point. He ground his teeth, tempering the anger that wanted to force him into telling the general where to go. Too many years of serving under the man kept him from doing it.

"I'm not the one who walked away," he finally forced out.

"How hard did you fight?"

"She made her choice. I wasn't going to go chasing after her like some lovesick fool with a broken heart—"

"Which is exactly what you were."

Nick pushed away from the wall and took two steps, distancing himself from the general. In two beats, his head was full of memories from that day. The day she told him she was leaving, pursuing the opportunity her mentors extended, and no doubt carefully executed to exclude him. The whole time, his fingers fisted around the small box in his pocket holding a ring.

"She was damn *young* when you were together."

Nick spun on his heels to face his former CO. "I didn't rob any cradles, General."

Castleton raised his hand. "Don't get your fangs out, Colonel. All I'm saying is that you've got blinders on when it comes to her. She was little more than a kid. Impressionable. *Controllable.* No one holds her leash now."

"So, what . . . I'm supposed to play nice and pretend nothing happened?"

"No." Castleton's eyes narrowed and he squared his shoulders, lowering his voice to a dangerous tone. "You are *supposed* to remember that we're all human, and that *none* of us are perfect. You included."

The general ground out his reply, pulled a bat turn, and walked away. Nick tipped his head back and drew a slow breath, puffing his lips as he released it. When he looked forward again, he barely hid his surprise to see Beverly standing in front of him, her jade eyes scrutinizing him. Nick cleared his throat and took a step back, making some space between them. He didn't know what it was, but there was something different about this woman. Not *off* as in bad or wrong, nothing that sent his mental flares to firing, but definitely different.

Beyond the fact that her voice came from a brooch on her left shoulder . . .

"I hope you've made yourself at home, Colonel."

Nick nodded. "Yeah, everything is just dandy. For being eighteen floors down."

She tilted her head, a small smile touching her lips. "CJ told me you live in a cabin on a lake. I have never been to a lake, but I imagine this must be very different for you."

"I've lived in military bases before. Most of my adult life."

Beverly nodded. "If there is anything you need, please be sure to let me know."

He tried to hide his wince. "I will. Thank you."

She smiled wider, showing a brief flash of white teeth. "You're welcome, Colonel."

"I'm retired. I can take the rank from the Bubbas and Black Shoes, but I'd rather you just call me Nick."

Shallow lines furrowed her brow and she tilted her head, her eyes focused on his lips. She looked up again to meet his gaze, puzzlement still obvious on her face. Nick chuckled softly, realizing to her he probably sounded insane.

"Just means the other military personnel."

Her lips rounded in a silent "oh" and she nodded. "I see. Certainly, Nick. Well, once again, I wanted to say welcome. We're glad to have you here."

*V*ictor took the damp cloth from Michael's forehead, the material hot from the short contact with his fevered skin. Trying to make as little sound as possible, Victor dunked the cloth in the basin of water in his lap and cooled it again. He sat on the edge of Michael's bed with the only light in the room a small square of silver moonlight streaming through the window near the ceiling. It was just enough to allow Victor to see the aftermath of Kathleen's amusements.

Michael hadn't moved since the night before, still lying prone with his arms spread out from his sides. His hair was dark with sweat and plastered to his forehead and his skin was coated with a fine sheen of moisture. Victor wrung out the cloth and patted Michael's cheeks, drawing a sharp hiss from the man, before laying it across his forehead again. Michael blinked and finally pulling out of the deep sleep he had been in since Victor slipped into the room.

He turned his head on the pillow, his eyes searching the shadows. "Victor?"

"Yes. Lie still and I'll get you some water."

Victor reached to the floor and picked up the cup he had prepared before sitting. Mixed into it was another cocktail of electrolytes, antibiotics, and analgesics he hoped would help Michael heal and ease the pain. He set the basin on the floor and shifted one knee onto the mattress to give himself the leverage he needed to lift Michael's head, touching the rim to his lips. Michael drank deep, and Victor finally had to pull back, afraid he would take too much.

Michael gasped a breath as Victor eased him back. Tightness gripped his chest as he looked at his friend, and anger simmered just below the surface of his skin. In two hundred years, he had never known such an extreme degree of any emotion, and his control was tenacious at best. Victor sat down again, curling his hands into fists and pressing them against the pounding at his temples.

"Do you know your parents, Victor?" Michael asked, his voice barely a rough whisper in the darkness.

Victor lifted his head, focusing for a moment on Michael before reaching out to remove the once again warm cloth from his forehead. He picked up the basin and began the repetition of soaking the cloth and cooling Michael's skin as best he could.

"We don't have parents, Michael. We don't view familial relationships the way you do," Victor finally answered, the lie a familiar bitter taste on his tongue. *But if he knew . . .*

Michael swallowed audibly, clearing his throat and the raw sound if it made Victor wince. "She wanted me to die this time."

Victor didn't know what to say, because there was no excuse for what Kathleen did. She claimed everything she did was for the better Areth good, to identify a way to remove the genetic keys that held the Areth back. Victor sought to isolate the same key, and he failed to see how her methods could possibly be *the* way. A deep-seeded hatred boiled in her for Michael, beyond Victor's comprehension. He had no understanding of being a parent—or a child—but he knew in his core this was just wrong. No matter the final goal, this was wrong. The familiar nausea rolled through his stomach and a slow burning sensation started at the base of his skull, but he swallowed hard and tamped it down, refusing to give in to the mystery ailment now.

Michael's ragged breathing turned into a cough, and he tried to move onto his side. Victor put a hand against the back of his shoulder, helping him roll, and the coughing eased off. With a deep, shuddered breath, Michael eased back onto the bed again. Uneasiness sat in Victor's chest. Even though Michael had only been awake a few minutes here and there since the last 'session', Victor senses there was something different in his friend. Something was gone.

Perhaps, this time, she had accomplished more than ever before.

"You need to rest."

Michael rolled his head against the pillow. "Talk to me."

Victor looked around the room, able to see clearer now that his eyes had adjusted to the darkness. The shelves Michael had been allowed to fill with science fiction novels and books on art and history now sat empty, and the reprint of the Monet's *Boats Leaving the Harbor* that had hung on his wall was gone. He had been stripped to the bare necessities, the precious personal items he had spent years working to earn—taken away after one vicious command from Kathleen.

"What do you want to talk about?"

"Do you know who he is?" He almost didn't hear Michael's voice. It died in the darkness of the room, eaten by the shadows.

Victor swallowed and dunked the cloth in the water again. "Who?"

"My father. I've known you since as long as I can remember. Did you know him?"

Victor shook his head, even though he doubted Michael saw him. "You were very young when you came here, Michael. I didn't know you before that." *When had it become so easy to lie?*

Michael nodded. He slowly raised a shaky hand and gripped Victor's arm. Victor stared at him in the darkness, biting back the angry bile that burned his throat. Several minutes passed and the hold on his arm relaxed as Michael's breathing deepened in sleep. Victor carefully eased himself off the bed and dumped the now lukewarm basin water in the small sink.

The hallways were quiet and empty, and Victor made his way out of the building without being seen. He moved without conscious thought, initiating and navigating his hover vehicle away from the facility to the simple, sophisticated dwelling outside the city where many of his kin lived.

By the time he entered the building, the blood pumping through his veins burned like acid and the incessant pounding in his skull reminded him of a snare drum. He entered his unit, and spoke the command to bring up the lights to an appropriate ambiance.

Victor looked around, and flexed his fingers into tight balls. White walls, white floors, and white furniture. No artwork and no color broke the monotony. It might as well be Michael's cell for all the personality it held.

Rage surged in him, overpowering the weak hold he had on control. Victor clenched his fists, his arms shaking, as a near-primal yell ripped its way from his throat. He swung around, slamming his knuckles into the nearest wall. The material cracked and gave way beneath the force, caving in around his bleeding hand.

A searing pain shot up his spine hitting the base of his skull like a flaming arrow. Victor braced his hand on the wall, gripping the back of his head with the other as he fought to keep himself standing. The world tilted and he dropped to his hands and knees, gasping to keep from vomiting as black spots invaded his vision and blood rushed in his ears, sounding like crashing waves in a barrel.

He heard someone screaming, but had no idea who, too far lost in the miasma of pain, rage and vertigo to care. He fought to breathe, his chest burning even though he sucked in lungful after lungful of air. Then something broke within his mind, a rush of cold heat flooding him, and he collapsed as the darkness took over.

CHAPTER SEVEN

"*E*at up. You're going to need your strength later."

Lilly looked up from the plate of chicken she had been picking at to look at her husband. Jace winked, wagged his eyebrows, and speared another piece of medium-rare steak. She smiled and flipped a stray lock of blond hair behind her ear.

"Sounds like a challenge, Mr. Quinn."

"Nope." He picked up the bread roll beside his plate and ripped it in half, dabbing at the juice. "More like a promise."

A warm flush shifted over Lilly's body, and she pulled her lower lip through her teeth, wiggling her foot free of the leather shoe she wore. She crossed her legs and glanced around the sparsely populated cafeteria. With a smirk, she straightened her knee until her foot came in contact with the inside of Jace's thigh. He shifted slightly and tried not to choke on his bread, but otherwise showed no signs that her foot was now pressed between his legs and her toes curled against the zipper of his pants.

Lilly set her elbow on the table and rested her chin in her palm, putting on her most innocent expression. "Maybe *you* are the one who needs to bulk up."

He cut another bite of steak and pointed to her with the end of his fork. "What do you think I'm doing? Protein, see? Baby making is hard work."

Lilly smiled again, and shifted to push her foot further beneath the table. Jace swallowed hard and his eyelids slid lower over his green eyes. Heat permeated her sock, and she felt the growing evidence of her effect on him. *Four years and I've still got it.*

"You know it could take time. I just stopped injecting the ovarian block three months ago. Even if I were here more, it could be months—"

"Yeah, but all the fun is in the trying," he interrupted with the same wickedly sexy grin that had weakened her knees and melted her insides since the first time she saw him.

Lilly pushed the half-eaten meal to the side and leaned forward on the table. She knew full well the new position gave Jace an unobstructed view down her blouse. His eyes shifted to somewhere decidedly south of hers, and she focused on the pulse point at the base of his throat as it sped up. Jace cleared his throat and dropped his half-eaten roll onto his plate.

"Let's go."

She slowly sat back, smiling smugly, as Jace piled their plates on the one tray he had used to carry supper to the table. He slid her a heated look as she reached beneath the table to retrieve her shoe. They stood together, and with the tray balanced in one hand, he pulled her back against his chest as his free hand snaked around her waist to hold her close. His breath whispered across her throat and he bent his neck and pressed a quick kiss to her cheek.

"You're going to have to stick close, darlin'," he whispered across her ear. Jace subtly rubbed his hips, and his erection, against the small of her back. "Otherwise, within the hour half the base will know what you were doing under that table."

*C*J sat in the corner of the cafeteria, a plate of cut fruit and raw vegetables barely touched in front of her, watching Jace and Lilly Quinn make their way out of the room. They walked so close it was almost comical, with Jace's hand wrapped around her body to splay across her stomach. Lilly covered his arm with her hands, a natural and beautiful smile spreading her lips as she glanced across her shoulder at him. Jace laughed and smiled, dipping his wife slightly to press a quick kiss to her lips before they disappeared through the doors into the hall.

Tears burned CJ's eyes, blurring her vision, but she forced them back and focused on swirling a piece of cantaloupe in the clear juice in the bottom of her plate. She felt selfish and petty for envying Jace and Lilly the love they obviously had for each other, and never before had their outward expression bothered her. In fact, she usually found joy in their happiness, especially when things like affection and love seemed to be a dying art in the world. People were so focused on genetic matching, and perfect compatibilities that old-fashioned concepts like falling in love and being together forever were falling more and more by the wayside in lieu of arranged child planning and marriages of opportunity.

Tonight, witnessing the affectionate exchange between them, the flirtatious contact and heat that nearly warmed the air for everyone else, it all left a heavy weight on her chest and tightened her throat. Tonight, CJ couldn't escape the memories.

The smell of bacon and spring mornings filled the cabin, and through the open kitchen window came the music of a distant songbird. CJ picked up a warm slice of toast and spread soft butter across the surface.

"Breakfast is ready, Nicky," she called out, but gasped as two long, strong arms circled her body from behind.

"Mmmmm, smells delicious."

"I didn't burn the bacon this time," she said with a smile and tilted her head so he could press a kiss just in front of her ear.

"I'm proud of you," he said, his voice earnest. "But damn, woman. How am I supposed to think about food when I find you wearing nothing but my old flannel shirt?"

CJ's body tingled as his long fingers expertly released the buttons of the oversized shirt and his hands slipped inside to skim over her skin. He slipped the collar away from her shoulder and buried his face into the curve of her neck, his tongue applying firm pressure to her skin before his lips sucked gently. CJ let her head fall back, supported by his chest, as his hands cupped her breasts and skimmed her stomach, plucking at the waistband of her panties.

"Nicky . . ." she whispered hoarsely.

He turned her around in the space between him and the counter, his hands coming up to cup her face. CJ looked up at him as his thumb stroked across her lower lip. He was bare from the waist up and the subtle flex of his arms and chest when he moved made her heart race and her blood heat. She reached up to lay her hands on his chest, enjoying the heat of his skin and the beat of his heart beneath her palm. He tipped her face and covered her lips with a deep, open mouth kiss that made her insides dance and her knees shake. His fingertips laced into her hair and he pulled her closer, kissing her longer, until they both had to stop to breathe. Nicky rested his forehead against hers, their rapid breath mingling in the space between them, and licked his lips.

"I love you, Caitlin."

Her heart jumped, and she wrapped her arms around him, pulling him closer. "I love you, too, Nicky."

Her first breakfast of unburned bacon was left forgotten on the counter as he swept her up into his arms and carried her through the cabin to the bedroom, laying her down on the blankets that still lay unmade from the night before.

CJ shot back to reality when a hot tear fell on the back of her hand. She sniffled, and wiped at her cheeks with a napkin, glancing around. No one had seen her, and she released a shaky breath. It was useless to try and eat any more of the food, so she went back to the counter and asked for the plate to be wrapped. She would just take it back to her quarters. Perhaps later, she would be able to force it down.

As she opened her door, her lights slowly rose to her personal preference level. CJ walked to the kitchen and set the plate of fruits and vegetables inside the cooler unit. She moved aimlessly, not knowing what she wanted to do or where she wanted to be. Standing in the middle of the sitting area, CJ paused and looked around.

If someone were to compare her simple, utilitarian quarters here in Colorado to the elegant, spacious, and airy apartment supplied to her in New Mexico, it would be easy to see that this was the place she called home. Here was where she kept those things that meant the most to her. Not that she had much. Some pictures of friends, a few of her younger brother, Connor, and one of her parents that they had sent her a few years before. It had been years since she had returned to Paris to see them. A cranberry colored blanket lay across the back of the seating lounge, and a painting of an open field in autumn hung near her bedroom door. It reminded her of Nick's lake. It was all she had to show this place was hers. That she existed outside of her lab and her work.

She left her parents' home when she was seven, living in dormitories at various boarding schools and universities until she was seventeen and earned her Masters Degree in Theoretical Genetics. While earning her doctorates, she lived in an Areth established apartment house with several other 'promising' scientists, but even now remembered very few names of any of her roommates.

Her life shifted from school to the labs, and at twenty years old she was a full-fledged doctor and scientist studying side-by-side with her Areth brethren toward the better good for all.

Then there was Nick.

One day he wasn't part of her life, and the next day he was, or so it seemed even now. She met him at an evening dinner party honoring several individuals in the Areth community, the science attachment, and the Earth Force ranks. Nick was there as a guest of one of the honorees. She had been twenty-two years, Nick was thirty-nine.

Two weeks later they were lovers.

For the next seven months, she actually had a life.

Until she threw it all away.

CJ crossed her arms and closed her eyes, swallowing the bitter emotion that choked her. She had no right to cry over losing him. It was her own fault and she had accepted that fact. All because of her own naïve stupidity and foolishness. It was only in the last two years that she had realized the true depth of her stupidity, but that knowledge didn't assuage her guilt or lessen the gaping black hole in her chest.

She missed him.

She still loved him.

Always would.

Suddenly, the filtered oxygen of the base smothered her and CJ needed to draw fresh air into her lungs. Let it cleanse her. She grabbed the blanket off the back of the lounge and left her quarters. Evening had settled on the base, though it was hard to tell this far down into the mountain they were buried in. She rode the elevator to the surface, her head resting on the back wall of the car with the wrap hanging over her arm. Thankfully, the elevator never stopped and no one boarded. No one to ask her how she was this evening, or to ask her where she was going. To offer to accompany her. She needed to be alone.

To breathe.

She stayed on the elevator until it reached the third level above the surface, where the limited quantity of gliders and transport ships were kept in a secure landing bay. CJ walked the halls to a door that led outside, immediately drawing in a cleansing breath of fresh air as it whispered across her face. She stepped out into the dark night and wrapped the blanket around her shoulders.

The night sky was a deep blue, almost black but not quite, the stars bright pinpoints of light through the trees. The moon was silver white, and looked larger than life, even though it was only three-quarters full. CJ scanned the sky, and caught the subtle movement of one of the lights, knowing it was one of the four Areth ships constantly in orbit over the planet.

"Beautiful, huh?"

CJ gasped and jumped, turning to the voice in the darkness. She could barely see the tall form in the shadows of the trees. "Nick?"

Twigs and leaves rustled quietly beneath his feet as he moved toward her, his features coming into focus as the light from the moon played across his face. The moonlight made his hair silver, and his face a composition of shadows and planes. He pushed his hands into the front pockets of his jeans and stopped several feet from her. He shifted his jaw, his lips separating, and CJ's pulse jumped. She wrapped the blanket tighter around her body.

"What the hell are you doing out here by yourself?" he demanded.

"I have nothing to worry about here, and I needed air."

He snorted a chuckle. "I get that."

"Is that why you're here?"

He took a hand from his pocket to motion over his shoulder with a thumb. "Dog."

CJ nodded and looked away, turning her attention to the stars again. Without consciously deciding to, her mind picked out individual constellations and scanned the horizon for others that were harder to see this time of year. She felt Nick move closer to her, standing behind her, but didn't dare move or react.

"Do you remember them?" he asked.

She slipped her right arm free of the blanket and pointed to the western sky, tracing a series of stars with her fingertips. "There is Cepheus." She moved her hand south and slightly east. "And Draco. I can almost see Cassiopeia, but she should be more visible in another two or three weeks." She turned, pointing past him even further into the southern sky. "And there is Hercules."

He followed her direction, and nodded his head. "You do remember."

CJ lowered her hand, and looked up at him in the semi-darkness, her eyes having adjusted enough that she could easily make out the details of his face. As he turned back, his chin tipping down to look at her, CJ drew in a slow breath.

"I remember everything," she said simply.

"Yeah," he said, his voice heavier than moments before. "So do I."

CJ wanted to believe he remembered all the afternoons of making love, the nights in each other's arms, the days they spent together just because they liked being together, but she doubted it. She heard a sound in the bushes and assumed it was Dog sniffing around, but it was distraction enough to let her find her bearings again. She took a step away from him, wrapping the blanket tighter around her shoulders.

"Has the general brought you up to speed?"

"Pretty much."

She nodded. *Okay, so conversation was going to be like pulling teeth.* With a quiver inside her chest, CJ accepted that she just didn't have the strength to do it—to dance the dance of denial—with him. Not yet. Maybe, in time, they would be able to pass in the hall or sit in a briefing and her heart wouldn't hurt. Not quite yet.

"I'll go and leave you and Dog to . . ." She trailed off and turned to walk back to the door.

"Caitlin," he said as she reached for the security lock.

She rested her palm against the cold metal of the door instead, and only turned her head enough to see his shadowed figure out of the corner of her eye. "Yes?" she managed to say.

"Do you regret it?"

She closed her eyes, vicious tears burning their way from her heart. CJ blinked, two trails of moisture running down her cheeks, but she didn't look at him. She swallowed hard, fighting the thick emotion in her throat.

"Yes," was all she could manage to say. He didn't make a sound, and she drew a fortifying breath, pushing away from the door to partially turn toward him. He still stood where she had left him. "I knew almost immediately how stupid I had been. At first I was too ashamed—" She choked on her own words, closing her eyes. "Then I knew I had no right to ask you to forgive me."

He took two steps closer to her, and as the dry leaves beneath his feet crinkled and crunched, CJ held her breath.

"You should have talked to me."

CJ curled her hands into fists, gripping the blanket until her knuckles ached and turned her back to the door, leaning heavily against it. She was tired, to the bone tired. Tired of keeping it all trapped and tightly boxed, controlled and restrained, yet, it wasn't time. There may never be a time to let everything go. She just had to hang on, just get through the next day, then the next two weeks. Small steps. Someday, somehow, a day would come . . .

"I didn't know how," she finally answered. "Nick, I had never—I didn't know what the hell I was doing. I didn't have anyone to tell me that what I felt was okay, and what I *was* being told was that we were wrong. I had no one to turn to. I was being guided *away* from you, not to you."

"You let the Areth decide *for* you."

She heard the anger laced through his words, and didn't blame him. Nick had never hidden from her the fact that he had questions about the Areth. He still believed in the freedom to speak one's mind, to have one's own opinions. He believed he was safe with her. He was. She never once told anyone what he said. That didn't mean that his views weren't known.

"There is nothing I can say that won't sound like an excuse. I don't want to make excuses. I know what I did was wrong, and I wish to *God* I could change it. However, I can't. I wasn't strong enough then." Even now, she felt the strength drain from her with each word, and yet a weight eased from her chest at the same time. It might not make a damn bit of difference, but she said it.

"You have the strength *now*?"

CJ lifted her gaze and looked into his face. His eyes were black in the moonlight, shining bright, as he looked down on her.

"It doesn't really matter, does it?"

He stepped closer, so close their bodies nearly touched, and CJ flattened her back against the door, keeping her chin up to look into his face. His gaze skimmed over her features and she felt it, almost as real as a caress. Her heart skipped and suddenly the blanket was too hot, her skin tingling with awareness. CJ held her breath as his hands slowly came up to cup her cheeks, his thumb smoothing over her mouth, gently pulling her lips apart.

"I need to know something." His voice was so low and rough she almost didn't hear it over the breeze shifting through the trees.

"What?"

He shifted closer, his legs bracketing hers. His hips pressed her against the door as he lowered his head and his lips brushed across hers. The first contact was barely there, just a moist slick of his lip over hers. His breath warmed her skin, CJ sucked in air as her heart pounded in her chest and her eyes fluttered shut. The tip of his tongue traced the seam of her mouth, and she opened her lips. When his mouth covered hers, all sensible thought disappeared in the flashing lights and pounding blood behind her closed eyelids. CJ released the blanket to reach out and curl her fingers into the front of his shirt.

Nick groaned softly, the sound vibrating against her lips as he pushed her harder against the door, his hands leaving her face to wrap his arms around her, hauling her against his chest. CJ moved her hands to his neck, burying her fingers into his short, gray hair, lost in the amazingly silky feel of it as he devoured her mouth.

Then he released her, stepping back, leaving her to fight for her breath and balance against the door. CJ raised her hand and touched her fingertips to her stubble-abraded lips, still tasting him there; a blend of coffee and something sweet he must have had after dinner mingled with the familiar flavor she knew as simply Nick. He stepped backwards, raking a hand through his hair, and she could hear his raspy breath in the darkness.

Neither said anything for several moments, both fighting for their own equilibrium. CJ bent over and picked up the blanket that had slipped from her shoulders to the ground. She had to keep her hand on the door to prevent herself from falling over since her knees were barely more than firm jelly.

"I'm sorry," Nick finally said. "I don't mean to be such an ass."

He turned and walked off into the darkness, leaving CJ alone.

CHAPTER EIGHT

*B*everly sat at the octagon holovid table, observing the choreographed dance of daily operations in Command. She made no attempt to read the lips of anyone, since most were on the move and turning away from her sporadically. Either that, or too far away for her to clearly see their faces. She liked just watching, observing.

Feeling . . .

The air in the room hummed with anticipation, everyone knowing the time would soon come that they would implement their plan. They had planned this mission for weeks, and everyone was ready to see it through, bring it to completion, and bring their lost people home. It didn't matter that they didn't personally know any of the human prisoners, the only one with a true name and face being Michael Tanner; it just mattered that they were somewhere they didn't belong. Phoenix would make it right.

Just another step on this long, hard road.

Movement to her left caught her eye, and she looked to see Jason and Lilly Quinn enter the room. Jace's arm was around his wife, holding her close to his side, and they spoke with their faces close. They sat down several chairs away from her, their hands linked together on top of the table.

"I'm going to miss you," she read on Jace's lips as he brought Lilly's knuckles to his mouth for a kiss.

Lilly stroked the back of his neck, her fingertips weaving into his short brown hair. She kissed his forehead and looked into his eyes, a watery smile on her lips. Beverly blinked against the burning tears as Jace pressed his face into the curve of his wife's neck and Lilly closed her eyes, resting her forehead on his shoulder.

The current in the air shifted, shocking her, and Beverly turned toward the source. Colonel Tanner—Nick—entered Command and took a seat, setting his handheld computer on the table in front of him.

Why did she feel him enter?

She understood why she felt the combined emotions of everyone present. When enough people felt the same emotion, she always knew. It danced over her skin and tickled at her nerves, sometimes like electrical charges and sometimes like the soft fall of rain. All depending on the emotion. What she felt when Nick walked in wasn't just an addition to the mass. It was different, and she felt him alone.

When they met, and he had taken her hand, her blood had hummed from her hand to the base of her skull. From his expression, she suspected he felt something similar.

But what?

What caused it?

Why him?

He glanced in her direction and smiled, but immediately looked away. Beverly didn't need to feel his emotions to know something troubled him; obvious in the tense hold of his shoulders and the deep worry lines at the corners of his eyes. He engaged the monitor in front of him, his fingers moving quickly over the keys to access the information he wanted. Then Beverly saw his head tip up slightly and his focus shift, his hands stilled.

A slight turn of her head found what grabbed his attention. CJ had entered, and now stood with General Castleton at the far end of the table. The briefing would begin soon, and Command filled quickly with key personnel to the mission. Beverly shifted her gaze between Nick and CJ, noting how they sought out each other, and yet avoided each other's eyes. She felt a pressure against her chest; a new hum tingled beneath her skin and made her hair stand on end.

She looked again to CJ, who spoke with the general, but her eyes looked past him to watch Nick. Beverly felt a ripple press against her walls, and she fought to keep them up. The sensation was foreign, the emotion unknown, and she feared opening herself up to it.

Nick looked up again, and his gaze connected with CJ. He drew a breath, squaring his shoulders. Another wave assaulted Beverly and she gripped the table edge. All eyes turned to her, and she realized through the attack on her senses that her voice synthesizer now vibrated against her shoulder. She had to have expressed some sound in response to the assailment. Lilly stood and came to her, crouching down beside her to lay a hand on her arm.

"Bev? Are you okay?"

The soothing flood of concern from Lilly washed over her, canceling out the disconnected emotions coming from Nick. She brought her hand across her body and laid it on top of Lilly's, squeezing gently.

"I think so, yes. I just—" She didn't know how to explain this. "Yes, I'm fine."

Someone set a glass of water beside her, and she sipped from it, heat rising in her cheeks at having everyone's attention on her. CJ sat down in the chair on the other side of her, concern drawing her features. Beverly waved everyone off, then motioned that they should all sit down.

"I'm fine. Honestly. Please, let's just begin the meeting."

*C*aptain Fields held out a small microslide to CJ, and she flattened her hand so he could set it in her palm. microslide was only half an inch square and an eighth of an inch thick, its rainbow metallic surface gleaming in the hydrogen-gel glow of the lights overhead. She tilted her hand and watched the colors change.

"Based on the information on the security system you brought to us, we've determined they use a hybrid computer program, Areth technology piggybacked on Earth computer operating systems. Load this into any computer terminal by the end of mission day. Once loaded, the program will record and correlate security system data, and will access the security system at precisely 2205 hours, creating a mirror or echo of all systems for thirty minutes. The data loop can be accessed by our hand held units, thus giving us complete control of the system at the time of insertion."

CJ nodded and curled her fingers over the slide.

"We've determined from the global weather net," Jace began from the other side of the table, and CJ turned her attention to him, "that a severe electrical storm is going to roll through the region that night. We anticipate that the combination of the security program override, the

71

inconvenience of the heavy rain and the havoc it will play on their motion sensing equipment, they will pass over any detection of us coming in as just system glitches. That will get us *in*, the hard part is going to be getting back out."

Nick tapped one finger hard on the tabletop, activating his console. "I've studied the schematics and our best extraction point will be here," he said pointing to the left quadrant of the glowing map. "In the event this area is inaccessible, I've also plotted two additional possible routes of escape, here, and here." Two glowing red dots joined the first. "In any case, you can be sure that if we get in, I'll damn well make sure we get the hell out."

The weight and conviction of Nick's voice sent a chill up CJ's spine, and she straightened in her chair. Even turning back to Captain Fields, she felt Nick's gaze on her, and she dared not meet it. Since he kissed her on the mountaintop the evening before, her skin hadn't stopped its constant tingle and she hadn't been able to find rest all night. There was an ache in her soul that she hadn't felt in a long, long time.

"Do I have to run any command for this?" Caitlin asked as she slipped the microslide into her pocket and zipped it closed.

"No, you just put it into the drive. In fact, you can drop it in and walk away. The program creates no visual presence on the monitor being used. The system just needs to be powered on and connected to the center's network."

"They won't be able to trace that back to her in any way?" Nick asked.

Captain Fields turned to look at him, and raised one shoulder in an abbreviated shrug. "We've done all we can to prevent that. This is why we've made it downloadable from any terminal. She doesn't need to do anything or log in anywhere. She doesn't even need to touch a key. Just slide it into a data port and it does the rest." The man grinned. "We even created it from a special base that resists any kind of fingerprint or DNA transfer."

"I'm staying in the building. I'll be monitoring the situation on the security band. If the override doesn't work, or the rain isn't providing sufficient cover, I'll be in place to create a diversion within the facility," CJ reminded.

Nick's fingers drummed on the tabletop.

"That's good," General Castleton said. "But, considering the events of last week be sure to stay alert. You see any signs of a trap, use the emergency link to contact us and we will abort. Better to pull back before this blows up in our faces, and have a chance of trying again later, than to go in guns blazing and find our sixes in a sling."

CJ nodded, but silently hoped it wouldn't come to that. She wanted this mission to be done, for so many reasons. She wanted Michael, and the other prisoners, free. She wanted Nick reunited with the son he never knew. Beyond all that, CJ wanted to be free herself. This mission ended her life outside Phoenix, a fact she had willingly accepted when she volunteered—no, practically demanded—to be the one to go to New Mexico. Even just a year ago the thought of losing her identity as *Doctor* Caitlin Montgomery, geneticist, would have terrified her, now she welcomed the thought of leaving it all behind.

"Good luck to you, CJ," General Castleton said as he stood and extended his hand to her.

Caitlin pushed her chair back and stood, taking his hand. The general sandwiched her fingers between both his palms and squeezed gently, giving her a warm smile before turning away and heading toward the front of Command.

She crouched down to pick up her bag from the floor, and slid a glance sideways to see if Nick was still in his chair. He had stood, his hands pushed characteristically into his pockets. His sculpted lips formed a thin, strained line and the creases near his eyes that were usually barely visible were deeper as his features tensed. CJ braced her hand on the table edge and slowly stood, her gaze holding his, her breath locked in her chest. His lips parted, his jaw cocking to the side, as he stared back. One eyebrow raised a fraction of an inch.

A hand touched her arm, and she broke eye contact to turn and look at Lilly and Jace. Lilly opened her arms and embraced CJ, squeezing her tight before pulling back.

"Promise me you'll be careful."

CJ smiled. "Of course. I'll see you when we come home." She turned to Jace and raised her arms to wrap them around his neck. He hugged her back, kissing her cheek. "You be careful."

"You kidding? Lilly would kill me if I come home with so much as a scratch," he said with a chuckle as he released her.

They spoke for a few minutes more, and then the Quinns excused themselves. She quickly glanced over her shoulder, and saw Nick was gone. A shimmer of disappointment moved over her, but she did her best to push it aside. One kiss after eight years, after what she did, certainly changed nothing.

She slipped the strap of her bag over her shoulder and headed for the hall, and the elevator that would bring her to the surface, her mind already on her complicated travel plans. Still, she'd be back in her sterile, utilitarian apartment within two hours. At the elevator, a familiar voice said her name just as she reached for the call button.

"Caitlin."

His voice was heavy, rough, and unclear. She paused her hand over the unlit arrow and turned to look over her shoulder at Nick. He stood several feet away, subtle tension still etching his features, narrowing his eyes at the corners. CJ turned to face him, shifting her bag on her shoulder.

"Yes?"

Nick glanced around, looking for what she didn't know, and took a step toward her. He cleared his throat and shifted his weight on his feet. For one brief moment, she remembered the first night she had met him. The entire evening he had been the confident, sexy Earth Force Colonel who had danced her off her feet with his charm. As the party wound down, and it was time for her to leave, she had witnessed a total shift in his demeanor. He was fidgety, tense, and unwilling to meet her gaze.

Just like now . . .

Course, that night it was because he had wanted to see her again. He admitted to her, weeks later, that it had been years since he had pursued a woman.

As the memory washed over her, CJ realized with a start that she was staring and ruthlessly pulled her emotions back in check, separating the past from the present and waited for him to speak.

He took one hand from his pocket and motioned toward an indiscriminate point down the hall. "Could we . . ."

CJ nodded and turned down the hall away from Command. Nick fell into step beside her and they walked in silence. He followed her lead as she turned them left down a branch hallway. At the end was a double vault door. CJ paused to punch her access code into the keypad beside the large steel frame. The vapor seal around the door released with a gush, and the doors slid open, revealing the expansive chamber beyond.

"Holy crap," Nick said just behind her as she stepped over the threshold into the seventy thousand square foot hydroponics chamber.

CJ hid her smile at his reaction by leaning over to smell a sunflower that grew nearly as tall as her chest. The change in the air was tangible and instantaneous, taking on a heaviness and a life as it tickled her nose and weighed heavy on her skin. The air smelled green and stirred her hair as the hidden circulation fans re-oxygenated and re-hydrated the artificial climate. She stepped off the six-foot square steel platform at the door onto the stones that followed a serpentine path through the patches and rows of fruits and vegetables. Nick's boots crunched on the stones as he followed her. The vaulted doors slid closed on their hydraulic tracks, and the airlock sealed again with a hiss.

"What the hell is this place?" he asked.

"It's our hydroponics facility for Phoenix. It supplies eighty percent of the fruits and vegetables we need to feed the compliment of the base. We affectionately call it The Farm."

Nick walked with his head tilted back, taking in the expansive space. The ceiling was seven stories above their heads, with observation windows at several levels from different parts of the mountain, and as far as they could see, everything was green. Trees of varying sizes ran the perimeter, some fruit bearing, some just there to help naturally oxygenate the air. Vines and climbing plants covered the walls and ceiling, hiding most signs that concrete and steel lay beyond the verdant life that filled the room.

CJ motioned for them to walk further along the path until they reached a thirty foot wide circle had been left clear of any plants, and in the center was a marble bench. She walked across the grass, enjoying the spongy give beneath her shoes, and sat down, waiting for Nick to join her.

He stepped to the bench, tugged down on the legs of his jeans, and sat. Nick leaned forward, resting his elbows on his knees and linking his fingers together. CJ tried not to notice how long his fingers were, coiled and woven together. She turned away, focusing on a copse of apple trees on the far side of the chamber, but her attention was drawn back to his hands. He swirled his thumbs around each other—rolling forward—then back.

"So, what's on your mind, Nick?" she finally asked.

He turned his head, looking at her along the line of his shoulder. She could almost feel his gaze shift over her, coming back to focus on her face. CJ curled her fingers around the edge of the bench and waited. Nick parted his lips, pausing before he spoke, thinking about what he needed to say.

"Don't stay in the building until we get there."

CJ blinked, tilting her head. "Excuse me?"

"Don't stay there. Get out before we ever get there and come straight here."

CJ shook her head. "I can't. Nick, the plan is that I stay. I make sure everything is ready and running smoothly for you to get in. And if not, I create a diversion."

"I'll get us in."

She shook her head and closed her eyes, taking a moment to digest the swing in conversation. Stupid her, she thought he wanted to talk about the kiss. Even if it was to tell her it meant nothing. *No*, it was to tell her he didn't think she could do her job! After drawing a calming breath, she looked at him again.

"You're still the cockiest son of a bitch I've ever met, Nicholas Tanner."

He twisted his body, resting one elbow on his thigh with his hand on his other, deep furrows creasing his brow. "What the hell is that supposed to mean?"

"It means that you haven't known me for eight years, Nick. You don't know what I've done and you don't know how I've changed. You don't know that I can hit a moving five-inch target at three hundred feet with a Glock 100 pulse charge pistol, or that I know five ways to break your arm without breaking a sweat. I don't need to be rescued, or led around by the hand, and I *don't* need the big, bad, kickass Earth Force colonel to charge back into my life and start throwing around orders." She snapped off the last words, and moved to stand.

Nick's hand snapped out, grabbing her wrist. CJ looked down at the way his finger wrapped around and lapped over each other. She grit her teeth, and raised her chin to meet his gaze.

"Is that what you think? That I don't think you can handle it?"

"Isn't it?"

He shook his head and a muscle jumped along his jaw and white lined his lips as they pulled tight. CJ eased back onto the bench and he released her wrist, running both palms vigorously up and down his thighs. The sound of his calloused skin against the denim whispered between them. He stopped the action, curling his fingers into loose fists. CJ waited, but he said nothing, staring straight ahead into the neat rows of corn and lima beans.

Was that all she was going to get? A shake of his head?

"Nick—"

"I've hated you for eight years."

His voice was cold and hard, hitting CJ in her chest with the force of a battering ram. It was different, somehow, to know the truth than to hear it. She held no misconceptions in her heart that he felt anything for her other than detest and anger, and didn't begrudge him any of it. To hear the words from his lips hurt more than she ever imagined. CJ blinked rapidly, swallowing against the hard lump of emotion in her throat. She stared away, focusing on the edge of the clearing as the leaves on the corn swayed gently in the fabricated breeze.

"The way you feel about me doesn't change my involvement in Phoenix, or this mission," she finally said when she felt she could trust her voice. CJ bent forward and picked up her bag, standing in one fluid movement. "Good luck, Nick. Come back safe."

She walked with determination toward the door, which seemed a mile away. Her insides shook and her eyes burned, but she couldn't let go. Not now. Not yet. After an eternity, she reached the end of the path, and sucked in a breath. Almost there. She was almost there. She reached for the keypad to open the airlock, to escape . . .

CJ cried out when he grabbed her arm and spun her around to face him. She looked up into his face, and her heartbeat faltered. *His eyes . . . she hadn't seen his eyes that dark since . . .*

CJ stumbled backwards, but his hold on her kept her from moving. He gripped her other arm, pulling her toward him, her hands sandwiched between them. CJ fought to keep from panting, her heart pounding fiercely in her chest as his hot gaze shifted over her face, his nostrils flaring with each rapid breath he took.

"Nicky . . ." she rasped.

"I should hate you," he growled. "Why can't I hate you?"

His words barely clicked through the fog in her mind before his mouth devoured her lips, all air rushing from her lungs as he slammed her back against the wall, his hand protecting the back of her head. CJ groaned against his mouth, circling her arms around his neck as his hands pressed hard against her side, forcing her to stand on her toes. She had to suck air in through her nose as Nick relentlessly kissed her, his hard lips bruising hers, his tongue delving past her teeth to send shocks of electricity through her body.

CJ gasped a high-pitched cry, her head falling back, when Nick's hands pushed beneath her shirt and his warm palms slid over her ribs and back, the contact scorching her skin. Nick took the opportunity to bury his face against the arch of her throat, drawing sensitive skin between his teeth to caress with the tip of his tongue.

Her body shook with the sudden jolt of arousal shoved into a state of being it had not known in years. Nerves sparked and skin hummed, blood pooling and heating, muscles tensed and coiled.

Then Nick jerked away, leaving CJ slumped against the wall with knees like jelly and her chest heaving. He crossed the platform in three long strides and slammed the heel of his hand into the far wall, the sound echoing through the chamber.

"Damn it!" he shouted, his voice returning back to them threefold.

CJ used the wall as support and watched Nick as she tried to regain some equilibrium. He stood with his back to her, his hands braced above his head. Barely trusting her legs, she took a step, one arm extended behind her with her fingertips trailing the cool metal. Her throat was a desert, and she licked her lips.

"Nicky . . ."

He pushed off from the wall and turned back to her, striding half way back across the space before stopping again. Nick twisted partially away, raking his fingers through his hair, and stood for several moments with his head bowed and his hands set as his waist. CJ could only watch; lost in the whirlwind she was suddenly swept up in. Then he looked up, his shoulders rising and falling as he took a deep breath.

With a slow, purposeful stride, he walked to her and gently took her face in his hands, closing his eyes as he rested his forehead against hers. A tremor shifted through her body, and CJ wrapped her fingers around his wrist as their raspy breath mingled in the space between them.

Nick kissed her forehead, his thumbs stroking her cheek. "Come back alive."

CHAPTER NINE

*V*ictor splayed his right hand on the granite lab table, examining the red edges of split skin around his knuckles. After two days without any kind of treatment, the damaged skin had the beginnings of infection swelling beneath the surface, and flakes of dry blood still clung to the lesions.

He would have treated the damage before now, but had only awakened that morning on his apartment floor, his head throbbing and his hand a sticky mess of dried, congealed blood from putting it through the wall. After quickly wrapping his hand in gauze and scrubbing the macabre mess from the floor, he had reached the lab and now tried to treat the wounds before too many of his Areth brethren could question the cause.

With a glance around the empty room, he slipped his hand into his lab coat to remove the small vial of Dermaseal liquid and the stratum basale stimulator. He tried to hold the vial in his right hand to open it, but pain shot up his arm from what he suspected to be one carpal and at least three metacarpal fractures. The broken bones would have to wait until he could get to the infirmary and access the osteoskeletal sonic binder. For now, he just needed to hide the visible evidence. He winced as he again tried to twist open the vial.

"Damn it!"

His entire body tensed, and he nearly dropped the vial, when he felt the presence of someone behind him. He curled the vial of Dermaseal into his left hand and slid a look over his shoulder. CJ Montgomery stood behind him, her hands in the pockets of her lab coat, and her blue eyes trained on his injuries.

"Doctor Montgomery," he said, trying to tamp down any indication in his voice that anything was off. "This is nothing. Just an accident."

She sat down on the stool beside him, her fingers curling around his wrist to bring his hand closer to her. The first contact jolted him; he was so unaccustomed to physical touch. Her fingertips traced over his knuckles, following the outline of the blue and purple bruising that spread over most of the back of his hand. When she lifted his hand, he flinched as pain shot straight up his arm. She immediately looked to his face, meeting his stare.

She held her hand out toward his left, silently asking for the vial he apparently hadn't hidden very well. Victor set it in her palm, and she twisted it open, smoothing the dauber over his split skin. The anesthetic blended bonding agent quickly suppressed the momentary sting. He could almost feel the liquid soaking down through his cells, knitting them together.

"Do you have a SBS?"

Victor nodded, and handed that to her as well. She adjusted the settings on the stratum basale stimulator, and he took the few moments to study her, remembering the instructions Barnabas had given him days before. Somehow, he didn't think this was what Barnabas had in mind. Doctor Montgomery aimed the stimulator at his knuckles and turned it on, his hand illuminated by a bright white-blue light. His skin tingled as the photogenesis process created new skin instantly, healing, and knitting the damage together again. The bruises faded slightly, and some of the ache eased as the swelling diminished around the broken bones.

She clicked the stimulator off, setting it down on the table. Victor withdrew his hand, examining the skin now whole again, with only the slightest pink lines to indicate the damage. He almost flexed his fingers, but stopped himself. Doctor Montgomery leaned her elbow on the table and set her fist against her temple.

"I'd get to the infirmary soon and spend a couple minutes with the osteoskeletal binder. I don't think anything is snapped, but you could have a fracture or two by the looks of the bruising."

Victor nodded. "Thank you, Doctor."

She sat watching him, and Victor wondered what she might be thinking. After what she saw the week before, Michael's escort to Kathleen's torture chamber some called a lab, she had to wonder what secrets were being kept behind locked doors and pass code encrypted computer files. CJ Montgomery presented herself to be a humanitarian, here to better the lives of her fellow man. What would she do if she knew what the Areth did to better their own existence?

A large part of him wanted to know.

He looked up, meeting her blue eyes. She raised one light eyebrow in a graceful arch, and he found himself thinking that among human women, she was very attractive. High, round cheekbones accentuated her large blue eyes and her lips were full and wide. She was relatively tall for a human woman, though not for an Areth, and although her long lab coat often hid her form, he knew she was well shaped. Victor pulled his attention away, focusing again on his hand.

"Thank you for your assistance, Doctor Montgomery."

"Of course."

Victor slipped his injured hand into his lab coat as he left the room, hiding what visible swelling and bruising remained from inquiring eyes until he reached the infirmary. While he was there, he intended to obtain more antibiotics and analgesics for Michael. A heavy weight sat on his chest, not knowing how Michael was or if he had survived the weekend. His unknown ailment had kept him from coming back and checking his friend, and now he would have to wait until the end of the day before going to the cell. He flexed his hand inside the pocket, pain searing up his arm.

This time he didn't flinch away from it.

Michael had endured far worse. Was he worth so much more that he deserved relief when relief was denied his friend? The only reason he healed himself at all was to keep any questions at bay. *Was it not for that . . .*

Victor bit down hard, fighting to control the rage that surged out through his limbs, hot in his blood. Hate simmered beneath his skin. Hate for Kathleen, for the sadistic pleasure she harvested from Michael's pain. Hate for the cold, heartless existence that was his destiny. Hate for his own ancestry, his own lineage, and his own kind.

*N*ick poked at his pile of mashed potatoes, swirling his fork through them, making a valley for his gravy. When there were too many valleys, he just stirred until the potatoes were brown goo and he tossed his fork down, letting it clatter against the side of the plate. He slouched in his chair with a groan, scrubbing his face with his hands.

This sucked!

"Eating alone sucks."

Nick chuckled and uncovered his face to look up at Jace Quinn, who stood beside his table with a tray of food in hand. "Yeah, I was just thinking the same damn thing."

"Mind if I . . ."

"Have a seat."

The lieutenant pulled out the chair across from Nick and sat down, his silverware clattering against his plate as he half dropped it. Nick sat up and made another attempt at poking at his food. After a few more mouthfuls, he gave up, deciding to take the rest back to his quarters for Dog. He stole a glance at Jace; slumped down in his chair swinging his fork from his fingertips with a piece of meat skewered on the end. Jace looked up, and when their eyes met, he chuckled.

"We're pathetic. You know that, right?" he said, tossing his meat-laden utensil onto the tray. "Our women are gone twenty-four hours and we're —" He motioned between them in frustration.

"Crying in our beer?" Nick offered.

"Exactly!"

"Except for the glaring lack of beer."

Jace leaned forward, motioning for Nick to do the same. "I can fix that, Colonel."

Nick popped up his eyebrows. "You have beer?"

*M*ichael sat on the edge of his bed, curled forward with his elbows resting on his knees and a damp cloth pressed to the back of his neck. His body ached, every muscle protesting the simplest movement. Exhaustion pulled at him, making his limbs twice as heavy as usual and his head a boulder on his shoulders.

He'd lived. How, he wasn't sure. She'd taken him to the edge.

His tiny corner of hell was once again in darkness, the sun having set hours before. A thin beam of silver moonlight slashed through his window, illuminating a square on the far wall where a shelf of books had once hung. He wondered what had happened to them. Had she just ordered them taken away, or had she gone so far as to have them destroyed? His mind filled with the image of curled and burning pages, the words of Asimov, Wells, and Lewis disappearing in consuming flames, and his chest ached for a loss he didn't know for sure was real.

The soft click of the door lock disengaging echoed through the hollow room, and Michael raised his head to watch the triangle of light spread across the floor as the door opened. He wasn't surprised to see Victor slip into the room and close the door behind him, glancing out through the small security screen at the top. Victor looked in his direction, and in the dim moonlight, Michael saw a smile on the man's face.

"You are looking much better, my friend," Victor said, bringing the only chair in the room to the side of the bed to sit facing him. "How are you feeling?"

Michael sat up and dropped the now warm cloth back into the shallow basin of water beside him. He groaned at the stiff ache hindering his movements and pushed his hand into his side as the muscles around his ribs pulled. "I'm . . . alive."

Victor nodded. "You worried me those first two nights." He reached into the pocket of his lab coat and produced a wrapped sandwich, holding it out to him. "I didn't know if they had begun bringing you food yet."

Michael hoped Victor forgave his greedy grab for the package, and unwrapped it as quietly and quickly as possible, his stomach immediately rumbling at the potential of food after four days. He bit into the sandwich, not even caring what filled the bread, and moaned in satisfaction.

"Thank you," he mumbled around the food crammed in his cheek. Michael caught the shift in Victor's expression in the silver moonlight, and shook his head as he forced down the first dry swallow.

"Don't thank me. I do nothing to stop her."

"There is nothing you can do, and I know that."

Victor raised his head and their stares locked. His jaw clenched, his lips pressing into a tight line. Michael nodded, taking another bite of the sandwich. He took the time to savor the taste and realize it was ham and cheese. They sat in silence as Michael finished the sandwich, and swallowed the half dozen mixed pills Victor handed him with a glass of water. With the empty ache in his gut appeased, Michael braced his hands behind him on the rumpled bedclothes and leaned back on his arms. Victor sat straddling the backwards-facing chair, his arms crossed on the high back and his head down.

"You remind me of Mr. Spock" Michael finally said.

Victor raised his head, but didn't answer. He stared at Michael for several moments, his only movements the blinking of his eyes. Then a slight grin cracked his face. "I assume this Mr. Spock is from one of your books?"

Michael nodded, lacking the energy required to fully explain. "He was an alien."

"Of course."

"No physical resemblance. Your ears don't point and your blood isn't green. Is it?"

"My blood is as red as yours, Michael."

He sat forward, finding that a shift in position every few minutes helped stave off the worst of the stiffness before it had a chance to grab hold of him too hard. "Mr. Spock was *half* alien. He was also half human. That's more me than you, isn't it," he said, stating the fact more than asking the question.

Victor's eyes shifted away for a brief moment before coming back to him. It wasn't something Michael needed confirmation on. Kathleen was his mother, and she was Areth. He wasn't Areth. He was, for all intents and purposes, human. Someday, he wanted to know what twist of fate and science put him in a cell. What monumental transgression he had committed, other than the unforgivable act of being born, was terrible enough to deserve a lifetime of hell?

"All you have told me is how I am *unlike* this Mr. Spock. How do I remind you of him?"

"Spock was always fighting this internal battle. Trying to be one thing, when by nature he could have just as easily been something else." Michael drew a slow breath through his nose, staring at Victor as he thought about all the times in the last years that this man had shown him friendship—and even compassion—when every other Areth around him saw him as something akin to a lab rat or yesterday's garbage.

Victor chuckled and stood, swinging the chair back to its original position. "You have read too many of those psychology textbooks, Michael. IQ of one-hundred and seventy-two and you think you know everything."

"*We* were running standard lunar training flights—slingshot maneuvers for low burn re-entry—and I broke formation as we skimmed the northern polar cap. I was fifty miles away and hovering at a forty-five degree angle cherubs five down an ice crevasse before my CAG knew I was gone."

Nick arched his eyebrows and bobbed his head. "Holy crap! Five hundred feet? How long did you maintain that position?"

"Right up until my go juice was approaching bingo and I figured if I didn't back track I'd be stuck down there until the whole damn polar cap melted. I heard my playmates on the radio, and they thought I'd crashed and burned. I flew at the speed of heat to the nearest airfield, greased a palm or two to get capped off, and dry-footed it across Asia to Nepal. I contacted some people there I had met over the years, and waited. It took seven months before I met with General Castleton and came back to North America."

Nick took another long draw from his beer, draining the remains of his bottle. He sighed with the last swallow, and willingly took the next bottle Jace offered. In the two hours since retrieving the pilfered supply from the medical supply cooler outside the Quinn's quarters, the two of them had managed to knock back three-quarters of the supply. It had been a mixed lot: import and export, canned and bottled. However, Nick didn't really care. It was cold, and it was all beer. Close enough.

Right now, his head was feeling light and his limbs were feeling heavy, which in all was not an unpleasant sensation. He twisted off the cap of the new bottle, and took a drink. A little stronger than the last one, but smoother. Not bad.

"By then, Earth Force knew you weren't dead."

Jace shrugged. "Pretty much, yeah. I was declared AWOL and a deserter."

"What made you do it?"

Jace finished his own beer and took the last amber bottle from the cardboard six-pack on the glass top table between them. "Ever get a feeling in your gut that just says things aren't right?"

Nick nodded, his cheeks puffing out with a low belch. "Sure."

"That's all it was. I had no solid proof of anything. Not like most people who come here. I just knew things were too damn good to be true. Freedom and security doesn't come that easy. It doesn't just fall in your lap. My father was an Earth Force chaplain, and his daddy—Jedidiah Quinn—ran a mega church in Florida. My mother's father was a Marine before the Areth came. He fought in Desert Storm back the end of the century. I remember him telling me about what it was like, when we were the United States of America and not just another continent. Not that I think the world should go back to fighting with each other. Somewhere along the way we lost our pride. Our own strength. I don't trust anyone who can take that away."

Nick stared at him for several moments, then chuckled.

"What?" Jace asked.

"Do you ever shut up?"

Jace laughed. "My wife says I talk too much when I'm drunk."

"She's right."

In response, Jace drained half the contents of his fresh beer. Nick looked down at his own, and decided to slow down just a little. It had been awhile since he had drank large quantities of alcohol, and probably was beyond the point of avoiding a hangover in the morning, but wanted to avoid getting sick if at all possible.

"How long have you been married?"

"Four years," Jace answered, setting his own bottle down and crossing his arms over his chest, slouching down in his chair. "I met Lilly when I transferred to this base. She had been with Phoenix for two years already." He smiled the goofy kind of grin Nick recognized as a drunken man in love. "It took me six months to convince her I wasn't just a cocky glider pilot looking for a quick screw. Six months later, we were married."

Nick raised his bottle in salute, forgetting his resolve from minutes before to back off on the booze. "Well, good luck, congratulations, and all that."

Jace grinned and raised his own bottle. As both men lowered the bottles again, Jace used his to point toward Nick. "How long have you and CJ been a thing?"

Nick slouched down on the leather-upholstered bench and set his foot on the edge of the low table, resting his bottle on his thigh. "Caitlin and I haven't been a *thing* for a long time."

"Yeah? How long?"

"Eight years."

The younger man's eyebrows jerked upward and his mouth dropped open. Nick figured he was probably doing the math. Yeah, she was young. He was a cradle robber. Nothing he hadn't heard before. In his defense, she hadn't acted like any twenty-two-year-old he'd ever met, and she sure as hell didn't look like a kid!

"Shit. So, what the hell happened?"

"Can we change the subject?"

"Sore spot, huh?"

"Drop it," Nick snapped.

"Still love her, huh?"

"Remember that thing your wife said about you talking too much? You're doing it again," he said against the mouth of his beer before taking another swig.

Jace laughed loudly, his head falling back. "Okay, fine. New topic. How'd you get the call sign *Zeus*?"

"How do you know my call sign?"

Jace shrugged and grinned. "I told you when we met. I spent years trying to break your wormhole flight record. I saw it as a personal challenge. I studied your flight reports, your statistical data, everything. And I tell ya, I came damn close."

Nick nodded. "My old RIO got hold of me, told me I retired too quick because some smart ass wet-behind-the-ears space jockey was going to steal my glory."

"Is that why you flew like that? The glory?"

Nick leveled his gaze on Jace, his fingers absently picking at the foil label on the empty bottle in his hand. They were cut from the same cloth, Nick and this kid. He could tell the minute Jace started rambling about O_2 tanks and manual compensation. He tapped the bottle on his leg and shook his head.

"No way in hell," he finally said.

Jace grinned. "I didn't think so. It's the rush. The g-forces pushing on your body despite the inertial dampeners because you're going that damn fast. The way your blood almost bubbles and your head feels like it's going to pop off your shoulders. Knowing that with one extra twist you could be on the other side of the solar system like *that*," he said with a snap of his fingers.

"Damn straight."

A flash of understanding crossed Jace's alcohol-relaxed face and he pointed a finger at Nick. "God of the Sky . . . that's why they called you Zeus. You were the God of the Sky."

Damn, it sounded pretentious when said like that . . .

"You know mine. What was yours?"

Jace snorted, and retrieved the last two bottles of beer remaining from the stockpile they'd snagged from the cooler in the storage room. He handed one to Nick and twisted the cap off his own. "Anakin."

"As in Skywalker or Solo?"

"Does it matter? Both were kick ass pilots."

Nick chuckled. "Yeah, but one turned into one twisted son of a bitch."

Jace just shrugged and nodded, grinning before he drank from his last bottle.

*N*ick stumbled back to his quarters some time in the morning, he wasn't sure when. He just knew he had woken to a snoring Jace Quinn on the other side of the room, empty beer bottles and cans all around, and decided it was time to go. His head pounded and his legs seemed to bow out at the knees with ever step. He half-fell into the dark space, leaning into the door to close it.

Dog jumped off the bed in the next room, pattering across the floor to greet him, but Nick didn't dare bend enough to pat his head. Bending might put him flat on his back on the floor. He looked across the space to the bedroom door, and at that moment, the bed looked a mile away.

"Screw it," he mumbled and managed to half-walk, half-fall sideways to sprawl across the lounge.

His stomach lurched at the rapid change in position, and he took several deep breaths waiting to see if a quick dash to the bathroom was necessary.

That's what you get for getting drunk once every . . . what . . . five, six year?

Things settled and Nick huffed. Yup, the lounge would do just fine for the next twelve or fifteen hours. He shifted to find a comfortable position with his legs draped over the end of the lounge, and glanced towards the PAC sitting on the glass table beside him.

Nick reached out his arm, his fingers tapping the keyboard and bringing the computer to life. Belching loudly, he entered a series of programmed commands and the screen filled with a now all-too-familiar video clip. As it looped through the same thirty-second sequence, Nick touched the screen with his fingers.

He fell asleep, images of his lost son playing beside him.

CHAPTER TEN

10 November 10, Friday 15:24
Phoenix Compound
Outside Colorado Springs, Colorado
Former United States of America

*T*he mountain hummed with activity. On every level and in every section, preparations were complete. Temporary quarters were filled with beds and supplies for the new residents that needed no medical care, and extra space had been cleared in the infirmary for additional beds for those who did need help when they arrived. Shelves were stocked, food goods were prepared, and every kind of medication they had on hand at the ready.

The all-terrain stealth hovercrafts they would be using for transportation waited in the surface bay, already loaded with supplies; modified by some of the best engineers Nick had ever seen. The crafts could hit one hundred ninety miles per hour in less than four seconds, and their surface travel capabilities were amazing. Nothing slowed them down. When it came time to come home, speed and agility might be the only thing keeping them alive.

Nick lifted a Glock 100 pulse charge pistol from the pile of various weapons on the table in front of him. The black steel was cold in his grip, the weapon just heavy enough to settle comfortably in his hand. After twenty years of service, seven years of retirement hadn't lessened the familiar way the weapon felt. The weight was natural, an extension of his arm. He slid his finger through the trigger and flattened his hand, familiarizing himself with the balance.

"That your weapon of choice?"

He looked at Jace, who dropped into the chair beside him, choosing a Magnum SP-21 stun bolt pistol from the selection.

Nick aligning his site with a security camera on the other side of the room, one eye closed. "Yeah. You like the Magnum?"

Jace engaged the safety, removed the bolt magazine, and spun the black polymer weapon around on his finger, smiling. "A lot less bulk in the speed suit if I have to be armed when I fly. They're light, too."

"How many bolts per magazine?"

"Thirty."

Nick clicked his cheek. "See, that's why I like the Glock. Self-charging. No magazine necessary."

"Okay, but the mercury cell alone adds a good seven or eight ounces to the overall weight. It's *steel*! You don't think that thing is heavy?

Before Nick could throw back an appropriate jab at Jace's manhood, a female voice came from behind them. "Men and their toys."

"Lil," Jace declared, his Magnum clattering to the pile of weapons as he stood, pulling his wife against him in the same movement. "Why didn't anyone tell me you were on your way down?"

"I told the security guard he didn't need to. That I'd find you."

Jace kissed her, humming loudly his obvious pleasure at seeing his wife after two weeks. "You sure did."

Nick busied himself with studying the details of his weapon and cleaning the small grooves along the side as the two of them stood behind his chair. They kept their voices low, the sound just barely carrying to him. He shifted his chair, setting his elbows on the table, as he examined another pulse charger. When the words stopped, and the sounds coming from behind him were more ardent than conversational, Nick set the Glock in his hand down with a loud thump.

"You two wanna find a room?" he said over his shoulder, not turning to look.

He heard Jace's chuckle. "Don't worry about him, baby. He's just a horny old man and CJ won't be back until tonight."

Nick snorted, and focused on his gun again. He grinned at the distinctive sound of Lilly smacking Jace, not too hard, but smacking all the same.

"Jason Patrick Quinn," Lilly scolded.

"What? I'm not wrong . . ."

Damian approached the table and leaned over, his hands on the edge. "The global weather net is confirming our predictions. A severe weather pattern is forming off the coast of California now, moving southeast and expected to make landfall within the next hour and a half. It should be moving across Arizona about the time we're preparing to leave, and hitting New Mexico right on time." He smiled smugly, his teeth a white slash against his dark skin.

"It's not going to mess with the hovercrafts?" Nick asked.

"Our hovers will fly in anything," Jace answered, returning to his seat. Lilly perched on the arm of the chair, listening, her husband's arm draped across her hips.

Damian nodded in agreement. "The advance sensor array can read fifteen miles ahead of us in a constantly adjusting radius, even in fog as thick as soup and torrential rain, and the automatic compensation system will keep us from hitting any trees or rock jags."

"We're ready to move?" Nick asked, trying to ignore the thumping anticipation in his chest.

Damian nodded. "We're ready as we'll ever be. Now, we just wait for the right time and head out."

"On that note, if you gentlemen don't mind, I'm going to go spend some quality time with my wife," Jace said as he stood and took Lilly's hand, leading her down the hall.

Damian and Nick exchanged looks, and Nick shook his head. "Hey, the kid's been my shadow for the last two weeks. At least now I get some peace and quiet," he said with a smirk.

*C*J stared out into the dark night from one of the hallways on the fifth level of the facility, seeing nothing but black beyond the thick tempered glass. The steady pelt of rain on the window echoed through the quiet hall, the building nearly empty. Steady streams of water ran down the glass, merging with other drops, dividing, coming together again until they hit the steel edge of the window and diverted to run off. She stepped closer and touched the window, the glass cool to the touch.

She glanced at her watch. Less than an hour and Nick would breach the perimeter of the compound, an hour from now they and the others would be inside. God willing, five hours from now they would all be back in Colorado safe and sound. All of them.

Her insides quivered with nervous anticipation, and she drew a slow breath. It was important to maintain the veneer of calm, especially now. She had slipped Captain Fields' microslide into a terminal in the Hemo lab earlier in the evening and had surreptitiously paid attention to the security staff at each post for any sign that they suspected anything strange. Each time she passed and saw nothing out of the ordinary, her spine relaxed one small degree.

Of course, she wouldn't relax completely until this night was over.

The elevator at the end of the hallway dinged as it reached the level she was on, and she glanced toward the doors as they slipped open. Victor exited, his head down and two paper coffee cups stacked together in his hand. CJ stepped back from the glass and slipped her hands into her lab coat pockets. He looked up, and his steps slowed for just a moment before he smiled slightly and continued toward her.

"Doctor Montgomery. You're here late, especially for a Friday evening."

"I've been running a simulation all day, and the final calculations are just about complete," she explained, giving the answer she had already prepared. Even now, the computers back in her lab were churning away on the very simulation she spoke of. "I wanted to stay long enough to see the results."

"This is the Guillain-Barre study," he said, tipping his head.

CJ nodded, her eyes inadvertently shifting down to his right hand that held the cups. He followed her gaze.

"I wasn't able to fully heal the fractures, but it was enough to make the hand useable. I appreciate your discretion in the matter, Doctor Montgomery. You certainly were under no obligation to keep the information to yourself."

He met her stare. There was something different about Victor, something she couldn't quite define. She hadn't dealt with him much, only in passing when their individual research programs coincided, and two weeks ago when she found him trying to self-treat a badly injured hand, but even in their brief contact she picked up on it. When he met her eyes, it wasn't a challenge. Not like with other Areth. He smiled. Nothing outrageous, or to call attention to himself, but simply put, Areth didn't smile. They didn't laugh. They didn't joke. They claimed to have discarded the need for excess emotion, including affection and love.

When she'd first identified him as the man in the video with Michael, she had wanted to hate him for his obvious participation in the façade that was this facility. As she worked with him, she couldn't help but wonder about him.

"I didn't feel I was under any obligation to report it, either," she answered simply.

He dipped his chin slightly. "Well, thank you."

CJ fought the urge to glance at her watch. She could almost hear the time ticking away, but she had to maintain the façade. "Why are you here so late, Victor?"

"Didn't you hear? I live here now."

His expression was stoic, straight-faced, and CJ blinked, unsure how to respond. Then Victor chuckled and smiled. "I'm sorry, that was a very poor attempt at humor. I'm afraid I'm not very good at it."

CJ laughed, she couldn't help herself, and tried to smother it behind her hand. "No, no, that was good . . . I just wasn't expecting it."

Victor shrugged one shoulder. "Perhaps I need to work on my timing."

She wrapped her arms over her stomach and drew a shaky breath. "Perhaps."

He looked through the window into the darkness. "Actually, like you, I can't seem to leave tonight."

"Oh. I understand." She didn't, but without pushing further, his answer had to suffice. It was time to wander down near the security station and make sure no red flags were up. She lifted her arm and glanced at her watch. "My simulation should be ending shortly. Have a good evening, Victor, what's left of it."

He nodded, and she walked away. As she neared the security station at the end of the hall, through which she would have to pass to re-enter her laboratory wing, she wrapped her fingers around the remote detonator in her lab coat pocket. It was the diversion Nick would need, should he need it. A couple of computers exploding in her lab should be enough to draw most guards away from their monitors.

She walked to the locked door that led to her lab, and made a show of patting her coat pockets, knowing the guards would be watching. After a few moments, she backtracked to the security station and leaned onto the desk with a sigh.

"I seem to have left my security badge in my lab," she said to the guard seated in front of the panel of monitors. "Do you suppose you could buzz me through?"

"Of course, Doctor Montgomery," he said with a slight air of condescension and superiority. Any other night, CJ might have let it bother her, but not tonight. "If you could please step around to the back of the desk. We are required to report each time we override the passcard system. You will need to sign in."

CJ nodded and rounded the desk as the second guard stood with a handheld computer interface in his hand. He motioned for her to step inside the half-oval area as he entered data into the interface. She cast quick glances at the monitor array, scanning the images displayed on the multiple screens. Everything appeared to be progressing without incident. The security override had engaged ten minutes before, and it appeared that no one was the wiser. A small bit of relief relaxed a little bit more of the tense muscles around her spine.

"Sign here, Doctor," the guard said, handing the flat interface to her along with a long, thin stylus.

CJ took it and signed her name across the bottom. As she handed it back, a red light at the base of one of the screens started flashing, and a loud, buzzing alarm sounded. Her head snapped up, and her heart jumped. The guard beside her moved to lean over the desk. She slipped her hand into her pocket when her breath caught in her throat.

The picture on every monitor changed, all of them switching to what appeared to be the interior of a small cell. Three orderlies, dressed in white uniforms, were in the room attempting to hold down a fourth person that CJ couldn't quite see. He was a big man, and he was fighting them. *One of the human prisoners . . .*

Oh, crap . . .

The three occupants of the security station stared at each other, and then the guards exchanged a look that almost had CJ running down the hall. *This was so incredibly not good . . .*

"What is the problem, Joseph?" came a voice from behind her.

CJ blinked and swallowed, turning to look at Victor where he stood. He stepped into the semi-circle, his eyes shifting to the monitors, and CJ thought she caught a slight and momentary shift in his expression.

"There is a disturbance in—" The guard stopped himself, his eyes shifting from CJ to Victor. "We were about to call Kathleen."

"No," Victor said, cutting off the suggestion. "I will attend to it."

Joseph's gaze moved to her again, and she could almost hear the question hanging in the air . . . *But what about the human?*

"No need for concern. Doctor Montgomery is aware of the residents in D-Wing." His voice was flat and calm, and as he spoke he looked directly into her eyes.

CJ nodded her head slightly, her mind trying to process the sudden and dramatic shift in events. Of all the possible contingencies they had anticipated, a disturbance in the holding cells hadn't been one of them.

"I will still call Kathleen and Barnabas. You will need assistance in dealing with the patient. And we have not been informed of Doctor Montgomery's security clearance status change."

"Both Kathleen and Barnabas have left the facility for the day, and the hour is late. If you feel the necessity to contact them to inform them of a security situation which would be resolved before they could return, and of a staff update they are already aware of, it is certainly your prerogative." Victor's voice had taken on the characteristic dispassionate levelness of his Areth peers, and CJ could only stare.

The guard considered Victor's words, and then jerked his head in a curt nod. "Understood, Victor. We will simply note in our logs that Doctor Montgomery will be assisting you."

A tight muscle jerked along his jaw as his gaze slid toward her. "Fine. If you will follow me, Doctor."

CJ followed Victor away from the security station, glancing back once at the guards. One entered data into the system, while the other returned the monitors to their usual display of the facility. Nick and the others could very well be inside the building by now, and the security system hadn't yet alerted anyone to their presence.

She followed Victor to the elevator, her insides twisting, and her pulse jumping. He pushed level three and the elevator jerked into motion.

"I apologize now for your forced involvement in this situation, Doctor Montgomery. In the end, the solution may not be a favorable one because we both will be required to answer for our elaboration on the truth. But with this solution, we have at least postponed the inevitable for another day."

She stared at him with wide eyes, nodding. *What the hell could she say?*

"I know you have become aware of our third floor residents, and while I can't yet determine what your opinion on this matter is, I am not in a position to question you further. One of our patients needs help, and if you and I are unable to properly give him what he needs, I find the consequences most unpleasant."

The elevator bumped to a stop, and the doors opened. The hall was completely empty and stretched on for what seemed forever. Not a sound carried to them. Victor gripped her elbow and propelled her from the car, leading her down the hall to a locked door. He slid his passkey and pressed his thumb to a bioscan pad before the lock disengaged. CJ felt caught in a whirlwind as he led her down another hall. Loud screaming echoed back to them the further they moved, and the painful resonance chilled her blood.

"The patient's name is Alexander," Victor said, turning sharply to face her before unlocking yet another door. "I warn you, Doctor, his appearance will be a shock. But I suspect it will take two of us to calm him."

"What's wrong with him?"

They were in another hall, lined with doors along both sides. Each door having a small, screened window near the top. At each end was a security desk, and the shouted voices of several men and women came from the cells. That was exactly what they were . . . cells. CJ knew exactly where she was.

Victor jogged to the far end of the hall, past the orderlies who stood outside one room, seeming not to care about the screams of pain and sounds of thrashing that came from inside. He opened the door, and CJ stepped into the room. Her heart froze in her chest.

Lying on the floor was the largest man she had ever seen. Were he standing, he would have easily reached over seven feet, and had to top four hundred and fifty pounds. Her stomach jumped to her throat as he rolled onto his back and she saw his face. Twisted and distorted like some melted wax sculpture, his features hung from his skull in odd places and at bizarre angles. His skin was an ashen and translucent white, with blue veins throbbing close to the surface. Tufts of yellow hair sprouted randomly from his head, with no pattern. An oversized tongue hung from his cleft-split lips and massive hands on arms the size of logs lashed out, knocking over a nearby table as he howled again. His booming cry resonated in the small cell.

"Dear God . . ."

"He's in pain," Victor finally answered.

CHAPTER ELEVEN

*A*lexander's cries echoed through the cellblock, each bellow a punch in the center of Michael's chest. He paced his small space, hands planted at his waist, bare feet slapping on the cold linoleum.

Why didn't they help him?

Another pain-filled cry reverberated off his walls, and Michael braced his hands against the frame of his door, leaning into his arms with his head bowed. Frustration gnawed at his insides, knotting his muscles and heating his blood.

"What have you done for his pain?" came the question from the hall.

Michael raised his head, listening to Victor's voice.

"Kathleen has left strict instructions to comply only with the regimen she has outlined," Dorjan answered.

"He is in pain," Victor snapped. "I don't give a damn about his regimen. Get me a hypo of Dolpaman and a hypo of Poldamax." There was a pause. "Now!"

Alexander cried out again, and Michael heard the scuffling as he assumed Kirk and Paco attempted to hold the big man down. His hands curled into fists as Alexander's slurred tongue called his name, desperate for rescue.

He held his breath, listening to each individual sound that relayed to him what happened, imagining it in his mind. *Dorjan returned with the syringes filled with sedative and nerve-numbing painkillers. Victor entered the cell again, and as Kirk and Paco held a frantic Alexander down, he pushed the abusive needles through paper-thin, transparent skin.* There was the sound of shattered glass, and Michael imagined a bottle of some drug now lay broken on the hard floor.

Alexander cried—his sobs sometimes a bellowing wail and sometimes a whimpering whisper.

"He is still in pain."

Michael focused on the soft, feminine voice now in the hall outside his cell. It was unfamiliar and he tried to angle himself to see the speaker through the mesh window in his door. All he saw was a flash of golden hair standing near Victor.

"He has worked himself into a panic, and I'm not sure the sedatives will help him," she continued.

"Victor!" Michael called out. "Let me help him."

Victor came to the door, looking at Michael through the mesh. "Do you think you can?"

"I know I can. Alexander trusts me. He's calling for *me*, Victor."

Victor motioned toward one of the security guards who stood nearby, indicating they should unlock Michael's door. The guard hesitated, glancing at his partner, but after a harsh look from Victor, he came forward and slid his passkey through the lock. Moments later, the lock disengaged, and Victor pushed the door open. Before Michael could step into the hall, the guard had his weapon drawn and trained on him.

He didn't know whether to be annoyed or complimented. Barefoot and unarmed, his strength still depleted, and they felt the need to hold a pulse weapon on him. Victor gripped his arm and led him toward Alexander's cell. Michael made brief eye contact with the blond doctor who stood along the wall, and immediately recognized her as the woman from the elevator weeks before. She stared at him with wide blue eyes, her lips parted slightly, and Michael wondered for a brief moment what had put the flush of pink in her cheeks. She looked as though she might jump out of her skin at any moment.

Alexander curled into as tight a ball as his hulking form would allow on the floor of his cell. His hands fisted tight, his arms crossed over his chest as he rocked on his side. Deep cries rumbled from his chest and tears poured unabated down his cheeks. Michael moved quickly into the room, dropping to his knees beside Alexander to place his hand on the big man's shoulder. Alexander immediately jerked, crying out again.

"It's me, Alexander. It's Michael."

"Miffll?" he asked, his voice nearly lost in the rasp caused by hours of screaming.

Michael nodded. "Yes. No one is going to hurt you, Alexander. Victor is here, and he is going to stop the pain. If you calm down, take deep breaths, the pain will start to ease."

He looked over his shoulder to Victor, to confirm his instructions were correct, and Victor nodded. The blond doctor had stepped into the room and stood near the door, her gaze shifting from the activities in the room to the hall.

"Afffraid," Alexander slurred, spittle flying from his lips.

"I know, but there is no need. Victor will not harm you."

"Should we give them some space?" the woman said to Victor.

He nodded and motioned for Paco and Kirk to leave the room. Michael sat on the floor, drawing up one knee to rest his arm and kept his other hand on Alexander. For the next few minutes, he calmed Alexander just by talking and as the minutes passed the tension left his body and the crying calmed.

"Good, Alexander. You're doing fine," he said when Alexander drew a long, shuddered breath. "Do you feel better?"

"Yeff, Miffl."

Michael patted his arm and looked up to Victor and the woman. "They were heavy handed with him before you came. It's no wonder he was upset."

Victor shook his head, his expression twisting into the shadowed mask of anger and frustration. He turned on his heels, one hand curled in a fist, but stopped short when several high-pitched pings of pulse weapon discharge echoed through the hall. Michael came to his feet when he saw Dorjan stumble backwards in the hallway, his body encased in white-blue threads of electricity, before he fell limp to the floor. Maurice and Rocco drew their weapons, firing and shouting to the as of yet unseen attackers.

"What is going on?" Victor asked to the room and headed for the door, but the other doctor stopped him, her hand on his arm.

"Don't go out there."

"Move aside, Doctor Montgomery."

She blocked him from the open door, the intent absolutely clear in her expression that he would not leave. Her blue eyes stared, determined, and cold, and she braced her lower arm across Victor's chest. "No, Victor."

Michael raised an eyebrow, torn between his curiosity over the events in the hall and the ones right here in the room.

The muffled pulse fire rang out again, and Alexander cried in fear.

99

Michael crouched and laid his hand on Alexander's shoulder. "Don't be afraid."

Several men dressed in black ran past the cell, weapons drawn, and one stopped to secure Dorjan's hands with plastic cuffs. A tall man with mostly silver hair and sharp features filled the doorway, pulse pistol immediately aimed directly at Victor.

"Nick, wait!" the woman shouted, pressing her hand to his chest.

He stopped short, his finger flexing on the trigger. Michael observed, taking in everything, especially the new arrival. Something pulled at him, a niggling knowledge like he knew this man. He should know him. Slowly, he stood, rising until he saw past Victor's shoulders to look directly into the man's face. His gaze moved, and when their eyes locked, something inside Michael's chest tightened. He saw the man tense, draw a breath, his eyes widen as he examined Michael. For one brief moment, the angle of his weapon dropped as all his focus shifted.

*N*ick couldn't breathe, and all he could hear was the rush of blood pounding in his ears. A metallic tinge sat bitter and raw in the back of his throat, and he knew it was the adrenaline of the fight. He forgot the gunfire and the security entourage that could be on them any moment when he saw Michael.

He stood behind the dark haired doctor, dressed in a loose linen tunic and baggy pants that pooled around his bare feet. His hair was slightly long, and the natural haphazard tendencies that he seemed to have inherited from Nick had it ruffled. Their stature and stance mirrored each other, in height and build, Michael having the hard angles of youth on his side.

His chest burned and he sucked in air.

Michael stared at him, his head tilting the smallest degree, and Nick wondered if he realized—if he knew or suspected.

Another pulse fire echoed through the hall and Nick's instincts kicked back in. He leveled the weapon once again on the Areth doctor, but didn't fire. His gaze shifted to the giant man lying on the floor, over which Michael stood protectively.

"Can he travel?" he asked Caitlin, nudging his chin toward the man.

"He's been sedated and given a strong pain killer. It's not going to be easy."

"Where are you taking him?" Michael demanded, and Nick heard the challenge in his voice. He almost smiled.

"Somewhere safe," Caitlin answered. "All of you are going someplace safe."

"Damian and Seb are the biggest guys we've got. They can help—" Nick paused, looking down at the hulk of a man on the floor.

"Alexander," Michael offered.

Nick met his gaze, holding it. In just the few moments they had shared the same space, Nick already recognized the emotions behind Michael's eyes. So familiar, and to anyone else, most likely masked. Challenging. Skeptical. Wary. Who could blame him? Soon enough, he would know. He would learn.

"They can help Alexander to the hovers."

"I should go with him," Michael said.

Nick just nodded, finding it hard to look away. His hands itched to reach out—to touch him. Make sure he was real. Finally, he swallowed and pulled his focus in once again. If he didn't keep his mind on getting everyone out, everything could come crashing down around them. Shouting over his shoulder, he called for Damian.

Damian's bulky form filled the doorway, his bald head glistening with sweat, shining black against the lights behind him. He braced a hand against the frame, pulse charge weapon in hand.

"Yes, sir."

"Grab Seb. We're going to need help in here."

Just as quickly as he appeared, he was gone again. Silence settled in the cell, broken only by Alexander's soft whimpers. Nick shifted his gaze between Caitlin and Michael. When he glanced down at her, he found her watching him, her blue eyes intense, and the smallest bit of tension released in his chest. She wasn't supposed to be here, but at least now he would know she was safe and away. He could protect her like he couldn't before.

"You will need Alexander's medical records."

The doctor's voice surprised him, and Nick shifted his attention. "It would be helpful," he said, guarded.

"If you allow me to go to the desk, I can access it for you. Along with the other patients."

"Do I *look* stupid to you?"

Caitlin touched his arm. "Wait, Nick. Let's think about this. Lilly could use those records, especially for Alexander. What I was able to obtain is very limited."

"You trust him? Caitlin, he's *Areth* . . ." he said, waving the muzzle of his Glock in the doctor's general direction.

101

"I'm not saying I *trust* him, but—"

"He's my friend."

Nick's eyes darted to Michael, who had stepped closer to the doctor. Michael focused on him as he spoke.

"I trust him."

Nick clenched his jaw. *Christ, this was going to hell in a hand basket!* He squinted as he stared at the doctor Michael indicated as Victor. "Why would you help?"

The man stared back, unwavering but lacking the Areth arrogance Nick expected. "We are not all monsters."

Damian and Seb returned with Jace, and the two big men moved toward Alexander. The big man shouted and tried to scurry away when they approached, but Michael quickly crouched beside him.

"Alexander, listen to me. Would you like to leave this place?"

Alexander lifted his head, and Nick did his best not to react to the a-symmetrical malformation of his face. He blinked large, clouded eyes at Michael, spittle running from the corner of his lips.

"Leeff?"

"Yes, Alexander." Michael turned back to them with his jaw set firm and his eyes dark. "Promise me, swear to me now that he will be safe."

Nick nodded his head once. "I swear to you."

"No experiments. No torture."

He shook his head. "No. Not ever."

"We'll take care of him." Caitlin's voice was tight, and he wanted to look down at her, but couldn't pull his attention away from his son.

His son.

Michael turned back to Alexander and laid a hand on his arm. "We are going away, Alexander, to someplace safe. No one will hurt you anymore. I trust them, Alexander. Do you trust me?"

Alexander nodded, and only flinched slightly when Damian and Seb each took a trunk that somehow passed as an arm and helped him to his feet. Nick gave both men credit. Neither of them acted the least bit put off by his mutated and bizarre appearance. When Alexander looked to Damian, he flashed Alexander a big smile. Alexander frowned, his cleft lip splitting over crooked teeth.

"Dit you get burnt up?" he asked, his voice a low, loud timbre that echoed through the room.

Damian laughed. "No, big guy. I'm fine."

Alexander nodded, accepting the answer, and the three of them headed for the door. Jace stood out of the way for them to pass.

"We need to go soon," he said. "I think the firefight in the west corridor drew more attention than we expected."

Nick nodded. "Take the *good doctor* here to the station in the hall. He says he'll download the medical records of all the humans we're taking. If he does *anything* else, if you even suspect it, shoot him."

Jace nodded and pulled the Areth doctor from the cell, leaving Nick alone with Caitlin and Michael. The sub-frequency radio in his ear clicked and Nick pressed his finger to the small button that opened the communication channel.

"Tanner."

"Colonel, we're running into a problem here," came Captain Levandowski's voice. "Patrol presence has increased near the hovers. I'm concerned we may be detected soon."

"Take any precautions you deem necessary to assure the patrol doesn't have the chance to report your presence. Understood, Captain?"

"Yes, sir."

The line clicked off again. Nick laid his hand on Caitlin's arm. "We've got to get out of here now." She nodded and he looked to Michael. His son stood half way across the cell, his feet apart, and his hands linked together in front of him. With the force of a steel fist, Nick's throat tightened and his chest squeezed around his heart. He tried to swallow, but the thick lump of twenty-five years of loss choked him.

Michael stepped forward, their heights so close that they stared eye-to-eye. Nick wanted to speak, but the words wouldn't form. *I'm your father. I'm sorry. For everything. Just trust me and we'll be fine.*

"Nick, we need to go," Caitlin said softly beside him. "There will be time later."

He nodded, his logical military mind knowing she was right. Something had shifted inside him, had snapped around his heart and messed with his thinking. His son! In one moment, it was real. Until then, he had accepted Michael's existence, had driven himself to do everything possible to come to this moment, but Michael was still just a goal. An idea. Now, he was real.

Nick's chest hurt and he sharply sucked in a breath.

"Yes," Michael said, his voice level and calm. Just the slightest hint of a smile pulled at his mouth. "There will be time."

Nick took in the details of his son, absorbing them. Memorizing them. He nodded curtly and holstered his weapon. "Let's get you some shoes and get out of here."

They stepped into the hall as Jace and the doctor returned.

Apparently, the doctor had kept his word; otherwise he'd be a twitching mass on the floor. Jace handed Caitlin a microslide and she slipped it into her pocket.

"No funny business?"

Jace shook his head. "No. He accessed the medical files, and that's it."

Nick spun on his heels when the sound of automatic energy blast rounds echoed from an adjoining hall. Simon and Kamal rounded the corner at a dead run, firing behind them. Bursts of condensed power exploded off the walls as their shots missed their targets, and the pursuing security force's ammo did the same.

"Go! Go! Go!" Kamal shouted as he covered with more fire.

Nick grabbed Caitlin's arm with one hand, and Michael's with the other, herding them away from the fight toward the far exit door. Jace followed, dragging the doctor behind. Nick kicked open the exit door, and with his Glock trained on the approaching enemy, held them off as the others escaped into the stairwell. The echo of their footsteps dimmed, letting him know they had at least descended a flight if not more. He rallied another array of blasts at the security force that now held their positions behind desks and open cell doors, and let the door slam shut behind him as he jumped from the top of the stairs to the landing below.

The radio clicked in his ear again. "Sir, we are taking fire!"

"Shit." Nick took the next flight of stairs three steps at a time. He caught up with the others two flights down, and tapped the radio. "Take them out if you can, Captain. Ali and other reinforcements will reach you soon. My ETA is seven minutes."

"I don't think we have seven minutes, sir."

They hit the ground floor landing, the sound of frantic footsteps echoing above them. "Shit." Nick fought to steady his breathing and focus his thoughts. "Shit! Shit! Shit!"

"I still have this." Caitlin held up a small detonation device, twirling it in her fingers. "I intended to use it if I suspected the security override didn't work, but I couldn't monitor it from the cell block."

Nick took the black, elliptical shaped switch. "What does it do?"

"Several computers in my lab are wired with explosives. It will cause quite a show," she said with a smirk.

Nick bounced the detonator in his hand, ignoring the urge to kiss her. "Might even the odds a bit."

"I can help you," the doctor said from where he leaned against the wall. Nick glanced at him to see him eyeing Jace and his pulse pistol.

What the hell . . . why not? "How?"

"I can get you to the glider bay. Can you fly?"

Jace snorted and Nick threw him a hard glance. "Yeah, I can manage," Nick answered, not even attempting to hide the sarcasm.

"Perhaps that will distract the security force long enough to allow the others to escape?"

He looked to Jace, who shrugged. "It just might work," Jace said.

"On one condition."

Nick shook his head. *Damn it!* "What?"

"Take me with you."

CHAPTER TWELVE

*T*he resonation of Simon's pistol echoed in the confined stairwell as he fired straight up at their pursuers. With each shot, CJ and Michael flinched and she held a hand over one ear. They wouldn't be able to hold off the security force for long.

Nick flipped open the protective shield on the detonator, and pinched the device between his fingers. CJ half-expected to hear the distant explosions or feel the building shake, but her labs were several floors up and too far away to feel. He snapped the shield closed and slipped it into his pocket.

"Kamal, take Caitlin and Michael to the hovers. Make sure there are no stragglers between here and there. Simon, you're with Jace and me. We're taking the doc with us."

Both Simon and Kamal nodded their understanding. Michael looked between CJ and Kamal, and she saw the hesitation in his eyes. He had to be confused, wondering just who they were and why they had come. And whom he could trust. She smiled, trying to express confidence, even though her insides twisted with fear of leaving Nick and the others behind.

"We'll move together down this hall to the exit door at the far end and then split there," Nick ordered, and with a cursory glance into the hall, he pushed the door open and led the way for all of them to follow.

They barely made it half way down the dark hall before Areth security rounded the corner behind them and blasts of energy ricocheted in the tight space. Balls of fire exploded on the walls over their heads sending burning clumps of building material raining down around them. Nick curled against the wall, pulling her down with him to protect her with his body. He fired back, the air around them humming with the static discharge of their weapons. Jace took up the rear, sandwiching Michael and Victor between them.

"Give me a weapon!" Michael shouted.

"Have you ever fired a pistol?" Nick asked.

"I watched." Michael extended his hand, palm open.

CJ shifted her gaze from father to son, cringing as another blast hit over their heads and sparks arched over them. With a low growl in his throat, Nick pulled free the spare Glock he kept on his thigh holster and slapped the grip into Michael's hand.

"The safety is at the top of the grip, and you—"

Michael deftly released the safety, initiated the charge, and took aim. His first shot clipped one of the Areth in the arm.

"Damn."

Michael looked toward Nick. "I watched," he repeated.

Nick grabbed CJ's arm and they all sprinted down the hall, followed by the echo of weapon blasts. They collapsed in a dark access way, and CJ glanced toward Victor as he curled into himself against the wall, his hands clutching the sides of his head. Keeping low to the ground, she turned to face him, laying her hand on his arm. His lab coat was damp, soaked through by his own sweat, and his body trembled. He jerked away from her touch, and raised his head to look at her. Black hair plastered against his forehead, his dark eyes glassy. Sweat glistened on his skin, each breath ragged and shallow.

"Victor, what's wrong."

He suddenly gripped her arms, his fingers digging in painfully. "Leave me here, Caitlin. I—" His body shook, his eyes squinting shut. Victor slammed his head back against the wall, the impact echoing through the room, and drawing everyone's attention. Michael was immediately beside them, unmasked concern on his face. Victor opened his eyes again, his lips pulled back tight in obvious pain. "I'll tell you the security codes."

"Victor? What's wrong?" Michael asked.

Victor just shook his head, slamming it back against the wall once again, hissing through his clenched teeth. "You need to go, Michael. I don't want to hold you back."

"What the hell is going on?" Nick asked, coming up behind them.

"I don't know," was the only answer CJ could give. "Victor seems sick. He wants us to go without him."

"Bull shit," Nick snapped. "You're along for the *whole* ride, doc." He grabbed Victor's arm and pulled him to his feet.

Victor didn't fight, bracing his other arm against the wall to keep himself on his feet. His knees buckled, and the only thing keeping him up was Nick's grip. Michael stood, sliding his shoulders beneath Victor's arm, bracing his weight.

"I'll see he gets there."

"You can't. You're going with Caitlin."

"I can't leave him."

Nick raked his hair with long fingers and swore under his breath. "Just . . . let's get out of here and discuss this *later!*"

Nick moved to Victor's other side and pulled the man's arm around his shoulder's, supporting his almost completely limp form. Michael reluctantly released him, and looked past them to meet CJ's stare. She nodded, hoping he understood that Nick would do everything in his power to bring everyone home safe.

"We split here. Don't mess around. Get back to the base like the devil is on your ass. We'll be there when we can," Nick said to Kamal.

CJ's insides clenched again and she forced herself to remember all the training General Castleton had drilled into her over the last several months. Personal fear had no place on the battlefield. She had to push past it and get the job done. There would be time later for celebration, or for mourning. Focus, or die.

She allowed herself one final glance as they moved apart into the darkness. Nick looked over his shoulder at the same moment, and their eyes connected. CJ drew a shaky breath and mouthed the words "Be safe".

He nodded, one short jerk of his head, and disappeared into the dark.

"*L*et's kick the tires and light the fires, ladies."

Nick's voice echoed through the hanger bay. Jace ran past the first glider, leaving it for the Colonel and the Areth doc—*man, the guy looked like he had seen better days*—and hopped up onto the curved tip of the next glider's wing. As he ran along the smooth slope, he re-holstered his weapon and looked back to make sure the colonel and Simon had buckled their passenger into the second cockpit seat. Simon hopped down and headed for his own glider as Jace dropped into his plane and picked up the helmet left behind on the craft's floor. As he slipped it on, he heard the crackle of the radio in his ears.

"We ready to rock and roll?" Simon asked.

"Let's make ourselves dots," Jace answered, and flipped the O_2 ignition switch.

Immediately, the glider came to life, the craft humming around him. Jace smiled. It had been too friggin' long since he'd ridden the lightning of a glider; the familiar adrenaline rush hit him. The cockpit shield lowered with a hydraulic hiss and sealed into place. Jace familiarized himself with the control panels and positions of readouts and weapons arrays as he buckled the safety harness into place. The flight would be interesting without a G-suit, even with the glider's inertial dampeners.

"Opening hanger ceiling now," Nick said.

Jace looked straight up through the glass canopy as the ceiling cracked open and folded back like an accordion. Foot by foot, the night sky came into view and rain poured in, the water darkening the floor like a spreading shadow. He hated flying in the rain, but there wasn't a damn thing he could do about it. As the ceiling spread, Jace lowered the nose until the glider leveled and engaged velocity thrusters enough to inch out of line. As he turned the craft, a blast of energy ricocheted off his nose and he flinched.

"Shit!"

"We've got company!" Simon shouted into the radio.

"Suck in your sides and fly, Lieutenant!" Nick ordered.

Jace knocked back the glider, pointing her nose to the sky, his canopy already doused with rain, and aimed for the moon. He punched his thrusters, his body slamming back into the seat as he shot into the night. The readouts on his altimeter read Angels Twenty before he leveled the nose and turned south. Seconds later, Simon and Nick joined him, Nick taking point.

"Here's the plan. I'm assuming we'll have company up here in about fifteen seconds. We're going to fully engage. Fire at will at the *south* and *east* wings of the complex. This should give the others sufficient distraction to get the hell out."

"Got it, Colonel," Jace said, scanning the skyline around them for approaching bandits. "Enemy approaching at five o'clock, sir. I see five."

"Time to kick some ass, gentlemen."

Jace banked hard left, rolling tight to double back. The glow of multiple engine burners filled the night sky around him, but he knew exactly who was friend and who was foe. Picking a target, he punched his thrusters and dove in. Moments later, his sonic cannons locked on, the shrill beep echoing around him, and he fired. A solid blast hit the bandit's wing and he spun out of control, spiraling back down to earth.

"Wooohooo!" Jace shouted. "Damn, it's good to be back in the saddle again!"

"We're receiving a transmission, sir," a young man said from the front of the hovercraft as he crouched on the floor, a headset held tight against his ears.

The craft shifted over the rough terrain, moving at maximum speed, pinning CJ back against her seat. They had broken free of the rain five minutes before and the ride was smoother, but she still felt like a ball bearing in a pinball game. She curled her fingers into her armrests and glanced toward Michael, who sat beside her. His gaze shifted around the compact and crowded craft, apparently absorbing every detail around him. Even in his profile, she saw Nick.

"Who is it, Lieutenant?" Damian asked.

The young man shook his head. "I can't make out who it is, sir. There's a lot of static on the line. They're over a hundred miles back and still transmitting in the storm."

"What do you have?"

The lieutenant squinted, cupping his hand over his ear as he struggled to hear. "I'm sorry, sir. I—" His features fell and his head jerked up. "I think we lost one."

CJ's insides seized—her blood as cold as her damp skin. *Oh, God . . . no . . .*

"What?" Damian demanded, shifting from his seat to kneel on one knee beside the radio. "Put it on the box."

The sound of static crackled. Silence filled the craft, as everyone seemed to collectively hold their breath. CJ waited for several beats of her heart. When the static broke, she jumped.

"Ah, shit! Do you see him?" shouted a voice.

CJ struggled to discern who it was. With all the interference, she wasn't sure if it was Jace, Nick, or Simon. The depth of the voice could have been Nick . . . *God, please* . . . but she didn't know.

"On—six! Get him! Get him!"

"Bank left, I've got the band—" Static interrupted the transmission. "—sights!"

"Eject, damn it! Eject!"

"I can't! Canopy—"

Tears burned her eyes, running down her cheeks. Someone laid their hand on her shoulder and squeezed gently, but she couldn't look away from the black radio the faceless voices emanated from.

"It's stuck. Ah, damn! It's stuck!"

"Zeus!"

CJ gasped, covering her mouth with her hands. She couldn't see now, her world blurred with tears. The voices disappeared in a new wave of static. The lieutenant shook his head after several attempts to reconnect the signal. Damian rubbed his fingers across his lips, his expression dark. His eyes shifted up to CJ and held.

"That doesn't mean—"

She nodded. "I know." Her words were lost in the crack of her voice. "I know."

CJ closed her eyes and rested her head back against the wall behind her, the motion of the hovercraft rocking her from side-to-side. She tried not to think about the panicked voices on the radio, the shout of Nick's call sign . . . it didn't mean he was the one who went down. It didn't.

It couldn't.

"He'll come back."

Michael's voice, even though her heart knew it wasn't Nick's, somehow helped soothed the ragged edges of her nerves. He had the same timbre, the same slow roll that came from somewhere deep in his chest. In another fifteen years, he would have the same aged bass as his father, like rippling water over stone. CJ drew a slow breath and opened her eyes, turning to Michael.

"He will. Getting you out meant everything to him. He won't give up now on the chance of coming back to you."

He looked at her, his eyes almost black in the dim light of the hover. "He's my father."

CJ nodded. "I know he wanted to tell you himself, but there just wasn't time."

Michael nodded and turned away, focusing to some distant point on the other side of the hover. CJ looked down at her hands, drawing a slow breath. She knew she had to believe in her own words. Nick would do anything to come back. He wouldn't let the Areth stop him now.

"I don't think I'm the only thing he wants to come back to."

Michael's statement was low, and heavy in the air between them. CJ glanced up, but his attention was still somewhere in empty space.

$\mathcal{C}$J stood near the foot of the examination table where Michael sat, hands folded in his lap and feet, still bare, braced on the metal framework. He tapped the pads of his thumbs together, his fingers laced, and CJ tried not to smile at how much his fidgeting reminded her of his father. Nick barely ever sat still, some part of his body always in motion.

The thought of Nick twisted her stomach and sent a wave of cold sweat over her skin. She waited here for Damian and General Castleton to come with news, because there was nowhere else she could think to be. Nick wasn't here, someone needed to be with Michael.

She needed to be with Michael.

The echoes of the crackling radio played again and again in her head, relentlessly . . . a slow torture.

"It's stuck. Ah, damn! It's stuck!"

"Zeus!"

Lilly moved around the room, seeing to her new batch of patients. Most of them were without any real need of medical care, appearing on the surface to be in relatively good health. Others, like Alexander, would require her in-depth attention over the next few days and weeks until it was determined just what had been done to them, and what could be done to help. Someone had told Lilly the details of the escape, and of the broken bits and pieces they had picked up on the radio. Every few minutes, she returned to CJ's side with a comforting touch and a compassionate smile.

They all thought he was gone.

Pain twisted through her chest. *God, was this what a broken heart really felt like?*

Her eyes burned again and she tipped her face to the ceiling, willing the tears not to fall. Later, in the darkness of her quarters, she would let them come. Not now.

"Okay, Michael. Your turn."

CJ looked to Lilly, who had come to their bed. She held in one hand a bioscan reader, and in the other a palm data recorder. Michael eyed the devices not with unfamiliarity, but with a definite apprehension.

"Would you mind taking your shirt off for me?" Lilly asked.

He crossed his arms over his body to grab the hem of his linen tunic. With a fluid motion, he pulled the shirt up over his head and tossed it onto the bed beside him. What CJ saw instantly made her nauseous, and she barely managed to stifle her gasp.

Michael's arms were laced with tracks, red welts left by large gauge needles that couldn't have been more than a couple of weeks old. Older scars left testimony that whatever had been done to him hadn't been a new experience. Circular scars marked his pectorals and abdomen. Lilly circled the bioscan reader over his chest, scrutinizing the data as it fed into her palm unit.

"Could you turn a little?" she asked.

Michael did as he was told, twisting on the bed so his leg was on the mattress, and his back was to CJ. Long white scars crisscrossed his back, as if he may have been whipped at one time.

Dear God, what did they do to him? And why?

Lilly finished her scan, turning the reader off and set both devices down on the bed beside him. "Some of your readings concern me. Your white blood count, iron levels and electrolytes are way off and your B12, dopamine, and oxytocin levels are very low. I'm getting signs of inflammation in several muscles and joints. Overall, your readings look like someone recovering from a pretty severe trauma. Do you have trouble sleeping?"

"Yes."

"Do you have headaches?"

"Frequently, yes."

"What has been done for them?"

"Nothing."

CJ saw the anger flash across Lilly's face. "I'm going to get some supplements for you to start with, get you a shot of B12, and some analgesics and anti-inflammatory medications. Should ease some of your discomfort. And a pair of slippers," she added with a smile.

Activity near the infirmary door caught CJ's attention and she turned to see General Castleton make his way through the mass of people toward them. The grim look on his face made her stomach clench. When he reached them, he laid his hand on CJ's shoulder, squeezing gently.

"I'm glad I found the three of you here."

Michael picked up his tunic and slipped it over his head. CJ crossed her arms and curled her fingers into fists.

"Have we heard anything?"

The general shook his head. "No. Communication has been sending out a call on our secured frequency for the last hour and a half with no response. They may have lost their radios, or can't answer for a number of reasons. We haven't been able to confirm anything about the broadcast we picked up earlier."

CJ swallowed hard. Lilly took her hand and squeezed, but cold dread had already settled around CJ's heart.

"This is a hard way to start things off, son," General Castleton said to Michael. "I was a friend of your father's, and I know he gave his heart and soul to bring you back. You should be very proud."

Damian jogged through the open infirmary door, his chest heaving as he reached them. "General, sir, we have news."

"What is it?" Lilly asked before the general had a chance.

"We've picked up two bogies on radar heading this way. Could be them, sir."

"Two . . ." Lilly said softly.

The room tilted, CJ's vision wavered. Michael stood, his strong hands —so much like his father's—gripped her arms and held her steady until she could breathe again.

CHAPTER THIRTEEN

*T*he final descent into the mountain's hanger bay was a practice in balance and a test of Nick's strength as his damaged glider fought him for every foot. Two of his five thrusters were out, and his directional controls were barely functioning. The joystick moving like a thousand pound log through concrete. He grit his teeth, sweat running freely down his face as the landing gear jostled for position on the hanger bay floor. When all three wheels settled, he pushed the controls away and killed the ignition switch. The glider died with a shudder.

"You still with me back there, Doc?"

No response came from the still form of the Areth doctor who had fallen silent shortly after their ascent from the facility. Nick tried to turn to see past the high back of his seat, but only saw the man's slumped form.

As soon as the canopy cleared his head, Nick braced the sides of the opening and stood, launching himself free of the craft. He glanced back toward the hanger bay opening to see the other glider approach, wagging its wings in a sign that all was clear. He quickly assessed the external damage. If they managed to salvage the glider, it would be a miracle. If the base had a bone yard, that's where it was heading. The communications array still smoked, black ash trailing away to the fuselage.

The air inside his helmet was stifling, and he searched around the unfamiliar edges for the release. He needed to breathe . . . and then find

Caitlin and Michael. Not knowing for sure if they had made it out ate at his gut . . . *among other things.*

"Colonel Tanner?" said a voice from the hanger floor.

Leaning over to brace his hands on the wing's cold metal, Nick hopped down, his boots echoing through the cavern. His fingertip hit the latch and he ripped it free, yanking the helmet off his head. The cool night air chilled his damp skin. "Where is Doctor Montgomery?"

Sawyer shook her head. "I—I don't know, sir."

"Where are the people we brought back? My son?"

"In the infirmary, I believe, sir."

"Everyone make it all right?"

As he spoke, he took the Glock from his thigh holster and leaned against the wing, his helmet nestled in the crook of his other arm. The Areth in the back hadn't made a peep, and hadn't done anything yet to prove himself an enemy—other than being *the* enemy—but Nick wasn't taking any chances. He wiped the sweat off his face and rolled his neck. Every muscle in his back and shoulders hurt from fighting with the glider for the last two hundred miles.

The technician stared at him, wide eyed, and nodded. "As well as can be expected, sir."

Nick shifted his attention to her, and caught her expression.

"What?"

"We thought . . ." She swallowed, her smile barely touching her lips. "It's good to see you in one piece, Colonel. When the general reported you had—"

Nick threw the helmet to the concrete floor, the crack repeating back as he strode toward the exit. He ignored the call of his name as the engines of the second glider cut out. There was no time . . . he had to find Michael and Caitlin.

"Sergeant!" Nick shouted, pointing at an armed soldier who stood guard just inside the hanger bay doors. "Get over here, *now!*"

The sergeant snapped to attention, jogging toward Nick to meet him half way.

When he was within reach, Nick shoved his Glock into the guard's gut where his hands reflexively gripped it. "Guard him," he ordered, pointing back to the damaged glider. "Have someone from the infirmary collect him."

The sergeant nodded, but Nick was already gone.

He jogged the hall to the nearest elevator, and paced the interior as it took him to the infirmary level. *Damn it! They could reach the moon in a matter of seconds, but it took five minutes to travel a few hundred feet?* More curious and surprised looks greeted him as he pushed through the barely open doors, but he ignored them, marching down the hall.

The sounds of the active infirmary reached him a hundred feet before the entrance. Voices mingled with beeps of monitors and the clatter of medical equipment as the sick were treated. Nick stepped through the door, and within moments, the sounds faded away.

Caitlin sat on a bed half way across the room; her shoeless feet on the edge of the mattress and her bent legs drawn up to her chest. Her arms rested on her knees, cradling her head, and she faced Michael who sat beside her. Their lips moved and heads nodded in conversation. A gentle fist tightened around Nick's heart.

His family.

Caitlin raised her head, and he saw the tear streaks on her cheeks. She reached out a hand to touch Michael's shoulder and turned to look around the room. As she did, her eyes settled on him.

Nick was paralyzed, forced to watch as the realization played across her features.

Her eyes widened and her lips parted as she slipped off the mattress edge. He read his name on her lips, but the rush of blood in his ears drowned out all sound. Michael looked up as Caitlin moved away from the bed. She took a hesitant step, and then launched herself at him, wrapping her arms and legs around his body, and the sounds of the infirmary came crashing down around him again.

"Nicky!" she cried against his neck as she clung to him. "Oh, my God, Nicky! They told me you were dead!"

Nick held on tight, pressing his fingers into her back to support her as he drew her warmth and scent in. It revived him and immediately eased some of the pain.

"I'm right here," he whispered into her hair. "I'm here."

She cradled his face in her hands and kissed his cheeks, again and again, until her mouth covered his in a kiss that seared his soul and tore a moan from his throat. Slowly, he eased her down his body until her feet touched the floor. When his lungs burned for oxygen, he broke away and pulled her close to bury his face into the curve of her neck. Her tears slicked the cheek-to-cheek contact, and bouts of laughter mingled with her small sobs.

Nick raised his head to see Michael standing at the foot of the nearest bed, his hands pushed into the pockets of his loose pants. His expression was hard to read, jostling somewhere between clinical detachment and what appeared to be cautious relief. Nick shifted Caitlin against his side, his arm around her shoulder to keep her close, and reached out to Michael with the other. When his son stepped close enough, Nick laid his palm against Michael's cheek. Emotion choked him, burning his throat.

"Do you know who . . ." his voice failed him, and Nick pressed his lips together to try and regain control.

Michael nodded. "I do."

Nick matched the nod. "I would have done anything—"

"Thank you," Michael said simply.

A loud crash snapped their attention to the back of the infirmary. Michael shifted so Nick could see Lilly Quinn, standing with a shattered bioscan reader at her feet. Horror twisted her expression as she looked from Nick to Caitlin.

"No," Lilly whispered hoarsely, her voice carrying across the now deathly silent room. Everyone stared, trapped in the moment.

Caitlin looked up at Nick. "Oh, God."

Nick moved away from Caitlin to close the space between him and Lilly. The closer he stepped, the more violently she trembled. She crossed her arms over her body and bit her lower lip. His gut burned and twisted, and he hated being the one to tell her.

If only . . .

"Lilly, I'm sorry," Nick said.

"No." Her voice was weak, but insistent, and she jerked her head.

"Jace's glider was shot down by enemy fire during the air battle . . ."

Lilly's eyelids fluttered and her head tipped back. As she collapsed in Nick's arms, three nurses came forward to help him bring her to a bed. He stepped back, letting them tend to their own, and caught Caitlin's gaze across the crowded room.

They'd pay . . . someday those damn Areth bastards would pay.

*E*xhausted to the marrow of his bones, Nick punched in the code for his quarters and waited the eternity it took for the lock to disengage. He pushed the door open and was immediately greeted by a bounding mass of brown and white fur dancing around his heavy legs and nudging his hands for attention.

"Hey, Dog," Nick said wearily and made his way to the small

refrigeration unit for some cold water. It soothed his parched throat and splintered out through his limbs with each deep swallow.

He left the half-drained bottle on the counter and went to the bedroom, sinking down on the edge of the bed. The thought of flopping back onto the mattress, fully dressed, and sleeping for ten or twelve hours straight had a certain appeal, but he knew he needed to relieve some of the tension in his back or he'd never be able to move when he woke up. Dog jumped up onto the bed and flopped onto his side near the pillows with a deep sigh.

"I don't know who told you it was okay to sleep on the bed," Nick mumbled.

Dog sighed again. Nick chuckled. He probably deserved whatever attitude he got for leaving the mutt alone for fifteen hours with only the kid down the hall stopping by to take care of him. Dog would have his revenge . . . eventually. With a loud groan of protest, Nick leaned over and untied his boots, tossing them against the far wall with a loud thunk. He headed for the shower, letting the water temperature rise as he shucked his clothing. Nick stepped beneath the steaming stream, and moaned as the pressure pelted his back and shoulders. Leaning forward into the cold walls, he rested his forehead on his arms and breathed in deeply of the steam as the heat worked away the tension in his muscles.

A dozen thoughts churned in his mind at once, vying for priority. He needed to make room for Michael in his one-bedroom quarters until a larger one was available. For tonight, Michael slept in the infirmary. Tomorrow, he would be here. He needed to find a way to talk to his son. Every time he tried, all his words and thoughts got tied up and twisted and refused to cooperate.

He thought of what Caitlin had told him, the scars that marred Michael's body and the deficiencies in his system. They all pointed to recent, and possibly prolonged, torture of some kind. There were also other signs. Whatever he had gone through, it apparently was a part of life for him. Nick curled his fists, muscles already tight protesting with the abuse.

Sons of bitches . . .

121

C J doubted if she could ever say when she made the decision to come to his quarters rather than her own. Only that she had to. The past didn't matter anymore, and if she had to ask his forgiveness every day for the rest of her life, she would. She couldn't risk going one more day without Nick knowing how much she needed him. Her hands trembled when she punched in the old lock access code, betting Nick hadn't bothered to change it.

The apartment was almost completely in darkness, except for the dim light through the bedroom door. The soft sound of falling water echoed in the quiet space as she walked with weak legs to the open doorway. Standing at the foot of the bed, she saw his tall silhouette through the steamy glass door of the shower. He rolled his head on his shoulders and ran his hands over his wet hair beneath the heavy spray.

Languid heat spread through her body, making her skin prickle beneath her clothes and her breath catch. She stifled a moan and ran her hand along the back of her neck beneath her hair.

CJ stood in the open bathroom doorway, watching Nick. Rivulets of water ran down the door, and moisture hung heavy in the air, curling over the top of the enclosure. He faced away from her, his arms braced on the wall with his back to the pulsating water. His skin was red with the heat and he rolled his shoulders beneath the massage.

She unbuttoned her blouse and removed her clothing as she watched him, the pelting sound of the water muffling any noise she made. When she pulled open the door, Nick jerked, twisting to look at her over his shoulder. His gaze darkened as it roved over her body, and her breath quickened.

It had been so long since she had seen that look in his eyes.

CJ stepped beneath the almost harsh spray, gasping at the intense heat. Nick tried to turn to her, but she kept him where he was with gentle pressure.

"Stay still."

Nick held her gaze for several moments before turning away and assuming his previous position against the wall. CJ ran her hands over his back, the water making his skin slick. His muscles were hard, tense, and tight as they coiled out from his spine. She worked her fingers into each hard knot, urging it to release its hold on him. Nick moaned appreciatively as she pressed her thumbs along his spinal column. From shoulder to lower back, she kneaded until the twisted tension gave way.

She followed with her eyes the path her hands took over his body, memorizing and comparing to the man she had known eight years before, noting how very little he had changed. He was still beautiful. The muscles beneath her fingers were hard and contoured, strong. His torso was trim, hips narrow. CJ was anxious to run her hands over the sparse spattering of curls she knew covered his chest. His arms were thicker than she remembered, the muscles more defined.

CJ closed her eyes, letting her hands slide low on his hips as she leaned in to press a kiss to his spine. Water ran over his back, wetting her face and lips. "I'm so sorry, Nicky." Her voice was nearly lost in the cascade, and she wondered if he had heard her at all.

A low rumble shifted through his chest, vibrating against her lips. Nick straightened, and with slow deliberateness turned to face her. CJ raised her arms to slick her wet hair back from her forehead. He stared down at her, his expression intense and as hungry as the need she felt. He didn't move, his fists curled at his side. Her stomach clenched, her breath caught in the vacuum of her lungs.

CJ raised a trembling hand to touch the dark, curled hairs that sprinkled the broad expanse of his chest. She held his gaze, her nails skimming the sparse curls. Nick's hand snapped up, his fingers curling around her wrist, and CJ gasped. His dark eyes shifted rapidly, scrutinizing and consuming her in their intensity; she couldn't breathe.

Eternity passed in a heartbeat.

His strangled moan echoed in the small space and CJ cried out when he pressed her against the wall, the cool tile an exhilarating contrast to the thick heat. His large, strong hands slid over her body from knee to breast, searing her skin with the contact. His touch made her lightheaded and CJ closed her eyes. He framed her face, devouring her mouth. Hot breath mingled as their tongues vied for dominance, sliding and dancing together as he kissed her deep. His body pressed against her, wet, hard and smooth. CJ moaned again, unable to control the desire she had kept buried for so long.

Nick's hand left her face and the water cut off, the air around them immediately cooling by several degrees. CJ fought to breathe when he pulled back long enough to look into her face. She saw a battle waging behind his eyes, but before he could decide on any other path, she circled his shoulders with her arms and kissed him again.

He pushed open the shower door, a loud crack echoing through the small room as the frame bounced back. Nick pulled her from the shower, and still holding her close, moved them together into the bedroom.

CJ's body hummed with need as his large, capable hands moved over her skin, awaking parts of her that had long since lain dormant. Long, strong fingers kneaded and caressed her breasts and relearned the slope of her hips as they moved toward the bed.

"Dog, get out," Nick mumbled against her lips as they fell together onto the blankets.

She didn't bother to look and see if the animal had obeyed. She didn't care.

Nick's glorious weight pressed her down into the mattress as his mouth sucked and nipped at her throat and shoulders. CJ whispered his name, and felt the flex and bunch of his muscles beneath her touch as he moved over her.

The room spun and CJ had to close her eyes as Nick drew one nipple into the searing heat of his mouth, then the other. She held his head in her hands, lacing her fingers in his short hair, a shudder moving through her body.

Nick slid up her body and covered her mouth again, the kiss deep and hungry.

He settled between her thighs, her skin searing like a branding iron wherever they touched. His body emanated heat, and she relished it, soaked it in, and needed it.

Her skin heated and her blood turned to iced lava, chilling and scorching her from the inside out. Nick's own sounds of pleasure and need mingled with hers as they remembered in just a few moments what should have been forgotten after eight long years.

How to love each other.

Everything pulled inward, tightening and twisting until CJ thought she would blow apart. She clung desperately to Nick, anchoring herself to his warmth and his life, affirming in her heart that he held her and she hadn't lost him. He pressed his face into the curve of her throat, each thrust of his hips sliding their dampened bodies together, and she heard him whisper her name.

"Caitlin . . ." It was a strangled groan, half plea and half cry and it tore her apart from the inside out.

She shattered, her body arching off the bed to cling desperately to him. Nick groaned low and deep against her throat. His fingers curled almost painfully around her shoulders, but CJ was so lost in the sweet oblivion she didn't care. Replete and fulfilled, she closed her eyes and let her arms lie limp on the bed as she fought to catch her breath.

Nick trailed his lips across her shoulder, kissing the corner of her lips before levying his weight on his arms to look down at her. His damp hair fell haphazardly over his forehead, and he licked his lips before smiling. Deep dimples dug into his cheeks, and a soft chuckle bubbled its way up from CJ's chest. She didn't know why she was laughing, but it felt wonderful.

She touched his face, running her fingertip along the lines that bracketed his mouth and dug in above the arch of his nose. The marks were more shallow at the corners of his eyes, but if she looked close enough, she knew they were a little deeper than they had been eight years ago, and maybe there were more. His hair was soft between her fingers; silver threads of silk still slightly damp from the shower. As she traced his lips, he laid is own hand on her stomach.

She smiled and combed her fingers into his hair, tilting her head as she drew his lips down to hers. The kiss was slow, deep, drawing life from her very soul. Nick broke the kiss only long enough to grab the edge of the blanket covering the bed, wrapping it around them like a cocoon. He shifted beside her, sliding his arm beneath her head and she curled against him. The heat from his body wrapped around her and she sighed as the first tug of sleep pulled at her.

CHAPTER FOURTEEN

"*H*ungry?"

Michael had been so lost in his thoughts, he hadn't seen Nick Tanner walk into the infirmary or approach his bedside, or drop a pile of clothing on the bed near his feet. He looked up, still processing how he should regard the man. *Father? Colonel? Nick?* In answer to the question, his stomach rumbled.

"Yes," he answered simply.

Nick, which would do for now, checked his watch. "I think they're still serving breakfast in the mess hall."

Michael stared at him, waiting.

"Do you want to go eat?" Nick asked after several moments of silence.

Understanding then, Michael nodded and shifted to lower his bare feet to the floor. "I apologize. I didn't realize I needed to go elsewhere to obtain my own food."

"Didn't they feed you yet?"

The sharp edge to Nick's voice drew Michael's immediate attention, and he tried to gauge the situation. He had spent the majority of the morning studying the other people of the 'base' as they moved about their work, and found each of them fascinating. Already, he knew Colonel Nick Tanner was a different person than any of them, with a force of character that seemed to drown out others around him. He was powerful and respected, a leader among all of them. Among the Areth, personalities weren't widely varied except for the extremes—and Victor. Whom, he supposed, some might consider an extreme.

"Never mind. Let's just get breakfast. I'm starving," Nick said before Michael could try to form an answer. "I brought you some clothes. Figured you'd want to get out of the stuff they had you in there."

Michael looked at the clothing on the bed, picking up the first garment. It was a shirt much like the one Nick himself wore, with short sleeves and a round neck in a deep blue color. The fabric was soft and carried a clean, soapy scent in the weave. Also in the pile was a long sleeved shirt in a rich burgundy color that buttoned down the front. A pair of heavy pants, faded to white in spots like the pair Nick wore, was at the bottom of the pile. Michael ran his hands over the shirts, enjoying the soft feel. They were nothing like any clothing ever provided for him.

"I'll get you some new things when I can. I just figured we're about the same size and we can share for now."

Michael looked up. "These are yours?"

Nick shrugged. "Yeah. If you don't like them—"

"No," Michael said quickly, but tamped down his eagerness before he said more than he should. "May I wear them now?"

Nick motioned toward the lavatory in the back of the infirmary. "Sure. Go ahead. We'll go to breakfast when you're done."

Holding the gifts to his chest, Michael padded across the cold floor to the lavatory and closed the door behind him. He quickly shucked the baggy, coarse tunic and pants that had been his only clothing for as long as he could remember. The first shirt and pants went on quickly, but the long sleeve shirt confused him. Michael pulled it on, but wondered then the proper way to wear it. He assumed he should button it, but after that, he didn't know and he hadn't seen anyone else wear garments similar to these. Hoping he wouldn't offend Nick by not knowing, he folded his old clothing and went back to the infirmary.

Nick stood just where he had been, hands pushed into his pockets and his head down. A small smirk played across his lips as if he recalled a pleasant memory, and he rocked on his heels. Michael reached the foot of the bed and waited for Nick to look up. Several moments passed before he did, and when he raised his head, a look of surprise crossed his face.

"Why didn't you say something?"

Michael swallowed, and held out the clothes. "What should I do with these?"

Nick's eyes shifted down. "Burn 'em." His voice was cold and hard.

Michael stared, unsure how to process Nick's answer. Nick shook his head. "Sorry. Do you want 'em?"

"No," he answered honestly.

Nick waved to one of the women who had attended to the sick during the night and she came over to them. "Nia, could you take these things and get rid of them for Michael? We don't need them anymore."

"Of course, Colonel," she said with a smile.

"Let's go get some food," Nick said with a tilt of his head and turned to the door. Michael fell in step beside him, and Nick looked down. "After that, we're getting you some friggin' shoes."

They walked down the hall, matching stride for stride, to the elevator. Once inside, Nick pressed twelve and the car shifted into motion. They rode in silence. Michael wanted to ask so many questions, too many to keep them all straight and categorized in his mind, but he still didn't dare go that far. Everything was still too unbelievable. Too surreal. Could it really be that just twenty-four hours before he had been in his cell hundreds of miles away without the thought that anything could or would ever change?

"After we eat, I'll show you where we live."

Michael swallowed, trying to lubricate his dry throat before he spoke. "We, sir?" He noticed most everyone called Nick by Colonel or sir.

Nick's right eye flinched at the corner, and he paused to take a slow, deliberate breath before answering. "Okay, *first* . . . to you, I'm not 'sir'. I don't expect you to call me 'Dad' or anything like that, but . . ." He stopped, shaking his head. "How about Nick for now?"

Michael nodded, another apology on the tip of his tongue. He felt uprooted and transplanted . . . unsure what to say or do.

"Right now, I've only got one bedroom but I've asked for a family unit. We'll be in tight quarters, but we'll manage."

"I'll live with you?"

The two of them stared at each other for several moments, Nick's eyes shifting slightly. Michael studied him, trying to figure him out. Finally, Nick said with a tangible weight to his voice "Unless you don't want to."

Despite the rescue, and the obvious resemblance between them, Michael's first instinct had been to guard himself against Nick Tanner. To Kathleen maternity was nothing more than an excuse to inflict as much pain as possible on him. If Nick Tanner was his father, what part did he play? A small voice in the back of his mind warned that what was given could just as easily be taken away. He met Nick's eyes, knowing they were near mirrors of his own, and looked deep. More than once, he had challenged Kathleen by staring her down and had paid the price each time. Not only physically, but almost spiritually because of what he saw there. Coldhearted contempt. Evil. Hate.

He saw none of that now, and wondered if he could hide such a thing from himself.

"I didn't know where I would be," he finally said.

"With me. For as long as you want."

The elevator stopped and the doors opened. Immediately, a myriad of aromas hit him and his stomach rumbled in complaint so loud Nick actually turned back to look at him with a wide smile.

"Damn! Guess we'd better fill that hole quick," he said with a laugh.

They walked into a large room with multiple tables arranged in rows. Most were empty, with perhaps a dozen other people scattered around the room eating in small groups. Michael drew in the smells again. He had no names for any of them, he only knew they made his mouth water and his insides demand he eat *now*.

He followed Nick to the other side of the room where two long tables were set up with stainless steel basins on stands. There were baskets of whole fruit, and bowls of sliced fruit on either side, and more baskets of bread in various shapes and sizes. Michael's stomach grumbled again and his mouth salivated.

"They're starting the switchover for lunch, so whatever is left from breakfast is put out here for us to pick at. What do you want?"

Michael just stared. Every day for twenty-something years he had eaten cold oatmeal for breakfast, at least on the days they remembered to bring it to him. He blinked, scanning the tables.

"What smells so good?"

Nick drew in a long breath. "Bacon. Okay, what do you want with it? Eggs? Pancakes?"

"Pancakes?" He'd meant it as a question.

"Pancakes it is."

Nick took a dish from the end of the table and took the lid from one of the stainless steel bins. Using the tongs inside, he piled four large, round, golden brown cakes on Michael's plate. Beside it, he served several strips of what Michael guessed to be bacon, having only ever heard of the food in books.

"Here you go."

He handed the plate to Michael, the sheer weight of it bringing his hands down several degrees. Michael leaned over the food, inhaling the steam as it curled up under his nose as Nick filled his own plate.

"Go find a seat," Nick said, handing Michael his plate with a matching meal. "I'll get us some coffee and be right there. Coffee okay?"

Michael nodded. "Yes."

"How do you like it?"

"Any way I can get it," Michael answered automatically.

Nick gave him a strange look, but turned away to the large carafes at the far end of the table. Michael walked to the nearest empty seats and set the plates down, standing behind his chair until Nick came back.

"Go ahead and sit," Nick said, motioning to the chair after he set down their coffees. He pulled out his own chair and sat across from Michael.

Michael watched surreptitiously as Nick cut thin squares of butter and slid them between each pancake, flipping the pancakes around so the bottom one was on top when the butter on the very top began to melt. He mimicked each step, hoping he didn't look the fool for not knowing how to eat a simple meal. With the butter spread, Nick picked up a small stainless steel decanter and poured thick, brown liquid over the stack until it ran over the edges and spread across the plate to partially coat the bacon strips. When finished, he set the decanter down and slid it across the tabletop toward Michael.

"Syrup is my favorite part," Nick said, grinning.

The sweet smell of the syrup mingled with the bacon and pancakes, only heightening the ache in Michael's gut and he drained the last drops of syrup over his plate. As he finished, Nick picked up his fork and met Michael's gaze over the table.

"Enjoy."

They both cut into the pancakes with the sides of their forks, and Michael speared it with the tines. As he shoved the mouthful past his lips, he couldn't help the groan that escaped his throat. The blend of sweet syrup, rich butter, and warm pancake melted on his tongue and slid down his throat with barely any effort, but the effect was intense and beyond anything his imagination could have conjured from reading a book. He cut another piece and ate again. Closing his eyes, he slowly chewed to allow each flavor to dance through his mouth.

Nick chuckled softly. "I can see mealtime with you is going to be interesting."

Michael's eyes snapped open. "Am I doing something wrong?"

Nick's face grew serious and he set his fork down on the edge of the plate. He dropped his head forward, drawing a slow breath before he looked at Michael again. "I don't know what those bastards did to you. I wish like hell it had never happened, but that was there and you're *here* now. You don't have to live like you're back there. Understand?"

Michael nodded. "I'm beginning to."

"Good," Nick said with a lopsided smile. "Now, try your bacon. If you thought the pancakes were good, there's nothing in the world like fried strips of pig fat."

Michael arched one eyebrow and caught the amusement in Nick eye as he motioned toward the bacon with his coffee cup. Michael picked up a crisp piece, dripping with syrup, and bit. Nick was right. The bacon was nearly as good as the pancakes. However, before half the food was gone, his stomach clearly and loudly declared he had eaten enough. Instinct screamed again that he should eat everything given to him, because he might not see more for days, but he decided to test Nick's instruction. He pushed the plate away, with the food still on it.

"Did I give you too much? Those pancakes were pretty big. Don't think I can finish myself," Nick said, setting his own fork down.

Michael released a slow breath and took a sip of his coffee. It was good, but not as sweet as Victor usually made it. Okay, time to test the waters again.

"I would like to ask for something."

Nick shifted in his chair, leaning over his coffee as he swirled a spoon through it. "Go ahead."

"I want to see Victor."

Nick stirred more, clearing his throat. "You said he was your friend."

"He is."

"He's *Areth*, Michael. I don't understand . . . if he was your friend, how could he let them do the things to you they did?"

Michael met his gaze. His insides tensed, and he clenched his fists beneath the table. He wanted to take this man at his word, and that meant trusting. Trusting he could say what he felt, without consequence. This really would be the test. If, despite his own opinion, Nick let him see Victor, then perhaps Michael would believe this was all more than a pipe dream.

"He had no more power to stop it than I did. There were times I *would* have died if not for him." Michael paused, sorting his own thoughts. "If it weren't for Victor, do you believe we all would have made it out?"

"Not all of us did."

Michael's eyes slid closed, and he drew a deep breath. "I'm sorry. I didn't mean—"

"I know what you mean. I'm sorry, too. You're right. He did help."

"I want to see him."

Nick met his gaze again, nodding. "Then you will."

CHAPTER FIFTEEN

"I don't think it will take long before we move," Nick said over his shoulder as he punched in the security code to his quarters. "I spoke with General Castleton, and they'll be giving the single quarters to some of the new residents. Until then, we'll just make do."

He walked in, Michael following, and glanced around. The wall and ceiling lights mimicked late morning sunlight, but otherwise the space was silent. Nick glanced past the couch to the open bedroom door. The bed was neatly made and the clothes he had left scattered on the floor were picked up. He drew a slow breath. Caitlin's scent still lingered in the air. She hadn't been gone long, and had apparently taken Dog with her.

"Do you want anything? A drink?"

He turned to find Michael standing in the middle of the living space, his arms hanging at his side, as he slowly turned a full circle. His lips were parted and his eyes sharp as he took in the details of the space. Nick watched him, awe and regret fighting in his chest with the rage that always underlined it all. Everything was new and fascinating to Michael, Nick had seen as much just during breakfast. It was wonderful to watch him as he experienced something as simple as eating pancakes. Yet, it pissed him off, pure and simple. His son should have been eating pancakes and bacon when he was two, not twenty-five.

"This is where you live?" Michael asked.

"For now. Until all of this is over."

Michael twisted to face him. "Until what is over?"

"Until we get rid of the Areth for good."

Michael's brow furrowed and he frowned slightly. Nick knew there was so much to teach him, and he had no idea where to begin. He didn't want to overwhelm his son, but he wanted him to understand. After several moments, Michael just nodded and looked down to the long glass table that ran parallel to the lounge. Nick's PAC sat open on it.

"Where will you go when it's over?"

"*We* will go home."

Michael looked up again. "Where is home?"

"Do you know anything about geography?"

Michael nodded. "I once had an atlas."

"Parson's Point, Maine. On the shore of a lake. I have a cabin there. It was built by your great-great-grandfather."

An almost pained expression played across Michael's features, but it quickly disappeared. He sat, staring at the PAC, his fingers linked together in his lap. Nick sat in the chair adjacent to the lounge, leaning forward with his elbows on his thighs and his hands dangling, relaxed.

"Where are we now?" Michael asked.

"Colorado."

Michael pinned Nick with a dark intensity that startled him. "Where *was* I?"

"You didn't know?" Michael shook his head in answer. "You were in New Mexico, a couple hundred miles south of here."

Michael's lips parted as he prepared to say something, but the click of the door drew their attention. Nick stood as Caitlin came in, noting the rosy glow to her cheeks and her rapid breath. Her blond hair was slightly mused and she clutched one of his flannel shirts closed in front of her.

"Hi," she said, leaving the door open. "Boy, it's a brisk day out. The wind is whipping over the top of the mountain and it just takes your breath away."

Nick laid his hands on her arms, rubbing his palms over the flannel and leaned in for a slow kiss. Caitlin hummed.

"Damn, your lips are like ice," he said as he pulled away. "I'll get you some coffee. Where's the mutt?"

"Thank you. He's playing with Becca in the hall," she said as he walked away to pour the coffee. "Good morning, Michael."

"Good morning, Doctor Montgomery," he said, coming to his feet.

"My name is Caitlin or CJ. Whatever you prefer to call me. But I'm no longer *that* Doctor Montgomery."

Nick listened for any indication of regret in her voice, but heard none. If anything, there was a lilt and lightness in her tone that made him smile. He carried the coffee back to her and wrapped his arm around her shoulders as she sipped from the cup.

"Oh, that's good. Thank you."

Nick noticed Michael watching them with intense curiosity, and dropping his arm from Caitlin's shoulders, stepped toward his son. He realized, like a slap to the forehead, how odd and unusual they had to appear to him. He had no idea what, if anything, Michael knew of his parentage, relationships, families . . . anything at all.

"Don't be afraid to ask," Nick said simply.

Michael's gaze shifted focus from both of them to just Nick. He drew a long breath and pulled back his shoulders, tilting his head. His eyes were never relaxed, Nick always saw the thoughts churning and forming behind them. Never at rest. Always thinking, forming, processing, and always guarded.

"Mother never spoke of you."

All breath rushed from Nick's lungs, and he instinctively gripped the back of the chair nearest him, his knuckles white. Blood rushed in his ears, pulsing with the beat of his heart, and he barely registered Caitlin's hand on his back. He turned to her, speaking through clenched teeth.

"Did you know she was there?" he snapped.

Caitlin shook her head. "Not until last night. I heard Victor mention her name."

Rage simmered beneath his skin. Areth or not, how could she have let those *bastards* hurt him? Caitlin told him they were biologically, for all intents and purposes, human. She had to have a heart.

"You saw her?" he asked, focusing again on Michael.

Michael nodded, and had Nick focused more, he might have caught the one backward step his son took.

"Nicky," Caitlin said softly behind him, her hand sliding up his spine to curl around his shoulder.

"When? How often? Did she know what was happening to you?"

Michael stared without answering for several beats of Nick's pounding heart. Then he dipped his chin on a slow, single nod.

"She never stopped it? She just let it happen?"

His eyes were expressionless, dead, when he answered, "She was the one."

The room hazed over in a cloud of red. Nick clutched the sides of the chair and flung it across the room. It bounced off the far wall and landed on its side, cinder dust following it down from the dent left behind.

"Nicholas!" Caitlin shouted.

He clenched his fists, scanning the room for something else to throw, hit, or break. Bitter bile burned in the back of his throat. When he saw nothing, he stopped still and let his head fall back, his eyes closed and his fists clenched at his side as he sucked in air through his nostrils.

"Nick, you need to calm down." Caitlin's voice was quieter this time, spoken just behind him.

He had to breathe, had to focus. Had to . . . *something*. Nick didn't realize he had left the apartment until he was half way down the hall.

C J picked up the fallen chair, righting it on its feet, and slapped her palms together to clean away the dust. The chair now sat lopsided, one leg bent inward just enough to make it teeter on the other three. She sighed, resting her hand on the back as she covered her eyes with the other. A shudder moved through her as she fought to keep under control the threatening tears.

She ached for both of them, Nick and Michael. For the years lost, and the pain they both suffered in their own way. The outburst of rage from Nick had been a long time coming. CJ had expected it since the day at the cabin. He had released some of his grief that day, but not his anger. *This* was his anger.

"I'm sorry."

CJ raised her head and swiped at the moisture on her cheeks. "No, Michael. Don't be sorry. This—you didn't cause this." She sniffed and crossed her arms over her body drawing some comfort from the big flannel shirt she still wore.

"I angered him."

"No," she said firmly. "What happened to you angered him."

"Why?"

Just the fact that he asked why made her heart ache, and she drew a shaky breath. CJ crossed the space and took Michael's hand, guiding him to sit beside her on the lounge. He sat down, his attention on their joined hands while CJ tried to figure out what to say. When she said his name, he looked up to meet her gaze.

"Your father loves you."

Michael frowned, his brow pulling down toward his eyes as he stared at her. He tried to absorb her words, and she saw in his eyes her explanation caused him more confusion than clarity. She sighed, trying to sort through her mind what she might say to help him understand, when a loud yap made her jump.

Michael yanked free of her hand, scrambling into the far corner of the lounge, his eyes wide. CJ stood as Dog set off into a long series of barks, hunkering down on his front legs as he focused all his attention on the 'new intruder' in the room.

"No, Michael. It's all right. Dog, shush!"

Dog just barked louder, and trotted around the front of the table to approach Michael from the other side. Michael leaped to his feet on top of the furniture, bracing his hand on the wall, and ran the other direction.

"No, no! Dog! Stop it!" She reached out to Michael, hoping he didn't topple off the lounger and crack his head on the table. "Michael, please. It's all right. Dog, sit!"

Obediently, Dog sank onto his haunches, the long hairs that parted over his face shifting as he blinked his eyes. He panted, whined, and shifting anxiously in place but managed to obey her command. CJ turned her attention to Michael, who still stood above her with his back against the wall, staring at Dog.

"He won't hurt you."

Michael didn't look convinced, and she had to chuckle at the thought of Dog doing *anything* to *anyone* other than perhaps give them a headache.

"I don't think he'd know how to bite if his life depended on it."

Michael looked from Dog to her, and immediately back to Dog. "What is it?"

"He's a dog."

He tilted his head. "*That* is a dog?"

CJ chuckled. "Were you imagining something different?"

Michael smiled, perhaps the first genuine grin she had seen from him. Just one more way he reminded her of Nick. Deep dimples formed in each cheek, and his teeth flashed as his lips spread. He chuckled as he slid down the cushions to sit again.

"I suppose I was."

CJ sat beside him. "Come here, boy," she said with a slight lilt to her voice.

Dog stood on all fours and came toward them, tail wagging, and pink tongue lolling out one side of his mouth. Michael tensed beside her, but she decided the best thing would be to act like everything was fine and normal. Dog sat in front of them, panting as she scratched his head and rubbed his ears. He sniffed the air, but made no move to seek contact with Michael.

"This is Dog, and before you ask, that *is* his name. Your father wasn't very creative in that department."

"This is his dog?"

CJ nodded. "Yes. Came all the way with him from Maine. I think he likes it here because there are always children to play with."

Michael's head snapped around to look at her. "Children?"

"Yes." The look of wonder in Michael's eyes made CJ pause. Her hand stilled on Dog's head as she thought about the assorted array of people they had brought back the night before.

"Where did they keep the children?" she asked.

He shook his head. "I've never seen any children."

"None? Ever?"

"No."

"What about when you were a child?"

He shifted his eyes to look at Dog, but she noted he kept his hands carefully clenched in his lap. Some of the tension had left his body, but he wasn't yet willing to reach out. "I was alone," was his only answer.

"Come on," CJ declared as she stood, slipping off Nick's flannel shirt to leave it on the lounge. Michael remained seated, staring up at her, until she held out her hand. He stared at it for a moment, then wrapped his fingers around hers as he stood. "I have something for you to see," she said, leading him to the door.

She found Nick two hours later, alone in the smallest and remotest gym in the facility. The room was like a cave with only one small light shedding any illumination in the darkness, the only sounds she heard were his grunts of exertion and the slap of skin against leather. His back was to her, bare to the waist and glistening with sweat as he pounded his fists against the punching bag that hung from the ceiling. Huffed breaths filled the pauses between assaults, then his knuckles smacked hard on the bag in rapid succession. The muscles of his back rippled and bunched with each pull and push of his arm, silver hair appeared almost black as it clung damp and heavy against his scalp.

She walked slowly across the matted floor, not wanting to stop him before he had won the fight with the demons that haunted him. He paused, bracing his arms against the bag with his forehead resting on the leather. He panted each breath, and she wondered if he had been at this since he left them.

Then she saw his hands. The knuckles were raw and bloody, streaks of crimson coating him finger to wrist. He wore no gloves, and his skin had split under the abuse. How long had he continued? Oblivious to the pain?

"Nicky . . ." she said softly, taking the final steps she needed to reach him.

He raised his head, and her breath caught. The devastation in his eyes tore her heart out and tightened her throat. Nick stumbled back until his legs bumped a pile of mats that had been left to the side of the exercise area. He sank down, bracing his head in his bloody hands. CJ sat down beside him and wrapped her arms around him as best she could as he curled into himself and leaned sideways into her waiting embrace. She stroked his damp hair and kissed his temple, and said nothing at all.

CHAPTER SIXTEEN

*M*ichael sat on a wooden beam that served as one of the boundary sides for a large space filled with fine, white sand. Each side was at least twenty feet long. He had wiggled his toes into the sand and hadn't yet found a bottom. The soft grains were cool around his bare feet, unlike the dry, dusty earth he had grown accustomed to at the facility. Brightly colored containers lay scattered across the sand, and a miniature truck was half buried a few feet away.

He stared past the pit of sand to a large structure on the other side. Poles and boards formed what appeared to be a small obstacle course, with a rope bridge and a long, yellow slanted board of plastic that reached from the top to the ground, dipping and waving like water. Several children ran back and forth through the structure, gleeful shouts to each other carrying to him across the open space. They volleyed for the right to climb the ladder first, and then sat at the top of the plastic strip, and with their hands in the air slid to the ground usually landing on their backsides. Each time, they laughed and giggled. Each time, it made Michael smile.

One little girl slid down and landed on her feet. She seemed to be a bit bigger, perhaps older than some of the others, and better skilled at mastering the obstacles. When she stood, she looked in his direction. After several moments of silent study, she walked toward him. Her hair was long and hung in twisted curls past her shoulder, parted to the side of her brow so part of the golden brown waves fell across her forehead.

As she walked, she brushed them out of her eyes. She stepped over the far beam with expertise and trudged through the sand to reach him, sitting down adjacent to him.

"Hi," she said, her voice high-pitched and fluttery. "I'm Sabrina."

Michael shifted on the beam to better see her, leaning forward to rest his arms on his bent knees. The beam was so low his knees were even with his chest. "Hello. I'm Michael."

"I'm six years old. How old are you?" she asked with a tilt of her head, brushing the hair from her eyes again.

He remembered the doctor, Lilly, had said just how old he was. He had never known for sure. "Twenty-five."

"Ain't you too old to play in a sandbox?"

Michael straightened. "Should I not be here?"

Sabrina shrugged. "I don't think there's no rules that says you can't."

He squinted, trying to decide whether that meant it was okay or not. He assumed that Caitlin would not have brought him here if he shouldn't be here. Sabrina picked up a red pail and a small green shovel, and set to work filling the pail. Michael watched with fascination as she performed the task. When the pail was full, she tipped it oven and dumped the sand out again, the glistening grains flowing out like a spilled glass of water.

"You look a lots like Mister Tanner. My daddy says I'm s'possed to call him Ker-ker—" She huffed.

"Colonel?" Michael offered.

She nodded, working again to fill the pail. She knelt in the sand, her small knees burrowing into the mounds of sugary grains. "I can't say it right. Therefore, I just call him Mister. But you look like him."

"He's my father." It felt foreign to make the statement, but like many things he'd experienced in just a few hours, foreign didn't mean wrong.

Sabrina looked up, her blue eyes sparkling as she smiled. "Mister Tanner is your daddy? How come I never seen you before?"

"I just arrived," Michael answered simply.

"Oh."

Michael slipped off the beam to sit in the sand, pushing his toes deeper into the coolness. He buried his hand into the nearest mound, feeling the granules shift and slide over his skin. As he pulled his hand free, he let the sand fall in a long stream from his palm. Sabrina worked now at digging a deep hole, apparently one that she then intended to fill using the small truck she had freed from the sand. There seemed to be very little purpose to her actions, but she had a smile on her small lips and she hummed softly.

144

"What is that song?" Michael asked.

"Twinkle Twinkle Little Star."

He smiled. Just the way she said the words sent a small rush of giddy pleasure over him. Something he couldn't define, couldn't describe any further than that. As if he had just learned the secret of the world.

"Will you sing it for me?"

"You don't know it?"

Michael shook his head. "No. I've never heard it."

Sabrina giggled. "You're funny, Michael." Then she sang. Her voice was tiny and almost frail, wispy and ethereal as she sang about the stars in the sky. "Will you push me on the swings?" she asked as soon as she finished the final note.

"I don't know how."

"Didn't nobody ever teach you how to play?"

"No."

Sabrina stopped her digging to look at him. Then she stood up and dusted off her pants. With her hands still sprinkled with sand, she clutched a handful of his shirt and tugged at him until he rolled to his feet. When he stood too tall for her to keep her grip on his shirt, she slipped her hand into his and pulled him along.

"We gots some catching up to do," she said with determination.

"*Y*ou brought Michael to the playground?"

Caitlin nodded beside him. "It seemed right."

They walked together across the soft earth that had been transplanted in and formed to make a safe surface for the children of the base to play on. The next chamber over was the hydroponics lab, and both atmospheres fed off the same system, creating a feel as close to the outside as they could manage this far beneath the mountain.

"Do you see any kids?" he asked.

"No, but I think I hear them. Over this way."

They found Michael seated on the ground, his legs crossed Indian-style, in a circle with half a dozen children. A black haired boy walked the outside of the circle, tapping each child on the head, changing "duck, duck, duck." Nick stopped short of moving to close, watching from a distance. As the boy approached Michael, his grin got wider and wider until even Nick could see he was missing three of his front teeth. He hovered behind Michael, already giggling, when he tagged Michael's shoulder and ran, shouting "Goose!"

Michael scrambled to get to his feet, but the boy was already half way around the circle before Michael ever had a chance. His feet, still bare, slipped on the grass and he tumbled, rolling as his laughter echoed through the cavern. His tagger made it all the way around and to the spot Michael had vacated with a satisfied grin. The children clapped and cheered.

Rolling to his feet, Michael chuckled as he dusted the grass from his knees. Long streaks of green stretched from his knee to his ankles and he tried to wipe them away.

"Oh, man!" whined one of the little girls in the circle. "Michael, your daddy is here."

Michael's head snapped up, his hand stilled over the stains. Nick and Caitlin walked the rest of the way as all the children stood, clamoring together in a small mass. Nick was bombarded with varying pleas of "Does Michael *have* to leave?" and "Can't he stay a little longer?" Caitlin chuckled beside him, and when he looked down at her, he had to smile. This *was* pretty funny . . . Forty-seven years old and he has a bunch of preschoolers asking him if his son could play a little longer.

He looked to Michael, who stood behind the children with his hands at his side. His expression had lost the giddy fun from moments before, and Nick wondered why.

"It's up to you, Michael," he said. "We're heading to the infirmary, and I am going to ask about your friend." He was careful to hide how badly he wanted to choke on the words. "If he can take visitors, you might be able to see him. You can stay and we can go back later. If you want."

Michael shook his head. "I'll come now."

A collective "aaaaw!" went through the children.

"I'm sure Michael will be back," Caitlin added, and as soon as the words were off her lips they scattered back toward the swing sets and jungle gyms. She looked up at Nick, her smile melting some of the cold that had permeated his soul that day. "See? I told you this was a good idea."

Nick leaned over to kiss her forehead, keeping his hands securely in his pockets.

"Let's go," he said with a tip of his head toward the door.

Michael fell in step with them, but Nick felt the tangible tension emanating from his son. He glanced sideways several times as they walked the hall, and he made sure to stand across from Michael when they boarded the elevator. As the elevator carried them to their floor, Nick shifted and crossed his ankles.

"Everything okay?"

Michael looked up, meeting his gaze, but only for a moment. He bent to look down at the grass stains on the jeans. "I ruined your clothing. I'm sorry."

"They aren't ruined," Caitlin said quickly. "It's just grass."

"Doesn't matter anyway," Nick said with enough weight in his voice that Michael met his eyes again. Nick pushed away from the wall to stand near him. He wanted to touch him, lay his hand on his arm, but didn't want to frighten him with what he would see right now. "Michael, I'm the one who is sorry. For what I did before. I keep saying it, and I hope someday to prove it. You have nothing to fear here. Not me, not anyone else." He hitched his chin toward Michael's knees. "They're just jeans."

Michael nodded as the elevator bumped to a stop. Side-by-side, they walked together to the infirmary. Despite the damn rollercoaster he seemed to be on, Nick found extreme pleasure in the simple act. Michael walked on his right, Caitlin on his left. It felt good, right.

The infirmary was less crowded. Some of the beds had been removed

147

as the patients with no immediate medical concerns were moved to housing facilities on the base. Before last night, they had no idea how many humans would be returning, and now the shuffling process would begin. Finding a place for each and every one of them.

Lilly Quinn sat at a desk at the far end of the infirmary, her finger moving rapidly as she entered data into the computer. As they approached, Nick recognized her drawn expression and the unusual paleness to her skin. His gut dropped and another wave of regret slammed into him. Jace had been the only person lost.

She looked up, but no smile crossed her face. As they grew nearer, she pushed back from the desk and stood. The uncomfortable veil of wanting to help, to say something to ease the pain, and knowing there wasn't anything to say, settled over them.

"Hi," Caitlin said. The silent yet obvious question—*how are you*—hung in the air. Caitlin reached to lay her hand on Lilly's arm, but the doctor stepped back, avoiding the contact.

"I'm glad you came by," she said, her voice level and emotionless. "I have some medication for you to take with you, Michael. You need to take it every morning and night for the next couple of weeks. And I would like you to come by here every couple of days."

"I will," he promised.

"The man that came back with me," Nick said. "He's an Areth scientist named Victor. He was unconscious when I landed."

Lilly nodded. "He woke up this morning. General Castleton had me place him in a holding cell in the back of the infirmary where he can be guarded."

"Is he all right?" Michael asked.

She shrugged. "I don't know. I don't know what made him ill. I've run every standard test I have, and everything comes back normal other than the fact that he is running a low grade fever right now."

"Michael would like to see him."

Lilly looked at Nick, shock flashing through her eyes. "Why?"

"He and Michael are friends. He helped us last night." Even though he had no reason to like or trust the man, Nick felt he needed to defend his son. Because he knew instinctively that Michael wouldn't defend himself. He had spoken his mind this morning, but that was between them, and how far his courage went was too early to be told.

"Fine. I'll take you to him."

"First," Caitlin said, interrupting. Nick knew what was coming, and despite himself, he felt the heat of embarrassment. "Nick needs you to look at his hands."

"Your hands?" Lilly asked.

Reluctantly, Nick withdrew his hands from his pockets where he had kept them securely ensconced since leaving the gym. Caitlin had found some white gauze in a first aid kit and wrapped the wounds, but the gauze was already red and soaked, plastered to his knuckles. His muscles had stopped their fatigued twitching, but a dull ache and leaden heaviness had settled into his limbs. Even extending his arms out to Lilly was an effort.

"Damn," Lilly whispered and took his elbow to lead him to one of the beds. "Nia, get me a vial of Dermaseal and a stratum basale stimulator," she called over her shoulder. "I don't even want to know what the hell you thought you were doing."

Michael followed Doctor Quinn down the hall that led from the back of the infirmary to the area she said Victor was being held. Two guards stood outside a barred cell, dressed in dark green uniforms with pulse charge pistols strapped to their waists. Nick and CJ walked behind him, and he heard CJ softly reprimanding his father for 'fiddling' with the cold strips the doctor had applied across the backs of his hands.

Doctor Quinn spoke to one of the guards and he turned to open the door for her.

"The cell is small. It might be best if only one of you go in," she said to them.

"I'm not letting Michael go in there by himself—"

"Nick," CJ said softly. "Leave it to Michael."

Michael drew a slow breath and wondered if saying what he thought —what he wanted—would ever get easier. "I have nothing to fear from Victor."

Nick cursed under his breath, but nodded and Michael passed by the guard to enter the cell. It was dark inside, the environmental lights only running along the ceiling to cast a shadowy glow over the space. The contents of the room were sparse, reminding Michael of the cell he had inhabited for the last two decades. Except he had walls and not bars. Victor sat on the bed, his head down, and his hands hanging limp between his knees. His lab coat was gone, and Michael realized this was the first time he had ever seen Victor without it. It changed him completely.

"Victor," Michael said as he crossed the space and sat down in a chair adjacent to the bed. "Victor, it's me."

Victor raised his head, his expression distant as if he couldn't quite focus. He blinked slowly, several times. "Michael?"

"Yes."

Victor reached out and grabbed Michael's hands, gripping them tightly. His skin was clammy and hot, but his hold was fierce. "Michael, my friend, it is so good to see you!" he declared exuberantly.

There was something wrong. Michael saw it in the glaze of his eyes and the slight slur of his words. He tried to stand, but his whole body tilted and Michael maneuvered him back to the bed again.

"You're safe . . . you're safe . . ." Victor mumbled again and again. His head dropped forward, rolling half limp from his shoulders.

Michael twisted in the chair, his hands still trapped in Victor's hold. "What has he been given? What drugs?"

Doctor Quinn stood on the other side of the bars with Nick and CJ. "Nothing unusual," she answered. "I've tried some basic anti-inflammatory to try and reduce the fever, but it's the only symptom I can treat."

"Something is wrong."

"I know, but I don't know what."

Michael focused again on Victor, prying one hand free so he could lift Victor's head to try and look into his face. "Victor, what's going on? Why are you sick?"

His body tensed, his hand squeezing Michael's so hard pain shot up his arm, and a sheen of sweat glistened on his face. Victor clenched his teeth, hissing each breath. "Retribution . . ." he finally spat out.

"Retribution?" Nick said from the hall. "What the hell is that supposed to mean?"

"He hasn't been this bad since he woke up. Something is making it worse," Doctor Quinn said in a low voice. "We need to sedate him." She disappeared back down the hall to the infirmary main room.

Victor released Michael's hands to clutch the fabric of his sleeves, pulling Michael partially off his chair. "Do you remember . . ." He paused, seeming to push back a wave of pain to speak. "Do you remember, Michael, when you asked if being your friend was allowed?"

Michael nodded. His heart pounded in his chest and he wanted to scream for them to come quickly, to help. *How? Would they listen?*

"I remember, Victor. You brought me coffee."

Victor laughed, but the humor was lost in another deep hiss through this teeth. "Perhaps . . . perhaps this is what happens . . ."

The door clanked open and Doctor Quinn came in, a hypo in her hand. She pulled open the front of Victor's shirt and pressed the tip directly to his chest. The drug released with an audible hiss. Moments later, Victor's grip relaxed, and his weight slid forward. Michael caught him, and with the doctor's help, eased him back onto the bed. His eyes were heavy-lidded, his breath more even as his head rolled on the pillow.

"Michael," he said softly, and Michael leaned over. "It is good that you are safe. Free."

"Because of you, Victor."

Victor blinked slowly, each time his eyes opening less until they remained closed and his head turned to the side. His hand slipped free from Michael's shirt, leaving the material wrinkled and damp as his arm hung limp off the side of the bed.

Michael straightened and looked to the doctor. She shook her head. "I don't understand."

He turned to see his father standing in the doorway, and wondered at the look of concern on his face.

CHAPTER SEVENTEEN

*N*ick groaned loud and long, half in pain and half in pleasure, as Caitlin's hands worked across his lower back. She pressed hard against his lumbar, sliding the heels of her hands up the sides of his spine toward his shoulders, and he groaned again with each inch. The oil that slicked her hands warmed with her touch and seeped into his protesting body. Her fingers kneaded and focused on his arms then slid back to his shoulders.

"Oh. Gooouuuud . . ." he moaned, rolling his eyes back into his head.

She chuckled behind him. "Is that good or bad?"

"Keep going," he groaned against the bed.

He lay stretched out on his stomach, arms spread, with Caitlin straddling his hips as she massaged and worked his aching muscles. Going two hours with a punching bag at his age was stupid, plain and simple. His body had still hung to the tension and abuse from the night before, and he just abused it more.

"Turn over."

Her soft voice near his ear sent electrical charges firing through his body. Not one to disobey a direct order, Nick shifted beneath her weight until he was on his back and she settled again on his hips. Blond locks of hair fell forward across her cheeks and forehead as she worked on him, making her look sexy as all hell. She was so damn beautiful . . . fair skin with cheeks flushed from the exertion of the massage, blue eyes that sparked with life. Young and beautiful.

Caitlin filled her palm with more of the massage oil and warmed it by rubbing her palms together before she leaned over him and laid her hands against his chest. Her eyes held his gaze as she slid her fingers over his shoulders and down his arms, coming back to his chest. She shifted her weight back, settling more heavily on his hips, eliciting a spike of erotic pleasure through his groin, as her ministration moved over his abdomen. Nick slid his arms along the bed to rest his hands on her thighs. Caitlin smiled, slow and sexy.

Nick drew a slow breath through his nose, the aroma of almond oil filling his senses. "Caitlin, I'm old," he said as he released his breath.

If anything, her grin widened and she lowered herself down until their mouths were inches apart. "Yes. You are."

She pressed her lips to the center of his chest before slowly rolling back onto his hips. Nick stared at her, mouth open. Caitlin tilted her head, her fingers playing across his stomach.

"Did you think I'd disagree?" she asked.

"I didn't think you'd agree so completely."

Caitlin chuckled, the laughter vibrating through her. Pleasant tension coiled in his gut and blood sought out the point of contact. "Didn't we have this conversation once? After we met? But *before* you took me to bed?"

"I'm eight years older than I was then."

She arched one eyebrow. "So am I." She sucked in a breath through pursed lips, humming as she released it, trailing her fingers over his abdomen. "Do you know how many men in their twenties would kill for a body like yours?" She slid her hands up his chest and looked at him with eyes that could start a fire.

They *were* starting a fire . . . in him.

Nick slide one hand behind his head, and Caitlin took advantage of the new position to run her hands along his sides. Her fingertips nudged the waistband of his boxers a fraction lower. With his other hand, he reached up and brushed the hair back from her cheek to curl it behind her ear. She turned into his touch, but her gaze stayed on him. She studied him, her eyes asking him what was on his mind.

"It's not this easy," he finally said.

Her hands stilled and her eyes shifted away for a moment before returning back to look at him. "I know."

"Things are different. We're different."

She nodded as he spoke, and shifted down his hips to his thighs, her toes pointing over the edge of the bed. "I had just hoped—"

Before she could finish, Nick sat up and clutched her face in his hands. He stole her words with an open-mouthed kiss, and devoured her moan as his tongue slipped past her lips. Her fingers curled around his wrists, anchoring herself in his lap as he kissed her until his head spun. Only breaking the contact long enough to draw in air, he kissed her again and eased back onto the bed, bringing her with him. Her easy weight pressed against his chest and she gave as much to the kiss as she got, and soon Nick's body throbbed with need to be inside her.

"Where did you say Michael was?" she asked against his lips.

"Went exploring—" He sucked the skin of her throat between his teeth, eliciting a low purr from her. "—the base."

"He'll be gone awhile?"

"Sure as hell hope so."

The autumn air had a bite to it that had Michael's fingertips numb and his cheeks tingling, but he couldn't leave yet. Couldn't turn his back on the glorious view spread out before him. The sky was black; yet not so black the far tree line didn't contrast against it with a deeper hue. Each star was a white pinpoint, clear and sharp and spectacular. The moon was huge, or so it seemed to Michael. He swore he could see the craters on its silver surface.

Beautiful . . . it was beautiful.

He walked further into the trees, his hands in front of him to touch the cool exterior of each trunk he passed. The trees served as supports. Since he stepped out of the bunker door, and started his walk across the landscape, he had felt the strength give in his legs. He wasn't falling over, but every few feet he stopped to let the spasms pass. A slight pressure pushed against the base of his skull, the early signs of a headache, and he dreaded it. Sometimes, his headaches were nothing more than a nuisance, sometimes they left him nearly blind and incapacitated.

His sneakers slipped on the damp leaves, and he steadied himself against a white barked tree. The shoes made him feel clumsy, and his toes ached to be free. Why his father insisted they were comfortable, he didn't know.

The trees opened some at the top of a slight slope, and Michael stopped short when he saw the figure of a woman sitting with her back to him. Her white shirt, rolled at the sleeves and too big for her, stood out in the darkness and gave her an almost ethereal glow. She turned to look over her shoulder, her golden hair shifting where it brushed her shoulders.

"Michael?" she asked, and he realized it was Doctor Quinn.

"Yes."

She turned away and ran her fingers over her cheeks, drawing a shuddered breath.

"I didn't mean to disturb you," he said softly. Speaking too loud seemed to be an intrusion on the perfect beauty of the night.

"You didn't. Come sit."

He walked to her side and sat on the soft bed of leaves and grass that spread over the hillside. With his legs bent, he rested his arms on his raised knees and stared into the night. As his eyes adjusted to the semi-darkness, he noticed that each star had a different intensity, some almost seeming to wink at him and sparkle in the moonlight.

"It is true the longest drought will end in rain, the longest peace in China will end in strife. Still it wouldn't reward the watcher to stay awake in hopes of seeing the calm of heaven break on his particular time and personal sight. That calm seems certainly safe to last tonight."

"That's beautiful," Doctor Quinn said with a sniffle when he finished. "Who wrote it?"

"Robert Frost."

He looked at her in the moonlight, noticing how the angles of her face were softened by the shadows and the breeze stirred her fair hair. She nodded and sniffed again. Her arms were crossed on her knees, and in one hand she held a crumpled tissue. Her grief was almost tangible between them, pressing against him like a force field.

"Jace was always quoting scripture," she said softly, her face turned to the moon. "He knew a Bible verse for every occasion."

Michael looked up at the sky again. A cold breeze shifted through the trees, biting at his cheeks, carrying earthy scents that tingled in his nose. The air here had a weight to it that filled his lungs and revived him. He drew a slow breath in, filling his senses with the aromas of the forest. "Shout joyfully to God . . . How awesome are your works."

"Psalms sixty-six," she whispered and Michael nodded in affirmation.

Silence settled between them, disturbed only by the rustle of the wind through the trees and the sound of insects singing to each other. After several minutes, he heard her stifled cry and dared a glance to see the tears running freely down her cheeks. Her eyes sparkled by the light of the moon. Uneasiness made him shift and glance away, and he wished he knew what to do. He had so much to learn, and so much he had to understand.

"I'm sorry," he finally said and braced his hand on the damp earth to stand. "I'll—I'm going to go."

She shifted her gaze to him, pinning him to his spot. "No. Stay," she said so low he almost didn't hear her. "Please."

Michael nodded and settled again to the same position. He picked up a short branch that had fallen from one of the trees around them, running his fingertips over each texture. The branch was light, dried out, and the bark had peeled away on spots to reveal grayed wood beneath. The leaves had long since curled in on themselves and lost the deep green of the summer. He lifted the branch to his nose and inhaled. Earth and life still clung to the decaying bark.

"You're the first person who hasn't tried to tell me everything will be okay," Doctor Quinn said after a few minutes. Her voice carried a weight that made the words sit between them, almost corporeal.

Michael studied her. The tears had stopped, but her lips were turned down in a slight frown and her eyes were distant. She wasn't even looking at him, but to some far off place in the dark.

"Will it be?" he asked.

Her eyes shifted to him and he waited for the answer. She slowly shook her head and shrugged one shoulder. "I don't know. Right now, nothing feels like it will ever be okay again." Her voice faltered, and she sucked in a sharp breath. "I'm going to have a baby."

Michael faltered, unsure what to say. He knew he was ignorant of many things, but he understood that a child was more often than not a source of joy to the parents. "You and your husband must have been happy," he finally said.

"Jace didn't know yet." Her voice quivered as she spoke. "I had been waiting for this trip home to tell him. I wasn't going to go back to Florida. I'd already worked it out with the general, and he agreed I was needed here more than in the field."

Michael didn't know what was in Florida, or why she would have to leave, so he just listened. She sighed deeply, and looked out over the valley again. Silence settled between them, and Michael wished he understood what to do. Victor always told him he was intelligent, and that was one of the reasons the Areth worried about what he read and saw. Right now, he felt inadequate.

"I shouldn't have waited so long," she said barely louder than a whisper.

Michael dropped his head forward and closed his eyes. He ran a hand slowly over his face and pushed his hair back. "I'm sorry," he finally said. "Your husband died to—"

"No!" she snapped, cutting him off. "Michael, don't apologize. Jace is gone because of the Areth, not because of you."

He slowly nodded and looked at her, sitting up straighter. "What will you do?"

She shrugged and sighed. "I don't know yet."

Michael stared at her in the moonlight, and found himself studying her. She caught him staring, and smiled. Not much more than a slight upturn of her lips. "What?"

"I've never seen a pregnant woman."

Her smile widened, and he wondered what he said to bring it to her lips.

"I'm not *that* pregnant."

"How does it feel?"

"Not that different yet. Ask me again in a couple months."

"Okay."

She smiled again. "Would you like to go have some tea and cake with me, Michael? I have a triple chocolate layer cake in my quarters that's calling my name."

Michael smiled wider. His first experience with chocolate had been that day at lunch, in the form of chocolate pudding. If triple chocolate layer cake tasted anywhere as good as pudding, he couldn't pass up the chance. "Thank you, Doctor Quinn."

"Please call me Lilly."

He nodded and stood, his legs stronger after the rest, and offered her his hand to help her to her feet. Walking ahead, he led the way back to the door hidden in the side of the mountain.

CJ heard the change in Nick's breathing as she slipped on her last shoe and ran a hand over her hair. She knew she wouldn't make a clean escape. He rolled from his stomach to his side, his arm reaching out for her. When his hand found nothing, he raised his head from the pillow and opened his eyes.

"Hey," she said, tucking her shirt into her jeans.

"Hey. What are you doing?"

"I'm going to go."

Nick sat up, the sheet sliding down his body to pool in his lap. CJ's pulse quickened just at the sight of his bare chest and the hint of exposed hip. "Why?"

CJ leaned over to kiss him, her insides immediately melting when his response wasn't a quick peck but a deep kiss that begged her to return to bed. She groaned softly and pulled back, stroking his lips with her thumb. "Michael will be here soon."

"Yeah. And?"

"And this is his first night with you."

Nick arched his eyebrows, his hand skillfully reaching up to tug her shirt free from her waistband. "And?"

She gave in and sank onto the bed, straddling his sheet-covered lap. His expert hands that knew her so well slipped beneath her shirt and rubbed her back. CJ tilted her head to the side, giving him easy access to nuzzle his slightly stubbled chin against her throat, ignoring the argument in her head.

"And . . ." she said, already breathless. "He needs to acclimate himself to a new place . . ." Her last words were lost in the purr his kiss inspired.

His hands slid along her sides, his thumbs finding the edge of her bra. "And he can't do that with you here?" The vibration of his voice against her skin made her insides shake and she shifted closer to him.

"I don't want to confuse him."

Nick pulled back, his dark gaze skimming over her face. "What would confuse him?"

CJ tried to focus again, her mind hazed by his touch and kiss. She ran her hands along his bare shoulders, feeling the flex and bunch of his muscles beneath her touch.

"Everything confuses him, Nick. Watch his face when he sees something new. He's processing everything, absorbing everything. What seems normal and every day for us is beyond anything he's ever known."

Nick nodded, his hands stopping their caress to hold her. He leaned his forehead into her chest, and CJ kissed the top of his head as she stroked his hair.

"He needs his father to teach him."

"Just tonight," he said, his voice muffled against her breast.

"We'll see."

He raised his head and took her face in his hands, covering her mouth in a deep, long kiss that stole her breath. When he released her, he looked into her eyes. "Just tonight."

She opened her mouth to offer another argument, but Nick's arched brow and the determined set of his jaw told her it was pointless. CJ nodded in concession, and wrapped her arms around him, burying her face against his shoulder.

Reluctantly, she kissed his lips and slid from his lap to stand. As she tucked her shirt in again, he tossed back the sheet. She allowed herself the guilty pleasure of surreptitiously watching him as he stood and walked across the room without an ounce of modesty for his naked state. Heat rushed to her cheeks, and she quickly had to convince herself again that a night apart was the best thing.

"*G*ood night, Michael," Caitlin said over her shoulder as she opened the door to the hallway. Standing in the open doorway, she turned to face Nick with her back against the jamb and a smile on her lips.

"Good night, Caitlin," Michael said from the lounge.

"I'll see you both for breakfast?"

Nick stepped close to her, his body against her hip as he looked down at her. He set one arm on the jamb over her head so he could lean closer, and touched her cheek with his other hand. She smiled, the simple act making his blood pound in his temples and rush south of his belt.

Hot Damn . . .

Twenty-four hours ago, he had been preparing for the mission. No son, no lover. Except for Dog, his quarters had been empty. He had been waiting for his life to start again. *Boy, had it ever.*

"Come get us at oh-seven-thirty."

She nodded, pulling her lower lip through her teeth to try and suppress her smile. Nick wondered if she had any idea how sexy it made her look. Caitlin turned into him, sliding her hands up his chest, her eyes glancing sideways to make sure the door blocked them from Michael's view. Nick shifted, fighting the urge to press her against the wall and kiss her until neither one of them could think straight. Even though they'd been together less than two hours before, his body loudly and adamantly proclaimed his appetite for Caitlin Montgomery was not satisfied. He shifted his hand to her hip and pulled her against him.

"Keep that up, woman . . ." he whispered in warning, his voice rough.

Caitlin drew him down for a kiss, her lips parting beneath his, and he swore he'd make her suffer for this kind of sweet torture.

"Good night," she said against his mouth before moving from the space between him and the jamb to walk down the hall.

Nick watched her until she reached her quarters, and waited until she disappeared inside before he stepped back into the apartment and shut the door. Michael quickly hunched over, studiously working on untying his shoelace knot. His other sneaker was already off, set neatly beneath the table. Nick ran a hand along the back of his neck and crossed the room, sinking down into the desk chair.

Michael's eyes shifted up once, but he immediately went back to his shoes. He straightened each lace with meticulous care, slipped the sneaker off, and setting it beside the other. With both shoes off, he set his elbows on his legs and linked his hands loosely in the space between his knees. Nick cleared his throat and slouched down in the chair, crossing his arms.

"What's on your mind, Michael?"

His son looked up then, meeting his gaze. Nick was getting better at not feeling like a specimen under a microscope when Michael studied him. Michael read people, before, during and after he ever posed a question.

"You and Caitlin."

Nick nodded once, letting Michael know he could continue.

"She's someone special to you."

"Yes. Very."

Michael looked down at the sneakers he had so carefully set beneath the table, nudging one with his sock-covered foot. His expression flinched, revealing the effect of whatever thoughts churned in his mind.

"Go ahead, Michael."

Michael's eyes inadvertently shifted to the far side of the room, and Nick knew where he looked. The chair was gone, but the gouge would be in the wall for a while yet until he had time to have it fixed.

"I don't want to upset you again."

"Just ask."

"Was it the same between you and Mother?"

The anger burst inside him like a balloon of acid, twisting his gut and jolting his heart rate into overdrive. Just the mention of the bitch was enough to make him see red. Nick tamped it back, fisting his hands within the folds of his arms and clenching his jaw until he felt the surge ebb.

"No," he finally answered. "I cared for her, loved her even, but what I had with her was not like what I have with Caitlin. Everything that happened between Kathleen and I was a lie." Nick stood, nervous energy driving him to his feet.

Michael watched him pace, his own foot bouncing a steady rhythm on the floor. "She is Areth."

Nick paused, focusing on him. "I know."

"You didn't at first."

"No."

"You hate the Areth." His voice was steady, his words statements and not questions, but his tone carried a weight that pushed against Nick's chest. Something dreaded . . . wrong.

"I hate what they've done. To you. To the world. To me," Nick bit out.

Michael stood slowly, stepping around the furniture to meet Nick. Eye-to-eye they stood, practically mirror images with time the only variance. Michael swallowed and pushed his hands into the pockets of his jeans.

"*Say* it, Michael."

"I'm half-Areth."

Nick squared his shoulders, blinking as he tried to process the point. His gut sank like a lead ball, and he shook his head. "God, no. No, Michael. That doesn't—that doesn't matter to me. You're my *son*."

"She hated me because I was half-human."

Nick couldn't take hearing it again, doubted he had the willpower to control his murderous rage if he did. He reached out and clamped his hands on the sides of Michael's head, needing to make the connection, to make him realize. Michael tensed, and Nick felt him pull back, but he held firm.

"Michael . . ." The words were lost somewhere between the raging emotions in his chest and the part of his brain that would let him get them all out. "I could never . . . I *hate* that bitch and what she did . . . I hate when you call her Mother because *no* mother should treat her child like that. But I do not and could *never* do anything less than love you."

Michael stared at him, his lips parted on the verge of speaking, but he stayed silent. His eyes barely shifted as he focused on Nick, and in his gut, Nick knew he didn't understand. How could he? Nick stepped back and walked to the kitchen island to lean his hands onto the edge. He drew a breath, feeling it shudder through him.

"I've loved you since the day Kathleen told me she was pregnant," he said slowly, staring down at the utilitarian gray countertop. Emotion squeezed his throat and he swallowed against it. He turned his hands over and stared at his palms. "I used to put my hands on her stomach and feel you move. I'd push—just a little—and you'd push back. I loved you before you were ever born."

Nick looked up and saw that Michael had moved closer to him, deep lines furrowed his brow and frown lines bracketed his mouth. Silence sat between them, heavy and corporeal. Michael slowly shook his head.

"Why didn't you ever come?"

Nick curled his hands into tight fists. "They told me you were dead," he managed to push past the dam in his throat that wanted to keep the words at bay.

Just like the day at the lake, when Caitlin told him his son was alive, memories of his birth came flooding back. They burned from the inside out, Nick fought to breathe through the physical pain.

"The Areth doctors . . . they told me the two of you died in childbirth. I didn't—I couldn't believe. I shoved them out of the way." The room was out of focus through the hot haze fogging his eyes. "Kathleen was on the table, covered in a sheet. I demanded they help her, but they wouldn't. They said it was too late. They let me see you . . ."

He had to stop, sucking in a shaking breath. Nick pressed his eyes closed, wishing he could wipe the memory from his mind. "They gave you to me, wrapped in a blanket. You were blue and cold. God . . ." He opened his eyes and met his son's seeking expression. He had to know now, had to understand. "I thought you were dead."

Michael turned away, but not before Nick saw the single tear run down his cheek. He walked half way across the room before turning back.

"Why?" he demanded, the first spark of raw emotion Nick had seen edging his tone. "Why would they do that? Why would they lie?"

"I don't have all the answers, Michael. However, I promise you this . . . I intend to find them. For both of us."

*M*ichael's body jerked violently, yanking him with a swallowed scream from the nightmare that gripped him. He fell from the lounge where he had fallen asleep, his elbow hitting the glass table with a sharp jolt of point. He gasped for air, swallowing against the nausea that twisted his guts. Sweat dripped from the tip of his nose, falling on the back of his hand as he rolled to his hands and knees.

Bits and broken moments of the nightmare flashed behind his closed eyelids, each one pulsing through his body like bolts of lightning—or pain-inducing stabs from Kathleen's tools of torture. Michael leaned against the edge of the lounge, sitting on his ankles to press the heels of his hands to his eye sockets. Flashes of light replaced the images, but his gut still twisted and his lungs ached with each breath. He couldn't get enough air . . . couldn't stop the floor from tilting.

Pain throbbed in his skull, and every beat of his own heart in his ears ricocheted like echoes in a canyon. A final, violent twisting of his insides had him stumbling across the room to the open door of the bedroom, and into the bathroom. The remains of his lunch ripped their way from him, leaving him depleted and gasping for air.

CHAPTER EIGHTEEN

19 November 2051, Sunday
Phoenix Compound
Outside Colorado Springs, Colorado
Former United States of America

The small base chapel was filled to capacity, with at least three-dozen men and women lining the side and back walls. Those who had once been official military wore their dress uniforms to show respect for Lieutenant Jason Patrick Quinn. The chapel had been constructed in the highest level of the base, and was one of the few places that had actual windows. At this time of the morning the sunlight streamed through leaded and stained glass to light on the congregation. At the end of the service, the camouflage shutters would be replaced and the windows would disappear into the mountainside again, but for now sunlight bathed the chapel in its warmth.

A week had passed since Jace's death. It was no easier now than it had been seven days before.

Lilly sat in the first pew, her back straight and her body still. She hadn't moved since sitting down, and CJ wondered if she would snap in two from the tension that clenched her body. Sorrow permeated the small sanctuary, thick, heavy, and real. CJ glanced around quickly, and realized Beverly had not come. If she herself could feel the prevailing emotion of everyone here, it would be overwhelming to Beverly.

She looked sideways to Nick, who sat with his head tipped forward and his eyes closed. His hand slid across his lap to find hers, curling his fingers around her own. CJ squeezed gently, but left Nick to his thoughts. Michael sat on her other side, his hands linked in his lap, and his face turned up to the stained glass mural that made up the wall behind the pulpit. The Crucifixion and Resurrection were depicted in shards of gold and blue glass, sun streaming in from behind. The colors played across Michael's features as his eyes shifted to take it all in.

CJ reached out her free hand and touched his arm. "Michael?"

He looked briefly to her, his eyes wide with wonder, but immediately went back to the mural. "It's beautiful, Caitlin," he said reverently as he covered her hand with his.

She smiled and looked up. With Nicholas on one side of her, and his son on the other, her hands joined with each, she felt some of the weight lift off her chest. Perhaps they weren't a typical family, but it felt right. A small, yet persistent, voice in the back of her mind still warned her it could all end tomorrow. Nick could remember how badly she had hurt him, how stupid she had been, and he could stop cold this new chance. At least half a dozen times each day, her stomach clenched and a cold sweat permeated her skin at the thought that he might do just that.

Nick squeezed her hand and leaned over, speaking close to her ear. "You all right?"

CJ nodded, his lips brushing her skin. She realized tears trailed down her cheeks, and brushed them away with her fingers. "Yes."

He pressed a long, slow kiss in front of her ear before sitting back again. A hush fell over the congregation as the base minister took his place behind the podium. He spoke of Jace's life, his commitment, and his passion. Somehow, the words fell flat to the memory CJ held of him. She couldn't imagine, didn't want to try, how the words seemed to Lilly. CJ had lost Nick once, but not to death. Nothing so permanent and cruel. Nothing so without hope. Even though it had felt so at the time.

When the minister called on him, Nick stood and tugged the jacket of his uniform sharply into place. In the style of the old United States Air Force dress blues, the deep blue accentuated his tall frame and silver hair. Medals and ribbons of service adorned the jacket over his heart, and the insignia of his rank sat proudly on each shoulder. He stepped behind the podium, the carved oak stand too short for him, and braced his hands on each side. Michael shifted his hand, and CJ felt the tentativeness in his touch as he laced his fingers through hers. She looked at him and smiled, letting him know the contact was fine.

Nick cleared his throat, his gaze roaming over the crowd as he gathered his thoughts. He shifted, cleared his throat again, and looked directly at CJ, holding the stare for several moments before looking away.

"I didn't know Lieutenant Quinn for very long," he began, his voice graveled and rough. "But I didn't need to. In the short time I did know him, I learned everything I needed to know.

"Jace was a man who gave everything he had to everything in his life. Flying. Fighting." His gaze shifted to Lilly. "Loving. With Jace, what you saw was what you got. No games, no pulling punches. Honest. And you have to respect that."

Nick shifted again, sniffling softly as he brushed his nose with the side of his finger, clearing his throat. When he raised his head and looked out over the crowd, CJ saw the strain in his expression that he struggled to mask. Eight years ago, Nick had been a man living behind walls. He had let some of them down to let her in. She knew that, but there were still walls. In the few weeks since he learned of Michael, she had seen his resolve to hold up those walls crumble more and more. Too much had happened; too many things battered him down. He tried, he fought to keep the control he knew was expected of him. Her throat restricted and her chest hurt, wishing she could lessen the burden for him.

"I have my son back," Nick tried to say, his voice cracking, and he lowered his head to huff a breath. Michael's grip on CJ's hand tightened a small degree. When Nick raised his head, his lips formed a thin, straight line as he clenched his teeth. "But I lost a brother."

Without conclusion, Nick stepped back from the podium and down off the pulpit. CJ took his hand as soon as he sat beside her, and he held on tight, his gaze straight-ahead and unwavering. The minister returned to the pulpit, his own eyes reddened with emotion that Nick's short but powerful eulogy inspired in everyone.

"Today's service is going to be short at Lilly's request. She knew her husband wouldn't want us to dwell in mourning, but to continue the fight and to rejoice in the lives saved by his sacrifice. She has asked that we all sing together a very old hymn that was Jace's favorite. If you all would come to your feet."

Everyone in attendance stood, CJ standing between two tall Tanner men, each holding a hand, Michael's grip only slightly less firm and intense than his father's. Soft piano music filled the chapel, and in unison every voice came together to sing, even those who didn't know all the words. Nick's deep baritone was loudest of all to CJ, resonating in the air around them.

"Some glad morning when this live is over, I'll fly away. To a home on God's celestial shore, I'll fly away."

Her own singing was lost in the thick lump that kept them from escaping, but she mouthed the words as the chorus of four-dozen voices echoed around them.

"When the shadows of this life have gone, I'll fly away. Like a bird from prison bars have flown, I'll fly away."

The song ended, and the crowd slowly dissipated. Nick stepped into the aisle, leading CJ by the hand. Lilly left the front pew and walked around to meet them, her face a mask of calm that belied the grief CJ knew had to be beneath. She embraced each of them and thanked them for being there, the standard required dialogue for events of sorrow and loss. When Lilly hugged Michael, CJ noticed he barely hesitated to put his arms around her and nodded when she whispered something in his ear. She pulled back, a hesitant smile on her lips, and then moved away to the next group of well-wishers.

CJ glanced at Nick, who raised a single eyebrow.

"Colonel, might I have a word with you," came General Castleton's voice from behind them.

"Yes, sir," Nick said as they turned.

"You did well by the lieutenant in your eulogy today, Nick," the general said, shaking Nick's hand. "You didn't say much, but it was enough."

"Thank you, sir."

"Some things have come to light that warrant discussion. I've scheduled a meeting in Command at fifteen hundred hours."

"Yes, sir. We'll be there."

"We're only discussing new Intel, so if both of you can't make it, I'm sure you can fill each other in later," the general said with a smile

"Understood, sir," Nick answered, his hand sliding to the small of her back.

General Castleton patted Nick's arm and nodded at CJ and Michael in farewell before he blended into the crowd again. Nick's arm circled her shoulder, drawing her close to his side and they made their way toward the door.

*L*aughter drifted into the bedroom from the living area as Nick pulled a tee shirt over his head and fluffed his damp hair with his fingers. He tucked the shirt in to the waistband of his pants as he walked to the doorway, taking in the scene in front of him. Leaning his shoulder into the jamb, he took a few minutes to watch.

Michael sat cross-legged and barefoot on the lounge, leaning forward over the Scrabble game Caitlin had set up on the glass table. Caitlin knelt on the other side, her back to Nick, sitting on her ankles. Michael finished setting his tiles into place, and grinned at her.

"There. Twenty-eight points."

"Wait a minute," she said, coming up on her knees. "Zucchetto. Zucchetto? What kind of word is that?"

"By your own descriptions of the rules, it is a valid word."

Caitlin shook her head. "I don't think so. What the hell is a zucchetto?"

"The skullcap worn by Roman Catholic ecclesiastics," Nick said, stepping away from the doorway to cross the room.

Caitlin twisted to look up at him as he approached, with deep dimples digging into her cheeks as she smiled. "This is not fair. I'm being ganged up on."

"She tried to use slickery a minute ago," Michael said, immediately eliciting a loud gasp of shock from Caitlin.

"It *is* a word!"

Nick laughed and crouched down beside Caitlin, resting his elbows on his knees. "No, darlin'. It's not."

"Michael is killing me!" she proclaimed, flailing an arm in the direction of the game board. "You can't hold it against me."

Nick leaned in and stopped her mini-tantrum with a deep kiss. Her body relaxed and her hands came up to touch his face as he pulled back. Nick slid his cheek along hers until his lips were near her ear.

"Later," he whispered.

"Promise?"

Nick kissed her again quickly before standing. "If I'm not back by dinner, go ahead without me and I'll meet you there."

"And you can fill me in," Caitlin said, sitting back again on her ankles with her hands sandwiched between her knees. "You sure you don't want me to go?"

Nick nodded. "No need. Sounds like a quick in-and-out."

Caitlin smirked, her eyes sparkling and Nick winked at her. "Okay. We'll be here," she said.

Nick paused at the door, his fingers curled around the handle. He wondered if either Caitlin or Michael realized how right they looked sitting there. With one last smile and raise of his hand, he opened the door. Caitlin argued her choice of words before he had the door shut behind him.

Damian and Beverly were already seated in Command when he arrived, and Nick took his place in the chair beside Beverly. She looked tired and more pale than usual, and her eyes were heavy and shadowed. Each movement she made was slow and weighed down, the physical effort obvious. Before Nick had a chance to ask her if she was all right, General Castleton came out of his office and sat down at the head of the table.

"Thank you, everyone, for coming. The last week has been rough, but it's time to get back to work." The general turned to Nick with a wide smile. "How is your boy settling in, Colonel?"

Nick nodded, remembering the animated game between Michael and Caitlin. "Just fine, sir."

"Good to hear. This mission obviously wasn't without its casualties, but I believe Lieutenant Quinn would appreciate the good that has come from it. Bring Michael by. I'd like to get to know the young man."

"I will, sir."

Castleton nodded, a quick jerk of his head, and turned his focus back to the monitor set in the table before him. "I brought the three of you here to discuss some information that has come to light. I want your opinions on its validity, and just what the hell we should do with it."

Nick leaned forward over the table, linking his fingers together. "What kind of information, sir?"

With a few quick punches of the keys on his command board, the general initiated a data feed to all the monitors at the table. Nick stared at the information as it scrolled up, decoding the Areth language in his head. It was a rough download, obviously encrypted and translated from some other program than anything they ran at the base. Streams of information ran right to left, wrapping back again in a reverse typewriter effect until the entire screen was full of tiny green font symbols.

"Where did we obtain this?" Damian asked.

"It was piggybacked onto the medical files the Areth doctor provided you with during the extraction."

Nick popped up one eyebrow and looked at the data again. Even though he was fluent in Areth, both spoken and written, most of the information didn't make much sense and he wondered if it were written in some type of code to hide the details.

"Does it appear that he intentionally attached these files?" Beverly asked, tilting her head to the side as she leaned forward. Her green eyes shifted between the faces of the three men.

"The computer geeks are studying that now, as well as finding a way to decode the data into a more reader friendly format. But right now, they're saying it looked intentional."

Nick tapped his fingers on the table. "Okay, so what does it say?"

"Not a damn thing about the Areth. This," he said, waving his hand at the monitor. "Refers to an entirely new alien race."

"Another race?" Damian said, his eyes widening. "Huh . . ."

"I can't say I'm surprised," Beverly interjected. "It would be pretentious of us to assume that of the entire universe, the only cognizant beings are ourselves and the Areth. And of course, according to them, we are one in the same."

"And?" Nick pushed.

"This race and the Areth are enemies. They fought a war a couple thousand years ago, but don't ask me who won. Don't know yet," Castleton provided.

"The enemy of my enemy . . ." Damian began.

"Is my friend," Nick finished, looking across the table at the man.

"Bingo," Castleton said, jabbing the air with his finger.

"But why would an Areth scientist purposefully provide us with information about his people's enemies? Obviously, this is not information the Areth ever intended for the people of Earth to know about. Why would he do this?" Beverly asked.

"Why would he help us free a bunch of human guinea pigs?" Damian added.

"Is he setting us up?" Nick's first instincts told him not to trust Victor, but an annoying voice in the back of his head kept reminding him how Michael trusted the man. How Michael claimed he owed Victor his life. A double-cross didn't fit.

"We need to find out," the general said. "That's where I need you, Nick. And you, Beverly."

"How?"

Castleton looked to Nick. "I want you to talk to the Areth. See what he'll tell you. How forthcoming he'll be about the information. Beverly, I want you to go with him. See what kind of sense you can get of him. You know I wouldn't ask usually—"

"I know, Robert," Beverly said, a smile on her lips.

Castleton rapped his knuckles on the table. "Good! We'll meet again tomorrow to discuss what you come back with. Agreed?"

The three nodded and everyone slid back from the table. Beverly touched Nick's arm briefly. His turn to her was in reaction more to the quick zing of electricity that shot up his arm, than the subtle touch. He looked down at her, and another flash of concern at her weary appearance hitting him.

"Would you like to go now, Nick?"

"Yeah. Might as well." He squinted, focusing on her. "Beverly, are you all right? You look tired."

She nodded, a strained smile pulling at her lips. "It has been a hard week. Everyone's emotions have been so intense and overwhelming; I haven't been able to fend them off."

"Is there anything I can do?"

"You are," she said softly. "Even without touching you, I can feel the peace and happiness that has taken over your soul. It sooths away everything else."

Nick smiled, unsure what to say to something like that. He motioned with his hand that she should lead the way and they left Command for the infirmary-holding cell.

CHAPTER NINETEEN

*T*he midday sun warmed his back and shoulders, and sweat glistened on his upper body from exertion. His muscles ached from the persistent swing of his scythe, but his father said he was strong, and the lower field was his responsibility to clear by the late day meal. Next season, he would choose a wife and join his father, side by side, in the fields. The corn his family grew was enough to feed many families in the Maya city of Tikal .

He paused to straighten his back, wiping his arm across his damp forehead. The white loincloth wrapped around his waist was wet and dirty from work, his bare feet caked with dust. He looked behind him, and smiled at the rows of fallen stalks.

Father would be proud.

A tingling awareness prickled at the back of his neck and he turned to look toward the distant tree line. A flash of white disappeared behind a tree. Promising himself he would only pause in his work for a few moments, long enough to cool himself in the shade of the forest, he ran through the tall stalks, the brown leaves whipping at his bare chest as he pushed them aside.

With the sun behind him, he stepped into the shadows and allowed his eyes to adjust. "Ukatim'u," he called, leaning into the cool moss covering a nearby tree. "You're playing games with me."

A soft laugh reached him, and he crept deeper into the forest. White flashed again, dodging from one tree to another. He moved to meet her, circling the same tree so she ran into his chest with a shriek.

"Mekel!"

He wrapped her young, lithe body in his arms and held her close, laughing as she squirmed to escape. Ukatim'u did not yet have the softly shaped form of a mature woman, but holding her against him still brought a smile to Mekel's young lips. In the last year, he had begun to see his childhood friend as more than just a playmate. As his thirteenth year approached, and his father spoke more and more of choosing a wife, his thoughts lingered more and more on Ukatim'u. Her long black hair swept over his arms, her dark eyes wide as she looked up at him.

"Since you were old enough to walk, you weren't fast enough to get away from me, Ukatim'u."

She stilled, her hands resting on his chest. "You speak as if I were trying."

He laughed and bent his neck to steal a kiss, but she eluded him, shaking her head. One more time, he moved for her lips, and she gifted him with a quick brush of her mouth against his before she broke free of his embrace and ran away into the field. Ukatim'u looked back at him over her shoulder, her smile flashing at him as she waved and disappeared into the corn stalks.

*V*ictor blinked rapidly, trying to bring the ceiling over his bed into focus. Something had jolted him from his fitful sleep, leaving him disoriented and fuzzy. His head pounded, his brain pushing against the inside of his skull even as something squeezed his temples in a vise. He slipped his arm from beneath the triple layer of blankets and covered his eyes.

The fever had subsided, now he was so cold he wondered if his bones would break like shards of ice if hit hard enough. His body trembled and shook from the inside out, his stomach clenching with each quake until it was impossible to eat without feeling sick.

He had spent the last seven days contemplating every disease and disorder he could recall, which might explain the torture his own body had inflicted on him. None fit. The human doctor ran test after test, discussing with him the results in an effort to help him, but none had provided any physiological reason. No infection, no virus . . . nothing.

Yet, he grew sicker with each hour. His periods of mental clarity grew shorter. Victor knew it, recognized when his mind began to slip, and could do nothing to stop it.

The clank of his cell door drew his attention. Doctor Quinn entered, followed by Nicholas Tanner and a woman Victor didn't know. The top of her head just met Colonel Tanner's shoulders. Red hair, laced with golden strands, curled and fell down her back, partially clipped to reveal her face. As the three people stepped into the cell, the unknown woman looked directly at Victor, her jade green eyes unwavering as she focused on him.

Doctor Quinn crouched beside him, quickly moving her bioscan reader in the space over his head and chest. "How are you feeling, Victor?" she asked as she studied the handheld med recorder in her hand.

"Cold."

She shook her head. "Your core temperature is down to ninety-five-point-four degrees. I'll bring back some warming blankets to see if that helps."

"Thank you."

Doctor Quinn stood, turning to Michael's father. The red-haired woman still stared at Victor, and he fought the compulsion to turn away from her scrutiny. What did she see? Did she imagine him as the Evil Areth embodied solely in him? Did she pity him as just a pathetic creature dying a slow and unexplainable death.

"Seventeen hours ago, his temperature was one-hundred and five. I had him packed in ice and had to give him fluids with an IV because he was severely dehydrated. Now . . ." She shook her head. "I don't know what to do."

"Can we talk with him?" the woman asked, and Victor knew he had to be slowly losing his mind. He looked right at her, heard her voice, and through the haze of his mind he swore he never saw her lips move. "We don't want to endanger his health any further, but the colonel and I have something important to discuss with him."

"A few minutes should be fine, but without knowing what is wrong, I don't want to aggravate a bad condition by causing him stress."

"We understand, Lilly. Thank you."

Her voice was feminine and soft, with a slight lilting accent Victor couldn't place. He knew the voice had not come from her lips. Victor closed his eyes and rolled his head on the pillow.

He mentally added delusions to the list of symptoms that haunted him.

Chair legs scraped across the floor, and Victor sensed someone sitting at his bedside. He was so tired. His body had turned to concrete weighed down with lead, the weight of his blankets smothering him and yet he needed them. Exhausted muscles and nerves screamed for sleep, but there was no rejuvenation in the few minutes he snatched here and there. Whispered voices and haunting dreams he didn't understand stole rest from him.

"Victor." The voice grated on his eardrums, echoing and stretching until it was so distorted he almost didn't recognize his own name. He blinked, slowly opening heavy eyelids, and turned to look to Nicholas Tanner.

Michael's father sat beside the bed, leaned forward with his elbows set on his knees and his hands clasp in front of him.

They want you dead . . . he's going to watch you die slowly and enjoy it.

Victor shook his head against the pillow, moaning against the strange voice that whispered in his mind. It wasn't his thoughts, his words, and yet the voice resonated within his own head.

"Victor, we found the information you hid on the medical file microslide."

The haze slowly cleared, and Victor swallowed against the dryness in his throat. He nodded. A slow, rolling heat popped like a balloon against the base of his skull and slithered out through his body, wrapping around his neck like a noose.

"Did you intend for us to find it, Victor?"

It was difficult to focus as the blankets became suddenly stifling and sweat broke out over his body. His empty stomach roiled and knotted and his joints ached.

"I hoped you would, yes," he finally managed to answer. His voice caught up with his thoughts and he forced them into alignment enough to speak.

"Why?"

Why? Questions he had no answers to from a man who expected an explanation when there wasn't one. Not one he understood.

"I'm not sure I can tell you what you want to hear."

He heard Nick's sigh as he pushed his blankets away, his shirt already plastered to his chest with sweat. Victor wanted to move, to escape the fire that branded his skin, but he was too tired and too weak to sit up or even roll off the bed.

"Our translators are working on the file. You helped by giving it to us. Help by translating it."

"I'll tell you what it says."

Nick looked sideways at the woman who stood at the head of the bed. Victor hadn't even realized she had moved to stand there, but the shift in Nick's stare made him look. She gazed down at him, her forehead knit together above the arch of her nose, her lips turned down in a frown. Her arms laced over her stomach, long fingers clutching her own elbows.

Tingling sensations danced up the back of Victor's neck as their gazes connected. The hairs at the base of his skull stood on end and an unseen hand flittered over his skin. Goosebumps raised on his arms despite the heat that boiled beneath the surface.

She looked to Nick, one golden red eyebrow arching.

"He's not lying." Her head tilted and her expression tightened. "But he's in pain. Somehow, all this causes him pain."

Victor blinked. No, he wasn't insane. Her lips were *not* moving. Was she telepathic or something? No . . . no . . . he didn't hear her in his head. The other voice, the evil slithering liar . . . *that* was in his head.

Who's the liar!

Pain shot through his skull, piercing his spine and spearing his temples with such ferocity it arched him off the bed and ripped a scream from his throat. Heavy hands kept him from flying away, searing his skin with the contact.

"Holy crap!" he heard Nick say. "Beverly, go get Lilly. He's burning up."

On the hazy edges of his peripheral vision, Victor saw the woman run from the cell. Details around him clouded in a miasmic sea of red as his eyes boiled in their sockets. Nick moved to stand. With the final burst of strength he had, Victor reached out and clutched the front of Nick's shirt, keeping him from moving away.

"Wait . . ."

Nick stared down at him, his eyes squinted as a wince shifted across his features. "We're getting the doc."

Victor shook his head. "I have to tell you . . ."

"*L*illy!" Nick shouted, his voice echoing off the concrete walls. "Damn it. Lilly! Get in here!"

"U-u-ummmmmani," Victor said, sweat from his lips flying to leave dark spots on Nick's shirt. "They are the Umani."

The grip on his shirt pulled him down until Nick knelt on one knee beside the bed. Violent tremors shook Victor's body with such force, his bed scraped the wall with a broken rhythm. Nick pushed against Victor's shoulders until he finally gave up the fight and laid back on the pillow, his breath coming in shallow, rapid bursts. Nick looked over his shoulder.

"Lilly!" he shouted again.

Finally, Lilly Quinn ran down the hall toward the cell, Beverly right behind her followed by two nurses. Lilly dropped to her knees beside the bed and Nick tried to move, but Victor's hand gripped his shirt, his knuckles white and his hand shaking with his tenacity. Lilly took his vitals, shaking her head as she read the data on her handheld. She leaned over Victor's sweaty, shaking body to lay her ear on his chest, closing her eyes as she listened.

"His breathing is labored and raspy. There could be fluid building in his lungs," she said as she sat back on her heels. "These rapid changes in body temperature . . . the pain he says he suffers . . . None of it makes any sense!"

When she looked at Nick, he winced at the truth he saw in her eyes. She doubted the Areth doctor had much time left. It was plain and simple as that.

"Umani," Victor said again.

Nick turned back to Victor and shifted closer, leaning in to hear him. "They're called the Umani," he said back, so Victor knew he understood.

Victor nodded. "Pen. I need a pen."

Nick looked over his shoulder to the nurses who stood, wide-eyed and mesmerized, near the cell door. He held out his hand, wagging his fingers impatiently, and the brunette handed him the clipboard she carried. A silver pen hung from a beaded chain at the top. Nick set the clipboard on Victor's chest.

"Here."

Victor rolled partially onto his side, positioning the clipboard to scribble something across the forms held firmly on it. His hands quaked and he dropped the pen twice, Nick handed it back to him each time. With each stroke of the pen on the paper, a small grunt accompanied it, and by the time he finished Nick knew he was in excruciating pain. He had seen too many men fight through pain to do what they had to do not to recognize it.

When Victor finished, he dropped the pen and fell back on the bed, his eyes drifting shut. Nick lifted the clipboard and turned it around to read what Victor had written. Scribbled across the form in deep, jagged lines of blue were a series of numbers.

"Coordinates," Nick said, focusing on Victor again. "This is where they are."

Victor nodded slowly, rolling his head toward Nick as he opened glazed, reddened eyes. "Find a way." Then he yelled and scissored into a sitting position, one arm wrapped around his body, the hand of his other pressed against the base of his skull.

Nick looked to Beverly, and immediate concern hit his chest. She stood near the head of the bed within an arm's reach of Nick, her green eyes glued to Victor, with her arms wrapped around her body. Small tremors shook her, and she looked as if her own arms were the only things holding her together. Nick touched her hand and her eyes darted to him.

"Bev?" he asked.

"He's afraid," he voice echoed in the cell.

"Afraid? Of what?"

She shook her head with her eyes glistening as one tear rolled down her cheek. "He doesn't know. He's confused. He doesn't understand . . ."

Nick squinted, glancing from her to Victor.

"He's trying, Nicholas," she said, her synthetic voice softening. "He wants to help. But he's afraid."

"What the hell is he afraid of? We're not going to hurt him."

"He's afraid if he tells us the truth, he'll die. That whatever this is ravaging his body will kill him."

"What does one have to do with the other?" Lilly asked.

Beverly shook her head. "I don't know. Neither does he."

Victor's hand snapped out with surprising speed to clamp down on Nick's shoulder as he rolled again onto his side. His olive tone skin was sallow and ashen, glistening with sweat, and his black hair clung to his forehead. Dark eyes darted back and forth, without focus.

"Were at war," Victor said finally, fighting to steady his ragged breath. "Four hundred years. We lost . . ." he trailed off, and rolled back onto the bed. Victor's hand slid heavy and limp from Nick's shoulder, his eyes staring at the ceiling as he licked cracked lips. "Plotted revenge for two thousand years . . . found you."

"He believes the Umani are our only salvation," Beverly's voice carried softly.

"I have no interest in trading one pain-in-the-ass alien race for another," Nick said, shaking his head. "They could come here for the sole purpose of blowing the Areth to hell and back, and who gives a damn if the human race goes along with them."

"No!" Victor shouted, but as soon as the word left his lips, he screamed as his body arched off the bed. Agony tinged the air, leaving gooseflesh on Nick's arms.

"That's it. Everyone out," Lilly demanded, standing to lean over Victor and hold him to the bed with her hands on his chest. "Now!"

Victor hissed, sucking air through clenched teeth. "They are you."

Then he went limp, his body flopping down on the mattress like a discarded dishrag. Nick rolled onto his feet and moved back to give her the access she needed as she scanned his vital signs again.

"Damn," she mumbled. "He's slipped into a coma."

One of the nurses left the cell without waiting for Lilly's next command. Nick stepped back until he stood with the bars to his back. He gripped Beverly's elbow, her body still shaking with small tremors, and pulled her to stand beside him. In moments, the nurse returned with more assistance rolling a gurney. They lifted Victor's limp body from the bed to the gurney.

"Doc—" Nick started to say.

"I don't know," Lilly cut him off, pausing only briefly at the cell door to look at Nick and Beverly. "I don't know."

"I've been worried about you," CJ said softly as she rolled to turn into Nick's embrace. "It's after midnight."

"Shush," he whispered in the dark, his lips skimming across her forehead, his breath warming her skin. "I'm here now. Go back to sleep."

CJ slid her hands over his side and chest, loving the heat his body threw off. Sleeping with Nick Tanner was like sleeping beside a pile of hot coals. She smiled against his skin as the realization that she shared his bed once again drifted over her like a warm breeze.

"Is everything all right? What kept you so late?"

Nick's long fingers followed the line of her jaw, brushing her lips, as he sought her out in the darkness. His thumb stroked her mouth with tender care, and CJ felt something else in the touch. She shifted to rise above his chest, looking down at him. Her eyes adjusted to the darkness, finding enough light to see his face. His brown eyes appeared black as he looked up at her. He brushed hair back from her cheek, curling it behind her ear.

"Nicky?"

His fingers curled behind her neck and drew her down until their lips met, and CJ moaned softly as her sleepy body came to life with his kiss. With their lips locked and her head held firmly between his palms, Nick rolled them until his weight pressed her into the bed and she relished the delicious sensation. She pressed her hands against his back as his seeking mouth found the curve of her throat, eliciting a soft moan from her.

All other thoughts vanished as his hands slid beneath her tee shirt.

CHAPTER TWENTY

C J felt the tension in Nick's body as he sat beside her; it radiated out from him like a force field and made her skin tingle. At a glance, nothing appeared unusual for him, his hands linked together on the table and his eyes trained on the data scrolling on their monitors. His jaw was firm set, his shoulders tight, and his eyes sharp as they read.

When he had run down the details of the meeting with the general, and the subsequent session with Victor, CJ had been stunned. Never had anyone within Phoenix ever imagined an opportunity like this. To assume that Humans and the Areth were the only sentient beings in the Galaxy would be arrogant, and she preferred to leave the arrogance to the Areth. To suddenly know who 'the others' were, and where they might be . . . she wondered if it was a dream come true, or a dream too good to be true.

She glanced sideways again at Nick, watching his fingertips drum on the table.

The center of the table glowed blue and a three-dimensional image of the galaxy appeared over their heads. A white core marked the center, with strings of pink/purple nebulae and clusters of bright starts swirling out until the edges faded and disappeared into the blurred regions of the galaxy's edges. A red dot glowed off center from the core indicating the coordinates.

"According to Victor, the home planet of the Umani should be here," Damian explained from the other side of the table as he tapped commands into his station. "In comparison, we are here." A blue light flashed and glowed on the opposite side of the core.

Nick shifted forward. "About fifty-thousand light years."

"That's a very close estimate, Colonel. The science of measuring galactic distances isn't exact, but our solar system is approximately twenty-four thousand light years from the center of the galaxy, and the Umani coordinates are approximately twenty-five thousand light years in the other direction."

Nick leaned back in his chair, pinching his lower lip between his fingers. Part of her wanted to focus on him, try to read what was wrong. She knew now wasn't the time or place. Instead, she scrolled through the data and read it again quickly.

"How confident are we of this information?" she asked.

Damian shook his head. "There's no way for us to be absolutely sure. We have no way to corroborate any of it. Only Victor's word."

"And . . ." CJ prompted.

"Victor believed it to be true," Beverly said, her synthesized voice low. "So much so that he may have given his life to tell us everything he could."

CJ shifted her stare between Nick and Beverly. *What the hell happened in that cell?* More had to have gone on than the succinct, bullet-point breakdown of events Nick had rattled off during his explanation. Beverly was obviously shaken up, and Nick looked ready to eat nails.

"How's he doing now?" General Castleton asked from the head of the table.

"Lilly reported there has been little change since last night," Damian answered, reading from a piece of paper he picked up from the table. "His temperature has stabilized, so has his respirations and heart rate. But he is still completely unresponsive."

"She still doesn't know the reason?" the general asked.

Damian shook his head, looking directly at the general. "No, sir."

General Castleton sighed, rubbing his fingers over his mouth in thought. "So, chances are the only information we might ever have is what we've got. Unless we manage to hack into an Areth database and find where they're hiding their information on the Umani." He shook his head, tapping the table with his knuckles. "It's too soon to try right now."

"What do we do?" Beverly asked. "Victor was adamant that we should make every effort to contact the Umani."

Nick drew a slow breath, sitting forward. His tone was metered, slow, and almost heavy. "The Umani are nearly fifty-thousand light years away from us. We can't exactly send a 'hey, how ya doin' and invite them for dinner." He waved his hand and arched an eyebrow. "Hell, we don't know for sure if we *want* to. We all keep forgetting the source of this information . . . an *Areth*."

"*If* we wanted to, what would our options be?" CJ asked, glancing between Nick, Damian and the general.

Nick remained quiet and the general nodded to Damian.

"We have no ships that can travel that far. I'm not talking just within Phoenix. I'm talking at all. Earth Force gliders have wormhole initiators and the ability to manually navigate the anomalies, but for short jumps only. The Areth ships in orbit over Earth can travel that far, but they're not going to share. In the last forty years, the focus of Areth 'sharing' has been in medical technology, not astrophysics."

"And any form of communication would take thousands of years to reach their side of the galaxy," CJ said with resignation.

Nick pushed back from the table and stood, his hands shoved into his pockets to pace slowly away from the table to the wall, and back again.

General Castleton's gaze followed Nick. He said nothing, and after a few moments, turned back to the monitors. "Still, it's good information to have. More than we had before, which says something. We just keep working on the problem and look for an opportunity to find out more."

He rapped his knuckles on the table and nodded, casually dismissing the small group. CJ slid her chair back, but didn't stand as the others filed out of the room. Nick still stood several feet from the holovid table, his back to them and his stance rigid. General Castleton walked to him, and Nick turned the moment the general spoke. CJ couldn't hear what they said, only saw Nick nod at the general's words and then tilt his head in her direction. The general nodded and left for his office.

Nick walked back to her, holding his hand out as he approached. When his palm slid across hers, he pulled her to her feet and guided her arms around him until he held her in a gentle embrace. Despite the smile on his lips, CJ saw shadows behind his eyes and tried to see past them.

"What's wrong?" she asked.

"I need to stay and talk to the general." Nick pressed a kiss to her forehead. "I'll be back soon. We have a date tonight," he said with a grin and a bob of his eyebrows.

"Nick—"

He stopped her question with a kiss, holding her face in his large hands. "I promise."

CJ crossed her arms over her body as he walked away, swallowing against the knot in her gut that told her something was wrong. Especially when she realized Nick had neither confirmed nor denied anything was wrong. He hadn't lied. She'd give him that. He was hiding something, and that frightened her even more.

"I'm not tryin' to get in your pants, sweetheart."

The weighted baritone of Lieutenant Jason Quinn followed her down the hall, and Lilly slowed her step before she turned. She carefully schooled her grin, not wanting him to know just yet how much she loved his persistence. He strode toward her, his walk rolling and loose, and he didn't stop until he stood close enough for the scent of his leather jacket and cologne to mingle and tickle her senses. He raised an arm and leaned into the wall, his stance cocky and casual. Typical pilot stuff.

She arched an eyebrow. "You're not? I'm not sure if I'm delighted or insulted."

One corner of his nicely shaped lips—and Lilly couldn't help but notice how the lower lip was just slightly fuller—tipped up in a cocky smile and he dipped his chin before looking at her again. His green eyes were disarming enough to make three-quarters of the single women on base practically fall prostrate before him. Heck, probably half of the married women as well. One of a dozen reasons why she didn't date pretty flyboys.

"I assure you, Miss Lilly, my intentions are completely honorable," he said in a low, slow voice tinged with a slight southern drawl as he pressed a hand to his chest.

Lilly laughed and shook her head. She leaned closer to him, angling her chin so her lips almost brushed the dark stubble that shadowed his jaw. "How disappointing, Lieutenant."

His deep laugh echoed off the base walls as she walked away.

Lilly blinked and forced herself to focus again on the world around her, a gentle ache settling around her heart as she let go of the memory. Thoughts of Jace crept over her at the oddest moments, spurred on by the simplest things. At first, she braced herself against them, afraid of the painful backwash. None came, not like she expected. Just a heavy melancholy mingled with the sweet comfort each trip into the past brought her. Eventually, she knew the pain would come. For now, she accepted the moments of peace.

She sighed and analyzed the bio-readings on the monitor beside Victor's bed, the task she had come into the small isolation room to complete. Lilly shook her head, rubbing her hands across her forehead to ward off the headache that was almost always inevitable after trying to find the source of Victor's mystery ailment. He had half a dozen symptoms at any given time, all subject to change at will, and none of which could be connected with any medical semblance to any known disease.

She had attempted treating the symptoms themselves, rather than the source of their cause, but that had proven to be ineffective. Antibiotics and analgesics to bring down fever seemed to force his body temperature to plummet to dangerous levels, only to rocket sky high again when she tried to warm him. She had finally resorted to the one treatment all doctors hated . . . none at all.

He had finally stabilized.

His core temperature was slightly elevated at one hundred and one, but it had maintained that level within a point or two for the last twelve hours since she ceased all IV treatments except for fluids. Blood oxygen readings were within acceptable parameters, and she kept the saturation level of his CPAP tube at fifty percent. His pulse had been thready when he first slipped into the coma, and had seesawed between tachycardia and bradycardia for the first several hours. That, too, now seemed steady and rhythmic.

His brain scans were another matter. Despite his unresponsiveness to outside stimulus, including physical pain, his brain activity readings were erratic and excessive, even for someone fully conscious and aware of their surroundings. The output from the Thalamus and Hypothalamus regions of his brain was intense and unpredictable, leading Lilly to believe that even in his comatose state, Victor was haunted by whatever fear had held him prisoner before his collapse.

She stood near the head of his bed, taking in the details of his relaxed features. His olive-toned skin had regained its color, although his slightly sunken cheeks indicated that he hadn't eaten well since arriving at the mountain. Perspiration no longer plastered his short black hair to his head as fever wracked his body, and his skin didn't glisten with moisture. Thick lashes lay against his cheeks as he slept. He looked like any of her patients, just as human as she or any other person on the base. His blood ran as red, his heart beat the same steady rhythm.

Yet, something set him apart . . . and tortured him to the brink of death.

The calm of his sleeping expression belied what she knew went on within his mind, and the caregiver in her wished she could ease it for him. Sedatives could only calm the body, not the mind. If his mind was the enemy, she was at a loss as to which weapons to use.

"Will he live?"

Lilly startled, and turned to see Michael standing at the foot of the bed. So engrossed in her thoughts, she hadn't heard him come into the room and had no idea how long he had been there. His gaze stayed on Victor, his hands curled around the footboard. She recognized the same silent strength in him she had seen in his father from the first moment they met, restrained and controlled, and yet Michael's control didn't hold the fierceness Nick's did.

She shifted her eyes from Michael to Victor, her shoulders dropping. "I don't know." As a doctor, she hated two phrases. *I don't know* and *I did everything I could* because both were always inadequate.

Michael left the foot of the bed to stand behind her, his chest almost brushing her shoulders as he moved between her and the monitoring equipment set up alongside Victor's bed. He reached past her to lay a hand across Victor's forehead, holding it there unmoving. Lilly felt like an intruder, knowing the two men had some connection she didn't understand, and stepped free of the space between Michael and the bed frame.

"I'll leave you with him. If you need me, I'll be right outside."

Michael turned his head, his gaze shifting over her with a slight furrow forming between his eyes. "I interrupted your work."

"No," Lilly said, shaking her head. "Stay with your friend. He needs you as much as he needs me."

Michael nodded and looked down to Victor's still features. Lilly stepped backwards through the doorway and pulled the metal-framed glass door closed. The isolation room was set in a corner of the infirmary and equipped with air filters in case of air-born contagions or the need of purification for the patient. The walls that faced out into the open space were made of glass with blinds inside for privacy. As she walked away, she glanced back to see Michael pull a chair to the side of Victor's bed and sit down.

He would be there, waiting and watching, until it was time to come see her.

"*H*ow are the headaches you told me about?"

Lilly ran her hands along the sides of Michael's neck and pressed her fingers to the glands beneath his jaw as she asked the question. Her bioscan reader told her many things, but her hands, eyes, and ears often told her more. The tendons along the column of his neck leading into his shoulders were taut and unforgiving, his muscles hard bunches beneath her touch.

"They aren't as severe," he answered, and she caught his flinch as she pressed against the top of his right shoulder.

"What about frequency?"

His eyes followed her as she moved around him, but he didn't seem at all self-conscious sitting on the exam table shirtless. Some of the other survivors who came with Michael were almost violently afraid of being exposed; two ends of the same terrible spectrum. She had pulled the curtain around them for privacy, but was pretty sure having his body exposed at someone else's will, for whatever torture they chose to inflict, was something Michael was accustomed to. The thought prickled at the back of her throat and made her bite down.

"Fewer. In the evenings most often."

She asked him more questions, and was relieved to hear his answers. His blood work showed better levels across the board, and the inflammation in his muscles and joints had lessened a great deal. The fatigue she saw in his eyes worried her, and the tension in his body. Both would contribute to his headaches, and she could treat them, but she preferred to cure them at the source.

Lilly picked up her handheld recorder and entered some information to Michael's file as he pulled his black tee shirt over his head. She turned to lean her hips against the edge of the exam table and crossed her arms.

"You're not sleeping well."

She didn't ask the question. Lilly was pretty sure Michael wouldn't lie to her if she asked him directly, but didn't want to leave it to chance. His gaze shifted down for a moment before meeting hers again, and he just shook his head, barely more than a slight jerk to the side.

"Do you know why?"

He looked away completely then and slid off the table to his feet. Lilly waited while he walked to the curtain and took some of the blue cotton between his fingers, rubbing it as if examining the texture and feel. The moments stretched, and Lilly hopped up to sit on the table.

"Whatever you tell me stays with me, Michael," she finally said. "Even if I weren't your doctor, you can trust me. I trusted you with my secret." He looked over his shoulder at her, and she caught the way his eyes dropped to her stomach, but pushed on. "Tell me."

Their gazes met and held for several beats of her heart before he walked back to her. He pushed one hand into his pocket and rested the palm of the other on the white sheet that covered the table.

"I wake up screaming," he said in a low voice

"Nightmares?"

He shook his head. "I don't know. I wake up so fast, I don't remember." Michael dropped his chin toward his chest, his never-idle fingers toying with the sheet.

Lilly reached out to rest her hand on his arm, and his eyes shifted to the point of contact. "Have you had nightmares like that since coming here?"

"In New Mexico I didn't dream."

"At all?"

"No."

The firm levelness of his voice confirmed for Lilly what she had suspected the moment he mentioned the dreams. "You're fighting sleep."

His eyes shifted to her, and then away again.

"Michael, you can't do this to yourself. You need to rest. If you have one—" His fists curled into the sheet. "Are you worried what will happen if you have a nightmare?"

He winced, hiding it by keeping his chin down.

Lilly moved to her feet to stand immediately in front of him, close enough that he had to look right at her. "Michael, you *know* nothing will ever happen to you like the things that happened in New Mexico. No one will hurt you for having a nightmare. Especially not your father. Tell me you know this," she said adamantly as she fought to keep her voice low and personal.

He nodded. "I know."

"Then help me understand—"

"It hurts him to know," he said, cutting her off.

Lilly couldn't breathe for several seconds as the reality of Michael's words sank in. He had known his father a handful of days, and even after the hell he had lived for the last twenty-five years, his soul forced him to hide his own pain to protect a man he barely knew. Tears prickled her eyes and emotion choked her, and all she could think to do was hug him. His entire body tensed when she threw her arms around his neck, but moments later, he hesitantly returned the embrace, his hands splayed on her back with the barest of touches.

"It would hurt him more to know you're keeping this from him," she said against his shoulder because she wasn't ready to pull back yet. "I know this is hard, and you're both learning. But he'd want to know."

She felt his nod and his hold on her tightened.

"*I*s he asleep?"

Nick guided Caitlin into the apartment, his hand at the small of her back, and glanced around the dimly lit room. "I think so."

"I'm awake."

Nick gave the command for the lights to increase to a low level, just enough so he and Caitlin could walk without tripping over Dog or Michael's shoes. Michael partially sat up and twisted to lean on his elbow and Dog lifted his head from where it was draped over Michael's legs. He wore no shirt, and as the blanket uncovered his torso, Nick had to tamp down the surge of anger that burned in the back of his throat like acid. Even in the low ambient lighting, he saw the scars and marks that flawed his son's body.

"Why are you still up?" Caitlin asked, sitting down on the table beside the couch.

She reached out and brushed back some of Michael's hair with her fingers; a natural act of comfort and familiarity and something squeezed around Nick's heart. He supposed that if he were a man prone to jealous thoughts, he would have felt something different at seeing his lover touch his son with such ease. It wasn't jealousy.

If anything, it was heartache.

"I haven't fallen asleep."

Nick suppressed his smile, but doubted he was successful. *Of course . . . he was up because he hadn't fallen asleep. Made perfect sense. Duh!*

Caitlin glanced up at Nick, smiling herself. "Okay. It's late. Try to get some rest." She rubbed her hand on Michael's arm as she stood and headed toward the bedroom.

Michael pillowed his arm behind his head, his eyes set on Nick. Even in the low light, Nick felt Michael's gaze. He started to follow Caitlin, but paused, staring down at his son.

"Everything all right, Michael?"

He didn't answer right away, and Nick waited, watching him. Then he nodded, a slight tick of his chin. "I'm fine."

"Good. We'll be in the other room if you need us."

"I know."

Michael stared at the ceiling, his arms tucked behind his head. The room was in darkness save the small line of light beneath the bedroom door. He listened intently, hearing the muffled tone of Caitlin's voice followed by a deep chuckle from his father.

He closed his eyes, letting the calm wrap around him.

Moments passed, and finally the light went out. The sounds of their voices stopped. Michael was tired, so tired it pulled at his limbs and pushed him into the lounge. In the past few days, he'd found his strength tapped out after even a few minutes activity, and he had dared only find moments of rest when his father was away from the quarters. Lilly was right. He knew she was right. He couldn't sustain this pattern much longer.

He swallowed hard, and blinked his eyes in the darkness.

Perhaps she was right about everything.

Nick jerked awake, instinct immediately breaking through the fog left behind by sleep. He blinked and raised his head off his pillow, glancing around the darkness of the bedroom. Nothing was out of place. Nothing seemed unusual.

He was on his right side, his arm stretched out along the mattress, and Caitlin lay curled against him with her back to his chest. Her cheek rested on his arm, using him as her pillow. Nick carefully brushed her hair back from her cheek and she hummed softly in her sleep. He wanted to kiss her shoulder, but she wore one of his tee shirts tonight and her bare skin was covered.

Wide-awake, Nick rolled onto his back and stared at the ceiling, wondering what woke him. "Lights," he said softly. "Night. Very dim."

A small row of lights along the headboard of the bed glowed softly, casting a gray shadow over the bedroom. In this position, his fingertips soon started tingling and he gently worked to slide his arm from beneath Caitlin's head. She shifted, grumbled softly, but quickly settled back into the pillows.

As he sat up, flexing his hand to resume the flow of blood to his fingers, a muffled cry snapped his attention to the door. Nick tossed back the covers and managed to pull on his pants as he bolted for the door.

"Lights," he demanded, scanning the main room.

Michael was on his back on the lounge, the blanket kicked away, his arms spread out away from his side and his neck arched off the pillow. His muffled groans had pulled Nick from sleep, he realized now, as Michael thrashed on the makeshift bed. Dog whined and looked from Nick to Michael, pacing back and forth. Nick spanned the room in three long strides, kneeling in the space between the lounge and the table.

"Michael," he said firmly. "Michael!"

His son didn't respond, his entire back bowing off the couch as he dug his bare feet into the cushion for leverage and another strangled cry ripped from his throat. Nick held Michael's head in his hands, Michael's hair damp beneath his fingers from the sweat that covered him. He fought the hold, twisting his neck against Nick's grip, but his arms remained out away from his side.

Michael forced a muffed sound through clenched teeth, his cheeks puffing as he tried to speak.

"Michael, wake up!" Nick demanded. "Caitlin!"

She came through the bedroom door seconds later. "Dear God," she whispered as she rushed to them and knelt at Michael's head.

"I can't wake him up," Nick told her panicking, bitter bile lodging in the back of his throat.

"You shouldn't," she said in a soft voice, leaning over to speak near Michael's ear. "Shush, Michael. It's all right. It's all right."

She continued to speak in a low voice, and with a gentle touch, urged Nick to move his hands from Michael's head to his shoulders. "Just hold him, keep him from hurting himself."

Michael kicked out, his ankle impacting with the concrete wall above the back of the lounge, and Nick flinched. Everything in him demanded he shake his son awake and end the nightmare, but he grit his teeth and braced his lower arms against Michael's chest as Caitlin stroked his hair.

"You're safe, Michael. You're safe," she repeated, smoothing his hair back from his forehead.

Moments passed and his body relaxed his back easing onto the lounge cushions. His violent fight for breath eased to a steady rhythm again, and the rapid pounding of his heart against his ribs slowed. Finally, after what felt like an eternity, Michael drew a long breath, his body shuddering as he released it and all tension dropped away.

Nick looked to Caitlin, who still smoothed Michael's hair but had stopped whispering in his ear. She met Nick's stare, tears glistening in her eyes.

"He'll be okay now." She reached out and touched Nick's cheek. "He probably won't even remember."

Nick sat back on the floor, setting his elbow on one raised knee to run a shaking hand over his face.

"I swear to God, Caitlin," he said in a low voice that hissed past his clenched teeth. "If I ever find her, I will choke the life out of her with my bare hands."

She scooted toward him on her knees and leaned over to press a kiss to his forehead. Nick wrapped his arms around her and she turned within his hold to sit in the space between his legs. They sat together for the next hour and watched Michael sleep.

CHAPTER TWENTY-ONE

"One thing you have to learn about women, Michael," Nick said as he used his leg to hoist up the boxes he held. "For every one possession a man has, a woman has four."

Michael smiled widely, and looked past Nick to the bedroom door behind him. "Does that explain why we moved out of our quarters in one trip, and this is Caitlin's third?"

"*Ex*-actly."

Caitlin came out of the bedroom, a small box balanced on her hip and a disgruntled look on her face. "If moving my things is too much work for the two of you, I can find someone else."

Nick chuckled, leaning over to kiss the top of her head when she stopped beside him. "Michael and I can handle it just fine." Caitlin tipped her head back to look at him, and Nick took the opportunity to kiss her lips.

Michael paused, a box held in front of him, watching them. Nick was starting to expect his son's silent study, not with just him and Caitlin, but with most everyone and everything. Watching. Absorbing. Taking it all in. Nick hitched his chin toward the door.

"Take that box to the new place. I'll make sure she didn't forget anything and we'll be right there." He exaggerated the grunt when Caitlin elbowed him.

"Watch yourself, Tanner," she warned.

Michael's grin tipped up and his shoulders shook with a silent chuckle. The amount of restraint he still inflicted on himself grated on Nick, despite the fact that in the short time since coming home, Nick had seen a change in his son. Some of the 'fight or flight' tension that had pulled him tight as a bowstring when he first came to the mountain had relaxed. He stopped apologizing every time he didn't understand something, or thought he had done something wrong.

There had been no dreams the last two nights, and Michael looked more rested than he had in his first days at the base. Nick found himself waking at least twice a night and checking on his son, but nothing had ripped him from his sleep like that first blood-chilling scream.

He hoped it never happened again. The thought of leaving his son alone . . .

Nick blinked and focused when Michael spoke

"I'd like to go visit Alexander," Michael said. "Would you mind if I took Dog?"

"Sure. Go ahead," Nick answered. Michael nodded and turned to go, but Nick called after him and he stopped. "We're your parents, not your watchdogs."

Michael's eyes shifted between Nick and Caitlin. Then he nodded, and whistled for Dog as he moved to the door. Dog followed on Michael's heels, ears bouncing and tail wagging.

"I think Dog has a new master," Caitlin said as she stepped away from his side to make a slow walk around the single quarters.

"Fine with me. I don't have to fight him for the bed anymore." He waited until she looked his way, and winked at her. "Now, I just have you to contend with."

Caitlin's gaze slid away and she set down her box. She walked behind the long lounge, her hand running along the back. "Every night . . ." she said, her voice trailing off as she avoided looking in his direction.

Something squeezed in Nick's chest, but he pushed it aside and ignored it for now. Eventually, he knew he'd have to face reality. Just not yet. Not right now.

"Every night," he repeated.

Nick set his own boxes down and walked to her, taking her hands as soon as he was close enough. Caitlin raised her head, her eyes tracking up slowly to look into his face. She released one of his hands and slid her palm over his chest to rest above his heart, the simple touch enough to warm his blood. Her eyes shifted as she took in the details of his face. Nick stepped closer and curled his hands around her hips.

"Something on your mind?"

"Do you realize what you just said to Michael?"

Nick squinted, not sure where she was going. "Pretty sure. He's almost twenty-six years old. He doesn't have to account to—"

"His parents," she cut off.

Nick stared at her, not getting her point.

"You called *us* his *parents*."

He grinned, pulling her closer with a gentle tug. "Did I . . ."

"You don't think that won't be a little confusing for him? Hell, Nick, it's confusing for *me!*" She stepped free of his hold and walked away, her arms crossed. When she reached the now empty desk in the corner, she turned and leaned onto the edge, looking at him. "My logical mind reminds me I'm only five years older than him. But . . ." Caitlin sighed and closed her eyes.

"But what?"

"But he makes me feel so old sometimes."

"You? Try having your lover remind you she's barely older than your kid, then see how old you feel," he said, mocking a low grumble.

Caitlin smiled, just a small grin touching her lips, and her eyes sparkled when she looked at him again. "I mean the way he looks at the world, Nicky. Everything is so new, so interesting. I know he probably had to 'grow up' years before he should have, just to be able to deal with *everything*, but in some ways he's like a child. When I start seeing him that way, I remind myself just how old he is . . ." She huffed. "And then I feel old."

Nick walked to her and bracketed her body with his thighs, bending his knees to look her straight in the face. He laid his hands on her shoulders and nudged her chin with his thumbs until she consented to look at him.

"Okay, so we've established you couldn't actually have given birth to him." His gentle teasing earned him another small smile. "But there is no one I would rather have with me right now, helping me." *Taking care of him when I can't.*

"How do you know I'm any good at this?"

Nick popped up an eyebrow and tilted his head. "You're kidding, right?"

"It all feels very permanent," she said softly. Her voice cracked slightly, and she paused to swallow.

A knot twisted in Nick's chest, and for the first time since she came back from New Mexico, he questioned their return to being lovers. If he hadn't been such a hardass from the beginning, he would have seen it coming the first time he looked up and saw her at the cabin. It was inevitable. As undeniable as the first time he ever saw her and knew he had to know her name. It felt right. After the first kiss at the top of the mountain, he was a done man. Everything had been inescapable from that point on.

So he thought.

"Do you not want this?" he asked, finding it hard to say the words.

"You know I do, but I want to make sure this is what you want." Her voice was low and heavy, almost lost in the space between them.

"What makes you think it isn't?"

Caitlin swallowed and blinked. "Just weeks ago, you told me—"

"Forget what I said. I was wrong."

"No, Nicky. You weren't," she said, shaking her head enough that the ends of her short, blond hair brushed across her cheeks. "I know neither one of us wants to get into this conversation again, but we both know who was at fault when we ended."

"It doesn't matter."

"Doesn't it? Won't it always be there?"

"No," he said emphatically.

"Nicky—"

Nick stopped her with his thumb pressed against her lips as he slid his hand along her jaw. Her blue eyes shifted up. Holding the stare, Nick smoothed the pad of his thumb across her mouth. Her lips parted, her breath warm on his skin, and he leaned in to kiss her. He took his time, letting their breath mingle and their tongues slide together as he tipped her head to deepen the contact. Cold heat flashed through him, and he pulled her closer, fighting his body's need to tug her clothes free until he felt skin-on-skin. Instead, he pressed his fingers deeper into her hair and swallowed the soft purr as it escaped her throat.

When the rhythm of the kiss demanded either they stop or kick the door shut and sink to the floor, Nick pulled back and laid his cheek against hers as he wrapped her in his arms. Her hands slid along his sides to his back as they both struggled to find even breath.

"No more questions?" he asked against her ear.

She shook her head within the curve of his neck. "No more questions."

Nick pressed a quick kiss to her forehead before he stepped back to retrieve the boxes he had set down. "Let's get you moved in. Castleton already has people waiting for this place."

*B*everly raised her hand to catch Lilly's eye as she looked up from the bruised knee of her young patient. Lilly smiled, waving back, motioning for Beverly to wait near the door of the infirmary until she finished her work. After a few minutes, the little girl Lilly attended was back on her feet, heading out to play again, and Lilly crossed the room.

"Hi," Beverly read on Lilly's lips. "I wasn't expecting to see you until after dinner. You were just here a few hours ago."

Beverly nodded and smiled. "I know. I'm not in the way, am I?"

"No, not at all." The two women turned and walked side-by-side toward the back of the infirmary. "His care isn't very active right now. I'm keeping him warm, hydrated, and nourished. It seems when I do anything more, his condition worsens."

"You must feel almost helpless," Beverly offered, sympathetic to Lilly's frustration.

"There's no 'almost' about it. More than likely, the visits from you and Michael probably do more for him than anything I'm doing. Based on his brain activity, I don't believe he is in the deepest level of coma. He could very well be hearing everything around him, and knowing there are people here might be just what he needs."

"I don't know how much my presence helps," Beverly said as they reached the glass door of the isolation room. "We never met until just before . . ." She didn't know how to put into words the events of that night, so she let her thoughts trail off.

"It doesn't matter. Remember what I said. Talk to him. If it helps, bring a book. I've seen family members read through half a dozen novels waiting for someone to recover from a coma."

"Did it work?"

Lilly smiled and pulled the door open. "It didn't hurt."

Beverly stepped through the open door and immediately felt the change in the air. Within the enclosed space, the air was purer and cooler, rushing through her nostrils like a gust of wind on a winter day. The door closed behind her, and the pressure on her skin shifted as the airlock reengaged. She felt lightheaded for the first few breaths as her body adjusted to the higher concentration of oxygen. None of the sensations were a surprise. She had been here over a dozen times in the last five days.

The crackle in the air didn't surprise her, either. No one else felt it, and somehow the glass walls of the room worked as a buffer whenever she wasn't here. The fear and confusion that had pushed him to this state hadn't disappeared when he collapsed. It had lessened, but the feelings were still intense enough to push against Beverly and send gooseflesh over her skin whenever she was near him.

She walked to the chair that sat beside his bed. She and Michael had fallen into an unplanned pattern of visitation with Victor. Only once had she come when he was here, but his presence always lingered behind after he was gone. Whatever connection the two men shared, it was strong, and she was sure Michael had much more to offer than she.

She couldn't stop coming.

The moment she had seen Victor, his emotions had slammed into her like an out of control air tram. Never had she experienced such intensity from a single person. Strong emotions, yes, but once she felt the first nudge of their strength she had always been able to put up walls. When Jace Quinn died, the mass sorrow that had swept the base had been so vast she had been forced to shut herself away to defend herself from it. Attending his memorial service had been out of the question. This was one man . . . one man and more fear and confusion than she could measure.

Beverly sat down, folding her hands in her lap, and leaned forward so she could still clearly see his face. She didn't expect him to suddenly open his eyes and speak, but watching him helped her feel more connected to him. His countenance was relaxed, his head turned slightly on the pillow so his face tilted toward her. Thick black lashes curled against his cheeks, and his short hair fell across his forehead haphazardly. Two days' worth of unshaved beard darkened his jaw, accentuating the sharp lines of his features. The planes and ridges of his profile were subtle in comparison to men like Nick Tanner and Jason Quinn, his build more tendon than muscle. He reminded her of the track athletes from the Olympic Games held twenty years before. Tall and lithe, his size belied his strength.

"Hello, Victor."

She didn't know what else to say. What could she say to a man she didn't know?

Beverly shifted forward, sitting on the edge of the chair to be closer to the bed. She raised her arm to rest her hand on the bedcovers, but hesitated before letting her fingers touch the soft cotton. Victor's hand lay palm down at his side on top of the blankets, and her position brought her own hand within a breath of touching his.

Contact.

It was something she both feared and craved.

She flipped her long braid back over her shoulder and looked again to Victor's face. His lips were parted slightly, his chest slowly rising and falling with each breath. Despite her desire to keep the memories at bay, her mind filled with images of Victor writhing in pain, his face glistening with fever and sweat. He had looked at her, their eyes connecting, and she had felt a jolt. Like two live wires connecting.

"What haunts you, Victor?" she asked the silent room.

A sudden awareness shimmered over her, her skin tingling to the roots of her hair. She glanced around, half expecting to see Lilly standing behind her, but no one was there. Beverly looked back to Victor, but he hadn't moved. She raised her hand and held it hovering over his brow, an unseen force tugging at the center of her chest, nearly demanding she touch him.

"I'm afraid, Victor."

The air in the room closed in around her, pushing on her chest, and Beverly blinked against burning tears. Her blood ran cold and her stomach clenched, a bitter taste hovering in the back of her throat. She glanced over her shoulder again, and saw Lilly standing on the other side of the infirmary through the glass. Her back was to the isolation room. *Would she stop me?*

Swallowing the pungent taste of fear, Beverly focused on Victor once again. She fought to steady her breathing and her hand shook, but there was no doubt in her mind that this was what she needed to do. Closing her eyes, Beverly laid her palm against Victor's temple and drew in a sharp breath.

Help me!

She jerked her hand back and snapped her eyes open, gasping for breath. Her whole body trembled, coated in a cold sweat, and she slowly eased back into the chair, feeling depleted. With her elbow braced on the arm of the chair, she held her forehead in her hand and stared at Victor's unmoving form.

"Dear God," she said. "What is happening to you?"

"These are the schematics for the modifications," Damian said, handing Nick the clipboard-size computer interface. "The hanger chief says he can have this done in seventy-two hours, sir."

Nick examined the digital image on the screen, reading estimated input and output for the modified engines and O_2 recyclers. "Have McClintock review the drive source figures. I need them to be within no less than point-zero-two percent efficiency."

"Yes, sir."

"How are the eggheads coming with the data files?"

"They're progressing, sir. The glider systems will be equipped with a passive kill switch. Unless engaged, the system will wipe itself clean at a specified time."

Nick nodded, handing the interface back to Damian. "Thank you, Captain. Keep me updated." He focused again on the fuel burn estimates on his own monitor screen in Command.

"Yes, sir." Damian turned to walk away, but paused and came back. "Permission to speak with you, Colonel."

Nick looked up, then hitched his chin, and waved a hand at the empty chair beside him. "Pull up a seat, Captain."

Damian pulled out the chair and sat down, setting the interface on the table. Nick leaned back, bracing his chin against his hand, one finger running along the side of his face to his temple.

"Sir, I know you don't need to hear this from anyone, but I wanted to tell you how much I respect what you're doing."

"It has to be done, Captain."

Damian shrugged, shaking his head slightly. "Perhaps. Some say not. Either way, I know you are the one who brought this plan to General Castleton. In your position, sir, I'm not sure I'd make the same call."

Nick looked away, focusing on some non-distinct point on the other side of the room. What Damian didn't know was that he was within two seconds of calling the whole damn thing off about ninety percent of the time.

Every time he glanced across a room to see Caitlin's smile.

Every time he shared a meal with Caitlin and Michael.

In the middle of the night, when he stared at the ceiling with Caitlin curled against his side, her hand over his heart.

Each time he found something new to teach Michael, and got to see the look of enjoyment and wonder on his face.

Every time he said 'my son' and his heart didn't ache with loss.

Every time he looked into Michael's face, and saw himself, saw the future.

Hell, yeah . . . two seconds flat.

"I appreciate that, Captain," he finally said.

"Yes, sir," Damian said, and stood. He left Nick alone again, battling with decisions he wished he never had to make.

CHAPTER TWENTY-TWO

"*M*ichael? Caitlin? Anyone home?"

Michael rolled off his bed to his feet and set down the tattered copy of *War of the Worlds* he had found that afternoon. Dog jumped to the floor, following on his heels as he stepped into the main room.

"I'm here."

Nick turned where he stood near the door. "Where's Caitlin?"

"She went to visit Lilly."

Nick nodded and motioned with his hand for Michael to follow him. "Grab a coat and come on."

"Wait."

His father paused, hand already on the doorknob. "What?"

"I don't have a coat."

"Right." Nick said, pointing a finger at Michael. "Okay . . . hang on."

Michael stood in his spot as his father disappeared into the other bedroom. Something was off with Nick's actions. Usually very controlled and precise, his father seemed distracted and unfocused.

Nick came out of the bedroom wearing a buttoned flannel shirt, the tails loose around his hips. A leather jacket draped over his arm, and he held it out as he neared the door.

"Here you go. Should fit—fits me."

Michael took it, sliding his arms into the sleeves. The heady mix of well-worn leather and familiar scent he had begun to associate with his father hit him. "Where are we going?"

Nick smiled wide, his eyes crinkling at the corners. "You'll see. Let's go." He slapped his hand on the back of Michael's shoulder and swung the door open for them to exit. "You, too, Dog."

They boarded the elevator and Nick pushed a button marked S3— three levels above the surface. The ride took several minutes as the car stopped three times to pick up and drop off other riders along the way. All the while, Nick stood against the back wall with his hands braced on the stainless steel rail that ran the circumference of the car and his ankles crossed. Dog sat between the two of them, his tail thumping against the floor each time the door opened and someone stepped inside.

Michael took a similar position to his father, leaning against the railing, pushing his hands into the pockets of the jacket. His fingers found a flat, rectangular object inside and he pulled it out. Flipping the leather square, he revealed a photograph of his father and Caitlin. Michael held the photo closer, and realized it wasn't a recent picture. They stood together, arms wrapped around each other, smiling at whoever held the camera. Nick wore jeans and a flannel shirt, almost identical to what he wore now, and Caitlin was dressed in faded denims and a yellow sweater that slid off one shoulder to reveal part of her neck and collarbone. Her hair was longer, hitting almost half way down her back and swept from her face with a clip at her crown. Nick's hair was almost completely brown, with only the early signs of gray touching him at the temples. They looked happy. Very, very happy.

Michael looked to his father. His hair was almost completely silver now, and the lines around his eyes and mouth were deeper. He was the same, nonetheless. Nick's eyes shifted to the photo.

"I wondered where I left that."

"It was taken a long time ago?"

Nick pushed away from the wall as the elevator bumped to a stop and the doors opened. Two men dressed in blue jumpsuits boarded, carrying toolboxes in each hand, and nodded in their direction. When the elevator moved again, Nick took the photo from Michael and looked at it himself.

"Over eight years. Closer to nine now. This is at the cabin I told you about."

"In Maine."

His father nodded. "We took this the first time Caitlin came to the cabin."

Michael watched as his father stared at the photo, his thumb rubbing across the image of a much younger Caitlin Montgomery. The elevator stopped again and the servicemen exited. Michael waited until they were alone before speaking again.

"Am I right that the two of you haven't been . . ." He paused to find the right word.

"Together?" his father offered.

"Yes. That you haven't been for a long time."

Nick slid the photograph into his back pocket. "You're right." His gaze connected with Michael's and he reached out to rest his hand on Michael's shoulder. "I could tell you all the reasons, if you need to know. They're not important to me anymore. Right now, I have her . . . I have you . . . and all the crap that screwed us up before is ancient history."

The elevator stopped once again, and when the doors opened, Michael followed Nick out. Dog bounded ahead, his bark echoing back off the concrete walls as he bolted left. Cold air hit Michael and he zipped the jacket half way. He glanced up and down the hallway they stood in. It looked the same as the hallways below the surface, but the air was much cooler. It smelled fresh and crisp. He remembered coming this way the night he met Lilly on the surface.

They walked to the end of the hall to the access door that led to the outside. Nick pushed and held the door open for Michael to pass by. Before he even stepped through the door, Michael paused and stared.

The landscape was brilliant white, every branch and bush coated in a blanket of pure, glistening snow. Michael had tried to imagine many times what snow would look like, but nothing born of his imagination equaled the splendor of seeing it. It took his breath away.

Large, fat flakes fell straight down, quickly coating the leaves and foliage that covered the grass. The sky was gray with only small patches of blue peeking through the clouds. Michael stepped out, his sneakers crunching on the frozen earth, and he squinted against the brilliance of the sunlight reflecting off the snow cover. He held out his hands, palms up, tipping his face to the sky. A giddy sensation twirled in his chest, and as the flakes fell on his face and cooled his lips, he laughed out loud.

The door closed behind them and Michael jogged further into the white wilderness, Dog running beside him. With the ground covered, it was more difficult to find the path he had taken several days before, but he did and soon stood on the same hill he and Lilly had sat on to stare up at the night sky. The mountain range rolled out away from them, capped and frosted with white, the air thick with falling flakes.

He heard his father's footsteps behind him, and turned to see, blinking against the flakes stuck to his lashes. "*How strange it should be that this beautiful snow, should fall on a sinner with nowhere to go,*" he said, lifting his arms out. "I read *Beautiful Snow* when I was a child, and I never understood it. Now, I think I do."

Nick pushed his hands into his pockets, a fine dusting of snow gathering on his shoulders and in his hair. "I figured you'd enjoy this."

"Thank you." His cheeks hurt from his smile.

His father just nodded and followed Michael's footsteps to stand beside him on the hilltop. Michael turned again to look across the valley. The layer of white accentuated each treetop and ledge, bringing to sharp contrast what had been mingled greens just days before. He was cold, but he didn't care. He shook his head and snow fell from his hair, leaving dark spots on the brown leather jacket. With his head tipped back, he opened his mouth and let the powdery flakes land on his tongue.

"It tastes sweet," he said, chuckling. "I never imagined snow would taste sweet."

"This probably won't last two days," Nick said. "It's too early in the year for snow to stay on the ground. The winters are longer in Maine, harder. The snow gets as high as the windows and stays for months."

"I can't wait." Michael bent down and scooped up a handful, loving the bite on his fingertips. The flakes melted quickly, leaving small drips of water on his skin. "Does it take long to get there?"

When his father didn't answer, Michael looked up from his examination of the melting snow. Nick stared at him, hands shoved in his pockets, his mouth a straight, tight line. A bunched muscle jerked along his jaw, and as Michael stared back, his gaze slid away with a tight expression. An unseen band tightened around Michael's chest and he let the snow slide from his hand.

Nick shifted, toeing the white powder with his shoe. "Michael, I need to talk to you," he said in a low, rough voice.

"What is it?" The words were hard to say, his throat suddenly tight and dry.

Nick looked up, squinting at the cloaked sun, before turning to face him. Michael studied the tight pull of his mouth and the strained squint at his eyes. Whatever it was he needed to say, it was hard.

"I need to leave."

*N*ick wanted to kick himself as soon as the words were out of his mouth. *Damn it to hell!* Michael didn't say anything, just stared at him, and Nick wished he could back up about three minutes.

"Look, that didn't come out right."

"Because I'm here?"

The question was a slam in the gut, and it took Nick several seconds to wrap his brain around his son's words. "Christ, Michael. No!"

"If you don't want—"

"Stop. Right. There," Nick snapped off, pointing a finger at him. He curled his fist until his knuckles turned white. "Don't even say it."

Michael's eyes slid from Nick's fist to his face, then he looked out across the valley. Nick watched him swallow, a flinch pulling at the corner of his eye. "Why would you leave now?"

"I have to," Nick said. Michael opened his mouth to speak, but Nick raised his hand. "Let me tell you why, okay?"

Michael nodded and shoved his hands into the jacket pockets. "Okay."

Nick took a deep breath, and told Michael all the details Victor had given them before he had slipped into the coma. The Umani. Victor's adamant belief that contact had to be made. Everything they knew. Michael listened silently as he spoke.

"Right now, Earth Force doesn't have a ship capable of making that kind of flight. We don't have extended wormhole capability or automatic navigational systems. The best we've been able to do is artificially create wormholes that'll take us maybe a thousand light years. Tops. The Areth can do it, but they're not sharing," he finally said, hoping it all would help Michael understand. "We figure we have one shot at this."

Michael's eyes shifted and he looked past Nick to the sky. The snowfall had slowed, only a spattering of flakes falling now. The air was already warming. By mid-afternoon, most of the white cover on the ground would be gone.

"You're going to fly it." There was no question in his words, and Nick knew Michael had figured most of it out in his head already. *Damn smart kid.*

"We're adapting a glider for extended flight."

Michael nodded slowly, still not looking at him. "I read about your flight records when I learned to use the computer database search." Then his eyes leveled on Nick. "There's no one better at manual wormhole flight."

"I haven't done it in a long time," Nick admitted. "But if there's a chance—"

"When?"

"Three days."

Michael's eyes slid closed and his chin tipped toward his chest. Nick stepped toward him, his shoes crunching in the fallen snow. When he stood in front of his son, he laid his hand against the side of Michael's head and Michael looked up. Nick's chest squeezed and a tight fist clenched his heart at the emotions he saw reflecting in Michael's eyes, so near the surface.

"How long will you be gone?"

Nick had to swallow against the choking thickness in his throat before he answered. "A long time. It's going to take me months just to get there, if I—"

"You will." Michael tried to smile, but Nick knew it wasn't genuine. "You're the best."

"If there were any other way . . ."

"Does Caitlin know yet?" Michael asked, clearing his throat.

"No."

"This is going to hurt her."

Nick nodded. "I know."

"When are you going to tell her?"

Nick snuffed his nose with his hand and blinked. *Damn cold weather.* "As soon as I find her." He set his hands on Michael's shoulders, looking him straight in the eye. "I need you to know, before I leave, how *proud* I am of you. I couldn't have asked for a better son." His voice cracked and was lost in the wind that swept up from the valley.

Michael nodded, and Nick pulled him into a hard embrace, slapping his hands against the leather of the jacket as he held his boy close. "Come on. It's too damn cold out here."

They started back toward the mountain entrance, then Michael turned and Nick stopped, his hand on the trunk of a white birch. "What?"

"We'll be here," Michael said. "When you get back."

Nick patted his son's arm and smiled, because words were no longer an option.

"*I*'m sorry this turned out to be a 'working' visit," Lilly said as she sat behind her desk entering data into her computer. "With the influx of new patients on the base, and all the medical problems they brought with them, I've been too busy to think. Alexander alone has been enough to keep me busy six or seven hours a day."

CJ sat on the other side of the desk, her legs crossed as she partially slouched in the chair. She studied her friend, noting the fatigue that shadowed her eyes and the lack of any true spark in her expression. She worried about Lilly. When Jace was lost, she had expected Lilly to mourn, but she seemed almost determined to refuse all acknowledgement of her husband's death. Instead, she worked from early in the morning until late at night, her mind constantly on other people and other things.

"I can help," CJ offered with a smile. "I *am* a doctor, after all. Let me take a look at the files."

"Sure. I'll have the records copied for you." Lilly shook her head and leaned on her hand. "As a geneticist, I don't know if you'll be amazed or disgusted."

"I know what science is capable of. It doesn't amaze me." CJ said, tapping the desk with her finger. "Did you find proof of genetic experimentation on many of the New Mexico survivors?"

Lilly sighed. "I have a feeling that it happened in some capacity to all of them, either before or after birth, in varying extremes."

Cold dread settled in CJ's stomach and the hairs on the back of her neck stood on end. She tried to keep her voice level when she asked her next question. "What about Michael?"

Lilly met her gaze across the desk, looking as though she contemplated answering the question. "It's not as obvious, but yes, something has happened to him." She pushed her blond hair back off her forehead, and CJ caught the slight tremble in her hand. "I've read his file over and over, and it turns my stomach every time. It doesn't read like a medical record, it reads like a diary of the Marquis de Sade. This Areth scientist—Kathleen—she tortured him, CJ."

CJ's throat tightened and she blinked against her hot tears, looking down at her hands as she tried to keep the anger in check. "You don't know," she said in a strained voice.

"Know what?"

CJ looked up. "You know Michael's mother is Areth."

"Yes," Lilly said with a nod. "How, I'm not sure since the Areth are supposed to be sterile. But yes, I know the records you found . . ." Her voice trailed off as a flash of realization shifted over her face. "Dear God."

"Kathleen is his mother."

"How . . . how could . . ." Lilly stumbled over the questions, but she didn't need to finish them. CJ understood. Lilly bowed her head and wiped her hands across her cheeks, hiding her tears from CJ. "I never connected the dots before. Dear God. CJ, how . . . how is he the man he is? How can he be so . . ."

CJ shrugged, wiping at her own cheeks. "I don't know. I guess he inherited his father's heart."

"Afternoon, ladies."

CJ and Lilly looked up to see Damian Ali standing a respectable distance from Lilly's desk, his hands clasped behind his back in a relaxed military stance. CJ smiled, heat rushing her cheeks at her emotional state. Damian bowed forward, a lopsided grin on his face and brought a data interface clipboard from behind him.

"Doctor Quinn, might I have a few minutes?"

"Sure."

CJ stood. "I'll go and let you two talk."

"Okay. Thank you for the visit. And the offer to help."

CJ left Lilly and Damian to talk and crossed the infirmary to the hall. She was almost to the elevator when she remembered the small bottle of medication Lilly had given her for Michael. She spun and headed back into the infirmary, intending to just grab the bottle and go.

Lilly now stood beside her desk with her back to CJ as she approached. Damian stood beside her and they both read off the interface board he had brought with him. CJ started to say Lilly's name when a snippet of their conversation registered.

"Nick Tanner is as physically capable as any of us to make this flight. Maybe more so. He knows, at least on some level, what to expect," Lilly said to Damian.

CJ froze, her mouth open on the verge of speaking. Once she heard Lilly's statement, she could only listen. Her blood suddenly ran cold.

"Nonetheless, General Castleton said he would feel better knowing he's sending a healthy man into space."

"He is."

"What the hell are you talking about?" CJ demanded, and both of them spun around like two children caught with their hands in the cookie jar. They exchanged glances before looking at her again. "Answer me! What are you talking about?"

"CJ . . ." Lilly began, reaching out to her.

CJ pulled back, stepping out of Lilly's reach. She didn't ask again, the heavy answer already sitting in the center of her chest. CJ walked backwards until her legs bumped one of the empty beds, her eyes still trained on Damian and Lilly. She saw remorse in Lilly's eyes, and regret in Damian's, but she didn't care. Drawing a deep, shaky breath CJ straightened her spine and walked out of the infirmary.

CHAPTER TWENTY-THREE

*N*ick opened the door to their quarters to find it shadowed in darkness, the levels unusually low for the middle of the afternoon. He stepped in and draped Michael's jacket across the kitchen counter and squinted into the darkness.

"Lights," he said firmly, and the hydrogen-gel lights along the walls and ceiling slowly brightened, increasing the ambient light in the room.

It was then he saw her, sitting in one of the main room chairs with her knees drawn to her chest and her arms wrapped around her legs. From where he stood, he saw the small tremors shaking her body as her blue eyes bore into him, her lips pressed tight and straight.

Ah, crap.

Nick dropped his head forward and braced his hand against the edge of the counter. "How did you find out?" he asked quietly after several moments of silence.

"Does it matter?" Her voice was so low and rough it almost didn't reach him across the short space. The room wasn't large, but right then it felt like a canyon. "It wasn't from you."

Nick raised his eyes and looked at her. He saw the evidence of tears left behind, her eyes red, and her expression tight. There were no tears now. Caitlin was angry as a bobcat in a dunk tank. She slowly unfolded her legs from the chair and stood up, her eyes never leaving him. Half a dozen excuses, apologies, and justifications ran through his mind but Nick knew none of them would help.

He had screwed up.

Big time.

Neither said a word as she walked to him, her arms wrapped around her body defensively. She stepped right to him, tipping her head back to hold his gaze, the angry tremors that shook her more obvious this close. Nick wanted to reach out to her, but being with Caitlin wasn't new to him. He knew when to be close . . . and when to keep his distance or risk dismemberment.

"Are you going to say something?" she asked, her voice so strained it cracked.

Nick slid his eyes closed for a moment and shook his head. "Nothing I say will be enough."

Her eyes filled and she looked away, pulling her lower lip through her teeth. Nick's chest tightened and he clenched his hand at his side to keep from touching her. When she looked at him, she didn't try to hide or stop the tears that ran down her cheeks.

"I went to General Castleton," she said, her voice steely cold despite the trails of moisture on her face. "He told me the intent of the mission. That was all he would say. Even though I have been a member of the command structure on this base for the last year and half, suddenly I am being kept out of *major* decisions and being told to go *talk to my man* like some twentieth-century housewife!"

"I asked him, and everyone else, not to say anything until I had a chance to tell you myself."

"Hell of a lot of good that did," she mumbled, swiping her fingers across her cheeks. She drew a shaky breath, once again reining in her emotions, and looked up at him. "Whose idea was it? Did General Castleton ask you to do this?"

Nick looked into her eyes, the band around his heart tightening. Was he insane? He had to be to, even for a moment, think he could climb in that glider and fly away. He ran the tip of his tongue along the inside of his lower lip before answering her.

"No. It was mine."

Caitlin's breath hitched and she turned away from him, taking several steps to put some distance between them. Nick moved away from the counter, just one single step, and extended his hand toward her.

"Caitlin—"

"What have the last couple of weeks been to you?" she snapped, spinning around to face him. "You told me . . ." her voice broke, and her expression twisted into a mask of pain as she tried to speak. Nick took

216

another step toward her, but she warned him off with a raised hand. "You *told* me not to question us . . . not to question how you felt . . . not to . . ." Her last words were lost in a choked cry as she emphasized each point with a jabbed finger in the air.

"I'm doing this *because* of us, Caitlin. Because of you. Because of Michael."

"That's bullshit!" she shouted.

"No," he said almost as loudly. "No, it's not. Caitlin, three months ago I didn't give a rat's ass what the Areth did. I planned on living and dying on that damn lake," he boomed, pointing his hand somewhere in the vicinity of North as best he could tell. "If Castleton, or anyone else, had come to me and asked me to do this, I would have told them to go screw themselves."

"I don't believe that. Neither do you. You're a good man, and if you thought you could help—"

"You're wrong!" he shouted, stopping her short. Nick curled his fists at his side to try to pull it all in. Everything that had been bombarding him and battling him for days plowed into him all at once and he bit until pain shot down the sides of his neck. "You're wrong," he said lower, through clenched teeth.

Caitlin stared at him with large eyes, her lips slightly parted. Nick braced his hands on the back of the nearest chair, his knuckles white as he hung on. "I had nothing," he finally said when the warring fury in his chest let him speak. He raised his head and met her wide-eyed gaze. "Now, I have something worth fighting for. Worth dying for if I have to."

"Then stay here and *fight*!"

"I can't."

"Why not?"

"Because there's no one else!"

"There has to be!"

"Damn it, Caitlin. There isn't! You know it!"

Their voices mingled and echoed back to them off the concrete walls, filling the room with tension so thick it choked Nick and sat on his chest like a dead weight. He huffed, setting his hands at his waist, and turned away from her. Her soft sniffle broke the sudden silence that blanketed the room. Nick closed his eyes. His son's words echoed back to him . . . *This is going to hurt her.*

Her deep sigh made him swallow against the thick lump in his own throat.

"When do you leave?" she asked, her voice so small he almost didn't hear her.

Nick couldn't look at her when he answered. "Three days."

She sucked in a sharp breath and his eyes slid closed. He heard the soft sigh of a cushion and turned to see her sitting on the edge of one of the chairs, her hands clasped together in front of her as she stared off to nothing. Nick moved to her and crouched down, resting one knee on the floor to be at eye level with her. He wrapped his hands around her clenched fingers, rubbing his thumbs across her skin.

"Caitlin," he said softly, but she didn't look at him, her cheeks now damp from tears and her lip swollen from being pulled through her teeth. "Baby . . ."

Her blue eyes shifted to him and a tremble moved through her.

Nick looked down at their hands, how small hers looked within his grasp, how fair her skin was in comparison to his own. He pulled her hands apart and laid his out flat, spreading hers on his palm to palm so he could stroke the back of her fingers and knuckles with his free hand. Her hands were delicate, but he knew the strength they could weld. She wore no rings, no adornment, but her hands were feminine and beautiful. Like her.

"We don't know what's waiting for me," he finally said, still focusing on her hand. It was a finite point, a comfort, and a grounding spot. "If there is anything there, it will take me months to reach it."

"If . . ." she choked out. "Nicholas Michael Tanner, you damn well better come home to me, or I swear to God—"

She stopped speaking when he brought his head up to look into her eyes. "If it looks like I'm not coming back—"

It was her turn to cut him off by lunging to her feet, nearly knocking him on his ass as she moved away. "No."

Nick rose to his feet, watching her pace between him and the bedroom door. "Caitlin, listen to me."

"No!"

He grabbed her arm as she passed and swung her around to face him, gripping her elbows. "Yes! Listen to me, damn it! I don't want you to waste time waiting for me to come back if there's no way in hell I ever will. I want you and Michael to—"

She jerked free from his hold, a look of shock twisting her features. "God! What the hell are you saying? If I can't have you, your son will do?"

"No, I didn't mean . . . Jesus, Caitlin! I didn't mean that!"

"What the hell did you mean?"

Nick raked a hand through his hair and twisted to stomp away. He reached the far wall and kicked with the side of his foot, slamming the concrete with the heel of his hand. It hurt like hell, but it was nothing compared to the pain in his chest. Nick leaned his forearms on the wall and rested his forehead on his arm, his eyes closed against the burning sting behind them.

"You and Michael . . ." he began, his voice choking on the lump in his throat. "You are my *family*. You are everything to me." Nick opened his eyes, hot tears running down his own cheeks, but he was too worn out to care. Too drained. He snuffed his nose with his thumb and cleared his throat, but didn't turn to face Caitlin. "I need to know that you'll take care of him for me."

Her hands skimmed over his back and shoulders, a gentle touch that instantly filled some of the burning hole that ate at his chest. Nick swiveled, immediately taking Caitlin's head within his hands, and devoured her lips. The salt from both their tears tinged the kiss and slicked the contact, and Caitlin moaned as he plunged his tongue into the warm cavern of her mouth. Her arms circled his neck, and he released her head to wrap her body in a firm embrace, pulling her as close as possible.

Nick pushed all the pain and rage aside, pouring everything into kissing Caitlin Montgomery . . . his life . . . his soul. He slid his hands up her side to gently squeeze her ribs and lift her off the ground. She reacted instinctively, wrapping her legs around his hips as he used the new angle to draw the smooth skin of her throat between his teeth. With her backside cupped in his hands, Nick carried her toward the bedroom door.

Inside the bedroom, he kicked the door shut behind them and stopped at the foot of the bed to ease Caitlin down. She knelt on the mattress in front of him, putting them nearly at eye level, as her fingers tugged his shirt free of his jeans and graceful fingertips teased his skin when she pulled the shirt over his head. When his chest was bare, Caitlin leaned forward and pressed her lips to his breastbone, drawing a hissed breath from him.

With hurried need he barely managed to keep in control, Nick removed Caitlin's sweater and bra, exposing her perfectly formed breasts. She gasped and combed her fingers into his hair as he leaned down and drew one hard nipple into his mouth, rolling his tongue along its peak. She whispered his name and Nick locked the moment away in his mind.

He lowered her onto the bed, and with his mouth worshipping the slope of her stomach, he slipped her jeans and panties down her hips. Her own hands did the same for him, and Nick moaned in unadulterated pleasure when skin met skin as he lay down with her. Nick kissed the underside of her breasts, the gentle ripple of her ribs, the indent of her waist, and each new spot brought a round of gasps and moans from Caitlin. She shifted and moved beneath his touch, her hands caressing his back and shoulders as her head rolled on the blankets.

Nick's body burned, his blood pounding in his ears. He wanted her so bad it hurt, but not just to ease the ache . . . to show her what she meant to him.

Caitlin's eyes widened when he rolled to his knees, but moments later her eyelids fluttered closed when he pressed his lips against the inside of her knee.

"Nicholas . . ."

He smiled against her skin. It took a lot to get her to use his full name in bed.

"I need you," she begged, her hands tugging at his arm. Her voice was almost lost in the deep purr from the back of her throat. "Please."

He gently rolled Caitlin flat onto her back and shifted over her, settling his hips in the natural notch of her thighs, supporting his weight on his bent arms. Caitlin ran her hands over his shoulders to rest on his cheeks as she looked into his face, her eyes heavy-lidded and dark with arousal.

He stopped to look at her, the way her blond hair lay mussed and wild around her head, and rosy color darkened her cheeks. Her lips glistened from their kisses, her sweet breath warming his cheeks as she breathed in hitched pants. Nick stroked her temple with his thumb and leaned in for a slow, gentle kiss that barely touched her lips, pulling a soft purr from the back of her throat.

"Nicky . . ." she sighed.

"I love you, Caitlin." Her breath caught and new tears sprang to her eyes. As one ran free, Nick brushed it away with his thumb. "I don't want you to question that, not for a second."

She framed his face with her hands, a watery smile on her lips. "I love *you*, Nicky. Don't *you* question that, not for a second."

Nick covered her mouth and kissed her slow and deep as he slipped inside her heat. Their soft moans mingled somewhere within the kiss.

Nick moved his lips along her jaw to bury his face against the curve of her neck. He slid his hands beneath her back, curling his fingers around her shoulders, and watched every moment of pleasure play across her features as he made love to her. He memorized every moment, every touch, everything down to the scent of their love.

She called his name and Nick closed his eyes.

CHAPTER TWENTY-FOUR

1 December 2051, Friday
Phoenix Compound
Outside Colorado Springs, Colorado
Former United States of America

10:02:34 to launch

"The Wormhole Initiation Program has been streamlined and the course of each jump has been pre-programmed into the computer. Before you commence WIP, your system will do a long-range scan and plot a course based on your final destination—the coordinates provided to us by the Areth scientist."

Doctor Kaplinski spoke from his position at the front of Situation Room where he briefed a dozen and a half base personnel. He directed his commentary mostly to Nick, as he pointed out the details on the schematics displayed digitally on the screen for everyone to see.

"We've pushed the limits of the jump engines as far as the simulation programs say they can go, but without real testing, our calculations are hypothetical at best. We estimate each jump will progress you approximately nine-hundred-ninety-seven-point-four-three-five light years."

Nick snorted and mumbled *approximately* under his breath. Caitlin squeezed the fingers she held, and hid her smile behind her other hand.

He nodded at Doctor Kaplinski and smiled so widely his cheeks hurt, bobbing his eyebrows. "Sounds great."

The doc nodded, turning back to his rotating image of the glider that would take Nick into the 'great unknown.' "The solid oxygen used to power the engines will also serve as a back-up to the life support systems —should it be necessary—but the cabin itself has been refitted with CO_2 recyclers which will be able to produce more than enough breathable air to sustain you. The Solid O_2 Sequencers are estimated to be able to keep up with power production with sufficient supply for an eighty-thousand light year trip."

"So, it will get me there."

Doctor Kaplinski met Nick's gaze and shrugged one shoulder slightly. "Yes, Colonel. It will get you there."

The rest didn't need to be said. Nick shifted in his chair and brought his right leg up to rest his ankle on the other knee. Doctor Kaplinski nodded to the next 'speaker.' She was a redheaded woman who barely looked twelve, let alone old enough to program a computer system for deep space flight. Doctor Patricia Byrne was a genius in her field, no matter how old she *didn't* look. As she took her place in front of the presentation screen, Nick lifted Caitlin's hand to his lips and pressed a kiss to her knuckles. He leaned sideways and whispered softly near her ear.

"I love you."

She tipped her head toward him so her temple rested against his hair, her fingers squeezing his. As Doctor Byrne cleared her throat, Nick sat up again, doing his best to pay attention to the next leg of the presentation.

"The majority of the systems on the adapted glider are set to automatic functions, since eighty to ninety percent of your time within the craft will be in stasis. Long-range scanners will be set to detect any possible approaching threats, and rouse you from your rest state if necessary. Medical scans will keep track of all biological and neurological functions, and will compensate with nutrition and supplementation whenever and however necessary. Recyclers and power generators are all on automatic function, and the system will run a full diagnostic after each wormhole navigation and at the end of each stasis period prior to your next jump."

"And what happens if something *does* go wrong?" Nick asked. "If repairs are needed, et cetera." Doctor Byrne and Doctor Kaplinski exchanged glances and Nick waved his hand in the air dismissively. "Yeah. I get it. Move on."

Doctor Byrne cleared her throat and clasped her hands behind her slight frame.

"The database is loaded with an abridged format of recorded Earth history—"

"All of it?" he asked, raising his eyebrows.

Doctor Byrne smiled. "Yes, all of it. We have also provided a more accessible and detailed accounting for all events since first contact with the Areth over forty years ago right up through to the outcome of our confrontation with them in New Mexico. The database requires a code for access, and is on a passive kill switch connected to the biological systems. If seventy-two hours pass in which the system reads no life signs, it will wipe the database clean."

Nick felt Caitlin's body tense beside him, heard her slowly metered breath as she controlled her response to the morbid statement of facts. If he died in the empty vacuum of space, and someone found his floating craft hundreds of years from now, there would be no record of his home or destination.

"Well, it sounds like we're good to go," Nick said, unable to feign any enthusiasm. "When is the window?"

"Nine hours, forty-two minutes," Doctor Kaplinski answered from his seat.

Nick nodded, standing. With their hands still linked, he tugged Caitlin to her feet along with him. "Fine. I'll be back in nine hours."

05:22:54 TO LAUNCH

The remains of beef stew, brought to the apartment in a large ceramic bowl from the mess hall, sat cold and forgotten in the middle of the table. Cornbread crumbs scattered on a plate were the only evidence that anything had been there, devoured by father and son in what seemed to be a silent contest to see who could eat more of the golden cakes. CJ sat with her elbow set on the table and her chin resting in the cup of her hand, watching with a smile as Nick animatedly told his tale.

"I don't think I was more than six or seven years old, and we were in Maine at the cabin for my grandfather's birthday. I can remember sitting on this red and white cooler, watching the campfire and listening to the crickets singing in the dark. So, anyway, my grandma pours my grandpa a cup of coffee and goes to check on my mom who was serving up the cake and ice cream in the house."

CJ watched Michael watch Nick, his eyes attentive, a smile ready on his lips. He had been caught up in his father's stories for the last two hours, eating them up like a child with a bag of candy.

"Grandpa was asking me about the fish I had caught that day when Grandma and Ma came out of the cabin, plates of cake and homemade ice cream for everyone. Grandpa downs the last of his coffee and immediately digs into the ice cream, his favorite part." A smile already spread Nick's lips, and the further he went in the story the more random chuckles laced his words. "As he's sucking down the ice cream like there's no tomorrow, my Grandma turns and her shirt tails get close to the campfire."

"Oh, no . . ." CJ interjected theatrically, both men turned and smiled at her.

"So, Grandpa yells 'Sara!' I guess it was the combination of hot coffee and cold ice cream, but his dentures go *flying* out of his mouth and land *right* in the middle of the campfire."

Michael laughed, his head tipping back as the booming sound filled the apartment. Nick's matching baritone rumble mixed with it, as he was lost in his own story. "So, everyone goes nuts jumping to their feet and throwing everything they can find on the fire. Coffee. Fruit punch. Ice cream. Soon, the campfire is a smoldering mass of melting strawberry ice cream and sugar water just screaming for an army of ants to come along and find it. Sitting on top is Grandpa's teeth, sooty and slightly warped. Cursing words under his breath like my young ears had *never* heard, Grandpa picks up his teeth and heads in the house."

"Were they okay?" CJ asked.

Nick shook his head, pausing to take a sip of the beer he had somehow managed to round up from somewhere. Michael had tried it, seeing his father's obvious preference for it, but had decided after one sip and a seriously twisted expression, that he would stick to his mixed juice.

"No, but Grandpa refused to go without his teeth. Said it made him look like an old man. He put them in and talked with a serious lisp for the rest of the week and had a perpetual 'cock-eyed' look. Every time he smiled, all you saw were blackened, melted teeth. I had nightmares for three months."

"Awwww," CJ cooed, sliding her hand across the table as she reached for Nick. He linked his fingers with hers, the table small enough that the three of them could form a circle linking their hands without any one of them having to stretch. "Poor little Nicky."

Nick chuckled and finished draining his beer. "You have no idea." He sputtered on the mouthful of liquid and used the end of the bottle to point at Michael. "That's who you're named after."

Michael had taken advantage of the lull in conversation to pick at the cornbread crumbs left on the plate. His head snapped up at Nick's words.

"Named after?" he asked.

Nick nodded. "Yeah." CJ saw some of the lightness slide from his expression as he set the empty bottle down, and Nick sat forward to curl his hand around Michael's forearm where it rested on the table. "I'm sorry, Michael. I guess it never occurred to me . . . do you know your name?"

"Michael," he answered, his eyes shifting between CJ and Nick, and if unsure if he provided the right answer.

Nick smiled. "Yes, your first name. Your full name is Michael Sean Tanner. Michael is my middle name, and Sean was your great-grandfather's name. I named you when you were born. Why the Areth kept that name, I don't know. Maybe they couldn't be bothered to use anything else. But *I* am the one who named you Michael."

Michael shook his head slowly. "I didn't know."

Nick took his hand from Michael's arm and laid his palm on Michael's cheek. "Now you do. I'm glad I told you." He sat back, almost visibly shaking off the momentary melancholy that had swept the table. "When I come back, the three of us are going to the cabin. I have photo albums and videos I want to show you. I want to teach you about where you came from. Where you *really* came from."

"Give us ten minutes, and we'll be packed. Right, Michael?" CJ said, looking between the two men across from her. "I'll take the crisp Parson's Point air over the inside of a mountain any time."

Michael nodded. "We'll see it together."

"Together." CJ said again.

Nick took a hand of each of them, and lifted CJ's to kiss her knuckles.

227

*C*J curled her body against Nick, shifting as close as she could, wishing she could crawl inside his warmth and strength and stay forever. He tilted toward her, pulling her closer against him, his lips against her forehead. The scent of his skin filled her senses. She closed her eyes and ran her hands over his bare chest, loving the feel of the crinkly hair beneath her fingers. His hands stroked her back and arms, occasionally slipping beneath the sheet to touch her side and hips.

"Do you have time for this?" she whispered against his shoulder, enjoying the taste of him on her lips.

His long fingers curled her hair back from her cheek and he kissed her just in front of her ear. "Shhhh. I'm making time."

Her body still hummed from making love to him, muscles, and nerves firing in the ebbing tide of sensation. She wanted so much to hang on to him, to close her eyes and push the rest of the world away. Wanted it so bad it hurt. "Promise me you'll come back to me," she said softly, her voice almost lost in the hard lump that closed around her throat. "Michael and I need you."

His arms held her closer, his hand cupping the back of her head to hold her against the curve of his neck. One hot tear escaped to seal the contact between her cheek and his shoulder.

"I promise you . . ." His voice graveled, heavy and raw, his breath warming her ear. "That I won't give up."

She nodded against his ear, thankful he didn't make any empty promises he didn't know he would be able to keep. Nick's lips skimmed over her shoulder, barely kissing, barely touching, and sending a shiver down her spine. His fingers followed the trail his mouth left, traced her collarbone, and slipped down to float over the slope of her breast. CJ watched him as his gaze followed his own hand, deep lines creasing his brow.

His name was on her lips, but she couldn't speak. Couldn't break the silence of his hypnotic worship of her body. CJ slowed her breath, not wanting even that to disturb the moment.

Nick pushed the blanket down, exposing her to her hips, and with gentle pressure, urged her to lie flat. CJ did, resting her arm on the pillow over her head. He shifted down into the bed, bringing his head even with her stomach, his fingertips continuing their gentle travels.

He curled his large hand around her hip, pressing against the juncture where her thigh met her body. A sensual jolt shot through her, and her spine arched off the bed, but his firm pressure on her abdomen pushed her back down. He pressed his open mouth to her stomach, the tip of his tongue scorching her skin.

Then he turned his head and laid his cheek over her navel, wrapping an arm around her thigh, urging her silently to slide her calf along his ribs to rest on his back. CJ stroked his hair and looked down at the top of his head, her eyes burning with tears she fought to hide. Tears would make it harder.

They lay silent for what could have been an eternity, but time passed all too fast. Too soon, Nick raised himself up, holding his weight on his bent arms, and looked into her face as he moved up her body. CJ laid her hands against his cheeks, smiling as she recognized the heated, focused look in his eyes.

"Making more time?" she said with a small laugh.

Her answer was his hungry kiss as he pressed her into the bed with his weight.

00:22:21 TO LAUNCH

The infirmary was nearly empty, except for one sleeping patient in a far corner and the nurse left behind to care for her. Everyone else, including Lilly, had gone to the glider bay to see off Nick Tanner.

Beverly wanted to be there. She had to do this. She had to try when no one would stop her.

Her hands trembled as she pulled down the blanket that covered Victor's chest. Beverly drew a fortifying breath and leaned over his body as far as the height of the bed would allow and laid her hands against the sides of his neck, her thumbs stroking his cheeks. She turned his head to look into his sleeping face. Blackness assaulted her mind, swirling and battling with ribbons of blue and orange light. She pressed her eyes closed and laid her cheek on his chest, focusing instead on the steady beat of his heart.

Instead of throwing up walls against the emotional onslaught, Beverly pushed out, struggling to find the essence of the man. When she did, even through the chaos, she almost breathed a sigh of relief. He was whole and he was fighting.

"Don't give up, Victor." Pushing the simple thought toward him took a tremendous amount of effort, but after a moment, she felt some of the darkness ease. She withdrew, exhausted and spent.

00:08:04 TO LAUNCH

The modified glider's hood lowered, the hydraulics hissing, as it closed Nick into the cockpit. He adjusted his position in the seat, tugging on one of the straps on his G-Suit, and slid his flight helmet over his head. The seal formed, creating an airlock within his suit.

"You are a go for flight, Colonel," said a voice in his ear.

Nick raised his hand and gave a thumbs-up through the front shield. Caitlin and Michael stood side-by-side. *His family.* Fractured and not quite whole, but the only family he had. The only family he wanted.

His reason for taking this mission, and his reason for wanting to stay.

00:02:15 TO LAUNCH

CJ held her breath, swallowing against the hard lump in her throat. She would not let Nick see her lose the faltering grip she still held on her control. She would stay strong until he was gone.

This was not forever.

Not forever.

God would not be so cruel as to give Nick back to her only to take him away again. She clenched her fingers together in front of her, jumping when she felt a large hand rest on her shoulder.

She turned and looked up at Michael. His gaze was on the glider, the sound of the O_2 engines echoing through the hanger as the ship hovered above the floor. Michael's jaw was set firm, his lips drawn tight, and CJ's heart ached.

00:00:00

The Colorado Mountains echoed the blast of Nick Tanner's escape from the atmosphere, the super-sonic boom making the air reverberate. Michael stood at the edge of the hanger bay, his hand shielding his eyes as he looking into the setting sun.

As the resonance died, the crowd thinned, returning to their duties. Michael stayed in his place as the sun disappeared. In his head, he knew his father was already on the other side of the system, and there was no chance of catching a glimpse. But still . . .

"Michael."

He turned to look at CJ where she stood just an arm's reach away. She reached for him and took his hand, squeezing gently. Michael looked down, turning their hands to look at her fingers. Contact still felt so new, and yet so natural.

"Come on. Let's go home."

As she pulled him away from the edge, Michael glanced one more time.

*J*ace leaned against the wall in the black hole the Areth had kept him in for the last . . . he didn't know how many days. Every part of his body hurt. He didn't know what the hell they were doing to him, but it was unlike anything he had ever known. Their 'interrogations' attacked him on a cellular level, tearing him apart from the inside out.

The cell door opened, and two big men dragged him to his feet, the light from the hall blinding him. Just as he was able to focus, they strapped him to a chair, and *she* came in. Involuntarily, his heart sped up. She was the most sadistic of all.

"This will end if you tell me what I want to know," she said, her voice low and almost seductive as she picked up a three-pronged silver device from the table beside him. Blue light arched between the prongs.

Jace bit down, bracing himself. Forcing words through his clenched jaw. *"Yea, though I walk through the valley of the shadow of death, I will fear no evil . . ."*

His body arched against the restraints and his words turned into screams.

Lilly!

CONTINUED IN

THE PHOENIX REBELLION BOOK TWO: OUTCASTS

Something dark and sinister haunts Victor's thoughts, threatening to steal his sanity. Turning his own mind against him. He doesn't understand it, has no true name for it. He only knows the malicious darkness in his mind he calls his demon wants him dead for his treachery in helping the Humans. Now, Victor is at the mercy of Phoenix and their mission to be free of the very enemy Victor represents. Only in the empathic presence of Beverly Surimoto does he find some fraction of peace. She silences the demon . . . most of the time.

Beverly Surimoto was born to, raised, and educated in the world of Phoenix as the child of some of the first founders of the rebellion group. To be associated so closely with the enemy could undermine her authority and perhaps everything Phoenix has built, but she senses deception like some smell flowers. There is no deception in Victor, only confusion and fear. Phoenix exists to end fear and find the truth, so how can she deny him safe haven even when he wears the name of the enemy?

The mask is ripped away, the face of the enemy is revealed, and Earth is plunged into a war it isn't prepared to fight... and unequipped to win. There may be allies somewhere far beyond the edge of Earth's system, but will the messenger sent to find help survive the voyage? There is no way to know who will be found: allies, or even worse enemies.

PLEASE ENJOY THE FOLLOWING SAMPLE CHAPTER OF

OUTCASTS: CHAPTER ONE

13 March 2052, Wednesday 06:32
Phoenix Compound
Outside Colorado Springs, Colorado
Former United States of America

Doctor Lilly Quinn flipped the infirmary's main overhead light on as she stifled a yawn behind her hand. If she had a hard time getting out of bed now, she wondered what she would do in a few months when she had a newborn. Running a hand habitually over her expanding waistline, Lilly picked up her handheld data recorder and headed for her first check of the day.

Victor.

Four months had passed with very little fluctuation in his condition. Since his vitals had stabilized, he had remained comatose with no indication of waking any time in the near future. Higher than usual brainwave activity in the hypothalamus had her confused, but other than that, the Areth scientist-cum-Phoenix-guest was a typical coma patient. No movement, no reaction to stimuli . . . nothing.

Michael sat inside the glass isolation enclosure, in his normal chair at Victor's bedside. In his lap was an open book, and as she reached for the door handle, Lilly saw his lips moving as he read aloud to Victor—his daily ritual.

"Many were they whose cities he saw, whose minds he learned of, many the

pains he suffered in his spirit in the wide sea, struggling for his own life and the homecoming of his companions—" Michael's voice was steady and sure as he read, his voice carrying to her as she opened the door. He looked up, pausing, as she stepped inside. "Good morning."

"Good morning. You're here early."

"Yes," he said in answer.

Lilly smiled and moved to the monitors that kept a constant record of Victor's every vital sign. "What are you reading to him?"

"The Odyssey of Homer."

"I read that when I was young. It's very fitting . . ." Lilly trailed off as she scanned the record from the night.

She heard the slap as the book closed and the squeak of the chair's leather before Michael stood behind her. "What is it?"

"I'm not sure. It could be nothing. But look here," she said, pointing to the cardiograph from several hours before. "What do you see?"

"Tachycardia."

"Almost, yes. His heartbeat didn't accelerate enough to set off the alarms, but it *did* accelerate. His respiration increased right around the same time, and again around 0447 this morning."

"Could he be dreaming?"

"Coma patients don't dream," Lilly said, her voice dropping as she turned and looked at Victor. His head was turned away, his chin dipped toward his chest, and a niggling feeling tickled at the back of Lilly's mind. *That wasn't the position I left him in last night.* "Michael, did you touch him at all?"

"No."

Lilly yanked open a supply drawer in the bedside table and dug around until she found a small penlight. Michael watched her with avid interest as she turned Victor's head to face her, and gently slid back his eyelid, flashing the light across his iris.

"Is there a response?"

She repeated the process with the other eye, then flicked the light off and sighed. Lilly looked at Michael, but even before she spoke she saw in his eyes he knew her answer. "No." He stepped back from the bed and walked away with his hands pushed into his pockets. "I'm sorry, I thought maybe there was a ray of hope for a minute there, but his pupils are fixed and dilated. I'll keep a close eye on his readings, to see if—" Her voice froze in her throat when she looked down again to see Victor's dark eyes staring at her. Lilly blinked, making sure she actually *saw* what she thought she saw and then raised her hand to lay it across his forehead. "Hello, Victor."

His lips parted, shifting as if he wanted to form words but they wouldn't quite come to him and deep lines furrowed his brow. Lilly smiled and slid her fingers to his wrist, checking his pulse. It was slightly elevated, but not overly so. Good and strong.

"Michael, come here," she said softly, just loud enough for Michael to hear her across the room but not loud enough to startle her newly awakened patient. "How are you feeling, Victor?"

He shook his head, his warm skin rubbing across her palm. *Good. No sign of shock. Skin isn't clammy. Temperature isn't elevated or dropping.*

"I don't know," he finally said, his voice rough as dried leaves.

Michael stepped behind her and Lilly stepped back. He set his hand on Victor's shoulder, leaning forward so Victor could see his face. "It's all right, Victor. They're going to help you."

Victor rolled his head on the pillow, his eyes squinting slightly. "Michael . . ."

"Yes. It's me," Michael said with a wide grin.

Victor's features twisted and he winced, a hiss whistling through his clenched teeth. Michael looked at her over his shoulder and she reached past him to lay her fingertips against Victor's carotid artery. With a guttural howl, Victor snapped his arms out and viced his fists around Michael's throat. Michael jerked back, pulling Victor off the bed with him when he wouldn't give up his hold. Both men fell back, Michael's shoulder slamming Lilly back into the thick tempered glass wall of the enclosure. Equipment and monitors clattered and fell as the wires and cords connecting ripped off Victor or pulled the machinery in his wake.

"Michael!" Lilly shouted, but both men were oblivious as Victor slammed his body into Michael and sent them both into the wall.

Lilly yanked open a drawer of the supply cabinet in the corner of the room and removed a pre-loaded sedative syringe.

Michael gripped the front of Victor's scrubs, pinning him against the wall even as Victor fought to find leverage and get his hands around Michael's throat again. "Victor! Stop this!"

Victor howled again and fought with everything he had against Michael, even though Lilly could see his struggling to stay on his feet. With a new surge of fury, Victor shoved away from the wall and Lilly barely managed to get out of the way before the two men tumbled into the monitors along the side of the bed.

She was outside the isolation room in seconds. Her next decision made in a split moment as she shut the vacuum-sealed door behind her. No one else had reported to work yet, and it would take far too long for security to reach the infirmary. Lilly punched her private code into the keypad beside the door as Michael and Victor slammed against the glass in a physical battle for dominance. Seconds later, she heard a hiss and white fog filtered into the airtight chamber.

Victor fought until the Neurophynal gas finally overtook his neurological systems and both he and Michael slumped to the floor. Lilly entered another command to reverse the air filters and suck the room clean, leaning her forehead on the glass as she tried to calm her suddenly frazzled nerves.

"How long do we have before we have to go outside the mountain for supplies?" Beverly Surimoto asked, scanning the food supply report on the PAC in front of her. She glanced up to read Damian's answer on his lips.

Only a few other people sat in the cafeteria with them, scattered around at various tables. The majority of the breakfast shift had come and gone, leaving those who had worked through the night and only now managed to come eat, or those who enjoyed the pleasure of sleeping in. She sat beside General Castleton, and Damian was on the other side of him. Major Yun, Chief of Security on the base, and Lieutenant Major Reichek, Operations Officer, sat on the other side of the table.

"Based on the current compliment, and the level of consumption, we can go another seven weeks comfortably. After that, we're going to have to start either rationing or get in some supplies. The Farm is producing plenty of fruits and vegetables, but we need the staples. And meat."

Beverly nodded. She could get the details from the report, Damian was always very thorough, but she was able to get a better feel for the situation by talking to him. She walked away knowing whether things were dire or just tight, surplus or just fine.

"How about medical supplies? Especially with the addition of the New Mexico residents."

"That's much tighter. Doctor Quinn reported she has sufficient supplies of the staples: bandages, sutures, analgesics and whatnot. However, she is running low on antibiotics and some less commonly used medications she says she has had to use in gaining frequency in the last four months. I've provided a full list."

"And these are necessary medications for the new patients?"

"Yes."

Beverly nodded. "Then, we will have to see about getting her more, won't we?" She smiled as she projected the thought, hoping the words rang with confidence. Confidence she didn't necessarily feel.

It grew harder and harder to keep the base supplied with everything they needed. Five years ago, even two years ago, the base ran with a surplus of supplies ninety-five percent of the time. They came and went as they pleased, and were able to obtain what they needed as they needed from a variety of sources. With the increased focus from Alliance Forces, they didn't dare go too far and try to obtain too much.

"Get me a list of our most recent sources for medical supplies, as well as a viability report for their use now," General Castleton said. "We will need to organize a mission outside the mountain and I want to minimize the risk by contacting only the best possible resources."

"Of course. I'll have it to you this afternoon," Damian said with a smile, his teeth a flash of white against the rich, dark brown of his skin.

"Is there anything to discuss from Operations or Security?" General Castleton asked, already closing his own PAC. There usually wasn't, and like the general, Beverly expected the pat answer of 'all is clear'.

"We had an incident this morning, sir," Major Yun said. "Nothing of concern at this point, but Neurophynal gas was implemented to subdue an individual."

"Explain," General Castleton ordered.

"It seems the Areth in the infirmary woke up this morning and became violent. Doctor Quinn had no choice but to use the gas to sedate him."

The hairs on Beverly's arms bristled and her skin tingled. Her eyes darted from Major Yun to the general. She quickly slid her hands beneath the table to hide the sudden tremble that seized them, and she had to tamp down the urge to jump to her feet.

"Michael Tanner was also involved in the situation, but we've received notice that he is recovering."

"And what of Victor?" Damian asked.

"Sir?" Major Yun responded.

"The Areth."

"He appears to have suffered no ill effects from the gas, sir."

Her heart pounded against her ribs like a caged bird. "If you'll excuse me, General, I'll go to the infirmary myself and get the details from Lilly."

General Castleton's aged eyes settled on her for several moments and Beverly felt the traitorous heat rise in her cheeks. Finally, he hitched his chin in a curt nod. "Fine. Report to me this afternoon. We'll go over these numbers then."

"Yes, sir."

She pushed back from the table and managed to walk out of the cafeteria. It was a struggle to keep herself from running to the elevator or cursing when the doors didn't open immediately. Beverly contemplated the stairs, but before she turned for the stairwell door the elevator arrived. The trip to the infirmary floor was excruciatingly slow and she paced the small car. Four months . . . four long months . . . what would bring him out of the coma so suddenly now?

Three service men stood in the hall waiting to board the elevator when the doors open, and Beverly brushed past them with an apology. She rushed through the open doorway into the infirmary, finally pausing long enough to process what she saw.

CJ and Michael sat on the edge of one of the beds. Worry and concern strained CJ's expression as her hand nervously flittered over Michael's bare shoulder and tussled brown hair. CJ looked up as Beverly walked to them.

"I just heard what happened," Beverly said, shifting her gaze between CJ and Michael, noting the deep bruises that circled Michael's throat and the purple shading over his left shoulder. "Is everyone all right?"

"We're all fine," Lilly answered, looking up from her examination. "Surprised. But fine."

Beverly crossed her arms to disguise the nervous fidgeting. "I didn't get much detail from Major Yun just said Victor woke up suddenly. And that he was . . ." Her gaze shifted again to the bruises around Michael's neck. "Violent."

"That's one way to put it," CJ said, a scowl twisting her features. "He was trying to kill Michael."

"He wouldn't have killed me," Michael said, looking at CJ.

CJ and Lilly exchanged glances, and Beverly got the sense that she was coming in late on a conversation that had been going on for a while. Michael closed his eyes, the muscle along his jaw bunching.

"Is the headache back?" Lilly asked. He just nodded, raising his hand to rub his fingers across his forehead. "I'll get an analgesic. You should lie down. It's going to take some time for the effects of the Neurophynal to completely wear off."

Michael didn't argue and CJ stood so he could swing his body onto the bed and recline onto the pillows. He draped one arm across his eyes, his other hanging limp off the side of the bed. CJ moved to stand beside Beverly, her lips pulled taut in a deep frown as she shook her head.

"I swear, Bev, my heart was in my throat when Lilly called me and told me Michael was unconscious. I haven't been that frightened in a long time. I didn't even know he was gone."

Beverly's gaze shifted to Michael, her eyes unmistakably drawn to the scars that marred his body. As a link in the chain of command, she had read all the detailed reports made on the people they had taken out of New Mexico, Michael among them. She had seen the categorized list of abuses and tortures—at least the ones they knew about—that had been inflicted on him. She had sat with CJ talking about the nightmares that still haunted the young man. She couldn't understand a mentality that could justify the treatment of a human being in that way.

CJ touched her arm, drawing her attention back. "I don't care what Michael says, Victor was trying to kill him. I saw the security tapes."

"But why would Victor attack Michael? It doesn't make sense."

"None of it makes sense, Bev," CJ said, a deep 'v' forming between her brows as she scowled. "Come here. You need to see."

With one last glance towards Michael's sleeping form, CJ motioned for Beverly to follow her to the back of the infirmary. They walked past the glass isolation room where Victor had lain dormant for the last four months, and Beverly couldn't help but stare as she passed at the destruction within the sealed walls. Monitors and equipment were shattered and broken on the floor, cables, and wires strewn like multi-colored spaghetti. A crimson stain smeared the floor and she wondered whose blood it was.

They walked down the hall in the furthest back corner of the infirmary. Doors lined each side; some storage rooms, some cold lockers. The cell where Victor had spent his first few days in the mountain sat barren and cold as they passed. CJ turned her head to look at Beverly as they walked.

"Lilly said this room hasn't been used in probably forty years, maybe longer. Well before the original military base was decommissioned. Victor was too violent to strap to a bed. She was afraid he'd hurt himself."

A heavy pressure squeezed around Beverly's chest, making it hard to breathe. She crossed her arms and pressed her clenched fists against her sides, drawing in a tight breath. They reached the end of the hall, where an armed security officer stood outside a closed door, with his hands behind his back and a pulse charge sidearm strapped to his thigh. He stepped aside when CJ and Beverly reached him so CJ could look inside the two-foot-by-two-foot window in the door.

"What is this room?" Beverly asked.

"A padded cell."

CJ stepped aside so Beverly could look inside.

Her heart froze in her chest and her hand flew to cover her mouth. Victor was in the corner of the small room, with every surface covered with thick padding that may have once been white but had aged to a dingy gray. His back was wedged into the corner, his knees drawn to his chest and his face curled into the circle of his arms. He rocked a steady rhythm, his spine slamming against the wall with each backward movement.

"Why doesn't Lilly help him?" she asked, looking to CJ.

"She's tried. He's sedated right now. You didn't see him before, Bev. I've never seen anyone like that. He was . . ." CJ shook her head, her gaze shifting to look at Victor through the glass. "I knew Victor in New Mexico. He was always so calm, so pleasant. Not like the other Areth. This is like . . . like Jekyll and Hyde."

Beverly touched her fingers to the steel enforced glass and watched him, her throat suddenly dry, and her temples throbbing with the beat of her heart. Victor raised his head, his face cast towards the ceiling, and her chest seized when she saw the heavy trail of tears on his cheeks.

End of Sample

Please enjoy the following bonus content.

"A Lifetime Ago"

a Prequel novella to

The Phoenix Rebellion Book One: Revolution

A LIFETIME AGO

Soft music, laced with subtle string melodies, echoed through the expansive ballroom as military leaders, political figures, and scientific pioneers mingled with Areth dignitaries and ambassadors. Subdued conversation hummed just below the surface of the music, blending with the tinkle of crystal and china.

Doctor CJ Montgomery stood at the top of the sweeping staircase that led to the ballroom floor, taking in the crowd as a giddy excitement danced up her spine. She tightened her hold on the arm of the gentleman walking beside her. He patted her hand affectionately.

"I take it you've never attended a soiree on this grand a scale, Miss Montgomery?"

"No," she said as she released a pent-up breath, then blinked and turned to look at Professor Abernathy. "No, Professor." Her voice was stronger this time.

He smiled behind his full, white beard and took a step forward. CJ walked with him, the flared hem of her silk skirt whistling around her ankles as they took the stairs. "You are the next generation of Genetics

245

Engineering geniuses, Miss Montgomery. It's high time you rub elbows with the men and women that will lead our world into a future full of promise and advancements like none we have ever imagined."

They reached the bottom of the stairs, and Professor Abernathy led her directly to a small crowd of people gathered together in conversation. She immediately recognized Warrick, High Commander of the Areth fleet, and her heart jumped into her throat. He was dressed in a long robe of deep brown, five gold cubes on each shoulder the only indication of his rank within the Areth chain of command. He needed no insignia to set himself apart. There wasn't a person on Earth who didn't know Warrick by sight. She barely heard the exchange between Professor Abernathy and the Areth leader until the saying of her own name snapped her out of her daze.

"I consider Doctor Montgomery my prodigy, and predict her contribution to the study of theoretical genetics will be groundbreaking. She is a brilliant doctor."

Heat rose in her cheeks and she glanced away from the professor and Warrick . . . and found herself looking into the most intense brown eyes she had ever seen.

"Doctor Montgomery, allow me to introduce Colonel Tanner," said someone's voice on the edges of her perception. "Colonel Tanner is one of our honorees this evening."

Colonel Tanner towered over her, or so it seemed. CJ was five-foot-ten and had on heels and yet she still had to raise her chin to meet his gaze. He was at least six-foot-three, and the blue dress Earth Force uniform he wore accentuated his broad shoulders and a trim physique. His brown hair was cut close in standard military fashion, with the slightest hint of gray at the temples. That, with his rank, told her he had to be in his late thirties at least. Slight lines bracketed his thin, chiseled lips.

He extended his hand and CJ took it, his long fingers engulfing hers.

"Doctor?" he said, and his voice was like honey over gravel.

"Yes," she managed to say, her voice lost somewhere in her throat.

"I believe, Miss Montgomery, that Colonel Tanner is surprised by your age. Rightfully so. Yes, Colonel. CJ is young, but it certainly doesn't diminish her skill," Professor Abernathy said moving up beside her.

CJ realized Colonel Tanner hadn't released her hand. His fingers tightened around her wrist for just a moment before he let her go and she withdrew. The sense of loss that chilled her skin surprised her, and she slid her glance to him only to find him still watching her. The warmth that had settled into her cheeks spread down her throat, encompassing her.

"If everyone could please find your seats, we'll be serving dinner and beginning the ceremony," the MC for the evening announced from the front of the room.

CJ followed a uniformed server to a small table with several other guests while Professor Abernathy joined his fellow honorees at a long table on one end of the room. She smiled pleasantly at the people she shared her table with, but found her gaze shifting back to Colonel Tanner. He stood back from the table, his hands tucked behind his back, as the other men and women found their seats. When everyone else had found their places, he pulled out a chair, sat ramrod straight, and linked his hands on the tabletop.

He was . . . handsome seemed inadequate a word to describe the man. It was inappropriate for the rough edge that shrouded him. He was a gentleman and a soldier, honed and skilled, but there was something subdued about him that made her curious.

A steward walked along the front of the table, offering glasses of synthetic alcohol to the honorees. She watched as he shook his head and nodded to the ice water the steward had in his other hand. He lifted the crystal glass to his lips, and as he sipped, his gaze met hers over the rim.

CJ sucked in a small breath, her heart pounding in her chest like a caged bird, as he slowly lowered the glass but never looked away. Someone stepped behind him and patted his shoulder, breaking the connection as he turned away. He spoke briefly to the older man in the uniform of an Earth Force General, and when the man walked away, he glanced back to her again.

"Who is that speaking to Colonel Tanner?" CJ asked. He seemed familiar, niggling at the edge of her memory.

Doctor Abernathy followed her subtle point toward the head table. "That's General Robert Castleton. One of the most decorated generals in Earth Force."

CJ raised her glass of imitation merlot and wished for a real glass of alcohol to calm her rioting nerves. The awards ceremony began as a compliment of stewards brought each attendee their meal. The citrus-glazed salmon would have looked delicious at any other meal, and she would have enjoyed every bite, but her stomach flipped and fluttered like a mass of butterflies and she only managed to force down a few bites. She barely heard any of the half-dozen speeches given in the next hour.

The MC took the podium again, and CJ probably wouldn't have registered his introduction at all were it not for the man. "Our final honoree this evening is Colonel Nicholas Tanner of Earth Force. Colonel Tanner has shown exceptional skill and unwavering loyalty to the advancement of Earth's security. Every young pilot who must now follow in his shadow envy his abilities, and his leadership is an example to us all. Colonel Tanner . . ."

He stood, shifting his chair back and moving to his feet with smooth agility, adjusting his jacket with a firm tug at the hem. The other honorees had each taken the opportunity to speak for several minutes at the podium, but Colonel Tanner only took the plaque offered him and shook the hand of the presenter with a restrained smile and a nod. He returned to his chair and set his plaque beside his plate.

She couldn't help but watch him, and scoffed at her own foolishness for being awe-struck by a man she had just met. Every move he made was a practice in smooth restraint, no excess energy was wasted, and nothing about him was clumsy.

The dinner ended, and the attendees moved en masse to the far side of the ballroom. A small orchestra played and several couples moved automatically to the floor. Despite her own chastising minutes before, CJ found herself scanning the crowd for a tall, handsome Colonel.

Damn.

No . . . *hot* damn.

How the hell did an old codger like Avril Abernathy manage to get a hot woman like that on his arm? What the hell did she see in him?

Nick stood on the outskirts of the crowd, his jacket unbuttoned and his hands shoved into his trouser pockets, watching her through the horde of big wigs and fluff shirts milling around to name drop and play their angles. What Nick wouldn't do for a beer, but the chances of finding one around here was somewhere between slim and none.

Doctor Montgomery stood near a pristine white column, a glass of fake wine balanced in her hand. The deep blue silk of her form-fitting gown had his throat dry, and he wondered how long he'd go before he'd have to button his jacket again.

Damn.

Hot Damn.

Abernathy was nowhere around, and she looked lost and uncomfortable, her eyes shifting from group to group as she swirled the wine-wannabee in the glass. As Nick watched, three men approached her and—he assumed—asked her to dance. She declined each one with a reserved smile and a shake of her head. Blonde ringlets bounced off her cheek and dangled along the side of her throat, and he wondered how much hair she hid in the tight twist she wore.

Quit ogling her like some wet-behind-the-ears first year cadet!

She took a sip, her eyes shifting around the room. He smiled when he caught the slight wince when she swallowed. As least she had the good taste to not like the crap they passed as 'social beverages' any more than he did. Nick wondered what she'd do with a beer, and grinned. Doctor Montgomery shifted and ran her hand over the silk covering her stomach, her hand pausing just below the puckered fabric over her breasts. Her gaze shifted, and caught him watching her.

Nick expected her to look away. She didn't. She stared at him, her lips parting slightly.

Damn.

Hot. Damn.

Feeling weak as hell for doing it, Nick broke the contact first, looking away as he rubbed his thumb across his lower lip. What the hell was he thinking and who the hell was he fooling? *One*, she was what . . . twenty-one? Twenty-two? Therefore, she was legal but that was about it. She was in pre-school the last time Nick asked a woman to dance.

Crap. Had it *really* been that long?

There was a second point in there somewhere, but whatever it was went orbital when he glanced up to see her walking towards him. Dusky color stained her cheeks all the way down her throat to her bare shoulders. Even with the orchestra playing, he heard the soft swish of her skirt, and the sound heated his blood and sent it southward.

"Congratulations, Colonel," she said when she reached him, standing an arm's length away. "You must be very proud."

Nick winced, and bit back his true response. The award was a bunch of bull, and his 'loyalty' to the Areth-Earth alliance was a crock. "Would you like to dance?" The question was out of his mouth before he could figure out reason number three why it was a stupid idea, and was probably a hell of a lot smarter than actually commenting.

She nodded and set her glass down. Nick curled his fingers around her elbow and headed for an empty spot on the dance floor, buttoning his jacket with his other hand. The song changed and he turned to her, taking her in his arms, hoping like *hell* he remembered how this whole dancing thing worked.

Her hand slid into his, her other arm resting along his jacket sleeve with her fingers near his collar. Nick inhaled, drawing in the smell of flowers and sweetness, and before his better judgment could override, Nick slid his hand up her spine until he felt bare skin above the back of her dress. Her breath hitched.

Damn.

"What does CJ stand for?"

CJ looked into the night, standing at a giant wall of glass that was so pure and clear it was almost like standing on a balcony over the city. She looked over her shoulder to see Nick standing a few feet away, his jacket unbuttoned again with his hands in his pockets as he leaned his shoulder against the wall. Her heart jumped and her skin flushed at the way he looked at her; appreciatively without leering like the sex-starved juveniles at the Academy.

"Why?" she asked with a smile.

He pushed away from the wall and strolled towards her, and with each step, her breathing grew shallow and her body flushed. Nick stopped immediately behind her, so close she felt the heat of his body on her exposed skin. His buttons brushed against the silk of her dress and she couldn't fight the shiver when he barely touched the back of her shoulder with his fingertips.

"Just a question."

She smiled and turned to face him, the cold glass to her back. "Caitlin June."

One corner of his finely sculpted lips tipped up in a half-smile. "Doctor Caitlin June Montgomery."

CJ nodded. Nick's gaze shifted down as his fingers brushed across her shoulders. It was barely a touch, but a jumble of sensations rioted in her stomach anyway. Then he withdrew and pushed his hand back into his pocket, looking into her face.

"I want to see you again." His voice was rough and smooth at the same time, like whiskey and velvet.

Her breath caught and she couldn't answer. As tangible as a touch, his posture shifted . . . a tensing and withdrawal even before he moved.

"Yes," she managed to force through her lips.

His gaze shifted over her face, and she felt the tingle as real as a caress as he settled on her mouth. She involuntarily pulled her lower lip between her teeth, and swore she heard a soft moan rumble deep in his chest. He raised his hands and laid his palms against her cheeks, his fingers slipping into the curls around her face. CJ held her breath, wondering if he could feel the thundering pound of her heart as he leaned in.

His lips skimmed across hers, his breath caressing her skin. Her eyes fluttered closed and she slid her hands inside his open jacket, the trapped heat of his body warming her arms. She pressed her hands to his back as he shifted closer, sandwiching her body between his heat and the cold glass window. His muscles bunched and hardened beneath her hands as he covered her mouth fully, drawing a ragged purr from her throat when his tongue slipped past her lips and slid along her own.

Nick broke the kiss first, resting his forehead against hers as their rapid breath mingled in the space between them.

"Damn," he said, his voice rough.

All CJ could manage was a nod.

7 MARCH 2043, SATURDAY
PARSON'S POINT, MAINE
FORMER UNITED STATES OF AMERICA

"It's so beautiful here. I don't think I've ever been anywhere so beautiful."

Nick smiled as he sat down in the chair adjacent to Caitlin's, handing her a glass of iced water. The chairs faced the lake as the sun dipped below the far tree line, and the air smelled of hickory smoke from the fire in the cabin mixed with the fresh scent of pine and earth surrounding them.

"I get up here as often as I can," he answered.

She reached her hand across the space between them, and he wrapped his fingers around hers. "I can understand why. Your grandfather built it?"

"Great-grandfather. It's been passed down father to son."

He expected the weight in his chest, so he wasn't surprised when it hit him. Even after eighteen years, the weight of loss hit him hard every time. She curled forward out of her chair moved to slide onto his lap. Nick rested his hand on her thigh, supporting her back with his other arm and rested his head on the back of the chair to look up at her. Caitlin ran her fingers through his hair, studying him in the dimming sunlight.

"That's the second time . . ." she said, her voice soft.

"Second time *what?*"

"The second time I've seen the shadows in your eyes, like you're remembering something you don't want to. What is it?"

Nick grinned. "You think you've got me figured out after two weeks?"

She pressed a kiss to his forehead. "Not completely, no, but enough. You don't have to tell me, but don't think you can't, either."

Nick drew a heavy breath, rubbing his hand over her jean-clad leg from knee to hip. Even after two weeks, he still couldn't quite accept the reality that this beautiful, young, sexy, *young* woman wanted to waste her time with him. He had asked her to the cabin on a whim, and had to plan fast to have the place open and ready for her when she surprised him by saying yes.

He looked past her to the water, watching a soft ripple dance across the surface to break against the shore. Streaks of orange and yellow shifted with each wave. Caitlin shifted in his lap to curl against his chest with her head on his shoulder. Her breath whispered across his throat, warming his blood. Nick curled his fingers around the back of her neck beneath her long, blonde hair.

"I had a son," he finally said, the words harder to say than he expected.

"Had?"

Nick nodded. "He died when he was born. Both he and my wife."

Caitlin lifted her head, her features hard to make out in the fading light of the day. "I'm so sorry, Nicky."

He still bristled at the nickname she had conjured up for him, but somehow he found it sexier now more than anything else. As he stared at her, his eyes adjusted to the darkness and he saw the soft lines of her profile and the glisten in her eyes. No one had wept for Kathleen and Michael in nearly eighteen years, not since his mother stood at his side and held his hand as they buried his wife and son. His throat tightened but he tamped down the old swell of emotion.

"It was a long time ago."

She touched his mouth with her fingertips as he spoke, her touch seeking. Caitlin shifted closer and replaced her fingers with her lips, her kiss igniting a need in him he had buried for years; unwilling or unable to let them surface until her. The tempo and intent of the kiss shifted, arousal spiking through him. Her hand slipped inside the front of his shirt to rest on bare skin and he moaned against her lips.

Nick jerked back, laying his hand against her face. Her shallow breath was the only sound he heard.

"Caitlin," he said, trying to ignore his need long enough to speak. "I'm old."

She laughed, her voice carrying through the night. "What?"

"I'm old. Caitlin, I'm *seventeen* years older than you."

She shrugged. "So."

"So?" Nick popped up his eyebrows, chuckling. "That doesn't bother you?"

She leaned into him, nipping the skin along the side of his throat between her teeth as her hands unbuttoned his shirt, exposing his skin to the cool evening air. He didn't feel the cold.

"If it bothered me, would I want you as much as I do?" she said close to his ear before she drew his earlobe between her lips.

Nick slid his arms beneath her knees and behind her back, taking her with him as he stood. Without another word, he carried her around to the front of the cabin and pushed the door open with his toe, kicking it shut behind him. The only bedroom in the cabin was just off the living room, a wide doorway connecting the two rooms with no door. He carried her through the room, his lips finding hers as he instinctively avoided the sparse furniture to bring them to the side of the bed.

He set her on the edge of the bed, her hands already tugging his shirt free of the waistband of his jeans. Nick yanked the cotton free of his arms and tossed it to the floor, acting quickly so he could once again devour her mouth as he laid her back on the bed.

18 SEPTEMBER 2043, SATURDAY
PARSON'S POINT

The smell of bacon and autumn mornings filled the cabin, and through the open kitchen window came the music of a distant songbird. CJ picked up a warm slice of toast, hissing as it hurt the tips of her fingers, and spread soft butter across the surface. She barely managed to keep herself from whistling as she arranged the two plates of food and glasses of juice. Coffee was still a mystery to her, and she had decided to forego even trying.

"Breakfast is ready, Nicky," she called out over her shoulder, but gasped as two long, strong arms circled her body from behind.

"Mmmmm, smells delicious." His voice shimmied over her like a sweet caress, and she leaned back into his embrace.

"I didn't burn the bacon this time," she said with a smile and tilted her head so he could press a kiss just in front of her ear.

"I'm proud of you," he whispered, his voice earnest. "But damn, woman. How am I supposed to think about food when I find you wearing nothing but my old flannel shirt?"

CJ's body tingled as his long fingers expertly released the buttons of the oversized shirt and his hands slipped inside to skim over her skin. He slipped the collar away from her shoulder and buried his face into the curve of her neck, his tongue applying firm pressure to her skin before his lips sucked gently. CJ let her head fall back, supported by his chest, as his hands cupped her breasts and skimmed her stomach, plucking at the waistband of her panties.

"Nicky . . ." she whispered hoarsely.

He turned her around in the space between him and the counter, his hands coming up to cup her face. CJ looked up at him as his thumb stroked across her lower lip. He was bare from the waist up and the subtle flex of his arms and chest when he moved made her heart race and her blood heat. She reached up to lay her hands on his chest, enjoying the heat of his skin and the beat of his heart beneath her palm. He tipped her face and covered her lips with a deep, open mouth kiss that made her insides dance and her knees shake. His fingertips laced into her hair and he pulled her closer, kissing her longer, until they both had to stop to breathe. Nicky rested his forehead against hers, their rapid breath mingling in the space between them, and licked his lips.

"I love you, Caitlin."

Her heart jumped, and she wrapped her arms around him. "I love you, too, Nicky."

He smiled, a single corner of his lips tipping up. "Good," was his only answer as he swept her into his arms and carried her back to bed, leaving breakfast behind.

12 November 2043, Thursday
Sorentino's Café
Arlington, Virginia
Former United States of America

"It's bullshit, Caitlin."

CJ glanced around the café, her nerves jumping at the thought that one of her colleagues —or *anyone* of power—might hear Nick's rant. "Nicky, please . . ."

"You don't think this is crazy? They're taking over everything and wiping out anything that resembles what we were. What we're supposed to be. Soon, there's going to be nothing left of *us*. The *Human* race."

"You're jumping to conclusions. President Camrin has not agreed to granting political power to any Areth official, and until he does—"

"*Until* he does. Even you think it's going to happen."

CJ set her fork down and rested her hands in her lap, drawing a slow breath to try and calm her nerves. "Why are we fighting about this?"

"We're not fighting," Nick said, jabbing at his chicken.

"It feels like we're fighting."

He finally raised his head and looked at her, his tense features relaxing when their gazes connected. With a huff and a shake of his head, he let his fork drop onto the plate with a clatter and reached his hand across the space of the table. CJ brought her hand from beneath the tablecloth and laid it in his, sighing when he gently squeezed her fingers. Nick raised her hand to his lips, kissing her knuckles.

"I'm sorry," he said. "I just get—"

"I know."

He smiled at her, and some of her tension eased. They finished their meal, and after Nick gave the waiter his payment card, they left the café. The winter air bit at her skin and she tucked her chin into the collar of her coat.

"I can't convince you to take the afternoon off?"

CJ smiled, moving closer to him so he could circle her shoulders with his arm and pull her against his side. "I'm sorry. We're close to breaking the DNA code we've been studying. I'm surprised Jairdan let me go for lunch."

"He's a slave driver."

CJ laughed. "But he's also a genius."

"Have you ever met an Areth that wasn't?" he mumbled under his breath.

They reached the entrance to the tall glass and steel medical building where CJ's new office and staff were located. Nick turned her in his arms and kissed her, long and deep, and she wished she really could take the afternoon off to be with him. They had given up on maintaining two apartments in the city, and Nick had moved in several weeks before. She loved waking up in his arms, and falling asleep to the sound of his heartbeat, but on days like today she wanted more. More time. More him. Just more.

"I'll see you tonight," he said against her lips.

"Okay. I love you."

"I love you." With one more kiss, he let her go so she could enter the sterile interior of the facility. She watched him walk away through the smoky glass that let her see out but didn't allow any pedestrians to see into the lobby. When he disappeared from sight, she walked to the elevator and rode to the top floor and her labs.

She absently walked through the lab where several of her subordinates worked, and opened to the door to her office, stopping short when she saw the two men waiting for her. Jairdan, the Areth scientist overseeing her studies, stood behind her desk and Professor Abernathy rested in one of her chairs. Both men looked up, whatever conversation they were having stopped short. Jairdan features were tight as he glanced at the photograph of herself and Nick she had set near her computer.

"Jairdan, Professor Abernathy, this is a surprise," she said, closing the door behind her. "Is there something I can help you with?"

Professor Abernathy stood, bracing his hands on the armrests for leverage. "Let's take a walk, Miss Montgomery. We haven't had a chance to talk in the last few months."

She glanced between Professor Abernathy and Jairdan, the tension and weight tangible in the air. Jairdan drew a slow breath through his nostrils and tucked his hands behind his back as he came from behind his desk.

"I'll leave you to talk," he said, his tone heavy on 'talk', and nodded at

Professor Abernathy as he passed. "You and I will speak later, Doctor Montgomery."

Professor Abernathy took her hand as he reached her, and slid it into the bend of his arm just as he had at the awards ceremony months before. "Your life is about to change, Miss Montgomery," he said as they walked out of the office. "Like you never imagined."

"I'm in the kitchen," Nick called through the apartment when he heard the front door open and close. He slid the pan of seared salmon off the heating unit and wiped his fingers on the small towel draped over his shoulder as he walked to the front foyer.

It was empty, and he continued to the combined living-dining room where he found Caitlin standing beside the table he had already set for dinner. She toyed with the soft petals of the orchids he had placed in a vase. Nick stepped behind her and slid his arms around her body, resting his chin on the top of her head.

"I was beginning to wonder how long Jairdan was going to keep you."

"Busy day today," she answered, her voice distant.

Nick gently urged her to turn in his arms, and bent at the knee so he could look her straight in the eyes. "You look exhausted. Why don't you sit while I finish dinner?"

She smiled, but her features were still tight and strained. Nick leaned in and kissed her until he felt some of the tension ease and her hand lay against his chest. Pulling back, he moved to pull a chair out for her and she sat, immediately picking up the glass of wine he had poured for her. Not that synthetic crap, either. Tonight, the real stuff was in order. She hummed appreciatively at the first sip.

Nick returned to the kitchen to finish preparing their plates. Before he picked them up, he patted his pocket just to make sure the ring was still there.

This was it . . . He was going to do it again . . .

He paused in the doorway before entering the dining room, sighing when he saw Caitlin. Her elbow was on the table, her forehead supported by her hand with her eyes closed. A protective surge of annoyance hit him and he marched across the room, setting her plate down. She jerked back, obviously not hearing him.

"I don't know who the hell Jairdan thinks he is, abusing you the way he does. They work you until you're dead on your feet—"

"They don't abuse me, Nicky," she said softly, but he kept going.

"Christ, I know *they* don't have lives, but *you* do. Hell, Caitlin, there are nights I don't even hear you come in."

"Could we please not fight?"

"I'm not fighting." Nick paused, grinning. "Déjà vu." Her smile was weak, but there nonetheless. "Dig in," he said, pointing to her plate with the tines of his fork.

She poked at the food, pushing the salmon around more than eating it. After a few moments of her not eating, and him watching her not eat, Caitlin sighed and set her fork down. "Nicky, we need to talk."

"Absolutely," he said around the bite of vegetables in his cheek. "I have something I want to talk to you about. I think we need to take a vacation."

"I can't right now, Nicky."

"Now, listen . . . I'm not talking a weekend away. I'm talking two weeks, at least. Get the hell away from the city and enjoy some fresh air. Do some stargazing, some fishing, whatever. Just you and me. I went eighteen years without taking any leave, so I've got plenty coming—"

"I can't."

"Why not?"

Caitlin pushed her plate away and sat back in her chair, crossed her arms and avoided looking at him. "We're close to making a breakthrough, and I can't walk away from the study right now. It's too important."

"When it's done, then"

She shook her head. "No. Nicky, since I was eleven years old I've worked *hard* to get to where I am. I wanted to be a geneticist, and I made it. I can't just throw it away for . . ." She stumbled over her words, stopping herself short, her eyes shifting to him for a split moment as color rose in her cheeks.

A lead weight hit Nick's gut and he felt sick. Keeping a tight rein on his urge to snap, he drained the wine from his glass barely tasting the robust flavor. "For what, Caitlin," he said through tight lips.

"For an unplanned vacation." Her voice was weak and unconvincing.

They sat in silence for several moments as Nick poured himself another glass, downing it in two swallows. Caitlin worried the edge of her napkin, her fingertips tapping on the tabletop. Finally, she drew a deep breath.

"You knew what I was when you met me."

Nick raised his head and looked at her. "I knew you were a doctor, I didn't know you were the Areth's personal whipping girl."

"That's not fair, Nicky!" She slapped the table, her silverware clacking against her plate.

He set his glass down with a thud and stood. "No, it's not."

Nick crossed the living room to stand at the wide glass door that looked out on Barcroft Park. It had started to rain some time after he got home from Langley. Rivulets of water ran down the glass, branching off and joining again like lines on a map. The park was dark, only two or three streetlamps visible in the gloom. He heard her chair slide across the tile floor, and saw her reflection muted in the glass as she walked towards him, her arms crossed over her body. Defensive. Protective.

What had he ever done to make her feel that way?

"I'm leaving, Nicky."

He spun around. "What?"

"I've been offered a position at the Alliance Labs in Geneva. I can continue my research there. I can form my own team, and it's important work." She hitched up her chin and finally met his gaze for the first time since she came home. "I want to take it, Nicky."

Nick scrubbed a palm over his face, sucking in air. He looked past her for a minute, regrouping, before setting his hands at his hips, and meeting her eyes again. "How long?"

"Two years, maybe longer."

He closed his eyes. "I can't relocate, Caitlin. I'm stuck here until I retire."

"I know . . ." she said softly. "The Areth are accomplishing amazing breakthroughs, and I'm going to be part of it."

"Areth," he hissed, storming past her. "It always comes back to the damn Areth. It's all I hear . . . *The Areth* are making our lives better, *The Areth* are accomplishing amazing breakthroughs. *The Areth* are our salvation. It's crap!"

"You know, they said you wouldn't understand—"

Nick spun around. "They? Who the *hell* are 'they'? Jairdan? Who the hell are *they* to say *anything* about you and me?"

"They're looking out for my best interests. My career—"

Nick took a step toward her, jabbing a finger at his own chest. "And I don't—"

"I didn't say that."

"Sure as hell sounded like it," he ground out.

They were nose to nose, their rapid breath mingling in the space between them. "Don't put words in my mouth."

"Why the hell not? The Areth already are."

She snapped her mouth shut so hard, her teeth clanked together, and she glared at him. A tremor shifted through her body, and he knew she was either on the verge of crying or hitting him . . . which one, he wasn't sure. Nick marched around the end of the couch and headed for the foyer.

"I'm going to go out for a while." He stopped in the archway of the hall, turning to look at her as he drew a slow, steadying breath. "Maybe when I come back, we'll both be calm enough to figure this out." She swiped her fingers across her cheeks, nodding. "Caitlin . . ." He waited until she looked up, her glistening eyes looking at him. "I *want* to figure this out."

She nodded again, and Nick grabbed his coat before leaving the apartment.

The vast blackness of space spread out on all sides of Nick's O_2 glider, broken only by the distant twinkle of dying stars. He kept his boosters pointed at Earth, floating in the vacuum to try and clear his head.

That was the advantage of being a colonel, he supposed. If he wanted to take a quick jaunt around the moon, no one was going to say no. There was no better way to find his balance than to catapult himself into nothingness.

Space had been his net after Kathleen and Michael died. He couldn't function on Earth, the air smothered him, and his life was nothing but a pile of rubble. Everything he thought he had was gone in a handful of minutes. His wife . . . his son . . . gone. He had buried himself in his glider, taking every training mission, and volunteering for every flight schedule he could until his skills were second to none.

That's the way it had been . . . for eighteen years.

Until Caitlin.

He didn't care what he had to do. He would make it work. If he had to resign his commission tomorrow, he would. Geneva wasn't so bad, after all.

Static whistled in his ear before a voice carried over the line. *"Zeus, this is Base."*

"Base, this is Zeus."

"Global weather net indicates some nasty weather in this part of the world. Suggest you return to the roost."

"Roger, Base. Back in seven."

"Roger, Zeus. Base clear."

Nick flipped the switch that engaged his O_2 boosters, and the glider hummed to life around him. With a sharp yank of his joystick, the glider flipped back in a full one-hundred-eighty degree twist, pressing him into his seat despite the inertial dampeners. Earth loomed in front of him, swirling shades of blue, white, and green. He glanced at his navigational controls and manually calculated his rate and angle of descent. With a punch of his thumb on his red initiator button, the glider shot forward, heading once again for Langley, and home.

An hour later, he stood once again outside the door of their apartment. He pushed his hand into his pocket, his fingers curling reassuringly around the platinum and diamond ring inside. The metal was warm against his palm.

This would work. It would.

He opened the door and darkness greeted him. The same heavy weight that had hit his gut at dinner slammed into him again. Dropping his coat on the back of the couch, he walked into the living room.

"Lights," he commanded, and the ambient lighting slowly increased until the room was as bright as midday.

Dinner sat on the table, just as they had left it. Leaning against the bottle of wine was a folded note, his name written on the front. Swallowing hard, Nick picked it up and opened the fold.

I wish this would work. More than you know.

Nick huffed a breath and closed his eyes.

CJ stared into the dark night as her jet, bound for Switzerland, cut through the rain and weather. Her tears fell as fast as the rain, despite the exhaustion that pulled at her.

The door to her private chamber opened, and she quickly wiped her fingers over her cheeks before Jairdan saw how devastated she really was.

He sat down, his back stiff and his expression stiffer. Emotionless brown eyes, so unlike Nick's, stared at her as she attempted to compose herself.

"You have made a wise decision, Doctor Montgomery. Your skill deserves to be appreciated."

Sadness exploded in her chest and she looked into the night sky again.

Eight years later...
15 *October* 2051, *Sunday*
Parson's Point, Maine
Former United States of America

CJ stood at the corner of Nick's porch and inhaled deep. The air was heavy with the scent of leaves, pine, and earth, and the sky was a brilliant blue softened with long wisps of cirrus clouds. It had been a long time since she had been outside a city, or anywhere *green* like this.

A long time since she had been *here*.

She closed her eyes and reached out her hand to lay it on the rough birch log, enjoying the tactile sensation beneath her fingertips. CJ leaned into the wall, inhaling slowly to let the scent of the wood fill her head. With the smell came more memories than she could ever count or categorize, and she smiled.

She opened her eyes, dropped her hand away from the side of the cabin, and stepped down onto the ground. Stone and dirt crunched beneath her shoes as she walked along the side of the house toward the lake. Nick wasn't inside, but he might be down at the dock. The sound of a low voice carried on the breeze, accompanied by the scraping of wood against wood. Her heart skipped, and she paused at the corner of the cabin.

Nick was on the dock, crouched down on the edge as he tied a small boat to the mooring, his long, sure fingers knotting the rope. A soft breeze blew in off the water, swirling fallen leaves from the ground and stirring his hair. Last she saw him, his hair still had been mostly brown with just the slightest touches of gray at the temples. Now, he was almost completely silver with brown showing through to indicate what it once had been. Dear god, he was still the most beautiful man she had ever seen.

She knew he'd hate her choice of words.

A small dog, not much more than a mass of white and brown fur, sat on the dock beside Nick, its tail swishing back and forth. Nick said something, and the dog's tail went faster. He stood, and CJ swallowed the hitch in her breath.

Eight years ago, Nick Tanner had made her heart skip a beat with a glance and turned her body to molten heat with a touch. Seventeen years her senior, she never once saw him as anything but absolutely virile and masculine. Now, so many years later, the effect was the same. He wasn't perfection, wasn't the ideal in the eyes of most, but CJ thought any woman whose heart didn't skip when they looked at him just had to be dead. A square jaw and chiseled features gave him the look of strength, and his dark eyes were shadowed reflections of his soul. His lips were finely sculpted, thin, and straight, and the lines on his cheeks only brought out his features.

He ruffled the shaggy fur that hid the dog's face, and stood to his full height. The first time she saw him, he had been wearing his Earth Force dress blues and the uniform had accentuated his six-foot three-inch frame. Not nearly as much as faded denims and the blue plaid shirt he wore now. The breeze caught the open shirt, pulling away from his chest, letting her see the gray tee shirt beneath, and she knew he was as strong and lean as he had ever been. The silver hair added time to his forty-seven years, but everything else defied it.

CJ closed her eyes for a moment, steeling her resolve. She wasn't here to relive past love affairs. Nothing about this visit was for her. It didn't matter how seeing him made her feel. She was here *for* him, and to convince him of the truth.

Her heart knew there was no chance of anything else. She had hurt him far too badly for that.

"Come on, Dog. Let's go get some lunch."

CJ's eyes snapped open at the clear sound of his voice, and she stared transfixed while he moved off the dock toward her. She knew she should speak, but the ability was lost to her as he smiled at the antics of the mutt hopping along beside him. Then the dog stopped mid-stride and turned in her direction, sniffing the air. CJ held her breath, and thought momentarily about disappearing around the corner of the cabin and running.

No. She couldn't. This was too important.

The dog yapped and bolted toward her, and CJ held out her hand, wondering whether she would lose a finger or just end up with a slobbered palm.

"What's your problem . . ." Nick called after the animal, but the question trailed off as he looked up and their gazes connected.

CJ reached out her hand to find strength in the wall of the cabin. The smile on his lips dropped away in an instant, and his eyes darkened. Nick squared his shoulders a degree and shifted his stance, setting one foot uphill with his knee bent. He stared at her, showing no sign of surprise, but absolutely no sign of pleasure. If anything, the cold steel in his eyes almost frightened her.

"Hello, Nick," she finally managed to say, petting the dog who had chosen to sniff and lick over any kind of attack.

"Leave. Now." His voice was flat, emotionless, despite the demand.

"I have to tell you something—"

"No."

He strode toward her with purpose, and CJ held her breath as he brushed past her. She turned and reached for his arm to draw him back, but the fury in his eyes when he spun around to glare at her made her drop her hand away. CJ retreated, bumping the wall of the cabin.

"Do you hate me so much you can't even listen to what I have to say?"

"Hate," he forced through clenched teeth, and the cold levelness of his voice made CJ swallow her breath. He took the one step needed to close the space between them, stepping so near she had to hitch her chin up to hold his stare. "Now, *there's* a word."

Then he was gone, storming off to the front of the cabin, leaving CJ swaying in the space he left behind. She drew a breath, blinking rapidly, and leaned back against the wall. Perhaps General Castleton had been right. She wasn't the person to do this. They should have waited until the mission was done, the task accomplished, and then Nick Tanner could have been told the truth. If they failed, he never would have known.

She couldn't let things go. Couldn't let him go another day without knowing the reality. She owed him that much.

CJ steeled her nerves and pushed clear of the wall, walking back to the porch. The dog had already forgotten her, and was sprawled out in a spot of sunshine, not bothering to lift his head when she approached. The front door was closed, but she hedged her bet that Nick never fixed the lock. The knob turned and she stepped inside. The cabin was dark, and slightly warmer than outside from the glowing embers still in the fieldstone hearth. Very little had changed in eight years. The flat monitor on the wall had been upgraded, and the rug in front of the fireplace might be different, but everything else was just the same as she remembered, from the soft leather couch with the red and blue woven blanket on the back to the handcrafted wood cabinets in the kitchen. The air smelled of burning hickory and bacon, with an underlying aroma of the soap she knew he used.

Her eyes burned and she blinked hard to keep back the tears. She refused to let this turn into *anything* to do with her. Nothing she felt, nothing she wanted, would come into play. Tonight, she would condemn herself for being stupid and naïve, but not now.

She closed the door and stepped inside, her shoes muffled by the braided rug covering the wide plank floor. CJ walked past the end of the couch and looked to her right to the archway leading to the joining bedroom. There was no door, nothing blocking her view to the large wrought iron bed that sat against the far wall, or to keep her from seeing Nick where he sat on its edge, his elbows resting on his knees with his head down.

CJ swallowed the lump in her throat and forced herself to enter the room, unprepared for the onslaught of memories that bombarded her when she curled her fingers around the cool metal framework of the footboard. Nights of lovemaking, mornings of waking in his arms . . . they all came back in a vicious wave.

"What part of *leave* was confusing?"

CJ closed her eyes against the hate and anger in his voice. "I will leave—"

"Yes, you will."

"You have to hear this first, Nicky."

His head snapped up and he glared at her. "There is *nothing* you can tell me that I want to hear."

CJ released the footboard and slipped a trembling hand into the hip pocket of her dress, her fingers curling around the microslide she had tucked away there. She extended her hand, palm up, and unfurled her fingers. Nick sat up, staring at the slide, his dark brown eyes darting up to meet hers momentarily. She nodded, jutting her chin toward it.

"Go ahead. See for yourself. Then, if you want me to leave, I will."

Nick stood, the old bed creaking at the loss of his weight. His fingertips brushed her palm as he took the slide and strode past her into the main living space. CJ took a moment to breathe deeply, closing her eyes. Her skin tingled where his fingers had touched. Clearing her throat, she turned and followed him. As she stepped into the main room, Nick opened the data receptacle on the monitor and placed the disk inside. He didn't spare her a glance as she moved beside him, punching in the command codes to open the file and run the program.

The screen flickered and a video began to play. CJ was far too familiar with the contents, having watched it again and again. The image spanned a large common room filled with men and women of all ages, dressed in loose, light clothing. Some sat together in small groups, some curled into themselves near the wall, rocking to the rhythm of an unheard beat. Orderlies and nurses stood on the outskirts, distributing medications to some, removing one or two for experiments that CJ hadn't yet been able to define or determine.

"What am I looking at?"

She pointed to the far right corner near the bank of bar-covered windows. A single man stood, facing out into the sun, with his feet set apart and his hands linked behind his back in a stance all too familiar to CJ. He was tall and lanky in build, even that was obvious through the baggy clothing he wore. His hair was brown, the same color she imagined Nick's had been a lifetime ago. Even now, looking at the younger man, CJ's heart skipped. The reality excited her, yet broke her heart in the same instant.

"Here," she said. "Magnify and enhance."

Nick touched the screen and the image paused. He tapped with his pinky and a menu appeared. With deft fingers, he relayed the commands and the video shifted, magnifying the image two hundred percent so the single man filled the screen. His back was still to the camera.

"Resume."

Nick tapped again and the video restarted. CJ's pulse quickened. She knew the moment she wanted approached. She stepped closer to Nick, her shoulder brushing his arm. He didn't move away, his focus on the screen, and she wondered if he felt the same niggling sense of familiarity she had the first time she saw it. She glanced quickly up at him. His gaze was intent on the monitor, a deep crease digging in above his nose as he focused.

Another man entered the view dressed in a white lab coat with his hands pushed into the large front pockets—Victor. That was all she knew about him. His singular name he'd either adopted or had assigned to him when he and his race arrived on Earth. He had dark hair and defined features, and the two men stood nearly at the same height, the doctor only being slightly shorter. If she didn't know what he really was, she would suspect his family to be from Belize, or that general part of the world. He looked to be about CJ's age, around thirty, but as an Areth his apparent age meant nothing. Her own supervisor at the lab didn't look much older than Nick, and she knew he was nearly four centuries old.

"Get ready to pause again," she said softly.

He held his hand over the monitor, not touching it.

The doctor stopped and spoke, and the focus of their attention shifted. For one brief moment, he looked straight at the camera.

"Now."

Nick tapped the screen.

"What the hell . . ."

His words mirrored CJ's own reaction the first time she saw the young man's face. It was like seeing Nick Tanner twenty years before. The same eyes, the same angled features, the same lips.

"Who is this?" he demanded, only briefly looking at her before focusing again on the screen.

CJ cleared her throat to try and push through the thick emotions threatening to choke her. "His name is Michael Tanner. Your son."

ABOUT THE AUTHOR

 Gail R. Delaney is a multi-published, award-winning author of romance in multiple sub-genres, including contemporary romance, romantic suspense, and epic science fiction romance. She always wrote stories as a kid through her teens, but didn't decide to write 'for publication' until her early twenties after the death of her mother. While helping her father go through her mother's papers, she found a box her mother kept with everything Gail had ever written—from book reports to short stories. It was then she realized her mother saw her as a writer, and it was time to live up to her mother's vision.

You can find out more about Gail R. Delaney's body of work at:

http://www.GailDelaney.com

ALSO BY GAIL R DELANEY

Baker Street Legacy

Baker Street Legacy is a romantic suspense series with a Sherlock Holmes bloodline.

Book One: My Dear Branson

Book Two: The Empty Chair

Book Three: Indefinite Doubt

Coming Soon

Contemporary Romance

Something Better

Precious Things

Feel My Love

Fools Rush In

A Love at First Sight novella

CPSIA information can be obtained
at www.ICGtesting.com
Printed in the USA
LVHW101338161222
735291LV00013B/730/J